DARK MIRROR

His hand trembled as he reached for the doorknob.

Before he had a chance to lose his nerve, he yanked it open.

For a moment he saw nothing but a janitor's closet. Nothing but mops and pails.

Then it popped up out of the sink.

For one long, seemingly endless moment, Virgil could only gawk in stark disbelief. The thing that leered at him from over the porcelain rim of the sink—the *child* that leered at him—was hardly bigger than a cat, with malassorted features and skin the color of a bad spot in an apple. Every hair on Virgil's body rose at the sight of it.

What was worst of all was that he *knew* that face. In spite of the distortions, in spite of the fact that it was a face he had not seen for thirty years, he knew it well.

It was his own....

THE BEST IN BONE CHILLING TERROR
FROM PINNACLE BOOKS!

Blood-curdling new blockbusters by horror's premier masters of the macabre! Heart-stopping tales of terror by the most exciting new names in fright fiction! Pinnacle's the place where sensational shivers live!

FEAST   (103-7, $4.50)
by Graham Masterton

Le Reposir in the quiet little town of Allen's Corners wasn't interested in restaurant critic Charlie McLean's patronage. But Charlie's son, Martin, with his tender youth, was just what the secluded New England eatery had in mind!
"THE LIVING INHERITOR TO THE REALM OF EDGAR ALLEN POE"
— *SAN FRANCISCO CHRONICLE*

LIFEBLOOD   (110-X, $3.95)
by Lee Duigon

The yuppie bedroom community of Millboro, New Jersey is just the place for Dr. Winslow Emerson. For Emerson is no ordinary doctor, but a creature of terrifying legend with a hideous hunger . . . And Millboro is the perfect feeding ground!

GHOULS   (119-3, $3.95)
by Edward Lee

The terrified residents of Tylersville, Maryland, have been blaming psychopaths, werewolves and vampires for the tidal wave of horror and death that has deluged their town. But policeman Kurt Morris is about to uncover the truth . . . and the truth is much, much worse!

Available wherever paperbacks are sold, or order direct from the Publisher. Send cover price plus 50¢ per copy for mailing and handling to Pinnacle Books, Dept. 137, 475 Park Avenue South, New York, N.Y. 10016. Residents of New York, New Jersey and Pennsylvania must include sales tax. DO NOT SEND CASH.

SCHOOLHOUSE

Lee Duigon

PINNACLE BOOKS
WINDSOR PUBLISHING CORP.

For
Melissa and Patty

Also by Lee Duigon

Lifeblood

PINNACLE BOOKS

are published by

Windsor Publishing Corp.
475 Park Avenue South
New York, NY 10016

First printing: December, 1988

Printed in the United States of America

Prologue

The night the sun fell out of the sky, the shaman of the Spotted Turtle band was fasting on the holy mountain.

A falling star was a powerful portent. It foretold the deaths of chiefs and the humbling of mighty nations. At first the shaman thought he was seeing a star fall; but the tiny point of light grew and grew until it filled the sky with fire and outshone the moon.

And then it struck the earth. The holy mountain trembled. Knocked down by the tremor, the shaman clung to the mountainside and felt a huge, hot breath across his back. It seared his skin, raising blisters instantly. He thought it must be a god breathing on him, and he was unmanned. He could only tremble and cling to the lichen-covered rock.

When he raised his head again, the valley was burning.

By dawn the people knew that it was not the sun, after all, that had fallen. And by noon a fleet of black clouds filled the sky and set loose a rain that washed boulders from the hillsides. It made the river roar and put out the great fire in the valley.

Two young men went down to the valley to see what had fallen from the sky. They were never seen again. Afterward, none of the people went into the valley. Not for many years.

"The Owl God was jealous of the sun," the Spotted Turtles' shaman told them, "and so he made a false sun. He wanted to hang it in the night sky, to make a new kind of day in which he would be the chief of all spirits. But the Great Spirit was angry and threw the false sun down to the ground. That was the false sun that fell into the valley."

When this shaman was an old, old man and the valley was green with trees and meadows, when there was no sign that there'd ever been a fire, men began to hunt there again, and women went down to gather fruits and herbs. Some camped there.

In later years the valley became known as a place of bad luck, a place that drew ghosts, and those who camped there sometimes returned with strange stories to tell.

Some of these stories were still being told when the white men came.

Victory School
Tianoga, New York
The Present

Chapter One

1

Rudi Fitch was supposed to be unlocking the library as part of the janitors' routine of preparing the school for a new day, but he'd been distracted.

Gee, they sure look like worm holes. But how could there be worm holes here?

He had noticed them by accident; he didn't think he could have ever found them if he'd actually been looking for them. They were in the wall, in a dark corner where the light could hardly reach, about a foot from the knob of the library door. There were two of them, a couple of inches apart.

Rudi stared. This was a concrete wall with a brick facing, covered by forty years' worth of institutional green paint.

Young Rudi Fitch, with the looks of a Greek god and the brains of a puppy, tried to figure out how worms could be making holes in the wall inside the school. Rudi went fishing sometimes. He dug for nightcrawlers. These holes were exactly like the ones nightcrawlers made in the ground and through which they emerged to sprawl on the surface on damp nights.

7

His fingers were too big, so Rudi probed the holes with his keys. They were deeper than the keys were long.

"Jeez," he muttered.

But he was wasting time, farting around when he was supposed to be working. He unlocked the library and headed back to the boiler room to get a brush and pail. There were some cuss words scrawled on the tiles above the drinking fountains outside the ground-floor boys' bathroom, and Mr. Iacavella wanted him to wash them off before the kids came in.

The chief custodian was at his desk reading *Playboy*. He put it down when Rudi came in.

Cosmo Iacavella liked pictures of naked women; the rest of the magazine could go fuck itself. He did not aspire to become a playboy. He was a school janitor. He looked like one of those grotesquely carved souvenir coconut heads from Florida stuck on a big, fat, grimy, hairy body, and he didn't give a good goddamn. When he tried to read the articles in the magazine, he didn't know what the fuck they were talking about. He only bought *Playboy* because it showed the best-looking girls. The ones in *Penthouse* and *Hustler* looked like whores.

"You get them cuss-words yet, Rudi?"

"I'm gonna do it right now, Mr. Iacavella."

"Hurry it up, willya? There's filthy stuff scrawled all over this fuckin' school. I don't like to think what seein' that shit does to little kids' minds."

Rudi bobbed his head. He had the brightest, reddest hair Cosmo had ever seen. He filled a pail at the sink and added some ammonia to it.

"Mr. Iacavella?"

"What?"

"There's little holes in the wall, over by the library. I just saw 'em."

Cosmo sighed, wanting only to get back to his naked women.

"F'chrissake, Rudi, there's holes all over this fuckin' building! It's rottin' out from under us."

"But—"

"Don't *but* me. Go on, get to work."

Rudi picked up the pail and left. Cosmo shook his head. The shape this building was in, it was a miracle it didn't just fall down. There were places where the wood would come off in your hands, and on a rainy day the whole building smelled like a fucking haunted house. Cosmo was pretty sure the boiler was rusting away from the inside, too, and he was goddamned glad there was only one more winter to go. Fuckin' thing'd last one more winter, he guessed.

For the Board of Education had voted to close this shitter of a school, nail the doors shut and sell the property. With the building on its last legs, Victory School was in its last year of operation.

Not much point fixing anything, Cosmo thought. Not when they were just going to tear it all down.

He leaned back in his chair and contemplated Miss October.

2

When Victory School closed its doors for the last time, Cosmo and Rudi would still be janitors, but Virgil Bradley would no longer be a principal.

As was his habit, Virgil walked to school, getting there just as the earliest arrivals appeared on the playground. He'd taught, been principal for six years, and gone to elementary school here. What would life be like without it?

He was going to find out whether he wanted to or not.

He looked at the school and tried to imagine condominiums in its place. The town had the hots for condos: great ratables, if only they could find a developer who wanted to build some here. Maybe someone would want to put up single-family homes, or a modest office building. The Board of Education was looking to make enough money on the sale of the property to knock a few cents off the tax rate on the next school budget. One way

9

or another, the time would soon come when there would be no more Victory School.

Virgil went around to the boys' entrance and up the stairs to the office on the second floor. The school secretary, Millie Stanhouse, was already there, brewing coffee.

"Mr. Bradley, you look like something the cat dragged in," she informed him with her usual tact. "What's the matter?"

He shrugged. He'd known her all these years and still called her Miss Stanhouse, maybe because she still called him Mr. Bradley. It didn't mean they couldn't talk about the things that mattered, though. Virgil was a good principal, but he knew he couldn't run Victory School without Millie, and he didn't resent it. He just hoped she couldn't run the school without him.

"Sometimes it just hits me, like a whack to the head," he told her. "I just can't get used to the idea that this is my last year here, that they're really and truly going to shut down my school. I'm starting to worry about how I'll cope with it. I guess I'm a little depressed today."

He opened the door to his private office and went in to get started on the day's paperwork. The oil portrait of Eric Hargrove, the school's first principal, seemed to frown down on Virgil's desk with more than the usual measure of disapproval. The Boston fern hanging over the windowsill looked like it might be sick, and it seemed to blame him, silently, for its condition.

Millie followed him inside. "You'll be all right, Mr. Bradley. It'll just take some getting used to, that's all."

"I hope so."

He eased himself into the chair behind the big hardwood desk. He was a tall, lanky man with long legs that still served him well on rock-climbing trips during the summer. Just forty, he'd already acquired that ageless look that sits so well upon school principals and senior civil servants. His wife, Carrie, thought him a handsome man, but he didn't buy it. When he looked into a mirror, he saw a serviceable lantern jaw, thinning hair that was neither brown nor gray, a straight, all-purpose nose, and a mouth that was equally capable of mirth or sternness. But Carrie was in love with his eyes. "They're *young* eyes," she would tell him, "and they're kind. That's very important in a principal." He didn't see how it mattered. All he saw was a pair of ordinary, faded blue eyes framed by plain, gold-rimmed glasses.

"You have a quiet day," Millie said, and closed the door on him.

He wished she hadn't. Lately he'd felt uncomfortable when he was left alone. This was out of character, and he hadn't mentioned it to anyone. Alone in the office, he felt as if there were things going on outside his door that he was better off not knowing . . . undefinable things.

Not for the first time, he wondered if he were drifting slowly into paranoia.

How could he help it, though? They were taking his school away from him.

Oh, he wouldn't be out of a job altogether. He had friends on the board. He was a valued member of the team—they didn't want to lose him. So he'd either be taken on at the middle school as an assistant principal—a prospect he didn't relish at all—or slotted into a teaching position at one of the other elementary schools, to be held in reserve in case Harriet Fulham or Louise Hunt died, resigned, or was caught selling dope to the kids, and they needed a replacement.

Or he could always look for a principal's job in another school district. Maybe relocate, uproot his family.

As he sat alone at his desk, brooding silently on the demise of Victory School, hidden sensors tracked his thoughts.

3

Ned Bradley walked to school with his friends. Dad didn't believe the principal's son should be any different from the other kids, and for the most part Ned agreed.

11

He was in the fifth grade, Mr. Hall's class, so this would have been his last year in Victory School, whether they closed it down or not. Personally, he'd be glad to get out of there and he wouldn't miss it a bit. If he was on the school board, he'd vote to shut it down, too. Just because your old man was the principal didn't make it a great school, and it didn't mean you had to love it.

It was hard to believe Dad loved it. Not with the way he'd sit at the table and tell Mom all the problems he was having. Ned overheard more of these complaints than he was supposed to, and knew a lot more about the place than he'd ever let on. Given what he knew, he'd've thought Dad would be overjoyed to be getting out of there. If Dad really was upset, it had to be because they were demoting him, because he wouldn't be a principal anymore.

Ned and his friends walked onto the playground. There was some excitement brewing: the Wang brothers were picking on fat Mort Snyder again. Phil, Patty, and Marty stayed to watch, but Ned drifted over toward the sandbox, where Miss Vollmer was tending her flock of kindergarteners, pretending not to see what was happening fifty feet away.

The Wang brothers were one of the things Virgil Bradley complained about over supper. Doug and Jimmy, twins, were in the other fifth grade class, Mrs. Praize's, and they carried on like a pair of heavies in one of those kung-fu movies to which they were addicted. They never bothered Ned, but then he'd always given them a wide berth. And a good thing, too, because lately they'd been getting worse.

Ned watched them give it to Mort, who was too fat and soft to defend himself and too slow to run away. Doug and Jimmy were dancing around him, shooting fists and feet right under his nose, showing off the fancy moves they picked up from the movies, going *aiee!* and *haawh!* and *heeaaah!* so you could hear them all the way over by the sandbox. They never used to lay a hand on Mort, but now they were grabbing handfuls of his belly, squeezing and twisting it like they were kneading clay. A bunch of kids were egging them on: the twins always drew a crowd. Poor Mort could only stand there and take it, looking like he was just about to barf all over the playground. His face was red with pain. They were working him over pretty good.

And there stood Miss Vollmer as if she was deaf, dumb, and blind, letting them have their fun. Their own teacher, Mrs. Praize, was nowhere to be seen. Mort had to suffer until the bell rang, summoning all the kids to class for the day.

Mr. Hall, another thing about Victory School that Ned's father wasn't all that keen on, was in one of his pissy moods that morning.

"You know what happens to wiseguy little boys who can't be bothered to finish their homework?" he asked when he caught Phil Berg, Ned's main man, without the answer to a math problem. "It's too horrible to talk about in front of children. I could lose my job if I told you. Suffice it to say that only a lucky few of them become the presidents of major corporations. The majority are doomed to lives of bleakest ignorance ... but that's all I dare say about it. As for you, Berg, you're sentenced to burn the midnight oil. In addition to tomorrow's assignment, you will solve the odd-numbered problems on page 131. And you'd better hand it in complete, or there's even worse in store for you."

Phil said, "Yes, sir." Ned saw him flip Hall the finger under his desk.

Mr. Hall liked to dress like a late-night talk show guest. He never wore a tie; his shirt was always open at the neck so you could see his gold chain dangling above the triangle of hairy skin. He spent a lot of time in a tanning salon. His clothes were colorful, his black hair always combed in some fruity style, dyed to hide the gray—Ned had heard his father say so. He smoked foreign cigarettes with colored wrappers. For all his trendy clothes, he was flabby around the middle and he had a big butt.

13

For the first few days of the school year, most kids thought he was cool, but that soon passed.

He liked to invent problems to be solved in class, on the blackboard.

"The Ayatollah has seventy-two political prisoners who must be executed by firing squad as soon as possible in order to make room for more. If the prisoners are shot in groups of eight, and if it takes ten minutes to execute each group, how long will it take to dispose of all seventy-two?"

Everybody laughed because it was expected of them. He picked Marsha Hellman, the prettiest girl in class, to come up to the board and solve the problem—which she did correctly by dividing eight into seventy-two and getting nine, and multiplying that by ten to get a total of ninety minutes. The whole time she was up there, Mr. Hall ogled her like a bullfrog eyeing a fly. She got it over with quickly and scurried back to her seat.

"See, boys and girls?" he said. "A practical knowledge of arithmetic can be of incalculable value in real life. Here's another one.

"Congressman Jones tells a dozen lies a day, every day. At the end of ten years, how many lies will he have told?"

A boy was summoned to the blackboard. He multiplied it out, getting 43,800.

"Wrong!" shouted Hall. The boy checked his multiplication and looked confused. "You forgot *leap year!*" Hall crowed, getting another grudging laugh. "Every four years you have to tack an extra day onto the calendar. In any span of ten years, there will be at least two leap years, sometimes three. So that's a minimum of twenty-four more lies for the congressman to tell, with a maximum of thirty-six. Aren't they supposed to teach you these things before they send you on to fifth grade?"

Ned ate lunch with Phil. When they finished and went down the hall toward the playground, they passed Bob Diehl, who cut

14

loose with one of his favorite witticisms: "Hey, Jewboy!" They kept going.

"It's guys like that," said Phil, "who give turds a bad name."

Ned lived in fear that someday Phil would lose his cool and make a crack like that to Diehl's face. Diehl wasn't much to worry about, but his asshole buddies, Johnny Rizzo and Mike Dudak, were. Johnny and Mike made the Wang brothers look like a pair of good samaritans.

"I'm gonna write to Israel," Phil said as they went outside, "and ask 'em to send someone over to blow those jerks away. Why doesn't your old man do something about them? Like kick 'em out of school."

Ned knew his father would just love to do something about those three, but hadn't yet figured out what.

"Rizzo's been kicked out before," Ned said. "It didn't do any good." Johnny's father was a cop. "His old man made a stink, and the school board made Dad take him back. The school board won't let you do hardly anything."

"They wouldn't stop a couple of Israeli paratroopers."

"Bet they wouldn't stop Vincent Price, either."

Ned was hooked on horror movies the way the Wang twins were hooked on martial arts flicks. They showed plenty of both down at the old Empire Theater, and more on television. His parents weren't thrilled about it, but they made no effort to stop him from watching the films. They figured he'd grow out of it. ("And they can't be any worse for him than the evening news," he'd heard Mom say once.)

"What do you think Vincent Price would do about those clowns?" Phil said.

"Dip 'em in boiling wax and put 'em in a museum."

"I love it!"

"Bury 'em alive."

"Couldn't happen to a nicer bunch of guys!"

"Chain 'em up in a little tiny room under a castle," Ned said, "and brick up the doorway on 'em."

"From your mouth to God's ear!"

When he thought Phil wasn't looking, Ned gave the playground a quick look-see to make sure Rizzo and Dudak weren't anywhere within earshot. Phil didn't notice because he was doing the same thing. There were a lot of kids milling around, and you never knew who might be listening.

So far Ned had managed to avoid running afoul of the Rizzo gang. His friends thought this was because he was the principal's son, but he wasn't willing to bet on it. The secret was to get out of their way quietly, and in plenty of time so that it never looked like you were running.

Ned had assets which he had already learned to recognize and use. He was a handsome boy, and most adults liked him. They liked the look of him, for starters, and they liked the way he acted—bold, but not fresh. They liked you to stand up to them, look 'em in the eye, and trade a wisecrack or two, so long as you weren't being snotty. You could get away with things if they liked you; in fact, they wouldn't like you as much if you didn't try. They expected boys to have a little mischief in them. Nobody respected a guy who did his homework all the time and never got his clothes dirty.

And for the most part, the other kids liked him, too. He knew the girls liked to look at him; he'd caught them doing it often enough. And he knew the guys liked him better than they would've if he'd been too short, too tall, too fat, too skinny, cross-eyed, birthmarked, or just plain homely. He had an instinct that told him he was popular because kids liked to be seen with him. The same instinct warned him against making too much of himself, going overboard, trying to improve on nature. If you did that, they'd resent it. Ned worked hard at being a regular guy and was good at it, understanding it intuitively without having the words for it. He ran with regular guys and no one hassled him. Life was good.

They had Mr. Reimann for phys ed that afternoon, and he had a hair up his ass. He socked them with calisthenics for the whole period: jumping jacks, pushups, situps, laps around the playground.

"Move it, move it, get the lead out! I thought this was supposed to be *boys'* gym, fer cryin' out loud!"

He kept it up all period long. Football season was here, he admonished them. *So why don't we just play football?* Ned wondered. There were enough kids in the class for a good game of two-hand touch. It was getting hard to figure Mr. Reimann out.

By the end of the period, he was red-faced and sweaty from all his bellowing. At rest, Mr. Reimann looked like an SS guy in a World War II movie. When he got worked up, he just looked crazy. And he was starting to get a gut on him that Ned hadn't noticed until recently. He wondered how many laps Mr. Reimann could run these days.

Phys ed class over, the boys trooped back to their classroom. When they passed the teachers' lounge, Ned saw Mrs. Wilmot, the other kindergarten teacher, march stiffly out the door with Mr. Hall popping out after her, looking like he was going to chase her. But he stopped and watched her walk away from him. She didn't look back. He turned and saw the boys.

"Well? What are you staring at?" He clapped his hands loudly. "C'mon, c'mon, back to class! We've got work to do."

4

Doreen Davis, the school nurse, knew a thing or two about depression herself; but she wouldn't have dreamed of discussing it with her principal. She had enough to worry about without making Mr. Bradley wonder if she was going around the bend.

Victory School's days were numbered, and while the school district would be forced to honor its contractual obligations to the teachers, it was under no such obligation to her. Come June, she'd be out of a job.

She couldn't go back to being a floor nurse at a hospital; she'd tried it and failed utterly. She just wasn't made to withstand that kind of pressure. Sixteen-hour shifts, knowing that somebody could *die* if you made a mistake. No, thanks. She'd have to sign with an agency and go into private duty. And you never knew where you stood with that.

Right now all she wanted was to go home and curl up with a good romance and a glass of white wine.

So far, it had been a slow day, thank God. No scraped knees to clean and bandage, no pukey kids messing up the floor of her clinic while they waited for their mothers to take them home, no surprise visits from Mr. Bradley. Doreen wanted desperately to believe, as did everyone else, that Mr. Bradley was a nice guy who was only there to help, but she couldn't shake the conviction that he was trying to catch her slipping up so he could give her the old heave-ho. That, of course, was ridiculous, paranoid, even stupid—but that was how she felt. The principal made her nervous.

And so did the teachers, the kids, and their parents. About the only thing that didn't make her nervous lately was the wine. God bless you, Paul Masson.

Maybe it'd turn out to be a blessing in disguise when they closed Victory School. Doreen couldn't remember when she'd been happy here. The building was getting old. It made funny noises when she sat alone in her clinic on a quiet day: little creaks and groans, and half-heard rustlings in the walls and ceiling. It gave off funny smells during the heavy rains. And you'd swear there was something wrong with the air. Lately she felt like she was getting static interference in her thoughts, as if her brain were a poorly tuned radio.

She tried to ignore it.

5

Rudi was working outside on the blacktop, scrubbing more cuss words off one of the little wooden sheds that protected the two short stairways to the basement floor. He hummed tunelessly and wondered who kept defacing the walls with dirty pictures and words. Rudi didn't know what half the words meant, and Mr. Iacavella only got huffy when he asked him.

He worked energetically. Behind him Mr. Bennett had his second graders out for recess. They were playing kickball, shouting and squealing happily. Some of them called to Rudi and waved. He grinned and waved back. Mr. Bennett smiled and asked him how he was doing. "Fine!" Rudi said. He liked Mr. Bennett, thought he was a nice man. He didn't look a bit like a pansy. What was that supposed to mean, anyway? A pansy was a flower. But that was another thing Mr. Iacavella refused to explain to him. "People's private lives ain't none of your business, kid. You got enough to do takin' care of yourself. You don't need to bother about nobody else."

Rudi loved Mr. Iacavella, but sometimes the man just wouldn't talk. The world, according to Mr. Iacavella, was chock-full of things Rudi wasn't meant to know. Before you could even finish asking a question, he'd remember some job that needed doing. Consequently Rudi had a lot of questions that he never got a chance to ask.

And some of them concerned the school, which now had ghosts in it, sort of. Rudi couldn't see them clearly; he wasn't sure. But what were they, if not ghosts? Where had they come from? Why were they here? Rudi wanted to talk about it, but Mr. Iacavella just didn't have the time.

So Charlie Hall had just happened to park his car next to Joanne Wilmot's, and now he stood there, talking her ear off. Diane Phelps turned away in disgust—and a little fury.

Diane still had papers to grade before she went home; she preferred to do her schoolwork at school. She tried to concentrate on the results of that day's spelling quiz, but her eyes continued to stray to the window. From the hall she could hear Cosmo Iacavella getting on Rudi Fitch's case for missing a spot on the floor.

The parking lot was nearly empty as the clock's hands crept toward three-thirty, so Charlie and Wilmot stood out like a pair of sore thumbs. Diane couldn't take her eyes off them. How could their flirtations be so open?

Her own affair with Charlie had been immeasurably more discreet. No one had ever known about it; Diane had seen to that. She wouldn't have dreamed of allowing the damned fool to chat her up in the teachers' parking lot, where anyone could watch.

And he dumped me like a dead battery. . . .

Diane knew how that arrogant shit's mind worked. Time was running out for Charles Arthur Hall, the Casanova of the classrooms. From where she sat, she could see how the new, unwelcome pounds of flab clung to his waistline, and the unattractive rounding of his shoulders. Diane, who had buried her face in Charlie's hair a hundred times, knew he was dying it these days.

Sorry, Charlie, you don't stay young by romancing young girls. You're just like the rest of us: you don't stay young, period.

For God's sake, didn't that idiot girl see where he was coming from? How could she fall for an old fraud like Charlie? And what in blazes did Charlie see in her? Wilmot had a chest like an ironing board and an ass to match, and a squeaky voice that'd etch glass. She taught kindergarten, and when she got excited she sounded just like one of her kids. Charlie's interest in her bordered on pedophilia.

Besides, the little twerp was married.

Diane was married, too, but there was a difference. Mack Phelps was a waste of space. They were nearing their twenty-fifth anniversary, and as far as Diane was concerned, only the first two or three of those twenty-five years were worth remembering. She had tried to keep her marriage vows, God knew. Mack couldn't help being what he was, and a woman couldn't divorce her husband for being a bore, a stiff, a freeze-dried little toad. Verily, she deserved credit for having gotten involved with only one other man. It wasn't as if she'd given Charlie anything Mack wanted. She made sure Mack never found out, but she seriously doubted he'd care. Anyhow, what was she supposed to do, shrivel up and blow away?

What difference? That was easy. Years before Diane had met Charlie, she'd paid her dues to the institution of matrimony. She'd earned the right to a little happiness. And now, this ... this callow *girl*, this mincing little *shit*, was trying to supplant her. And she with a young, handsome, lusty husband!

Diane gritted her teeth. None of this was getting the spelling papers corrected, but damnation, how much could a person take? How much was she *expected* to take?

She looked out the window. Wilmot got into her car and drove off, leaving Charlie standing there, his eyes mooning over her. But then he shrugged it off and jumped into his Porsche.

Somewhere behind her, something slithered briefly across the floor. She turned and saw nothing.

Mice? Have we got mice in this dump now?

She felt a headache coming on and gave herself over to the blackest of thoughts.

Chapter Two

1

The deal was that if he finished all his homework by seven-thirty, and Mom looked it over and said it was all right, Ned could watch anything he wanted on TV. He could have friends over, if he wanted. But no homework, no tube.

"School is your job," she put it, "and grades are your pay."

"Isn't that terribly unenlightened?" Ned had once heard one of Mom's friends from the Historical Society say.

"Probably," Mom had said. "But he gets good grades and sticks to a job until he's finished it acceptably, whether he's interested or not."

Mom used to be a teacher, and she was thinking of going back to it soon. Dad was a principal. He ought to outrank Mom, just as he outranked all the teachers at Victory School; but Mom seemed to have the most to say about Ned's education. Ned wished she would get back into teaching so he could cut a few corners on his homework. She didn't expect him to be a brain, but she did insist on him getting all the work done on time and passing every subject.

Tonight he really wanted to watch *Inner City Humanoids* on

the eight o'clock movie. When he buckled right down to his homework after supper, Dad started giving him the business, standing over him with the TV Guide.

"Hmm, I wonder what it is that Ned is so bent on watching tonight. Let's see ... *MacNeil, Lehrer* on Public TV ... followed by *The Making of Brideshead Revisited* ... or will he turn to Channel 50 and *The Secret World of Club Mosses?*"

"Virgil, let the boy do his homework," Mom called from the kitchen.

"Yeah, Dad, let me study. You want me to grow up to be dumb?"

"Oh, that could never happen to a boy who watches *Inner City Humanoids!*"

Ned wondered if he had to take that from a grown man who still laughed at the Three Stooges. Dad reached out and pretended to squeeze his head.

"Still hard as a rock," he said. He ruffled Ned's hair and went off to bother Mom.

Ned didn't like the new American history textbook they were using. They listed questions for which answers weren't in the text.

> Would it have been a good idea to have made George Washington the king of the United States, as some people wanted to do after independence was secured?

Damn it, there wasn't anything in the book about it being a good idea or not. Ned had to wrestle with the sucker for several minutes before he wrote, *No, because we had just had a war to get rid of the King of England, and if George Washington were king, he couldn't be President. And everything would be different nowadays.* Mom wasn't terribly pleased with that answer and had made him tack more on to it before letting him off for the night. Peeved, because it was almost eight o'clock and he

23

didn't want to miss the start of the movie, he added that people don't get to vote on who becomes king, so it's fairer to have a president who gets elected every four years.

"All right," Mom said. He thanked her and fled to the rec room in the basement.

The humanoids were people who lived in old subway tunnels beneath New York City, where toxic waste fumes had turned them into ugly, cannibalistic monsters.

Ned's passion for horror movies was limitless. Some were better than others, but there was no such thing as a bad monster movie. He didn't care if it was Rodan flying over Tokyo, Frankenstein shambling out of the lab, or Jabba the Hutt tooling around in his giant sail barge: they were all great. He'd watched so many of them that it took something really far-out to scare him anymore. (Last week he saw *Aliens* on the VCR over at Phil Berg's house, and *that* scared him. But he was over his fright by now.) He liked Don Mattingly and Gary Carter, but his real heroes were the actors who made the monsters come alive: Lugosi, Chaney, Karloff, Christopher Lee, Peter Cushing, Vincent Price. He'd trade Mattingly's baseball card for a picture of a monster any day of the week—a habit which contributed to his popularity around the playground.

The only horror movies he couldn't quite get into were those of the slash 'em, gash 'em variety, *Friday the 13th* and its imitators: the ones in which the monsters turned out to be people with knives and hatchets. As Mom said, you might as well watch the evening news. Just the other day they'd had a story about a guy in Philadelphia who had a bunch of girls chained up in his basement, killed one, made stew out of her, and made the others eat it. Gross, man. What was the difference between that and a slasher movie?

Inner City Humanoids almost fell into that category, but it was saved by the fact that the Humanoids weren't all that human anymore. Their skin had turned mushroom-white and grown over their eyeballs; it was like the blind cave fish they sold in Nature World. The Humanoids had scraggly white hair and claws instead of fingernails. They got around in the dark by using sonar, like bats, making high-pitched squeaks and navigating by the echoes. They ate bag ladies, punks, and maintenance men, and their big dream was to derail a train so they could have a real feast on the injured passengers. Two supercops, a man and a woman, stopped them. The two heroes also fell in love, which was a big fat waste.

But the whole thing got Ned to wondering whether there really were weird creatures crawling around in the bowels of major cities, their presence unsuspected, their plans and appetites unknown. It just might be, he thought.

People wouldn't make or watch monster movies if they didn't think, deep down inside, that some of it just might be real.

2

Victory School was deserted and locked up for the night; but there was life in it.

And it was life that knew a sense of urgency. It was aware of an impending change, urgently preparing to respond to it.

It knew that some time soon it would be forced into a period of dormancy: that which nourished the sentient part of it would be removed. It was to be deprived of its prey.

The prey which swarmed so abundantly here was going to depart, never to return. The place was to be abandoned.

This sentience did not concern itself with causes. Why the prey was going to leave, why the artificial structure was to be destroyed, did not trouble it. It was not capable of posing questions to itself. Nor was it capable of processing all the information, all the details, which its sensors sifted from the electromagnetic energy emanating, in waves, from human brains. Its concerns were only to feed upon that energy and to

25

define broad patterns of information which it could understand on its own strange terms.

Having received the message that the prey would soon be leaving, it stepped up its level of activity. Not knowing how long its period of dormancy would be, it had to consume as much sentient energy as possible. Experience had taught it that the prey would eventually return; but when, and in what abundance, could not be known.

There was also nonlife in the school, aware and purposeful in its own peculiar fashion. It wandered in the darkened halls, neither prey nor fully predator. With this the sentience was unconcerned.

Sensors poised, it waited for the prey to return with the morning.

3

Carrie Bradley remained awake, listening to her husband mumble in his troubled sleep. Sometimes he thrashed, torpidly. When she could listen to no more, she turned on her reading lamp and woke him. His forehead was clammy with sweat.

"Jesus Christ," he sighed, and reached up to rub his eyes.

"You were having a bad dream. You woke me up."

"Sorry."

"Was it about the school again?"

"Yeah." Virgil tried to remember, but the details of the dream were already fading fast. "I was lost in it. I couldn't get out." He thought the dream had shown him as a boy again, but he wasn't sure. All that remained was a sense of helpless woe and a vague impression of the building slowly disintegrating all around him.

He rolled over to look at his wife and placed a hand on her waist. It was a more ample waist than it had been years ago, and a hint of gray had crept into her blond hair, but Virgil didn't mind. They had fallen in love at college and never fallen out of it. "What's a couple of pounds between friends?" he would say on those mornings when she'd climb onto the bathroom scale, cursing softly what she saw. But he meant what he said. Nature was taking its course with both of them, and it didn't matter to him. Her skin was still as soft and clean as a baby's backside, her bright blue eyes still sparkled, and he still adored the shape of her face beneath the blond bangs.

And she knew him so well: sometimes, he thought, even better than he knew himself.

She reached for him and they held each other. He buried his face in her breasts. She kissed the top of his head.

"Virgil, honey, you can't let it keep eating away at you like this."

"I don't know how to deal with it."

"Maybe you should get some help."

She meant psychiatric help, of course. He had nothing against psychiatry, but he didn't think he was quite ready to go that far.

"If it doesn't get better soon ..." he said. Damn it, other principals had had their schools shot out from under them, and it didn't make *them* crazy. "I don't understand why I'm reacting like this."

Carrie didn't understand, either; not fully. "I just hate to see you hurting," she said, "and I think a doctor can help. It's worth thinking about, don't you think?"

"Sure."

He snuggled up to her. She held him until he fell asleep, then gently disengaged herself and doused the light.

Chapter Three

1

There was an old piece of gum stuck to the floor of the hall outside the boiler room, and Rudi was scraping it off when he saw something out of the corner of his eye that caused him to slip with the scraper and gash the back of his left thumb almost to the nail.

"Aah!" he screamed, dropping the scraper and jamming the wounded thumb into his mouth. Jesus, it hurt like the dickens! But what he'd seen was so utterly strange that even the pain couldn't drive it from his mind. Still sucking on his thumb, he slid the scraper into his back pocket and stood up, staring in astonishment at the door to the music room.

It was closed. He unlocked it, opened it, reached inside, and turned on the light.

Victory School didn't have a band, but the school district did provide a floating music tutor who came once or twice a week to work with the few kids who'd shown some aptitude for learning an instrument. She wasn't here today.

Rudi sucked on his throbbing thumb and looked around. It was a small room, once a storeroom, nothing in it now but a couple of stools and music stands. It smelled a little musty, too. There were a number of rooms in this building that sometimes had a funny smell, but Mr. Iacavella always said, "I can't smell nothing, ain't you got enough work to do?"

Blood seeped into Rudi's mouth, giving him a mild case of the old jelly legs.

Will you look at that? Son-of-a-gun, there's nobody here. Nobody here at all.

He closed the room and went upstairs to see the nurse, Miss Davis.

Doreen had always been attracted to Rudi Fitch, and it made her nervous.

Attracted? That was hardly a good enough word. He was the most gorgeous hunk she'd ever seen, and he had the mind and personality of a well-behaved little boy—which made her feelings for him something that appalled her. No, she wasn't just attracted. He was the central figure in the dreams which shamed her when she woke.

And for God's sake, he was a *janitor!* Not even that: an *assistant* to a janitor. And feeble-minded. Where in the hell was the magic in that?

Her clinic door was open. She was at her desk reading a plantation novel when she heard the knock on the frame. Instinctively she thrust the book out of sight, ashamed of her taste in literature, embarrassed to be caught reading when she ought to be working; but when she looked up and saw Rudi, her cheeks burned.

Oh, holy Moses, he's sucking his thumb!

Her stomach twisted into knots, and she was thankful she was already sitting down, her trembling knees hidden by the desk. She'd just been reading the part of the novel where the lady of the plantation lures the strongest, handsomest slave into her boudoir *(. . . He was a black Adonis, his skin as glossy as a panther's . . .),* and she must've really been getting into it, be-

29

cause Rudi's sudden appearance at the door hit her like a ton of bricks. It literally left her breathless—and, of course, speechless.

"Miss Davis? I hurt myself." He took his thumb out of his mouth to show her. It dripped blood.

Well, that threw cold water on things. It was enough to get her thinking like a nurse again. She got up from her desk.

"Come in, Rudi. I'd better have a look at it."

He shuffled into the clinic as deferentially as any second grader, nervous and scared. She had him sit on the cot and hold out his hand. When her fingers touched him, the contact sent a violent *frisson* all the way down to her heels.

It was a deep cut, it might have scraped the bone; but it looked clean and she doubted there was anything to be gained by sending him to the doctor for stitches. You couldn't stitch the back of a thumb, anyway.

"Wash it off well," she said, helping him to move toward the open washroom. "Use plenty of soap. Then I'll disinfect it and bandage it up for you. You'll be all right."

She dropped his hand as if it were a hot coal and got up to fetch gauze, white tape, and a disinfectant. Rudi went to the sink and earnestly washed his hands. He dried them with paper towels, crumpling the bloody ones and tossing them into the waste basket beside the toilet.

He came out and sat back down, still wincing slightly when she took his hand. Doreen sat beside him, battling to concentrate on her work as their knees pressed warmly together.

She sprayed the cut liberally with Bactine, swabbed it clean with cotton, patched it with gauze, and wound white tape around it. He grunted softly once, when the pain flared up, but otherwise made no sound. The silence in the room was too much for Doreen, so as she bandaged the thumb, she tried to start a conversation.

"How did you manage to do this to yourself?" she asked.

"I was scraping some gum off the floor. I slipped."

"You'll have to be more careful."

"I couldn't help it, though," he said. "I wouldn't've slipped, only I saw that kid go into the music room and it really made me jump."

Doreen gave a little titter. "Now why in heaven's name would that startle you?"

"Kid wasn't wearing no clothes, Miss."

Doreen stopped bandaging and gawked at him. *Slow* was one thing, *addled* was another. "Which kid was this?" she said.

"I dunno, I never seen him before. He was naked. Kids shouldn't go running around the school with no clothes on. But when I went into the music room after him, he wasn't there." He made a motion with his free hand. "Cross my heart and hope to die. And the door was locked, too!"

Out of nowhere Doreen had an overpowering vision of Rudi standing naked in her doorway with his thing hanging down between his legs, and it was more real than anything she'd ever imagined before, or even dreamed. . . .

"Are you all right, Miss Davis?"

"I'm fine. Just a little dizzy spell." She got up and moved away from him, her heart still fluttering. "You can go back to work now. Just try not to get that bandage dirty. I'll look at it again in a couple of days."

He eyed her a little strangely, as if he'd caught a glimmer of what was in her mind, but couldn't quite grasp the meaning of it. He seemed to be on the point of saying something, then decided not to, but simply muttered, "Thanks, Miss." And then he shuffled politely out of the clinic, leaving her with a pulse that was like a desperate moth inside a jar. She closed the clinic door and leaned against it.

He's not for you, a stern inner voice reminded her. But what was the good of reminders?

Christ, what's wrong with me? She just couldn't think straight anymore. Not lately. *Like somebody's been using my brain for a basketball.*

And Rudi, the poor dumb fool—he had to be seeing things.

31

There were no naked children creeping around the halls, pulling vanishing acts in the music room.

Yet she could imagine it as clearly as if she'd seen it herself. Doreen shuddered.

2

Virgil sat in his office, his chair turned so he could look at Dr. Hargrove's picture.

He'd inherited it with the office, but he'd never liked that portrait, its colors now fading to musty shades of brown. The damned thing hung over him like a momento mori. *As you are now, so once was I.* And now he disliked it more than ever.

The plain truth of the matter was that Eric Hargrove, just weeks away from his retirement, entered the school alone one night—on what errand, no one ever knew—and was found dead the next morning when the custodian opened the building. He was stretched out on the floor with a broken neck, lying at the foot of the stairs that led from the landing at the boys' entrance down to the basement, a few yards from the boiler room. That was back in 1954, and Dr. Hargrove's likeness had hung in the office of his successors ever since.

Haunting it, Virgil sometimes thought.

I've got to get a grip on myself. Maybe Carrie was right. Maybe he ought to see a psychiatrist. *Want to end up like old man Hargrove?* Maybe he couldn't cope with losing this school, either. Maybe he couldn't face retirement.

Virgil had never liked to spend much time closeted in his private office. He believed that a principal should circulate around his school, talking with children, taking lunch with teachers, visiting the janitor in the boiler room. He liked to go out to the playground and punt a football with the kids, or hang around the faculty lounge for informal conversation on the daily business of the school, or just mundane chat about weather, sports, politics, family matters, whatever. He'd never bought the idea that a principal ought to be a remote, inaccessible figure of authority. Consequently he knew his school inside out, and his school knew him.

But with the school's termination close at hand, there seemed to be more paperwork than ever, and he'd been increasingly tied to his desk, filling out forms, writing summaries, reading reports written by others. And feeling oppressed.

Cabin fever. That was part of the problem. Sitting here climbing paper mountains all day. Adding stress to an already stressful situation.

Hargrove frowned down at him.

He had to beat this thing, and he'd never do it cooped up in here. Screw the goddamn paperwork. He shoved it aside and lit out for the teachers' room.

3

Rudi went back to the music room and had another look around. Still nobody there, and no sign that there ever had been.

He knew Miss Davis didn't believe him about the naked kid. In his own way he realized he'd seen something that wasn't really there: a ghost, for want of a better word. Rudi didn't know too many better words. He'd seen other things lately, too, that you might as well call ghosts.

Rudi knew he wasn't quite as smart as other people. Hadn't his own mother often told him so? But even if she hadn't, it'd still be obvious. So many things were said that made sense to everyone but him. And Mr. Iacavella would drop hints. "Leave the thinkin' to me, Rudi, you just ain't any good at it." Or, "Never you mind, there's plenty of smart people who ain't worth the powder to blow 'em away." He recognized these sayings as Mr. Iacavella's way of being kind, and appreciated them accordingly.

Knowing all this, Rudi understood that anything he said about ghosts would never be believed—not because it wasn't true, but because it came from him. He was Chicken Little, and the sky was falling.

His eye wandered toward the baseboard and stopped at a hole in the wall. He squatted for a closer look.

A mouse-hole? Here? It looked like a mouse-hole. *But this here's a concrete wall. Mice don't chew holes in concrete.* It was like the worm-holes by the library.

He shook his head and went back to the boiler room. Mr. Iacavella was reading one of his girlie magazines.

"Where you been?"

Rudi held up his bandaged thumb. "I cut myself, with the scraper. I had to go see Miss Davis."

"How many times do I got to tell you to be careful with the tools, Rudi? One of these days you're gonna hurt yourself but good."

Rudi almost came out with his excuse of having seen a ghost, but caught it before it escaped his lips. Now was not the time.

"Sorry, Mr. Iacavella."

"You gotta watch what you're doin', kid."

"I know."

Cosmo felt a wave of tenderness for the boy. Never mind what he looked like, or how old the calendar said he was; he was a boy, his mind wasn't ever going to grow up. Cosmo's own son, Joe, had long since grown up, and a lot of good it had done him, the smart-mouthed punk. He was probably in jail somewhere, and it'd serve him right. Cosmo would be god-damned if he ever let anything like that happen to Rudi.

But the tenderness embarrassed him, and he covered it up with a disgusted snarl.

"You can have *one* cup of coffee," he said, "and then it's back to work. You gotta earn the money they're payin' you, Rudi."

Rudi beamed. "Right!"

Cosmo had just about settled back into *Playboy* when Rudi

34

said, "Mr. Iacavella, I think we got mice." Cosmo closed the magazine.

"Horseshit. The exterminator was here just a month ago. You didn't *see* any mice, did you?"

Rudi sat down with his coffee. "Well, no ... but you can hear 'em. I've heard 'em rustlin' around in the ceiling upstairs."

"It was probably old wires or somethin' comin' loose," Cosmo said. "This is an old building, and it's goin' straight to hell. Just because you hear some noise don't mean we got mice. Decrepit old buildings make a lot of noise."

"There's a hole in the wall, though, in the music room. It looks like a mouse-hole."

Cosmo rested his head in his hands, and shook it. "Aw, grow up, Rudi! Mice don't make holes in concrete."

"Yeah, but—"

"Rudi, concrete ain't plastic. And we got *cheap* concrete. The stuff soaks up water like a sponge. It's the water that makes it crumble. Christ knows it's been a damp enough fall so far."

"I didn't see no water."

"You can't see it. It gets sucked up by the concrete."

"Okay. But I think—"

"The hell with it," said Cosmo. "Hey, did you nail some plywood over that hole in the shed yet?"

Rudi hadn't, and Cosmo made him hop to it.

4

One good thing about Mr. Hall was that he didn't make you go through a song-and-dance when you had to go to the bathroom. All you had to do was ask.

The boys' room was on the ground floor at the foot of the wide central stairs. Ned slid down the bannister and paused to look at the trophy case, where the fourth graders had set up an exhibit of the Age of Dinosaurs. He thought he recognized a brown Tyrannosaurus he'd lost in the sandbox that summer. What the exhibit really needed, he thought, was a bunch of scale-model cars and buildings, with mobs of tiny HO people fleeing the prehistoric monsters.

He pulled open the lavatory door and went in.

It smelled a little funny. Not so bad as when Rizzo and his gang had pissed on the radiator last winter, nothing like that. But for weeks after Mr. Iacavella and Rudi cleaned the radiator, it'd still give off just a little *hint* of pee, and it'd be enough to make you queasy. It was the same with this smell: it was so faint that Ned couldn't say what it was; but he sure as shit didn't like it. He stepped up to the urinal to finish his business and get out of there.

The boys' room was big, and the tiled floor and walls magnified sound: three boys acting up in here could sound like a major riot in the orangutan cage at the world's biggest zoo. The urinal flushed with a muffled roar, like a dam bursting far away. Ned zipped up his pants, getting a high-pitched echo out of that.

And what the fuck was that?

Ned had been about to go over to the sink to wash his hands. He hadn't even turned in that direction yet. His eyes had just started to move, his head had been just about to turn—and something had *moved* in the sink. *Something moved.* There was even a little bit of a smacking noise that went with it.

It was like a snake went up the tap. Ned hadn't seen it clearly, but that was how he thought of it. Right up the faucet, too quick to be seen. It was more like he'd sensed it.

He walked over to the sink. The sinks in Victory School all dripped, Ned knew that. Mr. Halasz on the board was always giving Dad grief over the school's water bill; but *this* tap wasn't dripping now.

It just sounded like it was dripping. The *puh-puh-puh* a faucet makes when it leaks.

Ned turned the tap. Somewhere beneath his feet an old pipe

groaned. For a second or two, no water came out. When it did come out, it was the color of rust, one of the school's trademarks. But it also had a faint odor that strongly reminded Ned of the time he'd caught a jarful of spiders, forgotten to poke airholes in the lid, left it overnight, and opened it the next morning. Phew!

The water stopped. Under the floor the pipe vibrated so emphatically that Ned turned off the tap. The pipe gave a last shudder and fell silent.

What's wrong with this freakin' thing?

Ned bent over and tried to peer up into the faucet. He couldn't quite get the angle he wanted, couldn't see anything. Maybe somebody had wadded a piece of gum way up there. Ned stuck his finger up the hole and wiggled it around as much as he could, but didn't feel any obstruction.

He'd have to tell Mr. Hall that the sink in the boys' room wasn't working, and Mr. Iacavella would have to fix it.

Ned pulled his fingertip out of the faucet and sniffed it. Mostly it smelled wet, but there was a trace of something else.

He took his finger out from under his nose and looked at it. It had some kind of slimy goo on it, like the gunk a slug leaves when it crawls over a rock.

"Yuck!" he cried aloud.

Maybe I ought to turn on the hot water and let it run, get really hot, and see what happens. Depending on the state of the school's hot-water heater on a given day, the hot water in the boys' room could stay lukewarm or get close to scalding. You had to be careful with it.

Ned turned on the hot water. It ran as usual. It never even got all that hot. He rinsed his hands and used several paper towels to get them dry.

He got all the slimy crud off his finger, but it still smelled a little funky if he held it right up to his nose.

Otto had the girls in line and ready to go, and still no Charlie Hall. The fat fuck was late, and Otto was supposed to be several minutes into his last free period of the week.

"Mr. Reimann—"

He wheeled and slammed his palm against the gymnasium door; it made several girls jump. "Shut up! No talking!" They stared up at him with something like awe and fear, the little witches. Hey, if they wanted to get tough, he'd show 'em what tough was.

Mr. Hall, meanwhile, hurried down the central stairs, knowing he was late to pick up his girls from gym and feeling the most godawful, light-headed, and strange he'd ever felt in his whole life.

He'd been sitting at his desk marking math papers, and suddenly he was looking up at the clock and it was past time to fetch the girls from gym, the boys from art. When he tried to stand up, the room spun wildly and his feet went out from under him, dumping him right on his ass on the floor. He had to wait for the floor to stop rocking before he could try to get up. This time he made it, holding onto his desk and feeling sick as a dog. He didn't know why he didn't puke.

He looked at the math papers. He'd only done a couple, and he'd been here the whole period.

That was when he began to get scared. Because Charlie did a line of coke when he could get some, he'd screwed around with LSD in college, he smoked pot regularly, he liked a drink or two. *And let's face it, folks, the bedroom scale ain't lyin', the doctor ain't lyin', and old Charlie's health and fitness would hardly pass muster at a retired mattress-testers' track meet.*

He'd conked out.

Heart attack? Couldn't be; he'd had no chest pains.

He gripped the desk hard and battled the onset of panic.

Take it easy, Charlie-boy. No need to fly off the handle.

You've just been living too high on the hog lately, that's all . . .
burning the candle at both ends. Cut the coke, quit smoking,
get some exercise. Get healthy.

Meanwhile, he had kids to bring back to the classroom. He let go of the desk and aimed himself at the door. His dizziness decreased a little with every step. By the time he reached the gym, he was moving normally.

The gym teacher, Reimann, was ticked off.

"You think I got nothin' better to do on a Friday afternoon than babysit your class?" Reimann demanded.

Charlie still felt sick, but he tried to hide it. "I'm sorry, man. I got bogged down in some work and lost track of the time." He held the door open. "C'mon, girls, let's go. Shake a leg." The girls filed out gratefully. Reimann glared once more at Charlie, then took off in the opposite direction.

By the time he got the boys out of the art room, he was more or less feeling his normal self again. He'd had a bad turn, that was all, a fluke. It'd never happen again. And he was going to turn over a new leaf, by God. Fitness . . . no more sitting around.

Hey, he might even shed a few pounds, take up racquetball. He wondered if Joanne Wilmot played racquetball. Joanne wouldn't give him the time of day, but now he was convinced it was because he was overweight. *Get down to one-ninety and she's yours, baby. Bet on it!*

6

On Fridays it wasn't unusual for Virgil to be the last one to leave the building; especially now, when he had extra paperwork to do. The teachers bugged out when the bell rang, eager to start their weekends, and the janitors usually had all the classrooms locked up by four. Virgil had his own keys to the office and the building, so Cosmo and Rudi didn't have to wait for him.

All afternoon he'd been stuck behind his desk, and his back was letting him know about it. He still had plenty to do, but he'd done enough for one day. He got up and stretched.

He put on his coat, turned off the lights, and locked up the office. He stood outside in the hall to stretch again. The hall lights had been left on, but it was beginning to get dark. Must be clouding up for the weekend, he thought. It figured.

Thump. A door swung shut and a pair of child-sized shoes pattered on the linoleum.

There's a kid downstairs. What was a child doing in the building this late? It was going on five. And anyway, the janitors should have locked the outside doors. They always did when they left and Virgil stayed alone. Couldn't have thieves or vandals sneaking in.

Virgil's skin began to prickle; he didn't know why. A child could have sneaked back in before the janitors locked the doors.

Suddenly he had a strong sense of déjà-vu. He wasn't particularly prone to that, and he certainly knew he shouldn't let it bug him; but it was disquieting nevertheless. *This has happened before. I've been through this before.*

It's an illusion. Just find the kid and go home.

"This is Mr. Bradley. Anybody here?"

The echo bounded down the corridor. He thought he heard the patter of feet again, but he wasn't sure. He'd have to go down to the ground floor.

There was only one long hall down there, and no stairways leading down to the basement. It ought to be easy to find the child. All the rooms were supposed to be locked, but it'd be simple enough to check.

The ground floor was a wing that had been added on in the early fifties; Virgil still thought of it as the "new wing," which was what everybody had called it when he was a student here. The gym was tacked onto the other end of it in 1963; now it did double-duty as cafeteria and meeting hall. The entrances to the gym should all be locked.

Virgil got to the bottom of the stairs and checked the boys'

40

room door, which was locked. He went around the corner and found the girls' room door locked, too.

With the school empty and still, the hall looked longer. Nothing stirred. Cosmo must have left a door open somewhere, and the child must have ducked in.

Let it go. Go home.

The irrational, irresponsible urge to back out of the situation grew stronger by the minute.

And suddenly Virgil *knew* where the child was. His adrenalin began to flow, his guts tightened, his pulse raced.

The child was hiding in the janitor's closet, between the girls' room and the kindergarten.

What was he supposed to do—lock up the building and leave some poor little kid stranded in it for the weekend?

His hand trembled as he reached for the doorknob.

Before he had a chance to lose his nerve, he yanked it open.

For a moment he saw nothing but a janitor's closet. He saw nothing but mops and pails.

Then it popped up out of the sink.

For a long, unmeasurable moment, Virgil could only gawk in starkest disbelief. The thing that leered at him from over the porcelain rim of the sink—the *child* that leered at him—was hardly bigger than a cat, with malassorted features and skin the color of a bad spot in an apple. It was stunted, with twiggy arms and a face that looked like it had been put together by a closet cubist. Every hair on Virgil's body rose at the sight of it. The air seemed to crackle around it, and there was a faint smell of ozone, like the fleeting odor left behind after an appliance shorts out with a hail of sparks.

Moreover, he could see through it. He could see the faucet and the stained back wall of the sink.

But what was worst of all was that he knew that face. In spite of the distortions and the fact that he had not seen it for thirty years, he knew it well.

It was his own.

Chapter Four

1

As Saturday afternoon drew to a close, Johnny Rizzo and his friends hid behind the multiflorabunda rose hedge that separated the Kanes's back yard from the Seitzers'. Flanked by Mike Dudak and Bob Diehl, Johnny was intently watching the Kanes's back porch door, to the knob of which he had tied an open can of pale-green paint. The can was sitting on the lower rail of the Kanes's new red cedar deck, and when somebody inside the house opened the door, it would pull the can off the rail and spill paint all over the clean new planks.

"She ain't never gonna open that door," Diehl complained.

"She will if we throw a few rocks," said Dudak.

Johnny ignored Diehl, but turned to Dudak and called him an asshole. "We can always throw rocks, jerkoff," he said. "Just keep your shirt on, okay? She ain't gonna know she got *any* problems until she pulls that door open. You chuck rocks at the house, you're gonna ruin the surprise."

Johnny was proud of the trick he'd devised, and he'd be damned if he'd let these two dickheads spoil it. They'd been all for it at first, but now they were getting antsy. Fuck them

. . . he'd bang their heads together if they got out of line. He'd done it before and he'd do it again without batting an eye. They knew that, so they shut up.

Baiting Doris Kane had become one of Johnny's favorite sports, ever since the day she'd seen him break a window at the Central School and had tattled to his old man. She was a teacher there, and that made her a double target: Mark hated teachers. *All* teachers. And her husband was a fucking wimp.

Finally it happened: the door opened from the inside. The can of paint fell to the deck. Mrs. Kane, hearing the dull clunk of metal on wood, pushed the screen door open to see what it was. Confronted by the mess on her porch, she stood and stared at it wordlessly.

Just in time, Johnny spotted Mike with a pear-sized rock in his hand, cranking up to throw it. He grabbed Mike's wrist and shook the stone free.

"Are you fuckin' nuts?" He gave the wrist a yank and made Mike fall backward. The smaller boy glared poisonously at him, his face tight with pain.

"With my luck," Johnny said, "you'd have conked her right on the head and killed her—and *I'd* get blamed for it!"

"Let go of my arm!"

Johnny gave it an extra yank, then let go. It was a damned good thing, he thought, that Mike was only half his size. Mike had been pushing him lately, and the only way to remind him who was boss was to hurt him. Johnny would hurt him plenty, if he had to, and he usually did. You wouldn't know it to look at him, for he was a scrawny little fucker, but Mike Dudak was tough: he wasn't afraid of a little pain. In this he resembled Johnny, who took the worst his old man could dish out without bawling. Of the three, only Diehl—the biggest of them, even if most of it was mostly flab—was a pussy. Bend his fingers back once, and he was yours for life.

"Look," Diehl interrupted, "here's Fuckface!"

Nelson Kane, all ninety pounds of him, had joined his wife

at the door to peer mournfully down at his new deck. Mike got up to watch through the hedge with the others.

"That *is* beautiful!" Bob Diehl said.

The Kanes looked so woebegone that Johnny had to hold both hands over his mouth to keep from guffawing out loud. The harder he tried not to laugh, the funnier it got. Man, *look* at 'em, they were gonna bust out and cry like babies!

"I can't take it!" he gagged. "Let's get outta here!"

Hunching over so they couldn't be seen beyond the hedge, they ran through the Seitzers' yard and out to Reardon Street. Once they were on the sidewalk, Johnny let it all hang out and laughed until his sides ached. Bob laughed, too, that distinctive *huh-huh-huh* that made his big, soft body quiver all over.

Mike only grinned.

"Did you *see* that?" Johnny cried.

"Fuckin' A!" Bob chimed in. Johnny whacked him backhand in the tummy and he still kept laughing. Johnny noticed that Mike wasn't whooping it up with them, and stopped.

"What's your fuckin' problem, Dude? You still sore because I wouldn't let you cream her with a rock?"

"I ain't your fuckin' slave, Rizzo."

He was getting mad again. Lately he seemed to have a short fuse. Johnny wasn't afraid of him. What the hell, Johnny was built like a miniature fullback, it'd take three or four Mike Dudaks to put him down. But he still didn't want to fight, not just now. Johnny had never studied management techniques, but he knew you didn't slap down a guy like Dudak twice in one afternoon. He'd twisted the Dude's arm real good, he'd made his point. If he made it again, he'd lose him. Instinctively he took another tack.

"Of course you ain't," he agreed "Shit, you can't be a slave. You ain't a nigger."

"Drop dead, greaseball."

Johnny grabbed Bob and yanked him to his side. "Hey, do you hear that, you hear the way this guy is talkin' to me? You gonna let him call me a greaseball, you big dumb kraut?"

44

Bob thought that was a scream and started giggling again. Mike called them both a couple of shitheads and let his rebellion slide for the time being.

2

Virgil couldn't talk about it.

By the time he got home Friday, late for supper, he could no longer accept his experience in the janitor's closet as real. Horrible, yes; real, no. He'd had some kind of hallucination.

All he could think to do was to try to continue his life normally. He watched TV Friday night. On Saturday he raked leaves, went out and got a pizza for supper, and spent the evening playing the Game of Life with his wife and son. He took his family to church as usual on Sunday morning, threw the football around a little with Ned and some of the other kids, and then settled into his easy chair to watch the Giants–Lions game.

He'd be doing just fine if it weren't for the dreams.

They roared into his sleep on Friday night like a band of Hell's Angels blasting down the main street of a little country town, and again on Saturday. He couldn't really remember them when he woke, stiff and sweating, his muscles sore from tension. But he knew they had to do with the janitor's closet and what he'd experienced there.

He tried to put them out of his mind and enjoy the NFL game; but a few minutes after the kickoff, Carrie came in from the kitchen and put the issue on the line.

"I'm worried about you, Virgil. You've got to tell me what's happening to you. I'm getting scared."

"You know what's happening to me," he said. "Nightmares." He was afraid to say more. She'd really be scared if she knew he was seeing haints in the schoolhouse. He couldn't

45

think of any way he could talk about it without sounding like a crazy man.

Carrie sat on the edge of the couch. "This is two nights in a row you've had your sleep broken," she said. "Honey, that's not like you! Take it from the woman who's slept in your bed every night for the last fifteen years. I *know* when something's wrong. And I know it's getting worse."

He couldn't deny it. He turned to the TV screen, but didn't see any of the game.

"I wish I could tell you what it is," he said. "I want to. But I don't know how. I don't know what's wrong."

She made him come to the couch with her, and held him.

"Honey, you've got to see a doctor. You need someone who'll know how to ask the right questions. If there's something hurting you and you don't know what it is, you need to find out. I don't think you can do that without professional help."

The phrase "professional help" made him wince, but he made no protest. She was right. He needed a shrink.

Carrie said, "I think you ought to get some clinical hypnosis, Virgil. At the very least, it'll relax you. Don't be mad at me, but while you were out yesterday, I made some discreet phone calls. There are several doctors in our area who do that kind of work. And we're not talking years of expensive therapy, either. You should be able to get some benefit out of it right away. *Please* let me make an appointment for you."

He stared at her. "Christ, Carrie, is it that obvious?"

"Yes, honey. It's obvious." She paused. He didn't interrupt. "On Friday night you had the screaming meemies. You woke Ned. He asked about it yesterday, Virgil. He's worried about you, too. I told him you just had a bad dream, but he's not stupid. He can tell something's wrong. You owe it to him to take care of yourself."

"All right," he sighed. "Make the appointment. I guess it's time to see the witch doctor."

Chapter Five

1

On Tuesday morning Doreen got to work bright and early. She walked into her clinic before a soul could bother her, closed the door, and tried to lose herself in her plantation novel.

Maybe it'd be one of those days when the school seemed to forget she was there: no kids hurt on the playground or sick in the classroom, no interruptions from the principal, no phone calls from the supervisor of school nurses. After yesterday, she could use a quiet day.

She'd had her hands full Monday with a parent threatening to sue her, the school district, the town, and anybody else she could think of because the woman's rotten little bitch of a girl had picked a fight with a rotten little bastard of a boy and gotten punched in the eye for it. She only had a shiner, but her mother—one of those aggressive, stupid fat women so common in this part of town—went into hyperspace over it and convinced herself that the bruising around the kid's eye was the result of some kind of malpractice on Doreen's part. She charged into the clinic like a rhino and scared Doreen half to death. Doreen was still shaking when she got home and needed more than the usual amount of wine to calm her nerves.

So please, God, a quiet day today.

She really had had too much to drink last night. She was a bit hung over, and her breath tasted sour. Sudden movements made her head hurt.

And she couldn't get into the book. Maybe it was just too early in the morning, but all she was getting out of it was a bunch of words on paper. She put it down, fidgeted a little, and got up to go to the washroom, thinking a bit of cold water on her face would snap her out of the doldrums.

She turned on the light and peered into the mirror.

Yeah, it showed. There were bags under her eyes, and she looked like she'd aged five years overnight. Even her hair looked sick.

Below the mirror, water sloshed out of one of the taps.

Something cold and wet and rubbery whipped itself around her left wrist.

She sprang back with a yelp, but it held her close to the sink. She looked to see what it was.

A ribbed pink coil, glistening with slime, had emerged from the hot water faucet to lash itself around her wrist. It felt like a gigantic earthworm. It tugged her closer to the sink. It seemed to stretch a little when she pulled against it, but it was much too strong for her ... she couldn't break its hold.

She shrieked. Her door was closed. There was nobody in the building close enough to hear her, and there wouldn't be for another fifteen minutes.

As if summoned by her shriek, another pointed pink tendril snaked out from the cold water faucet and threw itself at her. She tried to beat it back. With blinding speed it caught her other wrist and pulled her downward.

The drain gargled. As she was drawn toward it, a thicker tentacle burst from the hole and seized her neck, choking off her next scream.

Her mind boiled into chaos.

* * *

Slowly she became aware that she was lying in a fetal position on the washroom floor. She had no idea how she'd come to be there. She tried to remember whether she'd fallen, or fainted, or what, but nothing came to her. She couldn't even remember having gone into the washroom.

Panic touched her: no one must come in and find her like this. She gathered her strength and struggled to her hands and knees.

Brilliant splashes of red, like starbursts, appeared on the floor before her eyes. It took her another moment or two before she realized that her nose was bleeding.

Oh, sweet Jesus! Her thoughts were a useless whirl of panic. She shut her eyes and battled to think.

I fainted. I banged my nose on the sink when I went down.

She had to get up. She didn't feel like getting up; she felt like she was going to heave; but if anyone came through the clinic door and saw her . . .

She grabbed the sink and practically climbed it. She wet a couple of paper towels with cold water and wiped her face clean. She wet another one and held it to her nostrils, tilting her head back. She tasted blood in the back of her mouth, but the bleeding had already slowed to a slight seepage. Pressing the towel to her nose, she backed out of the washroom, groped her way to her chair, and sat down.

According to the clock on the wall, she'd been unconscious for a good half-hour. The bells had rung, the kids were all in class, the school day had begun.

It made her shudder all over. In all the time she was out of it, it was a miracle no one had come looking for her. *I'd have been out of a job faster than you can say bye-bye.* In a way that was scarier than the fact of having had a fainting spell—and that was pretty scary in itself. Doreen had never experienced such a thing.

It had to be the stress. That and the alcohol, and the restless

49

night she'd spent, and maybe suddenly rising from a sitting position ... all of it could easily bring on a faint. Her brother had once fainted during a softball game. He was catching, it was a ninety-degree day, it was during a long inning, and when he had to jump up suddenly to catch a pop-up, down he went. Anybody could faint, given the right circumstances.

It was still scary ... scary as hell. Her chest was tight with fear.

Her nose hurt inside. A headache was descending on her, and in no time at all it blossomed into one of those pulsating flowers of pain that made like it was going to pop her eyes out from the inside.

She sat at her desk and whimpered.

2

While Doreen Davis was trying to lose herself in her plantation novel, Ned was trying to figure out some way to tell his friends that his dad was going to be hypnotized.

"And you're not to tell anybody about it, either," Mom had said, when she'd sent him out the door that morning. "Not your friends, not your teacher, not a soul. This is private family business."

They'd told him about it last night. Compared to most kids, Ned got told a lot about family business. As the principal's son, though, he had to be careful what he said at school. Private family business was not to become the subject of schoolyard gossip. And it was too bad, because here at last was something to top Phil Berg's story about his mom being asked for a date by a murderer. Mrs. Berg worked for a lawyer, the murderer was one of her boss's clients, and that story had made Phil a freakin' celebrity around the school. It was kind of a neat story when you first heard it, but after twenty retellings, it was beginning to get on Ned's nerves. His mouth nearly watered as he imagined Phil's face if he told him, "Yeah, well, my dad's gonna get *hypnotized* today! And not just to quit smokin', either."

He couldn't exactly tell the rest, though, could he? "See, Dad's been actin' awful weird for awhile, and he wakes up screamin' 'cause he has bad dreams. And he doesn't know what it's all about, so he's gettin' hypnotized to find out." Which wasn't quite how his parents had explained the situation, but it was probably a little closer to the truth than they'd have liked him to get. Maybe they didn't realize how much he noticed about his dad's moods. The old man wasn't himself, that was for sure. Ned just hoped the hypnotist could set him to rights.

As usual, he walked to school with Phil Berg and Marty McManus, the beanpole who lived next door. Marty's kid sister, Patty, tagged along. Patty was all right. She played third base on the farm team and could conceivably join Ned and Phil in the Valley Realty Blue Jays' infield next summer. Ned had a hunch that the kid had a crush on him, but that was okay, so long as he didn't have to do anything about it. Actually, it was kind of neat.

Marty was talking about basketball, which was like Orville Redenbacher talking about popcorn. You'd be shocked if he suddenly started talking about something else. Marty already had his whole life planned out: CYO Boys' League, high school varsity, all-American at St. John's, and then the NBA, and so on.

Marty was on that kick now, and Ned didn't hear a word he said. He was wondering how something could bother a person so badly that it gave him nightmares, without that person knowing what it was. He was wondering how Dad would feel when the hypnotist put him under.

Something soft flopped into his face.

Daydream broken, he was back on the playground, holding a knit cap which he'd caught instinctively after it hit him in the face. For a moment it seemed to have materialized out of nowhere.

51

"My hat! My hat!" A little kid, a first or second grader whose name Ned wasn't sure of, jumped up and down in front of him.

"Throw it here, Bradley!"

And whaddaya know, there was Mike Dudak motioning for the hat, too, with Johnny Rizzo and Bob Diehl by his side. Now Ned knew what was happening. Rizzo's gang had snatched the little kid's hat and was playing keep-away with it, probably hoping they'd make the little kid cry. Nothing entertained them more than somebody crying.

Knowing this, and knowing it was dangerous to cross them, Ned still gave the hat back to the victim, who promptly ran away. He did it because he wasn't thinking about it; he was still thinking about his dad's impending session with the hypnotist, and all he really did was hold the hat out and allow the owner to grab it. Now that he realized what he'd done, he suspected he'd finally made the mistake he'd been carefully avoiding for years—coming to the notice of Rizzo and his boys.

"What the fuck did you do that for, huh?" Rizzo demanded.

Ned was on the point of apologizing when Dudak shrilled, "God damn it, Bradley, I told you to throw that hat to me! You deaf or somethin'?"

From Rizzo, Ned would have taken that. Rizzo was a fellow fifth grader, and he could wad Ned like a chewing gum wrapper if he ever got his hands on him. But from Mike Dudak, no way. The skinny little creep was only in the fourth grade. Ned gave him the finger and said, "Chew on this, Weasel brain!"

For some reason, that tickled the shit out of Diehl. "Hey, I like that! Weasel brain!" He pointed to Dudak and guffawed.

Mike didn't like it a bit. He couldn't decide whether to attack Ned or Diehl. He was so mad that you could feel it radiating from him like heat from an oven, and Ned suddenly thought that maybe he'd just made another mistake, getting on this crazy sucker's bad side. It suddenly came to him that Dudak might be a lot more dangerous than he looked—like finding a little snake under a log that might turn out to be a baby copperhead.

52

Then Mr. Bennett came up with the little kid whose hat was taken, and Rizzo and his pals beat it around the other side of the building.

3

Otto Reimann saw Richard Bennett talking to some boys on the playground and wondered how the hell he was the only one who could see that Bennett was a fag.

Otto turned away. He felt like he might be getting an ulcer.

4

Diane Phelps watched Charlie Hall sitting in his Porsche, drumming his fingers on the steering wheel, when he ought to be up in his classroom, getting ready for the day. Obviously he was waiting for that little slut Wilmot to drive up so he could arrange an "accidental" meeting with her. The fool was so transparent. And Joanne Wilmot deserved to be horsewhipped for encouraging him.

Diane was desperately tempted to confront them. The only thing that held her back was her dread of making a scene. And the moment she did that, of course, her own affair with Charlie would be exposed. On the whole, she would be boiled in oil before she let that happen.

She could hardly stand watching Charlie's new affair develop. The stress was unbelievable. These days, she brooded on it all the time. When she saw the two of them together, it brought on mammoth headaches, and she was up all last night with a nosebleed that just wouldn't quit. She had an appointment to see her doctor tomorrow afternoon; maybe he could prescribe something that would calm her down.

Some perverse desire for self-flagellation tried to keep her outside a little longer, waiting for Wilmot, but she fought it successfully and retreated to her classroom.

The headache descended on her anyway.

5

"Well, you've done it now," Phil said. He grinned at Ned, the sun flashing from the coke-bottle lenses of his glasses. "It's been nice knowin' ya."

"You gonna leave me anything in your will?" Marty asked.

Ned tried to laugh it off. He was in the soup now, that was for damn sure.

Maybe he could pay the Kung-fu Twins to protect him—although he doubted that even the Wang brothers would be a match for Johnny Rizzo.

Patty, however, was looking up at him like he was some kind of hero. He liked that, for what it was worth.

"Look," said Phil, "all you gotta do is leave town. They can't get you if they don't know where you live."

"You guys are a big help, you know that? Maybe what I need is some friends who aren't too chickenshit to stick by me."

Phil made chicken wings with his arms, scratched the ground with his shoe, and said, "Bawk-bawk-bawk!"

The bell rang.

Chapter Six

1

I'm just walking down the hall.

I gotta pee real bad. Miss Watson let me go, even though it's the middle of recess. We're playing kickball. "Just hurry back, Virgil," she says to me. "You don't want to miss your ups."

Well, I go to the bathroom and I wash my hands. I feel good because Miss Watson trusts me not to mess around. She's really nice.

It's neat to be here all alone, though. I can stop for a just a minute and look at the exhibition case. It's full of toy army men; they're havin' a war. Our guys are the green ones, the brown ones are the Japs, I think. We got tanks and cannons and planes. I wish I had more army men. . . .

What happens next? Umm . . . I don't know. I guess I just go back out to recess. I don't remember.

"It's only a dream, Virgil. You don't have to wake up. It can't hurt you. Let's go back to where you're looking at the army men, and try again."

It's kind of spooky in here. The hall is so big. All the class-

55

room doors are closed, so it's quiet, too. It's like I'm the only one in the whole school—everybody else is gone.

What's that?

I heard something. I heard a door being unlocked. A click sound. Somebody unlocked a door, only I don't see anyone.

I better get goin'. I'm gettin' scared. I don't like this.

Somethin's gonna happen. Oh, no ... I don't wanna go in there....

"It's only a dream, Virgil. You're all right. Go in where?"

The janitor's room. Mr. Cuppy, he's got this little room next to the bathroom. He's got a sink in there, and some mops and brooms and junk like that.... He's not there now. Nobody's there.

I don't want to go in. There's somethin' bad in there. Oh, man ... I'm goin' in! I'm gonna go in there! Oh, Jesus, I'm openin' the door, and I don't wanna....

Virgil was immoderately relived to find himself back in the psychiatrist's office.

Under his clothes, his skin was clammy with sweat. His muscles were tense. He let out a deep sigh and tried to relax on the couch.

"I think that'll be all, for the time being," the psychiatrist said. "We can take it up again Thursday afternoon."

Virgil nodded, finding himself looking forward to it. Now that the horror of the dream was beginning to wear off, he felt like he'd somehow accomplished something.

He'd found Dr. Lauther an easy man in whom to confide. Maybe it was because Karl Lauther looked like an all-American college boy who'd grown up to join the Jaycees, and not like a typical psychiatrist. He had short blond hair and an athletic build, and he dressed casually but well. Telling him your troubles was like sitting down with an old friend and talking baseball over beer and pretzels.

"Am I crazy, Doc?" Virgil added a sheepish smile to mask the tension that he felt.

"No more than I am," Lauther said.

"What's happening to me, then? I mean, sane people don't ordinarily see boyhood phantoms of themselves when they open closet doors. . . ."

The doctor leaned back on his chair and smiled disarmingly.

"It's not that simple, Virgil.

"Look, this is all preliminary; but for what it's worth, I do have an idea about it.

"I believe this nightmare of yours stems from an experience you probably had as a child but which you no longer consciously remember. Something that was at that time so frightening and so unpleasant that you unconsciously suppressed it. And now, for one reason or another, it's trying to come back to the surface, and causing nightmares."

Virgil had studied some psychology in college, but at the moment, he'd forgotten everything he'd learned. "You mean the dreams are caused by this repressed memory coming out of the woodwork after all these years?" he asked.

"Something like that."

"But what about the hallucination? I wasn't dreaming when that happened. I was wide awake!"

"Doesn't matter," Lauther said. "You'd been sleeping *very* poorly, you'd just put in quite a long work day, and you'd been under stress from two sources—the threat of losing your job, and consequently your status in the community; and the physical and emotional stress caused by your lack of sleep and these bad nightmares. It's all tied together.

"Everyone's unique, Virgil. We all respond to stress individually. But one hallucination doesn't make a psychosis. It was just your mind reacting to a culmination of major stressful stimuli."

Lauther stood up and put his hands in his pockets, which made him look thoughtful in a nonthreatening way.

"I think that when we root out this suppressed memory, and

really analyze it, you'll feel a lot better," he said. "What's really bothering you right now is that you can't understand this, you can't make any sense of what's been happening. When you do understand it, much of the stress will be removed. After all, there's nothing so scary as the unknown."

"Jesus, I hope you're right."

Lauther smiled at him. "Trust me. I'm a good psychiatrist."

2

Virgil got home in time to join his son in the living room for *The People's Court,* but Ned wasn't interested in Judge Wapner's decisions today.

"What's it like, Dad, when you get hypnotized? Were you scared?"

Virgil ruffled the boy's hair. "No!" he said. "As a matter of fact, being hypnotized is kind of pleasant. It makes you feel good.

"You don't go into a trance or anything, like in the movies. You don't even fall asleep. It's nothing but a state of complete relaxation. Your eyes are closed, but you're very much aware of things. At the same time, you're able to *concentrate* better— much better than you could otherwise. When the doctor asks you to remember something, you can remember it so clearly that it's like reliving it—even if you'd forgotten it a long time ago. If you try to imagine something, it becomes very real to you. And there's no way it can hurt you. It's one-hundred-percent safe."

Ned had seen his share of goofy movies and TV shows involving hypnosis, and he had the average eleven-year-old's misconceptions about it. Virgil did what he could to clear them up.

"I still don't get what they're hypnotizing you *for,*" Ned said.

Virgil wasn't about to tell his son that he'd had a hallucination.

"Ned, you know how much it bothers me that the school will be closing down, and I won't be principal anymore. That's part of the problem. But I've also been having bad dreams that I don't remember when I wake up. The hypnosis is to help me remember them, so I can understand them and not be so scared by them. Once I remember, I'll be right as rain again."

He said so more in faith than in actual belief, hoping it would turn out to be true. *Please, God, let it be true. . . .*

In point of fact, however, he didn't feel as frightened as he had before seeing Dr. Lauther. The man had reassured him that he wasn't losing his mind, and he clung to it with all the strength he had. The doctor was competent; you had to assume he knew what he was talking about.

Meanwhile, Virgil wasn't looking forward to his bedtime.

Chapter Seven

1

There was more to the dream that night, and he remembered more of it when he snapped out of sleep at 5 a.m.

He *did* go up to the janitor's sink, in his dream, and he *did* look into it . . . but that was all he knew.

"At least it was easier getting back to sleep this time," he told his wife over breakfast. They ate before Ned got up. "I really think the hypnosis did me some good. I really want to get back to it tomorrow."

"The doctor says the dreams are based on something that really happened?" Carrie asked. She looked tired. *My fault,* Vigil thought. But she wasn't blaming him.

"I do feel better," he said, "honest."

"We can still move the meeting to another place tonight, so you can rest," Carrie said.

Carrie Bradley belonged to the Tianoga Historical Society and it was her turn to host the monthly meeting.

"Have it here," said Virgil. "I was looking forward to sitting in."

"As long as you're sure ..."

"Sure, I'm sure."

2

Diane's day left something to be desired.

The sight of Charlie following Wilmot all over the teachers' room caused her to lose her appetite. It would have been bad enough, with Otto Reimann clumsily implying that Richard Bennett was gay, and everybody else trying to pretend it was just a harmless joke; but it was unendurable, the way Charlie carried on. He might as well have gotten down on all fours and stuck his nose in Wilmot's butt, like a stray dog besotted with a bitch in heat. It turned Diane's stomach. And Wilmot! Making believe nothing was going on and acting as if Charlie wasn't even there.

I will not stand for this. They cannot do this to me. I will not be insulted.

They were going to be sorry, Diane vowed to herself. They were going to wish they'd never been born, the both of them. *Just keep it up. . . .*

After lunch, the rest of the day had been an unmitigated disaster. The kids were blockheads. Diane dropped an eraser and tripped over it, damn near breaking her neck. Once or twice she was nearly blinded by the pain of her headache.

And now this damned fool of a quack doctor was trying to tell her she'd gone and stuck a *pencil* up her nose.

"Are you out of your mind?" she snapped. "Why on earth would I do such a thing?"

The doctor shrugged. "That's not my department," he said. "All I can tell you is, I see this kind of injury from time to time in children, and it's usually caused by the insertion of a long, sharp foreign object—like a pencil. You're lucky you don't have an infection. I'll prescribe an antibiotic, though, to be on the safe side."

According to the doctor, Diane had a hole deep in her nose, a perforated nasal passage, and this was the cause of her nosebleeds. He used a cotton swab to clean it out, a ham-fisted operation that had hurt like holy hell and started the damned thing bleeding once again. The swab came out with a soggy lump of semiclotted blood, and Diane had had to lie down on the examining table until the bleeding stopped. While she was recumbent, the doctor took her blood pressure.

"Up a little," he reported.

"Of course it's up! You're *scaring* me."

"Sorry ... there's really no cause for alarm. It's just a little wound, and now that we've disinfected it, it ought to heal well. I wish you'd tell me how it happened, though."

Diane didn't know how it had happened, and that was why her blood pressure was up. For all she knew, she'd hopped around plunging a knitting needle up there while singing *Camptown Races.* The truth was that she could not remember, not a bit. The truth was that there were getting to be a lot of little holes in her memory of late, a minute here, three minutes there. Her mind was starting to go. It scared her, and to cover it, she confronted the doctor.

"What about the headaches?" she snapped.

"Well, you have no medical history of migraine, although that doesn't rule them out. It's possible some slight infection has developed in the nasal passage, and that might cause a headache or two—but I'm only guessing about that. I can prescribe you something a little stronger than aspirin, if you want, but what I really think you need is a couple of days' rest. Come back if the headaches continue, and we'll see what else we can do. I may have to send you to a specialist."

Brilliant, she felt like retorting. *I'm lying here with a god damned hole in my nose and the worst headaches I've ever had, and all you can say is that I might have to see a specialist. What the holy hell am I paying* you *for, then?*

When the bleeding stopped, she got up, paid her bill, and left, calculating the money wasted. She'd have the prescriptions filled, though she doubted it would do her any good. Maybe she'd alert the AMA to this turkey, just for laughs.

She wished it was Joanne Wilmot's nose that was bleeding, and Wilmot's head that was splitting in two. This was all due to stress, and Wilmot was to blame. She *could*, after all, honor her marriage vows and tell Charlie to take a flying leap. She *could* stay out of Charlie's way. She didn't have to go flaunting her conquest right under Diane's nose.

I ought to stay home for a day or two, she thought. But that'd be giving them the green light, wouldn't it?

Diane shook her head as she started her car. If anybody wound up in a hospital, it sure as holy hell wasn't going to be her.

Chapter Eight

1

Virgil sat comfortably in his corner of the sofa while the Historical Society cleared away old business.

He'd had a good day, sort of. Halloween was coming, and the decorations were going up all over the school. Outside the kindergarten, the hall was festooned with orange construction-paper pumpkins. The windows were filling with figures of black cats, witches, skeletons. In the office, Millie Stanhouse had a crêpe-paper ghost hanging over her desk. And Virgil had pried himself loose from his paperwork to stroll the halls, enjoying the new color that brightened up what was, if the truth be known, a pretty grim old building. He'd even found the time to cut a chain of paper ghosts with the first-graders.

Now he was ready to enjoy the meeting. He wasn't a member, but the members were all friends of his. The society president, Fielding Jones, was more than just a friend . . . he was the senior member of the school board, so technically Virgil worked for him. So did another member of the society: Harriet Fulham, principal of the Central School. Harriet and her husband, John, had been the Bradleys' companions on many a camping or fishing trip. *By this time next year, Harriett'll have a school and you won't,* Virgil caught himself thinking. Angrily he tried to banish the envy.

"Councilwoman Bowers called me today," Fielding reported when the last of the old business was disposed of. "I think she may be trying to drag us into politics."

"What do you mean?" somebody asked.

Fielding tilted his head. He looked like Einstein, Virgil thought. Fielding had served on the school board since the sixties, had been a borough councilman before that, and knew Tianoga and its schools like an old rooster knows a barnyard. What he didn't know about Tianoga politics hadn't happened yet—and probably wasn't going to.

"You know Mrs. Bowers is feuding with the mayor and his merry men," Fielding said. Trish Bowers was the only Democrat and the only woman on the otherwise all-male, all-Republican governing body. "She's been looking for an issue to hang her hat on, and I think she'll try to get some mileage out of Victory School."

"What does that have to do with us?" asked one of the members.

Fielding grinned. "Mrs. Bowers knows we're working on a history of the school district. She asked me if we could prepare a special report on Victory, to be completed before the school year is out. I think she might be planning a drive to get up a referendum on the school closing and try to stir people up. I don't want us getting caught in the middle of anything like that."

Virgil felt a grinding in his guts. Damn the politicians! As if the situation weren't hard enough, did they have to go around raising false hopes? There was no way to save Victory School. The school board had voted unanimously to close it.

One of the society members, old Mrs. Van Horn, who hadn't had a child in school since FDR was President, spoke up.

"What do you want to get rid of the school for, Fielding? Seems a shame to me."

"Victory's a facility that's outlived its usefulness," he said. "Our job here at the board is to provide a good education to the children of this community at a reasonable cost to the taxpayer. It's not our job to preserve every old building—especially one that was never a very good one to begin with.

"It's simple economics, Elsie. For the past ten years there's been an overall decline in the number of children enrolled in Tianoga's schools. People just aren't raising the large families they used to. The board researched it carefully, and while the decline does seem to be leveling off, there's no reason to believe the trend will be reversed in the immediate future. The town's pupil population is not going to increase overnight."

How can anybody know *that?* wondered Virgil.

"Meanwhile," Fielding said, "it costs us money to run the school and maintain it. Fuel bills, supplies, repairs. As you all know, construction of the school began in 1942—two years ahead of plan. It should've been pushed back, not forward. It was supposed to be a real 'victory' school—like the victory gardens—but with World War II on, they just couldn't get decent materials and labor. The result: a shoddy piece of work. It was opened in 1946, in time for the baby boom, and we've had problems with it ever since.

"And we don't need it. If we send all our fifth-graders to the Middle School, Central and Cliburn can easily serve kindergarten through fourth grade. They have the space for it. We can stabilize class size at about twenty-five kids per room, and reassign Victory's staff to the other schools. I honestly don't think we'll have to RIF anybody."

Virgil had heard that before. The dreaded "reduction in force," however, could come like a thief in the night, sometimes; you couldn't always predict it.

"After we close Victory," Fielding said, "we plan to sell the property—which'll put the land back on the tax rolls. The money we make on the sale, plus what we'll save by not having to keep the school open, we can pump right back into the district. Upgrade the other schools, pay off some of our debts, and hopefully knock a few cents *off* the school tax rate. It's a sound plan, and all of us on the board are in favor of it."

Mrs. Van Horn hadn't followed the story in the papers. "But what'll happen to Virgil, then?" she asked. "He'll be losing his school."

"He'll be first in line when we need a new principal at one of the other schools," Fielding said. "Meanwhile, we're hoping he'll stay on as vice principal at the Middle School or as a teacher at one of the elementary schools." He nodded his white head at Virgil, and gave him a smile which was meant to reassure him. "Don't anybody worry about Virgil. We'll take care of him. We don't want to lose him."

But I'm *worried about Virgil!* Virgil thought. He caught Carrie's eye. She took his hand and squeezed it.

"I think it'd be a pretty good idea for us to get the history of the school down on paper before it goes out of business," somebody said. "Let's do it now, while we can still get pictures. After forty-plus years, I think the old place deserves some kind of send-off."

Fielding shook his head. "I don't," he said.

2

While Fielding Jones was explaining the economics of the school closing to the Historical Society, another kind of meeting was going on *chez* Dudak.

Mike's old man, a long-distance trucker, was back from Utah a week early, tired and cranky because a job he'd thought he had all lined up had fallen through at the last minute. He was in one of those not-so-rare tempers in which he sat in front of the boob tube all day in his drawers and cowboy boots, drinking Coors and swatting anyone who got in range. When he got tired of watching the TV, he'd turn the radio to a country station and listen to songs about truckers, cowboys, and the women who did them dirt. If he was drunk enough, he'd cry when he heard Willie Nelson's songs. That was when he was really *dangerous*. And after the crying jags, he liked to get the family together and lay down the law.

Mike had already had his butt kicked once today, when he came home from school, on general principles. Now he was out in the kitchen, munching on a Twinkie and listening to Ma take her turn in the barrel.

"Damn it to hell, Beth, there's gonna be some changes made around here!" Daddy was saying. "I drive that fuckin' rig from here to kingdom come, I only get home once in a blue moon—and *look* at this fuckin' place! Look at it, damn it! It's a pigsty!"

Ma spent the day watching talk shows and soap operas and washing it down with gin: she wasn't really into housework. But now Daddy's clothes were strewn all over the living room, Coors cans rolled around the floor, and even if Ma had tried to pick anything up while he was listening to the radio, he would've nailed her with the heel of his boot.

"And another thing," he went on. "*You're* a fuckin' mess, too! You're goin' on a diet, damn it. I'm tired of comin' home to find you lookin' like a pig. Do you *have* to have your hair up in fuckin' curlers all the time? And either wear nail polish or don't fuckin' wear it! I hate it when you put it on and forget about it for a month. You look like crap, y'know that? Do you hear me, Beth?"

Daddy was working himself up for a good one. Any minute now he'd start throwing stuff. Mike decided not to wait for the fireworks. He gobbled up the last Twinkie and sneaked out the back door.

He was going to go see if he could get Rizzo to come out and knock over garbage cans or something, but he found himself heading toward school. He didn't fight it. After dark, with the playground all to himself, he didn't mind school at all.

Fuckin' Daddy, though—why did he have to come home? Unless it was hunting season and there were deer to kill, Daddy couldn't be in the house five minutes without starting in. Once he'd pushed Mike down the cellar stairs. Another time he didn't like his coffee, so he dumped it on Ma's hand, sending her off to the hospital to get the burns fixed. Home alone with Ma, Mike did as he pleased. She never hassled him and everything was cool. With Daddy in the house, you never knew when he was going to belt you.

For about the millionth time, Mike wished he were grown, big enough to kick the old man out the door the next time he made a move on him or Ma. He wouldn't mind turning the tables on Johnny Rizzo for a change, either: knock him around a while, see how *he* liked it. Mike was so fuckin' tired of being a kid, he could kill somebody—or would, if he weren't so damned *small*.

By the time he reached the playground, his stomach was churning, his blood was hot. He stepped on a stick, picked it up, and broke it against a tree. "Goddamn shitters!" he cried, not meaning anybody in particular. Goddamn shitters in general.

Victory School had a vandalism problem, and Mike was part of it. To deter the window-breakers and graffiti-scrawlers, the school board had put up spotlights along the gutters. They were pretty half-assed lights, though. They shone down on the black-topped play area at the back of the school and weren't even strong enough to let you shoot baskets at night. Undeterred, Mike found a rock and headed toward the blacktop.

3

Ned was in the basement rec room watching *The Beast Must Die*, a werewolf movie with Peter Cushing in a supporting role. It was okay, but it wasn't scaring him. The commercial breaks were really messing it up. When they hit him with a news break, too, he took the opportunity to go upstairs to visit the john. He was in time to overhear Mr. Jones explaining why he didn't think Victory School deserved a send-off.

"I don't want this getting back to any of the politicians," Mr. Jones said. "Then there really would be a controversy, and not a very nice one. You'll all have to promise me that not a word of this will ever be breathed outside this room."

When they had all promised, he turned to Virgil. "Some might say that I'm violating the board's confidence by what I'm about to say, but I feel I owe it to you and Carrie. I think you have a right to know *all* the reasons for our decision to close the school."

This was the first Virgil had heard of any reasons besides economics and demographics for shutting down the school. He wasn't sure he wanted to know them. He was still finding it hard to accept the numbers on their own merits. But he let Fielding go on.

"I'm sure Virgil is aware of this, but the rest of you might be very surprised to know that, since it opened in 1946, Victory School has *consistently* yielded the lowest test scores among our elementary schools. Year in, year out, the kids at Victory finish at the bottom of the heap."

It had certainly been true for as long as he'd been principal—it had always troubled him—but Virgil hadn't realized that the problem went all the way back to the beginning. How could that be?

"We've racked our brains over this for years," Fielding said, "for as long as I've been on the board; but no matter who we put in to teach or administrate there, no matter what we try, we can't get those scores to go up. It's no reflection on you, Virgil, or any of your staff. *No one* has ever been able to make any headway there. Of course, I'm talking about the aggregate scores for the whole school. Victory has had any number of bright kids. It's just that the average for the school has always been dead last."

"But why on earth—" Carrie started to say; but Fielding held up his hand and said, "There's more."

"Year after year, Victory leads all the other schools in requests for transfer by members of the teaching staff. This has been true since 1946. Victory also leads the district, year after year, in teacher absences, sick leaves, and just plain resignations. The turnover there has always been a lot higher than at the other schools—and that's a matter of record."

"I've got one or two requests on my desk right now—and this when everybody knows the school's in its final year!" Virgil said. "And I'm aware that we lead the league in substitutions. I'm damned if *I* know why. I've tried to make it a nice place to work."

"We all know you have. And if it's any consolation to you, transfer requests and sick days are *down* since you took over as principal. They're still too high, though. In fact, Victory's numbers, if you see them as percentages, are even higher than the Middle School's. And that's with that little prick Niebauer cracking the whip over his teachers' heads all the time, and a building full of adolescents with their glands running hog-wild, to boot. We find it a very disturbing statistic."

Virgil nodded. Over the years he'd said good-bye to more good teachers than he cared to count. Many of them were still in the district, happy as clams at their new schools—or at least not as unhappy as they'd been at Victory, in spite of his best efforts to content them.

"Can't keep your people, Virgil?" one of the society members said.

"Why do they leave?" asked another.

If I knew the answer to that, thought Virgil, *I'd go into business as a psychic.*

A few were lured by the prestige of Cliburn School, but the majority were simply fleeing Victory. They were astonishingly reluctant to talk about it. *Personal reasons.* Translation: "Gee, Virgil, I dunno, I just can't stand the place!" Sometimes it was a problem with another teacher, to put it mildly. Virgil had

71

teachers there who hated each other's guts. Some got into feuds with kids and parents, too. And yet a lot of the transfer requests came from people who seemed to be getting along with everybody.

Fielding came to the rescue. "One reason has to be the behavior of the children," he said. "We don't have statistics to back this up, but it's common knowledge among the teaching force that the kids at Victory have always been a lot tougher and meaner than the kids at the other elementary schools. I don't know how you'd go about proving it, but I do know that Victory, over the years, has always kept the district psychologist busy. That's on the record."

"We do have our share of bad apples," Virgil admitted. The understatement brought a sardonic smile to his face. *Good God! They had Tommy Sheets with his screaming tantrums, and his mother handing out UFO literature on Meet the Teacher Night. They had Doug and Jimmy Wang terrorizing kids with their kung-fu nonsense, Johnny Rizzo and Mike Dudak beating kids up even worse . . . and sometimes they had good kids flying off the handle for no apparent reason. Oh, they had their bad apples, all right.*

"Do you feel all right, Virgil?" one of the members asked.

Virgil discovered that his face was sweating. He took a deep breath and tried to laugh it off. "I guess I just realized," he said, "what a bitch of a job I've had these past five years!"

"Virgil's been our little Dutch boy with his finger in the dike," Fielding said. "Frankly, old buddy, we're doing you a favor, pulling you out of there. But I've saved the best part of this story for last." He paused to relight his pipe, then continued.

"The thing that bothers me the most is the number of genuine personal *tragedies* we find associated with this school. Teachers and administrators, of course, are human beings, and human beings sometimes botch up their lives. But this . . . it's something else."

Virgil knew where he was leading, but his own knowledge didn't go anywhere near as far as Fielding's.

Fielding started with Dr. Hargrove's mysterious death in 1954, then jumped to more recent cases with which Virgil was personally acquainted, albeit shallowly. Fielding had done some digging.

"James White, teacher at Victory School from 1971 to 1974. Came with excellent references from the Stelton School District. By 1973 it became apparent that he'd developed a drinking problem. It killed him; he ran his car into a utility pole one night and went straight through the windshield. The autopsy showed he was drunk at the time.

"Sarah McPherson. Granted maternity leave in November of 1980. Never came back to work. According to the newspapers, she disappeared a month after the baby was born—without the baby—and hasn't been seen or heard from since.

"Marybeth Loes. You remember her, Virgil. A fine second-grade teacher, until she started using drugs. We had to let her go in March of '84 after she lost control in class. The district almost got sued over that. She left town shortly afterward. I don't know what's happened to her since then, but I doubt it's been good."

Virgil remembered the incident painfully. He'd had to call the police. Marybeth had become hysterical over some trivial classroom incident, belted a little boy with her purse, and screamed obscenities at the top of her lungs. Virgil and Peter Ludovics had had to drag her out of the room and restrain her in the office until the police could get there.

He remembered White and McPherson, too. Sad cases ... good teachers gone bad. Normal, healthy human beings whose lives took nosedives. But it had never occurred to Virgil that they could be part of an overall pattern.

"My God!" one of the members said. "Are you sure it isn't something in the water?"

"Believe it or not," said Fielding, "we checked. But it's the same water everybody else in town is drinking."

"Maybe the school was built on top of a toxic dump, or something."

"Nope. We checked that out, too."

"My wife Harriett always said there were problems at that school," said John Fulham. "Much more so than she had at the Central School. And I've heard a few tales from Virgil, too. Still, I had no idea it was quite so bad."

"I've had a lot of transfers from Victory," Harriett said. "They come to Central and they're fine. But they're vague about their reasons for leaving. It was always something like, 'the place got me down,' or 'I just couldn't work with So-and-so anymore,' or 'I just wasn't happy there.' Never anything specific. And never any complaints about the way Virgil was running things. One transfer told me she just couldn't stand the way the building *smelled* on rainy days! Said it gave her headaches. And of course, you get the usual horror stories about rotten kids and hostile parents. Which doesn't really explain it."

Fielding said, "Please don't get the idea that the board is using economics and demographics to cover up the real reasons for closing the school. The numbers *are* the real reasons. The rest only goes to show that Victory School will be no loss to the district. I think we'll be better off without it."

"I still think we ought to do a history of it, though," said one of the members. "After all, that's what a historical society *does.*"

She put it to a formal vote and it passed over Fielding's objection, which he accepted with grace. The society would try to complete the project before the school was closed, giving it priority over other projects.

But they're really opening a can of worms, thought Virgil.

4

Listening to Mr. Jones, Ned missed the rest of *The Beast Must Die*. He didn't mind, though. In a way, this stuff about the school was scarier.

Dad hadn't told him any of these things. The old principal falling down the stairs in the middle of the night, teachers turning into drunks and druggies, the one who ran off without her baby—too freakin' much.

Ned tiptoed back down to the rec room as the society was concluding its meeting. *Absolutely amazin'*, he thought, all that bad stuff happening at one school. And right from the get-go, Mr. Jones said.

No wonder they wanted to shut the place down. You'd think there was a curse on it.

5

Mike felt cold and stiff.

He was lying on the blacktop under the kindergarten windows, his back pressed to the brick wall. His head ached and the inside of his nose was sore. When he tried to sit up, he heaved.

He didn't know what he was doing there. The last thing he remembered was deciding to break a window. He leaned against the wall and stuck his hand out to touch one of the small vents that were in the wall out here, about a foot up from the blacktop.

All right, I passed out. I must be sick. He sure as hell *felt* sick.

He had no idea what time it was. He might have been out for just a few minutes, or it might have been half the night.

He licked his lips and tasted blood. It was all over his face below his nose, and mostly dried. He must have banged his nose when he fell down.

For a moment he was afraid of what Daddy would do if he came home late. But then it didn't scare him anymore. Fuck Daddy ... he'd be on the road again in another day or two. And someday Mike would be big enough to pay the old man back.

He could see it as clearly as if it were really happening: Daddy with his hair and beard turned gray, on his knees pleading for mercy like a bad-guy wrestler losing a match, and him towering over the old man—a Mike Dudak as big as Hulk Hogan himself, with muscles to match, getting ready to squash the old fucker like a bug. *"You wanna see what wallopin' is all about, Daddy? You ready to find out how it feels?"* Oh, yeah.

Mike stood up, His head spun like a roulette wheel and he almost fell again. He had to lean against the wall.

He felt ... *drunk!* That's what it was. Like Ma when she really got a load on, stumbling off to the bathroom and bumping into things without feeling anything.

It wasn't so bad. Sure hoped he could make it home, though. But he had his doubts.

Chapter Nine

1

Virgil walked north up Kirkwall Street the next morning, as he did every weekday morning, to school.

Kirkwall had been a dirt road when Virgil was a boy, and it hadn't received a permanent asphalt pavement until he was away at college. He would always remember it as one of those places his parents told him to stay away from—as in, "Don't want you playing over there, Virgil, those people on Kirkwall are nothin' but white trash." He remembered tiny houses with paint peeling from the shingles, rickety garages, cars rusting up on concrete blocks in the weedy front yards.

Well, that was all gone now, long gone. The street was paved, the houses had aluminum siding, the only cars you saw were still running on all four wheels. The people his father referred to as "white trash" had long since been driven out by rising property values, and rising taxes.

To Tianoga's old-timers, however, the neighborhood would always be known as Rivertown—even if most of the current residents had never heard the name.

The Tianoga River ran nearby. These dozen blocks or so

had been called Rivertown since the Civil War—meaning a place to go for cheap whiskey and even cheaper women. It was never big enough to be a slum; it had never even attained the status of a ghetto. It had simply been, for a hundred years or so, the armpit of Tianoga. It was better now, a hell of a lot better. But Virgil was old enough to remember one of his high school teachers lashing out at a classroom lout, "You hooligans from Rivertown are all alike!" It hadn't been meant as a compliment.

Now the shanties were gone, the streets were paved, and the neighborhood populated by middle-class folks who never dreamed that, to Tianoga's older residents, they were living in a place on a par with the scuzzier parts of Juarez City. But the old tradition was almost dead and buried. In its time, Rivertown had been a byword for alcoholism, unemployment, juvenile delinquency, and a lot worse. That time had passed.

In the center of Rivertown stood Victory School.

And there, thought Virgil as he walked to work, might lay the root of the problem. Victory was *Rivertown's* school. One of the reasons it had been built was to keep the Rivertown kids from mixing with those who lived in more genteel neighborhoods. Okay, the bad old days were already over when the school was opened in 1946, and even Kirkwall Street had been pretty much cleaned up by then. Christ, he thought, *I* live in Rivertown now! There was nothing in this neighborhood to be ashamed of, regardless of what some senile old farts in the Village thought.

Still, there had to be some way to explain Victory School's mulish resistance to improvement. The school, in some ways, was a lot like the way Rivertown used to be.

But if it wasn't the neighborhood that had dragged the school down, what else could it possibly be?

While Virgil was walking to school, Rudi was trying to wipe a message off the frame of the boiler room door.

Mr. Iacavella was mighty ticked off. Somehow, some kid had gotten up high enough to crayon JERKOFFS CLUB over the middle of the door. It was the first thing the janitors saw when they came in to work that morning.

"This is what we get for cleaning up their messes every day," Mr. Iacavella said. "It sure is nice to be appreciated, ain't it? Shit, I must be a jerkoff for goin' up to the roof and throwin' down the balls they hit up there. And look at all the bikes and skateboards and toys I fix, and never charge a dime. Welcome to the Jerkoff Club, Rudi!"

He went on and on about it, even while he got the coffee going and opened his morning paper to the sports page. Rudi could hear him muttering. He guessed Mr. Iacavella's feelings were hurt, and he didn't blame him.

Well, the sooner he rubbed this off, the better. He wiped hard.

A big piece of the wood came off in his hand. *Oh, shit, I busted it.* Aloud he said, "Uh-oh," which brought Mr. Iacavella out from behind his desk.

"Damn it, Rudi, what've you done now?"

Rudi held up the chunk of wood, "It broke off, Mr. Iacavella."

"Aw, fuck it," Mr. Iacavella said, making a gesture of disgust with his hands and turning to go back to his paper.

Rudi didn't know what to do. Should he glue the piece back to the frame, or throw it away? Mr. Iacavella was in such a rotten mood that Rudi was afraid to ask him. He stood fidgeting with the wood and getting himself agitated. He knew that if he threw it away, Mr. Iacavella would want to know why he hadn't glued it back to the frame; and if he glued it back, he'd get yelled at for not just throwing it away. There was no pleasing the guy, sometimes.

Rudi looked at the broken-off piece, noticed something odd, and held it up closer to his eyes.

"Huh!" he said. The wood had *strings* in it: a couple of white threads running with the grain. They looked like bits of dentist's string, floss, the stuff you were supposed to pull between your teeth every day. Rudi made sure he did that regularly.

The strings seemed to be set in snug little grooves in the wood, and there were tiny holes all over, like termite-holes, only Rudi didn't see any termites. And there were some little shiny spots, too, like dots of snail-slime—though snails made broad tracks, not little dots.

The wood smelled faintly like a dead frog in a jar. You could barely smell it, but it was there.

One of the strings moved. Rudi watched, riveted, as it slid slowly backward along its slot in the wood, leaving behind a narrow shiny track, disappearing finally into one of the tiny termite-holes.

"Mr. Iacavella, you gotta see this."

The newspaper rattled, and chair-legs rasped against the floor. "What the flyin' fuck is it now?"

"Look."

Mr. Iacavella looked at the piece of wood, then looked up at the man as if he thought he might be starting to lose his marbles.

"Look at what?" he said softly. "What am I supposed to be lookin' at, Rudi? Would you mind tellin' me?"

"These strings . . ."

"Strings?"

"Yeah! Look!" Rudi pointed.

"Fer shit's sake, Rudi, it's only some kinda fungus. Don't you know *anything?*"

"Fungus?"

"Yeah. It's a kind of plant. Like mushrooms, toadstools—athlete's foot's a fungus, too. There's all different kinds of fungus, kid. And a lot of 'em live in rotten wood, like we got all over this building. It'd mean a lotta trouble if they weren't gonna shut this place down in June."

"But it *moves!* One of these strings moved just like a worm! It went down one of these holes!"

"Are you gonna waste the whole morning on this shit, Rudi? Come on, we gotta open up the place before the early birds start poundin' on the doors."

3

Doreen decided not to take lunch in the teachers' room today.

This morning, for the first time in her life, she fortified herself with wine before setting out for work. Not enough to get drunk; just a cup to steady her nerves after a very rough night.

Bad dreams chased her from the moment she closed her eyes, grotesque visions of pallid pink snakes trying to crawl into her mouth, and gigantic earthworms getting under her clothes. Rudi Fitch was in them, too, but she wasn't anxious to remember what his role had been. All night long the dreams assailed her, and when she woke and found dried blood on the bedclothes, she realized that she'd had another nosebleed.

After a night like that, she deserved a little wine.

It did the trick, too. By the time she opened her clinic, she was feeling calm and competent. Mr. Ludovics brought in a boy with a sprained wrist, a casualty of early morning gym class, and she handled it like Clara Barton.

Then Rudi came along.

Doreen was returning from the office, where she'd taken the boy to wait for his mother, when she found Rudi standing by the clinic with a bucket and a rag.

"Hi, Miss Davis!"

She was in a huge fancy bed with silk sheets and a canopy, and clad in a negligee that was little more than a veil of smoke

81

around her body ... and there stood Rudi at the foot of the bed, naked from the waist up. He kept trying to look at the floor, but his eyes refused to stray from her. He was scared. She had the power of life and death over him. She owned him, body and soul. He was her slave.

"Take the rest of your clothes off, Rudi."

"Please, Miss ..."

"Do it."

"You okay, Miss Davis?"

She snapped out of the dream, which had roared out of her subconscious and swallowed her up so suddenly that it had been like falling into another world. She rose back into this one lost and trembling.

"Oh, gee, you don't look so good," he said. "Here, let me help you. . . ."

He reached for her, but she batted his hands away.

"Damn it, don't touch me!" she screamed. He drew back, looking hurt and confused, but she wasn't buying it. Still, it'd hardly do to make a scene in the hall. She forced back a rising wave of hysteria. "I'm all right. You startled me, that's all."

"I scared *you?"*

He might be a half-wit, but he knew all he needed to know. Doreen had to get out of this.

"What were you doing, hanging around my clinic?" she demanded. She was too shaken to be calm; the only way out was to put him on the defensive.

"I wasn't hanging around. I was just washin' stuff off the wall. . . ."

"Will you please move on? I've got a lot of work to do. I can't have you putzing around out here, disturbing me. Go wash the walls somewhere else."

Her bold front stood up. Mumbling under his breath, he picked up his bucket and withdrew.

4

"Miss Stanhouse, is there any way I could get a yearly list of our teaching staff here, going back to 1946?"

"You mean who was here each year?" Millie asked.

"Yes," Virgil said. "I don't want to put you to any trouble, but I was hoping you could look it up easily enough. It's for the Historical Society."

"Leave it to me, Mr. Bradley. I'll have it for you in a day or two."

"There's no hurry. Thank you."

She left him alone in his private office, where he'd been letting his paperwork slide, pondering the school's high rate of staff turnover. He was able, from memory, to make lists for each of the five years he'd been principal; and the only name he could put on all of them was Diane Phelps's. In just five years, she was the only teacher not to have moved on. Only one of twelve slots here had been filled by the same person for the past five years. He wondered what kind of outfit typically had a ninety-two-percent turnover rate in five years. Kamikaze squadrons, he guessed.

Why did they leave? Virgil, after all, had been a teacher at Victory for eleven years before becoming principal, and he'd never felt like applying for a transfer. Now that he thought of it, he'd been the only one to stick it out for the full eleven years—aside from Cosmo Iacavella and Millie Stanhouse, who'd been there forever. But they weren't teachers.

During those eleven years Virgil had dealt with his share of truculent kids and militantly stupid parents. It had never been more than he could handle. Honestly, he didn't think the kids at Victory were any worse than those at Central or Cliburn. As for the parents, Harriett Fulham could tell you that there were more than a few dunderheads living in the Village, too.

The transience of the staff at Victory was a fact; but in all fairness, Virgil thought, it'd be oversimplifying things to blame it on the community Victory served.

He didn't know what you could blame it on, but he would try to find out.

5

In the lunchroom, Diane Phelps watched Joanne Wilmot's every move, hating her a little more with every passing second.

Wilmot made the most of that little muppet-face of hers, you had to give her that. Thick blond bangs, big round glasses, wide gray eyes, and little-girl features. She was a regular cutesy-poo when she smiled, which she contrived to do quite often. She had fine, delicate hands which she waved around a lot, and a birdlike body language which seemed to serve her well. You could almost see how a certain kind of man might be taken in by that. Never mind the tiny tits and plywood ass.

And everybody doted on her. She had 'em all fooled. *Look at me, aren't I just the world's cutest little kindygarten teacher! And I can have any man I want—right, Di, old pal?*

The operative word was "old." Diane had a body that wouldn't quit and a face that could rightly be called handsome; but she was pushing fifty. Wilmot, on the other hand, was *young.* Undoubtably she made Charlie feel young.

And what a goody-two-shoes! She made Diane's flesh crawl. She didn't smoke, didn't drink, never used salty language, never lost her temper with the little brats, and *always* brought her own ostentatiously healthy lunch. She was too health-conscious to eat cafeteria food like the rest of the peasants. Skinny as a rail, she knew the caloric content of every vegetarian morsel she consumed, invariably capped by a shiny red apple for dessert. It was her cute little trade-mark. "*An apple a day . . .*" she never failed to remind her co-workers.

Diane watched her eat the apple, and suddenly had an inspiration.

Chapter Ten

Virgil took the afternoon off for his second session with his hypnotist.

"I'm still having the nightmares," he reported, "but these last two nights I've been able to get back to sleep with relatively little trouble. I guess that's a positive sign."

Lauther was wearing tweeds today, looking like a responsible young businessman who'd just taken over a struggling company and was eager to accept the challenge of taking it to the top. He nodded.

"That's a very good sign," he said. "I think we're going to make real progress today. You look a little less harried than you did the other day."

"I guess I'm more comfortable here, Doc. Last time I didn't know what to expect. I'd never been hypnotized before."

"Nothing to it, right?"

"Like falling off a log."

When he was comfortably settled on the couch, Lauther led him through some mental relaxation exercises until he was ready to go under. He had a deep feeling of peace and contentment, a sense that all was right with the world; but as the hypnotist steered him back toward the janitor's closet, all good feelings passed away.

He was nine years old again, and he was trying to decide whether to open Mr. Cuppy's closet, knowing there was something in it that would hurt him.

"I can't go in there."

"Yes, you can. It's all right."

"Do I have to open that door?"

"Yes . . . if you want to stop having nightmares about it."

He stood in front of it, vacillating. He wanted to go back out to recess, but that was impossible. What really happened was that he'd opened the door and gone inside. It couldn't be changed.

He reached for the knob. It seemed far away, but his arm stretched magically and his fingers touched the smooth, cold brass. He hoped it would be locked, even though he knew it wasn't.

"Am I still hypnotized?"

"Yes. You're perfectly safe, Virgil."

The knob turned freely. The heavy door swung open, just a little bit, on well-oiled hinges. It was dark inside, with that peculiar musty smell which certain nooks and crannies in the school had always had.

He reached around the doorframe and groped for the switch to turn on the light. He couldn't find it. But as the door opened wider, some of the grayish light from the hall seeped in, showing Virgil the big sink and a clutter of cleaning junk.

There's nobody in here, he thought.

Then who unlocked the door?

He forgot that he was under hypnosis. He wasn't remembering the experience, wasn't reliving it. It was happening now; he was going into the closet for the first time.

He went to look in the sink. It was a big sink, big enough for a little kid to hide in, if he could climb up over the edge. Virgil thought he could do that. If it turned out there was nobody hiding in the sink ... well, that would be that; there was no other place to hide in here.

He put his hands on the rim of the sink and stood on tiptoe to look in.

Something cold and wet and rubbery and strong shot up from the sink and snapped itself around his neck, pulling him off his feet and choking off his scream, making purple and maroon blots dance before his eyes. Ropy lengths coiled around his wrists and pulled his hands down into the sink. All he could do was kick his feet in the air, bruising his knees on the hard porcelain.

His mind screamed. He wet his pants and didn't even know it.

Once, in anger, his father had snatched him off the ground by the collar of his jacket. He couldn't struggle then, and he couldn't struggle now. He was a strong, fit boy, but against strengths like these, what strength he had was nothing.

He couldn't breath. He couldn't swallow. He could hardly see. He was all alone.

Something like a naked pink snake appeared before his face. It wavered like a cobra rising out of a snake-charmer's basket, then stood still.

It had a hole in its tip, a hole that was puckered like an asshole. Virgil stared at it. The orifice dilated, and slowly extruded a long, yellowish wand with a needle-sharp point.

Oh, God, it's going to sting me with that! That's its stinger, it's going to stick me in the eye! No ... !

But he couldn't scream out loud because he had no wind.

The pain, when it came, was like a Fourth of July inside his head. He couldn't see, but he could feel the stinger going up his nose, straight up his nose, all the way up to his brain like a long needle of fire.

... And then it was out. He felt it being drawn out, burning all the way. He saw it poised in front of him, the pale length of it slick with blood.

From the tip of it dripped a fluid that was not blood, endless drops, opalescent, milky white.

Oh, Jesus . . . !

Virgil gulped the air, swallowing it greedily.

He already knew he was back in Lauther's office, but he didn't believe it yet. His throat was raw from screaming. His eyes were full of tears. His nose ached. It was air conditioned in the office, but his clothes were limp with sweat.

"Take it easy, Virgil!"

He gulped more air. "What happened?" he panted.

"You emerged spontaneously from hypnosis. That's understandable, though. You were terrified."

Virgil tried to sink into the couch. His muscles were as sore as if he'd climbed El Capitan with a refrigerator lashed to his back. Dr. Lauther waited patiently, giving him time to get his psyche back together.

"I remember it now," he was finally able to say. "All of it."

"Do you remember what happened next?"

Virgil nodded. When he swallowed, his throat hurt.

"It just let go of me," he said. "It just let go. I slid back down to the floor and saw those . . . snakes, or worms, or tentacles, whatever you want to call 'em . . . disappear down the drain in the sink."

"Can you remember how you were feeling when you saw that?"

He remembered now. It was flooding back, wave upon wave. He had to pause to take it in. What he took in next astonished him.

"You'd think I'd've been feeling mighty lucky to still be alive," he said, "but that wasn't it. No. What I felt was really very strange." He paused again, searching for the right words. His sweat was already drying on him, making his skin feel cold.

"I felt . . . *rejected.* Like I'd been chosen for something and then put back. Like I wasn't good enough. Wasn't right. I don't know, it's crazy. But I felt *disappointed,* somehow."

"What did you do next?" Lauther asked.

"Nothing. Just went back out to recess, that's all. And I remember Miss Watson asking me what took me so long, recess was almost over. She was sort of disappointed in me."

"I take it you didn't tell her what had happened?"

"I couldn't! I couldn't remember! It was like nothing had happened at all—except that I had a bastard of a headache all day long, and after I got home, my nose started bleeding. And I think I was cranky and difficult the next few days. I know I had nightmares about it every night; but I couldn't remember them when I woke up, and after a while I stopped having them. Until now . . ."

"And how do you feel right now?"

Virgil thought it over, but he didn't have to think long.

"Scared, doctor. Like I'm losing my mind."

Lauther seemed to slip into a lecturing mode, which was all right with Virgil. He'd had enough emotional intensity for one afternoon.

"Repressed memory is like radioactive waste with a very long half-life, Virgil. You can bury it as deep as you like, but it's still there, pumping out its poison. When you repressed this childhood nightmare, you didn't get rid of it. And when the stress of losing your school jarred it loose, it came back up close to the surface to haunt you. Hence the renewal of the nightmares, and the hallucination that you had last week. Those were manifestations of this childhood thing."

"But why did my mind hit me with something like that when I was nine years old?" Virgil said. "What does it *mean?*"

Lauther waited before he spoke. "To find out what it *means,* we'd have to go into that period of your life in some detail. Quite frankly, that could get to be expensive. That's how people wind up spending ten years in therapy."

Virgil hardly heard that. The memories were still pouring over him. "Son-of-a-bitch, it seems so real! Like it honest-to-God, really and truly happened. And that last hallucination . . . that seems real, too, as real as this other. How can something so . . . *preposterous* . . . seem so real—without me being crazy?"

The doctor sat back down, leaning forward on the edge of his seat, his hands clasped casually in front of him. "Is that bothering you, Virgil? Do you think having experiences like these means you're crazy?"

"It *had* crossed my mind."

"I don't think you're crazy," said Lauther. "You don't appear, in my expert opinion, to be suffering from psychosis. You *may* have had a hallucination. But you aren't hallucinating in any way consistent with psychosis. You don't display any evidence of an anxiety state—beyond what's perfectly normal, under the circumstances—or mood disorder, or personality disorder. You're an excellent hypnotic subject, and I thought you made an honest attempt while under hypnosis to describe what you remembered.

"Then, of course, you've been holding down a responsible job for years, and done well at it, and you enjoy a stable, healthy family life. These factors militate very strongly against your being a psychotic. I could give you any number of tests, but I really don't think they're necessary." He paused and looked Virgil straight in the eye. "I have to have faith in my own professional judgment; and at these prices, so should you. In other words, if you're crazy, then I'm a *lousy* psychiatrist."

All this was very comforting, but it wasn't getting to the heart of the matter. "How can I have something like this in my head," Virgil demanded, "and *not* be crazy?"

"Well, hell, there's only two possibilities, logically," Lauther said. "One, of course, is that something like this really happened. I don't think we need to spend much time on that one. The other is that when you were nine years old, for some reason, you genuinely *believed* something like this had happened

91

to you, and the repressed memory has been festering inside you ever since.

"Now this experience you've recalled under hypnosis could actually be something else; some real experience that your nine-year-old mind found so upsetting that it repressed the events one step further by recasting them in this mythic, nightmarish form.

"For what it's worth to you, I think that this experience, whatever it was, is strongly linked to your school. Maybe something happened to you there when you were little. But that being the case, it would indicate a basis for what you might say has been a lifelong fixation on the school. It's not just a school to *you*, Virgil. It's not just a job. And if that's so, the prospect of forcible separation from the school would cause you extreme distress—which *superficially* would seem to be out of all proportion to the stimulus. Do you follow me?"

Holy shit, Virgil thought. It was a convoluted piece of reasoning, but it did make sense. Maybe his emotional ties to the school ran much deeper than he'd thought.

Carrie liked to listen to the phone-in shrink on the radio, and Virgil had listened with her often enough to appreciate the fact that the human mind worked in mysterious ways. He had heard stories of middle-aged human beings lost in labyrinths of bizarre and self-destructive behavior that they were at a loss to explain, only to discover—sometimes after years of therapy— that the root of it all sprang from some traumatic childhood incident no longer consciously remembered. Sexual abuse, battering . . . you name it.

"There's only one problem I have with this, Doc. *What really happened?* You've given me a line of reasoning that's missing a beginning. What do I do about it? What do I next?"

"Well, you could continue in therapy," Lauther said. "You could keep digging until you get to the bottom of it. I ought to warn you, however, that you could wind up trying to dig your way to China. *Or* you could wait a while and see how you feel. See what happens. If the nightmares stop, if you're able to cope satisfactorily with changes in your life, you might decide to let it go at that. Why not? All I'm saying is, watch out for therapy becoming a way of life. Let me tell you, it's a very expensive hobby.''

Virgil understood that. He'd heard such warnings before, on the radio. He couldn't afford to become a therapy junkie, anyway.

He did feel better when he left the doctor's office. If nothing else, the session today had been a catharsis. For the time being, at least, he felt like he'd gotten it all out of his system. Damn it, he was beat; he was ready for bed *now*.

And if he didn't sleep tonight, he didn't think he'd ever sleep again.

Chapter Eleven

1

Clouds began to roll in that afternoon, outriders of a cold air mass from Canada. Those teachers who lived some distance from the school resolved to leave as soon as the bell rang: some of the roads in this part of the county turned into trick-driving courses when it rained.

Joanne Wilmot, who lived just on the other side of town, was one of those who'd decided to stay for a while after school, despite the threat of bad weather. She and her husband planned to go out this evening, rain or no rain. It was the anniversary of their first date, and Geoff always took her out that night. So she would stay after school, revising some lesson plans she hadn't been able to finish on her break, clearing the decks for tonight.

She was lucky to have Geoff, and she knew it. He made good money, but he wasn't a business zombie, like some others she could name. The last time his boss tried to get him to work late on their first-date anniversary, Geoff said he'd quit first. "Ideally," he would say to her, "the company would like you to work round the clock, seven days a week, for free. That's impossible, so they settle for whatever they can get out of you. And you gotta teach 'em early that they can't have it all, or they'll expect it all.''

Jesus, he made her happy! Tonight they'd have dinner at Stello's, followed by a movie at the old Empire Theater (What was playing tonight? Was it a revival of the first *Star Wars?*), followed by a little wine in their living room (but not too much), and then ... oh, wow, she'd run home right now for just a preview of it, only Geoff wouldn't be home for another hour and a half. Maybe they'd do it in the shower. ...

Joanne was finding it difficult to concentrate on her lesson plans.

What on earth ... ?

There was a stink in the room. Not a big stink: after all, she hadn't noticed it until just now. But it sure as hell was there, you couldn't miss it.

Joanne knew how Victory School responded to changes in the weather. It leaked and it stank. It had a whole repertoire of odors, from *eau de rotting wood* to *memoire de cheap floor wax.*

This one was subtly different, though. This was more of a *meaty* smell, like there was a dead rat hidden somewhere in the room. Joanne wouldn't put it past this place.

Well, that wouldn't do. Had the janitors gone home yet? Probably not; but before she went looking for them, she thought she might as well have a look around the room herself.

This was a kindergarten classroom. The kids didn't have real desks, just tables where they sat in groups of four or five. So it wasn't a matter of some kid stashing a sandwich in his desk and forgetting it was there. No ... this was something that was tucked away somewhere along the perimeter of the room. She'd find it, then get Cosmo or Rudi to get rid of it if it turned out to be too much of a gross-out for her.

It wasn't anywhere around the baseboards, it wasn't on the shelf above the hooks where the children hung their coats. Joanne went around the room, peering gingerly into various nooks and crannies. Nothing on the windowsill. The closets, maybe?

There were two closets, one at each end of the cloakroom, where she stored reams of construction paper, jars of paste, bundles of pencils, boxes of crayons, this and that. The doors were decorated with brightly colored cardboard cutouts of Big Bird and other *Sesame Street* characters.

She opened the first one, shifting things around the shelves, sniffing. Nothing there. She went on to the second.

Now that it seemed pretty likely that she was about to find the source of the odor, she began to have qualms about it. What would it turn out to be? A dead mouse? A rat? Some rotten staring thing with a fuzz of mold on it?

She opened the second closet and looked in ... and was seized from behind.

Rough strength spun her around, pinning her against the shelves. An insupportable weight fell on her. Something pulpy and wet and odious forced its way into her mouth, gagging her scream.

Mr. Hall.

He was kissing her, bruising her lips, stifling her with a reek of cheap cologne. He had her arms pinned so that she couldn't reach up to scratch his eyes out. She was almost too horrified to think.

But Geoff, who knew a thing or two about the martial arts, had taught her a trick that she could use. Making a pair of fists with the knuckles of her index fingers sticking out like blunt blades, she sought Hall's sides, found spaces between his ribs, and dug in viciously. He jumped away with a gasp of shock.

Holding the sore spots on his ribs, he tried to screw his face into a disarming smile.

Still mad, Joanne punched him right in the nose, a good straight jab, a direct hit. He staggered back a step and reached up to his nose, but it had already started bleeding.

"Joanne—"

She spun around and snatched a pair of scissors from the closet, letting him get a good look at them.

"You fat old turd! See these? If you aren't out of here by the time I count three, I'll cut your fucking nuts off!"

He was out the door before she got to two.

She sat down, trembling all over, sick to her stomach, still emotionally numb with outrage.

I should've seen this coming. . . .

But how *could* she have seen it? She'd known since the beginning of the school year that Charlie had developed the hots for her—but Charlie Hall was a poor man's Don Juan, not a borderline rapist. He chased every woman he saw, but he'd never been known—or even rumored—to do something like this.

He was losing it, God knew why. Over the summer, for some reason, he seemed to have broken up with Diane Phelps, with whom he'd been carrying on for at least a year and a half. Had that done something to his mind?

Joanne's immediate impulse was to tell Mr. Bradley first thing the next morning, maybe even phone him at home tonight, so they could kick Hall's fat ass out of the school district. But after a minute or two, that idea had lost its luster.

Given the man's reputation as a harmless, even comical, wolf, it was unlikely that the school board would take her complaint seriously. They'd probably think she had led him on.

Joanne shook her head. She didn't need that.

She couldn't tell Geoff, either. Not on their first-date anniversary, for fear of ruining it; not ever. Geoff would *kill* the fat old son-of-a-bitch; he'd wind up in jail for assault and battery. God help 'em all if Geoff ever heard a whisper of this.

Joanne abandoned her lesson plans and left for home, hoping she'd be able to calm her nerves by the time Geoff got back from his office, hoping Hall had learned his lesson and wouldn't

bother her again, just hoping that the whole disgusting thing
was *over*.

2

Charlie fled down the corridor, dripping blood, praying no one
would see him.

*Oh, fucking shit, what got into me? Why, why, why did I do
that?*

Not only did he have a bloody nose, and the shame of having
been beaten up by a woman half his size.

He'd probably blown whatever chance he might have had of
someday getting together with Joanne. Just as bad, to his way
of thinking, he was acting like a crazy man. Losing control. *God
in heaven, what's next? Rape?* Charlie, whose bent for self-
examination seldom took him farther than a conflict as to what
color shirt he ought to wear, had suddenly discovered he was a
stranger to himself—an unpredictable, possibly dangerous, ya-
hoo capable of anything.

Oh, fuck, if she blows the whistle on me. . . .

He burst into the boys' room, which, by good fortune, the
janitors weren't cleaning at the time, and stumbled to a sink.
His nose was still bleeding, and he turned on the cold water
with one hand and reached for the paper towels with the other.

He washed the blood from his face, noting with chagrin that
there were a lot of fine, big blotches on his powder-blue Gucci
shirt. He saturated a couple of towels and pressed them to his
nose. *Fucking bitch, she Sunday-punched me!*

Then he looked into the mirror.

At first he couldn't believe what he was seeing. It refused to
register.

He saw a pale face creased with wrinkles, with deep furrows
cutting this way and that, like gullies in an aerial photo of the
desert. He saw toad's-belly skin spattered with liver-colored

spots, milky eyes with diseased red rims, a gaping mouth horrible with toothless gums. The mouth was leering, showing a blotchy tongue. And from a scabby scalp sprouted shapeless tufts of bone-white hair.

Charlie began to quake all over. A shuddering moan escaped his lips before he could stop it. He dropped the clump of soggy paper towels he'd been holding to his nose, filled his hands with water, and buried his face in it.

"... *Jesus God, no ... no ...!*"

He vomited into the sink with a sudden, violent clenching of his stomach. It came out mixed with blood. His head throbbed. But the physical reaction cleared his mind a little. He washed his face again, then summoned up the nerve to confront the mirror one more time.

He sighed thunderously.

He looked like hell, but at least he looked like himself, and not some eighty-year-old pimp at the most depraved cathouse in the world. His nose had started bleeding again and the blood was running down his lips, and under his sunlamp-induced tan, his skin was waxen.

I've got to do something. I've got to get in shape. No more reefer, no more booze. No more sitting around getting fat. I've got to get my act together.

His body, after years of slothful self-indulgence, was giving up on him, and his poor physical health was affecting him emotionally. That was it. It *had* to be. A little attention to fitness and he'd be a new man. Shed twenty or thirty pounds, build up the muscles, build up the wind, get out into the fresh air for a change. That was all he needed.

He hoped.

Chapter Twelve

1

Virgil didn't get home until it was nearly suppertime, and he didn't want to go into the details of his hypnosis session over the table, with his eleven-year-old son listening. Not that he wanted to hide anything from Ned: but he saw no point in passing his nightmares on to the next generation.

Carrie had spent a busy day with John Fulham (who was on early retirement), exploring local history via the microfilms of defunct newspapers at the county library. John was something of an expert on newspapers of the Tianoga Valley, past and present. If any item had ever appeared in print, however long ago, John would know how to find it.

"John and I are already off on an interesting tangent," she said, when the family had sat down to supper. "He thought it'd be neat to research the history of the site *before* Victory School was built there. One of the old-timers told him there used to be a firehouse there, during the twenties and thirties, and that there was an interesting story about it. So we dug the story out today, and uncovered a few things we didn't expect."

The town's present firehouse was on Main Street, across from the police station, with a cornerstone that was laid in 1930, the year the old firehouse, on the site of Victory School, was permanently closed down.

"There was a big scandal with the fire department in 1929," Carrie said, "as if people didn't have enough to worry about that year. It was in all the papers."

The big scandal, according to all reports, began one night with a fire out on Harrison Road. The alarm was duly sounded; but the men of Tianoga's Volunteer Hook-and-Ladder Company No. 1 never responded to the call. The house burned to the ground, causing the death of two elderly residents.

"They never showed up because they were *drunk*—the whole damned fire department!" said Carrie. "The *Gazette* actually had a reporter on the scene. He tagged along after the police and wrote an eyewitness account. He said they had one hell of a party going on at the old firehouse—bootleg whiskey, floozies, crap games, the whole nine yards. They'd started it some time before the alarm went off, and when the volunteers who were home when the bell rang reported to the station, they just pitched right in. A few men did try to get the engine under way, but they were too drunk to accomplish anything."

It'd be funny if those people hadn't been killed in the fire, Virgil thought. His imagination played it as a scene from an old Mack Sennet movie, in herky-jerky black-and-white.

"Volunteer fire companies have been known to get a little too wrapped-up in their extracurricular activities," he said. "That's why the big cities have full-time, professional firemen who have to measure up to standards."

"The county held hearings after the incident," Carrie said. "They inspected the firehouse and found it was a mess. All the equipment gone to pot, oily rags piled up in the corners, heaps of litter, worn-out wiring that should've been replaced, defective switches—the county fire marshal was flabbergasted. He said it was the worst damned firetrap he'd ever seen in all his life, and that it was a miracle they hadn't burned the place down over their heads. *That's* what made it a scandal!"

2

John Fulham's research hadn't stopped there.

Carrie said, "You'll never guess what was there before they built the building that became the firehouse."

"I don't know. An amusement park?"

"Close. Would you believe a *bordello?*"

"What's a bordello?" Ned wanted to know.

"It's a place where they house prostitutes," Carrie said, as Virgil cringed. Carrie believed in frankness and straightforward answers whenever Ned had a question about sex, drugs, or any of the myriad current topics that made most parents grind their teeth. "He's only going to hear about it on television, or from some other kid," she would say. "I'd rather he heard it from us." Virgil agreed, sort of. It was a necessary evil. Hence Ned already knew what a prostitute was, though Virgil doubted the boy truly understood the concept.

"It was owned by a man named Corwin," Carrie went on. "He was a big wheel in this town, back in the nineties. A big man in county politics. But he was a Democrat, and they had a Republican prosecutor in 1897, and that was the beginning of the end for Mr. Corwin."

That year, an unsavory incident had come to light. Virgil wanted to ask what the unsavory incident was, but that had to wait until Ned was sent off to the rec room to get started on his homework.

"One of the girls was murdered," Carrie said, "and that blew the lid off a nasty scandal. It wasn't just a cathouse, Virgil. Of course, you have to read between the lines when you're getting the story out of the newspapers. It was still in Victorian times. Certain subjects were just taboo, so you could only talk about them if you used a lot of euphemisms. But it looks like the place was some kind of sadomasochistic hangout. Really perverted stuff.

"The girl was killed by a regular customer who was apparently up to his usual tricks and just went too far. He was charged with murder, and in the middle of the trial, the house burned down. Everybody was sure it was arson, although it couldn't be proved. Mr. Corwin was charged with being an accessory to murder—in fact, they were going to throw the book at him. The prosecutor got him indicted on a dozen different charges. He never stood trial, though. He had a heart attack in 1898, and it killed him—right after the john was found guilty of second-degree murder.

"What do you think of that?"

Virgil shook his head. "What a sterling tradition!" he said. "An S&M club where a murder was done, and a bunch of boozy firemen who let a house burn down with people in it. If I were superstitious, I'd almost think the poor old school had two strikes against it before it was even built!"

"That *would* be superstitious—but I sort of felt that way myself," said Carrie. "John's going to take me down to the County Hall of Records tomorrow. We're going to look at deeds and try to trace the owners of the property as far back as we can. It ought to be a fascinating sidebar to the history of the school."

"I can't see them publishing stuff like that."

"History's history," Carrie said.

3

They watched *MacNeil, Lehrer* out of habit and because Virgil felt he needed a little breathing space before he told his wife how he'd fared at the hypnotist's office that afternoon.

He told the story cautiously, not wanting any exaggerations or understatements to color it, pausing frequently because it still sounded crazy to him and he was afraid it would sound even crazier to her. It took him over an hour to get through it.

Carrie let him recount it at his own pace, knowing that questions and comments would have thrown him. He was glad she didn't try to seduce him with facile explanations and home-grown theories of psychology.

"I do think the doctor was right," he said, "about me some-how getting fixated on the school, so that it became much more than just a school to me. Even when I went on to junior high school, I knew I'd come back to Victory. I always knew I'd be a teacher there someday, and always hoped I'd be the principal. It was all I ever wanted. And looking back on it from here, it does seem kind of strange. My friends all wanted to be soldiers, astronauts, doctors, skindivers, whatever. I just wanted to go back to Victory School. Wasn't that a queer ambition for a teenage boy?"

Carrie understood the question as rhetorical and didn't try to answer it. "Anyhow," Virgil added, "I think Dr. Lauther hit that one right on the head. But what actually happened to *cause* this fixation, Christ knows."

"If you really need to know, honey, you can stay in therapy. I'm ready to go back to work. I've kept my credentials in order, I'm sure I can get a good teaching job somewhere. If you need it, don't worry about the expense. We'll manage . . . I promise."

Virgil knew she meant it, and took her hand and squeezed it.

"I think I might be able to accept not knowing what really happened to me back then," he said. "I'm going to give it a try. Shit, I don't want us to be paying off a therapist when it's time for Ned to go to college.

"The thing that *really* confuses me, though—the thing that bugs the hell out of me—is the way I felt when that . . . that whatever it was . . . was pulled out of my nose. I know it's all symbolic of something else, I'm not taking it literally—but I'd still like to know why I felt so *disappointed*. After such a hor-rible thing, whatever it *really* was, why in heaven's name should I feel hurt and rejected? It doesn't make sense."

Carrie didn't try to answer that one, either. She was thinking of some of the people who called the radio shrink—people who'd been sexually abused as children and then felt rejected and worthless when the abuse *stopped.*

Had something like that happened to Virgil? Happened to him in *school,* when he was nine years old? Something that his child's mind, to keep its sanity, refashioned into an encounter with some kind of monster—something that simply couldn't have been real, and was therefore much less threatening? He didn't know, she didn't know, and they might never know. It was only a possibility.

"I think you're right to let it go for a while, honey, and see if you can cope with it as is," she said. "The doctor gave you a clean bill of mental health, which is more than some people ever get. You're the best husband and father anyone could possibly have, and you're a terrific educator. They may be about to close your school, but they'd hate to lose you. They're going to keep you on as a teacher or a vice principal while paying you a principal's salary. You can't ask for a higher testimonial than that."

"No," said Virgil. "I guess I can't."

4

The rain began just as they were turning out their reading lamps. Carrie fell asleep right away, but Virgil lay awake and listened to the raindrops on the roof.

Logically, the doctor said, there were only two possible explanations.

One was the chance that the fucking thing was honest-to-Pete, dyed-in-the-wool, fair dinkum *real.* That it all happened just as he remembered it. *Exactly* as he remembered it.

Oh, sure. There was a monster in the janitor's sink, it grabbed him and stuck its stinger up his nose; and thirty-odd years later, in the exact same janitor's closet, he ran into a ghost of himself as he was at nine years old. *Tell us another.*

The two voices debated in his head—the Sensible Party versus the Silly Party, as in the old Monty Python skit. The Sensible Party had reason on its side, good old reason. The Silly Party had fear.

Virgil only wanted to listen to the rain.

Chapter Thirteen

1

It rained like it was never going to stop.

Sheets of water rippled down the windows of the classrooms, obscuring the outside view and lulling some of the children, and nearly hypnotizing a few others. It worked its spell on teachers, too. Those on break were nearly somnolent. Those in class had to raise their voices: not because the children couldn't hear them, but because they could hardly hear themselves. The rain caused some of them to go woolgathering, and angered others by making them feel they had to compete with it for their pupils' attention. It was, in any case, a major distraction.

Cosmo and Rudi hadn't bothered to put up the flag today. It was raining cats and dogs when they arrived to open the school, and it was supposed to go on all day.

On the basement-level hall that ran from the boiler room to the library, a puddle or two had seeped across the linoleum. "Leaks in the foundation," Cosmo explained. Rudi mopped up the puddles while Cosmo made his rounds, unlocking the rooms and turning all the lights on. Today they would spend in the relative snugness of the boiler room, so they could be found easily in case a teacher needed them to stop a leak. On call, as Cosmo put it. He set his heels on his desk and started to reminisce about his Navy days, spinning yarns that contained kernels of truth, but not much more. Rudi paid him rapt attention.

A runnel of dirty water seeped from the lower corner of a windowframe.

2

Mr. Hall looked like he had dropped dead in his sleep but come in this morning to finish out the week.

"What's wrong with him?" Phil whispered as they hung up their raincoats. Ned pulled him close so he could whisper into his ear, *"He's dead!"*—which cracked Phil up and got them both a prickly reprimand.

"It's time you caught up on your reading," Mr. Hall addressed the class, after the Pledge of Allegiance and the attendance report. He told them to get out their geography books and read the chapter on the Great Plains states, and answer the questions at the end. It'd count as a quiz, he warned them. When all the children had their books open, he leaned his chair against the wall and pretended to fiddle around with his next week's lesson plans.

Between the pelting of the rain and the principal products of Nebraska, Ned was soon on the brink of corking off. He'd already looked at the questions—as Mom had taught him to do—and didn't think he'd have any trouble with them, so long as he could stay awake. What he really needed was to stretch his legs. He petitioned Mr. Hall for an excuse to go to the boys' room, and it was listlessly granted. What did Hall care?

Ned walked down the corridor to the main stairs. Outside the classrooms, the halls were hung with Halloween decorations. Next Thursday it'd be Halloween. And next year at Halloween, there'd be no school here to be decorated.

He reached the top of the stairs. Looking down, he saw a chubby man in a George Washington hat and knee-length socks go into the boys' room.

What the hell ... ? A teacher dressing up for an early Halloween? But it wasn't any teacher Ned knew. He was much too short and fat to be anyone who worked at Victory School.

Ned raced down the stairs, not thinking, for the moment, that there could be any danger in chasing the man into the lavatory to see who he was. There wasn't another soul in sight.

Revolutionary War clothes ... and they'd looked *real.* A costume would've been clean and shiny; this man's clothes were dirty and dull, like he wore 'em every day to work and would be needing new ones soon.

Ned hadn't gotten a look at his face.

He pushed open the washroom door and went inside.

There was a small, tiled hallway between the door and the room itself. You couldn't see anything from there, just a bit of wall and a trashcan. Ned paused there. He'd been about to sing out, *"Who's here?"* Suddenly he didn't want to.

One of the lightbulbs seemed to have burned out: it was darker than usual. Chilly, too—like somebody might've broken the bathroom window this morning. Ned felt goosebumps stand up all over his skin, and his hair felt like it was about to stand up, too.

And yet he wasn't scared. Well, not *that* scared. It was more like the feeling he got when he scuffed the rug and then got a shock when he reached for a doorknob. *Static electricity,* Dad called it. When there was a lot of it around, you could run a comb through your hair and the comb would pick up a piece of tissue paper, like a magnet.

He heard something slide softly across the floor tiles, followed by a muffled splash, as if somebody had dropped a soggy wad of toilet paper into the bowl.

What am I waiting for? This is the boys' bathroom, I'm allowed to be here.

Ned stepped into the washroom area.

Nobody here. Only the line of urinals opposite the three toilet stalls. The sinks at one end of the room, the unbroken window at the other. No sound but the rain washing down the glass.

But it was cold in here, and the air smelled like a thunderstorm was going to break any minute.

Could the man be in one of the stalls? Silently Ned lowered himself to the floor and looked under the green-painted metal partitions. All he saw were the bases of the bowls. So unless the guy was standing on top of a toilet, he wasn't here.

Which meant he *was* hiding on top of a bowl, because he sure as hell was in here. Ned had seen him go in, and he sure as hell hadn't come out.

That was when Ned got scared, because only some kind of wacko, one of the perverts they talked about on the TV news every other night, would sneak into a school bathroom and hide in a toilet stall.

The thunder-and-lightning smell grew stronger.

Outside it was completely overcast, and the light that came through the window was pale and sickly.

But there was another kind of light coming out of the farthest stall, a light that shimmered like a bright sunbeam full of dancing dust-motes—only this wasn't a beam. It was more like a huge *blob* of light.

Ned got out of there.

3

By mid-morning John Fulham and Carrie had a list of property owners going back to twenty years before the Revolution.

As yet, they had only a list of names, but that was something. It was the names that always hooked Carrie. You started with the names, and as you did your research, you clothed the names with dates of birth and death, business transactions, lawsuits ... until you had a living, breathing human being.

Rose Smollet. Edwin Smollet. Martha and Thaddeus Carter. James and Sarah Browning. Benjamin Bryan. David and Jonathan Hendrycks, William and Katrina Hendrycks. Josiah and Rebecca Mundy. They all waited to be drawn out of oblivion.

The Smollets worked a farm there before Mr. Corwin acquired the land and built his unhappy whorehouse there. Back, back marched the dates on record, back to the original claim staked by Josiah Mundy. Beyond him were only the Indians, who had kept no records.

"It always amazes me, how much information has actually survived!" Carrie said. "I'll bet everything's on record, somewhere."

The County Hall of Records had the births and deaths as well as the succession of ownerships. John was on a Bell Labs pension: he had the time and the energy to become expert at this sort of research. Carrie was learning from him. At one time she would have been hopelessly lost in the profusion of ledgers, file cards, and forms. Now she was able to do what John did, though it took her twice as long.

"We ought to go see Lillian next," he said. "She's got a whole bunch of stuff left over from the Bicentennial, plus whatever she's been able to dig up since then for that book she's writing. See if some of these names ring a bell with her."

Lillian Harker, Tianoga's chief public librarian, had chaired the town's Bicentennial Committee in 1976 and was still working on a book of local history. When and if she ever finished it, the Historical Society hoped to raise funds to have it privately printed.

"And we might want to check the newspaper records over the weekend," John continued. "Think Virgil will mind if you help me out with that?"

"We don't have anything special planned," said Carrie. "As long as I get home by lunchtime, I don't think he'll make a fuss. If it keeps raining like this, he'll probably want to sleep late and dawdle over his breakfast."

4

Rainy-day lunch periods were always a problem at Victory School.

The gym was converted into a cafeteria by pulling out tables with attached benches that folded back into niches in the wall. It was a tight squeeze, but there was just enough room to seat all the kids for half an hour. Then, normally, they'd be let out to the playground and the janitors would come in to fold the tables back and clean up the floor in time for the first gym class of the afternoon.

That schedule was thrown off when the kids had to stay inside. Virgil had experimented with sending them back to their classrooms after they ate, but that cut into the teachers' lunch breaks and made them cranky for the rest of the day. And you couldn't replace them with extra teachers' aides, because the budget wouldn't allow it.

So the children stayed in the cafeteria for the full hour, and the janitors had to get their job done there in a fraction of the time usually allotted for it. And that made Cosmo Iacavella angry. It was therefore tacitly understood that on rainy days, the janitors weren't to be bothered during the afternoon unless absolutely necessary.

With all the kids inside for sixty minutes, lunchroom duty was a real headache. The kids all shouted at once, tried to push each other off the benches, threw things, and generally kept the lunchroom-duty teachers hopping.

It wasn't very hard for Johnny Rizzo and his cohorts to sneak out to the halls in the middle of the period.

"That's better," Johnny said, when they were out. "You can't hear yourself think in there."

"What're we gonna do?" Bob Diehl asked as Johnny led them down the new wing, past empty classrooms.

"Shut up and let me think a minute."

Mike Dudak was restless, though he didn't say so. He hadn't

felt right since the other night, when he'd gone out to the schoolyard and later woke up on the blacktop. His nose still wasn't right. Every now and then, for no reason, it would bleed for a minute or two. He felt sore up there. He was also having intermittent headaches that hadn't improved his disposition.

And weird dreams, too. He kept dreaming he'd fallen out of his body, somehow, and watched it fade away. The worst thing about that was that it didn't seem to scare him as much as it ought to have. He really didn't seem to mind much at all. Yet the dreams left him feeling scared and queasy when he woke, and *very* relieved to find he was still there.

Just now, he felt like he wanted to punch somebody. He thought he probably would, before the day was over. He hoped it'd be Ned Bradley, who thought he was hot shit because he was the principal's kid. Mike was still sore at him for fucking up their game of keepaway a couple of days ago. He'd get Bradley for that, you could bet your balls on it.

Johnny had led them up the main stairway, then down the one that led to the girls' entrance and the basement floor. They moved quietly, not wanting any stray teacher to catch them and send them back to the lunchroom. For a moment they paused to look out the girls' door at the rain. It was still coming down much too hard to permit any thought of sneaking out of the building. Silently, they continued on down the stairs.

At the foot of the steps sat Rudi the Retard, eating a sandwich. He didn't hear them coming. Johnny stopped them, and motioned for them to go back up the stairs, all the way back up to the second-floor landing, where Rudi wouldn't overhear them talking.

"Wonder what he's doin' down there?" Bob said.

"He's eatin' his lunch, you dumb shit, what does it look like he's doin'?" Johnny said. He cogitated for a moment. "Hey! Maybe we can play a little joke on him."

They were up for that. One of the supreme moments of their lives had come last May, when Johnny had stolen a goldfish from a bowl in Miss Pfeiffer's room and put it in Rudi's bucket of water. Rudi the Retard was washing a crayon drawing of a dick off the wall between the kindergarten and the janitor's closet. Rudi dipped his rag into the bucket a few more times before he saw the fish—and then he *stared*. Oh, Jesus, how he stared! The boys nearly got hernias trying not to laugh out loud. The dope took the bucket back to the janitor's closet, set it on the floor, and turned on the taps over the sink, head tilted sideways, intently studying the water as it fell from the spigots—looking for more fish! They ran outside and laughed themselves silly.

Rudi the Retard was too dumb to see through their tricks, and he'd never figured out who was pulling all the pranks on him, so there was no reason not to pull another.

Mike wanted this to be the primo prank of all time, something *nobody* would ever forget. He didn't want to leave it up to Rizzo, who hadn't had a really good idea since the goldfish joke.

He wasn't crazy enough to tell Johnny this, but lately he'd been thinking that Rizzo was losing his touch. Maybe his old man's whuppings were finally taking some of the starch out of him. Of course Johnny would beat the crap out of *him* if he ever suggested it, so Mike kept his suspicion to himself. No doubt about it, though: Rizzo was going soft.

Mike's first notion was to grab a couple handfuls of soap from the boys' room, grease the steps up good and proper, and then get Rudi to chase them. He could almost *see* that. The big doofus's feet'd shoot right out from under him, he'd bust his fuckin' head. . . .

Only it was too complicated. They'd have to sneak back to the boys' room, some goddamn teacher would probably come along, and anyway, they might not have the time. Lunch period was almost over, probably. Fuck it.

Inspiration struck. Dazzled, Mike grabbed Bob and Johnny by their shirts.

"Hey, man—"

"Let's piss on his sandwich!"

For once Rizzo had nothing to say. Mike pulled him closer and whispered the plan that was pumping through his brain like electricity. "We can sneak up behind him and piss over his shoulder, right onto his sandwich! He'll probably take another bite out of it before he catches on!"

Johnny looked him in the eye and said, "You're nuts, Dude. *Crazy.* He'll hear us coming. We'll get caught."

"If he turns around, I'll piss in his eye! Come *on*, man, let's do it! We *gotta* do it!"

Having had his inspiration, Mike could no more have refrained from going through with it than a bullet could turn from its target. He felt like he was on a roll. He didn't give a good goddamn whether Johnny and Bob were with him or not. He let go of Rizzo's shirt and started back down the stairs, unzipping his fly as he went.

His friends followed.

Looking down from the landing, he could see the back of Rudi the Retard's red head. Mike reached down and pulled out his dick, then quietly began the final approach. Johnny and Bob were right behind him, but they hardly mattered anymore.

He held his breath, ready to let fly with a wizz in case Rudi turned around. But the big goon was intent on his sandwich.

Mike crept ahead, one step at a time. Johnny was beside him now, but Mike narrowed his concentration to a point just over Rudi's right shoulder, mentally mapping a trajectory from the tip of his peter to the sandwich Rudi held in front of him. This close, Mike could smell tunafish.

He stopped. He was in range. His bladder suddenly felt like it was going to burst. He fine-tuned his aim.

Now.

The yellow stream arched over the janitor's shoulder and splashed when it landed on the bread in his hand. Mike exhaled with what was almost a sob of glee.

Time ceased to exist, suspended on a glittering arc of piss.

Mike soared. But before he could laugh, Rudi dropped the sandwich and turned, taking the rest of the spray high in the chest.

His face went redder than his hair, his mouth hung open like a broken drawbridge. Fleetingly, Mike had a thought to shift his aim and go for the open mouth; but there turned out to be no time for that. Rudi shot to his feet, the muscles of his bare arms jumping into awesome bulges.

Johnny cried "Beat it!" and spun away. Mike came after him, abruptly having realized that Rudi had the strength to shred him into confetti with his bare hands. His dick shrank to the size of an acorn.

They plowed headlong into Diehl, who'd hung back to gawk like an idiot. The three of them nearly went down. Fortunately for them, Rudi slipped on his sandwich. They blundered up the stairs and through the fire doors at the second-floor landing, laughing uncontrollably as they fled down the hall.

Chapter Fourteen

1

Cosmo Iacavella wore a face like thunder, and loomed up in front of Virgil's desk like a black cloud. Beside him, taller yet seeming smaller, stood Rudi Fitch, nervously shuffling his feet.

"Tell Mr. Bradley what happened. Go on, Rudi, tell him."

After some stammering, Rudi said, "It's those boys, Mr. Bradley. Mike and Johnny and Bob. They ... they *peed* on me!"

Virgil wasn't sure he'd heard that right. "What?"

"I was eating my lunch, just sittin' on the stairs, and they came up behind me and peed all over my sandwich. On me, too." Rudi displayed a dark stain on his green workshirt.

"Tell the whole thing, Rudi."

"Aw, I don't know...."

Cosmo couldn't wait for Rudi to finish the story. "They been pickin' on him from Day One," he said, "and I ain't gonna stand for it no more. This is the last straw. You do somethin' about it, Mr. Bradley, or you gonna need a couple new janitors. We ain't gonna take no more of this shit. Jumpin' Christ, what kind of school is it where the kids *piss* on people?"

"I don't think their parents know how to discipline them properly," Virgil said.

"I'd give 'em some discipline! Nail their fuckin' heads to a door!"

Waiting for their teachers to deliver the boys to the office, Virgil surprised himself by wondering whether nailing their heads to a door might not actually do some good.

As a parent, he believed that some small amount of corporal punishment did a child more good than harm. Ned would get clipped now and then, when he got the old man riled. There were a few adults Virgil would've liked to clip, too, but that was beside the point. You couldn't always reason with a child. Reason didn't have all the answers, and other mammals got along just fine without it. You hugged your kid a lot, you carried him around until he was old enough to be embarrassed by it, you romped and tussled with him in play, and every now and then you batted him one because he'd gotten your goat. Mammalian parenting. Watch any good cat raise her kittens, and learn. If the kittens got rambunctious, they got bopped. It didn't happen often and it didn't make them crazy. The mother cat never cuffed them hard enough to hurt them.

But it worried Virgil a lot that he would have enjoyed, honestly enjoyed, hauling off and belting a kid like Johnny Rizzo right in the teeth.

With the boys standing in front of his desk, and Millie Stanhouse blocking the doorway behind them, Virgil phoned the parents, starting with Patrolman Neil Rizzo at police headquarters. Not surprisingly, Officer Rizzo wasn't in. The dispatcher promised to have him call back.

Next was the call to the Dudak residence. When Mrs. Dudak answered, she was so obviously drunk—at one-thirty in the afternoon—that Virgil decided to send Mike home in the district's van for handicapped kids, which would be free at the moment. He would follow it up with a letter explaining the reason for the suspension.

Mr. Dudak, he was told, was driving a truck down to Galveston, Texas.

Virgil had honest doubts about the wisdom of sending the boy home to such a household, but he had no doubt at all that Cosmo would make good his threat to quit if the little shit remained in school an hour longer. He supposed it was no wonder Mike was turning out the way he was; but there were some things that no educator could hope to change.

He hung up and started to dial Frederick Diehl's number, but Bob interrupted him.

"Mr. Bradley, you can't call my folks, nobody's home."

"Your parents both work?

"Is there a number where I can reach your mother or your father at work?

"I dunno, I guess so. But I ain't got it on me."

There was a quality to the boy's doltishness that made Virgil wonder whether his body fat had spread up into his skull and mashed his brain. Gradually, Virgil was able to pry out enough information to enable him to call Mrs. Diehl at her office.

She was at a meeting, he was told. Slipping into an adversarial mood, Virgil explained who he was and told them to get her out of the meeting for a minute; this was about her son. They put him on hold and he listened to Muzak for a while.

"Well, what is it?" a female voice broke in.

She listened impatiently while he explained. He thought he could hear fingers drumming on a desk. When he finished explaining, he said, "I strongly suggest we meet to discuss this, Mrs. Diehl."

"Write me a letter. I can't get the time off. We've got a big deal going down right now, and I'm putting in a sixty-hour week."

"Perhaps *Mr.* Diehl—"

"*Write* us, Mr. Bradley. Now, if you'll excuse me, I'm in the middle of an important meeting." And she left him listening to a dead phone.

Yuppies, he thought disgustedly.

His lecture to the boys was as brief as he could make it. He felt like he was addressing plaster mannequins.

"The law says you have to go to school," he told them. "Otherwise, frankly, we wouldn't have you here.

"But if you don't shape up, we don't have to keep you. Under some circumstances, the state will take you off our hands and put you in a supervised juvenile facility. And I can't think of anybody here who'd be sorry to see you go."

Rizzo was sullen, doing all he could to close his ears to this. Diehl looked a little worried, though, as if he weren't quite sure how much trouble he was really in this time. He also looked like he was trying to figure out just exactly what Virgil meant. The phrase "supervised juvenile facility" seemed to be going over his head. *Let it,* Virgil thought.

"Much as we would like it to be otherwise," he said, "we just have to face the fact that not everybody who goes through our educational system comes out a decent and responsible human being. We can't force you to become something you don't want to be. I'm telling you now, we've done about all we can for you boys. You're going to have to start motivating yourselves."

There was more he could have said, but the words dried up on him. What was the use? They didn't want to be anything but what they were—hooligans. Soon they would be entering the juvenile justice system as delinquents on their way to becoming full-fledged criminals. He was sure of it.

It wasn't exactly the kind of thought that warmed an educator's heart.

Rizzo glowered, playing the tough guy, while Diehl's dull eyes shifted this way and that and his hands looked like they wanted to pick his nose.

Mike Dudak was paying no attention to any of it. His eyes were locked onto a point on the back wall, over Virgil's desk. He was staring like a man to whom a profound religious truth has been unexpectedly and wondrously revealed; but Virgil knew without having to turn around and follow it that the boy's marveling gaze was fixed on—of all homely and unedifying things—Eric Hargrove's portrait. Acolyte and icon. He had a feeling that if he fluttered a hand in front of the boy's eyes, Mike wouldn't even blink.

That was when he truly began to be afraid of ten-year-old Mike Dudak.

2

The rain let up that afternoon, transforming the playground into a mire and leaving behind a smell of mildew all through the building. The sky looked like lead, auguring more rain yet to come.

Ned walked home with Phil and the McManuses. The schoolyard mud sucked at his boots with every step, trying to yank them off his feet, but he hardly noticed.

Look, fellas, I saw this Revolutionary War guy go into the boys' room, okay, so I followed him, only he wasn't there. . . .

Ned was starting to get bad feelings about this thing. *Very* bad. But he knew what his friends would say if he tried to tell them about it. *Well, looks like ol' Ned watched one too many monster movies, guys. His mom always said he'd wind up like this, poor boner's got bats in his belfry—vampire bats! Get it?*

Oh, yeah, he *had* seen a lot of horror movies . . . but damn it, Mom read those goofy murder mysteries all the time, and she wasn't thinking she saw dead bodies lying around. A movie couldn't make you see something that wasn't there. *Damn it, I saw the guy!* And besides—when had he ever seen a movie that had in it a short, fat guy whose George Washington clothes were about as clean and new as Mr. Iacavella's sleeveless T-shirts?

Ghosts look real. . . .

He was jarred out of his reverie when Patty, who was wearing brand-new red rubber boots and feeling mighty gay about it, took a standing broad jump into the middle of a big puddle and splashed her three companions, giving Ned a nice snootful of muddy water.

"Asshole!" Phil cried. His glasses were blinded by mud, and he had to stop to wipe them off. Patty's brother, Marty, jerked her out of the puddle by the wrist, provoking a yelp of pain and indignation.

"You hurt me, you big pig!"

"Serves you right, shrimp!"

They wrangled about it most of the way home, and it blew Ned's concentration.

Mom and Dad caught onto him halfway through supper.

"You don't feel well, do you?" Mom said.

"I feel all right," he said. He scooped a forkful of Niblets corn and dutifully slid it into his mouth. It had hardly any taste at all.

"Ned, you've been picking at your food. I'm the mother of a growing boy, I know what that means. It means you're coming down with something."

"Around here we don't punish little kids for getting sick," Dad put in, "although in your case we might make an exception. No TV for a decade."

"Go soak your head, dear," Mom said.

Usually Ned got a yuk out of it when his parents kidded around like this, but not today. He supposed it meant he really *was* sick.

Mom felt his forehead. "Hm. You don't feel feverish, but I'll take your temperature later. Do you feel queasy?"

"No." Actually, he felt cold, and tired—like he wanted to

curl up on the sofa with a wool comforter wrapped around him, or even go to bed. He felt drained.

"Well, it was kind of stinkin' weather when you walked home from school today. Maybe you caught a chill or something. You weren't fooling around in any mud puddles on the way, were you?"

Sometimes he could swear his folks had a crystal ball. But he shook his head and Mom didn't press the point.

"You'd better lie down for a while," she said.

"I can eat," Ned insisted. He didn't want them making a big deal out of this, although lying down sounded awful good to him just now. But he felt guilty when he wasted food: Mom took pains to serve meals that he liked, even if it meant preparing two different suppers. Not like at Phil's house, where you ate what was on your plate, or you didn't eat at all.

"Feed a fever, starve a cold," Dad said. "Or is it the other way around?"

Ned stayed at the table and finished his supper. It didn't make him feel any worse, but tonight he took no pleasure in it. He went straight to his room afterward, and no one said a word about his homework.

Ned lay in the dark and listened to the rain.

At 7:30 Mom took his temperature and found no fever, but he was so listless that she put him to bed anyway. It was very early for him, and he'd miss the eight o'clock movie, but he went without a protest. It seemed to start raining again as soon as Mom turned out the light and closed his bedroom door.

Shit, he felt run-down. He felt like a car with a dying battery, or a flashlight that had been left on too long. He'd *never* felt like this before.

And the more he thought about the other thing, the more he was convinced he'd seen a ghost.

It hadn't seemed like a ghost at the time; the thought had never even entered his head. Just a strangely dressed fat guy

123

walking into the bathroom. When you saw a ghost, you were supposed to scream. You were supposed to be scared, shit-in-your-pants scared. Run down the hall, screaming at the top of your lungs. You didn't go following it into a room.

Was it or wasn't it?

He didn't know what else it could have been. It was just impossible to believe in a man who dressed up like a Minuteman or something and sneaked into school lavatories to stand on top of the toilets. That was really ridiculous! Even a freakin' ghost made more sense than that.

And don't forget that funky light that was comin' out of the stall.

Ned shivered. There was something *in* that stall, something that was producing that light, that shimmering blob of light; and the fat guy in the Ben Franklin suit had something to do with it.

Yeah. He was dematerializing, like in the movies.

Or like when they beam you back aboard the Starship Enterprise.

Well, that was great. He'd gone from ghosts to *Star Trek.* Maybe if he really put on his thinking cap, he could come up with something even dumber.

He wished he could tell Dad. Dad was the principal. He should know about things like this. *Guess what, Dad. The school is haunted. . . .*

He couldn't stand the idea of Dad thinking he was buggy.

He had the blankets up to his chin and he couldn't stop shivering.

Holy shit—am I sick because of what happened today? Did seeing *that thing make me feel like this?*

What really tore at him was the thought of seeing it again. Fear kept him wide awake while his body begged for sleep.

Chapter Fifteen

1

The sentience inhabited a body, and without the body there would be no sentience. But there are other streams of evolution than the one which carries man and all the forms of life he knows.

For the body which housed this intelligence was independent of it. It looked after its own needs. Thus the sentience was only dimly aware of its own physical existence. It was free to dwell primarily in a realm of pulsating electromagnetic energies: its own, and those energies which emanated from the prey. Without the prey's energy, there could be no sentience.

Nor could there be those others, the nonbeings, the twilight people who were neither sentience nor prey.

In consuming the prey's energies, the sentience radiated its own. Some of what it consumed was wasted and remained virtually unchanged from what it was the moment it was drawn from the prey's brain, its source. As energy, it was imperishable. And in the field of energy that surrounded the alien sentience, it was channeled into a state of almost-being. It was the stuff of satellite entities, and it would endure for as long as there was a stronger field of energy to bind it to this place.

The rain seeped into the ground. Water molecules were picked up by far-spreading microscopic rootlets and siphoned back to nourish an alien physiology. Other rootlets absorbed needed minerals and organic matter originating from decaying plants, animals, and microorganisms. The earth was rich.

Not so the structure above, where the prey assembled according to fixed and easily predictable patterns.

The prey organism was complex, a highly developed being with a brain that emitted energy in a marvelous array of different wavelengths; and each brain was subtly unique. The sentience, which had evolved according to an entirely different scheme, would never be able to adapt to this with complete efficiency. There were individual brains which produced energies which could not be used at all, and others whose energies the sentience chose not to utilize. Consequently, it had to select those with whose energies its own were most compatible. And sometimes this could not be determined by sensors alone.

But the time was coming when all the prey would leave and the artificial structure would be destroyed; and the sentience could not predict when its source of energy would be restored, if ever.

In its own unfathomable way, it feared that time.

2

Ned drifted in and out of sleep all Saturday morning, feeling weak and spacy during the intervals when he was awake. He still had no fever; and although he had no appetite, he didn't feel pukey, either.

But when he woke again at noon, he felt well enough to sit up and take notice. Dad made him a couple of soft-boiled eggs, which he wolfed down.

"Where's Mom?" he asked.

"She's out with Mr. Fulham, doing some research for the Historical Society. She'll be home in a little while."

"How come she didn't stay home to worry about me?"

The wiseguy question was his way of telling Dad he was all right now, and Dad knew it. He grinned. "As a matter of fact," he told Ned, "I made her go. But you were due for a trip to the doctor if you weren't better by the time she came back. I guess you just caught a chill or something yesterday, and it knocked you out for a while. An adult probably would've come down with pneumonia."

Ned knew that wasn't so. He hadn't taken a chill, or anything of the kind, but he let it slide. He still hadn't figured out a way to tell Dad what he'd seen without it sounding crazy.

Mom was overjoyed to find him up and alert. When he asked if they could play Monopoly for a while, she fetched the game from the rec room and set it up on his bed, and Dad brought him a big glass of birch beer. Homework and housework took a back seat for a couple hours, and Ned was glad. Sometimes it wasn't such a bad thing to be sick. It made your folks appreciate you.

3

Ned was well enough to go to Sunday school the next morning, and out to play afterward. The sun was finally coming out again. Carrie made sure he understood that if she even suspected he messed around in mud puddles today, he could forget about going trick-or-treating on Halloween. Having delivered the message, she took off for another hour or two with John at the public library. Virgil retreated to his workshop in the basement, where he tinkered with an old radio he'd been trying to fix for weeks.

When Carrie came home, he gave it up and took a sandwich break. She was bubbling over with a story for him.

"John and I struck gold!" she said, her enthusiasm making her look twenty again. "We've been digging and digging, and we've dug up a story that has everything. No kidding, you could make a movie out of it. At least a TV movie."

It concerned Edwin and Rose Smollet, the father and daughter who had owned what was now the Victory School site from 1847 to 1873—the year Rose was murdered.

"How about *that?*" Carrie said. "Honestly, Virg, this family was a *beaut.*"

"I just hope your information's reliable."

"Oh, it's reliable, all right. Edwin's purchase of the land is on record, and we know he ran a small smithy there in the 1850s. We haven't yet been able to find out who he was or where he came from, but we've learned quite a bit about him and his family after they came to Tianoga. His wife's a problem, though. Her name isn't on record, but she was supposed to have died in Charleston in 1854. I guess she was a Southerner who went back home for some reason."

Smollet's son, Horatio, fought at Gettysburg, came out of that great battle unscathed and with a citation for bravery, and was killed in a meaningless little skirmish somewhere in the Virginia Tidewater in 1865, on the eve of Appomattox. His body was never brought home for burial, but his name was inscribed on the borough's roll of honor. "You can see it there the next time you go to Town Hall," Carrie said.

"I think losing his wife and son did something to Mr. Smollet," she went on. "His daughter, Rose, never married. She lived with him on the farm. We don't know what their relationship was like, but Edwin died in 1870 and they had a coroner's inquest. We're going to try to find the record of that—but I don't think they held inquests in those days unless they felt there was something suspicious about the death."

"You're reading a lot into this, aren't you?" Virgil said. "You sound more like a screenwriter than a historian."

"Well, they didn't summon a coroner's jury every time some-one died!"

"You're going to be disappointed if you find out they reached a verdict of death by natural causes."

"We'll see. Anyhow, Rose continued to live at the farm until 1873. A hired man named George McGrath killed her—clubbed her to death. And there's no mistake about that. The county court found him guilty of murder and hanged him for it. Hopefully, we'll be able to track down a transcript of his trial. If not, I'm sure we'll get the gist of it from the newspapers."

But McGrath had pleaded guilty and gone mutely to the gallows, and there was no record of his thoughts.

He was a drifter who took work where he found it, then moved on, soon forgotten. When he came to Tianoga, he was told that there was always short-term work at the Smollet farm, and that the woman who owned it welcomed drifters because none of the community's year-round residents would work for her. He asked why not, and received vague answers that struck him as so much moonshine. He put it down to the need of townsmen to spin yarns that would relieve the monotony of their lives. If the woman had poisoned her father, she would have swung for it by now.

Rose Smollet turned out to be a handsome, strapping, middle-aged farm woman who took him on with no questions asked, her last hired man having skipped out on her some time ago. The wages were agreeable, the work was what he was used to, and he would have a room in the house in which to sleep. If she's willing to take me on trust, McGrath thought, I owe the same to her. For all she knows, I could be a horse thief on the run.

She was a good cook, she was generous with her whiskey, and they sat up in her parlor for a good part of his first night there. She showed an interest in his travels, and he was happy to entertain her. If he told a few stretchers, she didn't seem to mind.

She warmed to him. In fact, she liked him so much that first night that she took him to her bed. McGrath was more than willing; he hadn't had a woman in months. And the invitation didn't surprise him. Miss Smollet was not the first farm spinster he'd bedded, and he doubted she'd be the last.

But he was surprised by her performance. More than surprised: he felt like a bather who's suddenly snatched up and flung head-over-heels by a freak wave. One expected a woman to snuff out the lamp, remove her shift in the dark, and lie acquiescently upon her back while he mounted her. Most of McGrath's women hadn't even gone in for a bit of kissing first.

Maid Smollet, however, practically ate him alive. They coupled in ways he hadn't dreamed were possible. McGrath had spent his whole life in the country, never having read a book; nor was he blessed with a lively imagination—all of the woman's games were new to him. She made him feel like he'd wandered into Gomorrah. It was almost frightening, and at the end it left him as limp and languid as a scarecrow.

"We've stayed up too long," she said. "Tomorrow night we'll go to bed earlier."

Work filled his days, pleasure his nights, and he found the pleasure more exhausting than the work. For a little while he considered himself the most fortunate of men, and even toyed with the idea of asking for the lady's hand in marriage. He wondered why in heaven's name any of his predecessors had left this happy berth. What more could a man want? Fertile land, a jug of corn whiskey, and a lusty woman—how could anyone have walked away from that? But he was grateful that the others had.

Yet his marriage proposal was never made, and misgivings soon intruded on his paradise like dark spots appearing on an apple.

Rose was insane.

There were nights when she thrashed in her sleep like a fish on a hook, howling and gibbering; and McGrath would get up the next morning to find himself bruised head-to-foot by her powerful arms and legs. She was also subject to nosebleeds, frequently while in the grip of one of her nightmares. When he suggested that she see a doctor, she denied that there was anything wrong with her, even as she washed the bloodstained bedclothes.

It wasn't long before McGrath's nerves were set perpetually on edge. The woman was a lunatic. One morning he heard her shouting in the barn. He came running, in case she'd aroused a surly tramp who'd bedded down there for the night; but she was alone, insisting that she hadn't said a word to anyone, much less shouted. "Your ears are playing tricks on you, McGrath," she said, "or else it was a trick of the wind." He decided not to argue about it with her, but he knew what he'd heard.

There were strange rustlings in the house, although he never saw any rats. There were peculiar smells. And one day he overheard her talking in the cellar, although he couldn't make out any words, because the door was closed. Again she tried to persuade him he'd imagined it. She flew into a right passion over it.

"You are not to prowl around my house, McGrath! This is my house and I forbid it! Don't think I haven't noticed the way your eyes rove, trying to find the hiding place where I keep the family jewels. You're thinking you can plunder me and scamper off!"

Nothing of the kind had ever occurred to McGrath, but he was given no opportunity to defend himself. She ranted on.

"There *are* no family jewels! I *have* no miser's hoard! I am a poor woman who has to toil like a man for every jot and tittle that I own. My mother is dead, my brother died in the war, and I buried my father in a pauper's grave. But I will not be made light of! Do you hear me?"

I could hear you if I were on the other side of town, McGrath thought. Rose's explosion of temper had unmanned him temporarily. For the moment, she seemed more than capable of

131

skewering him with a carving knife if he was unlucky enough to make the wrong reply. He didn't know what she wanted of him. Words filled his brain, but he truly did not know whether any of them would likely placate her or provoke her all the more. He could only mumble an abject plea for forgiveness and swear by his mother's grave that he had no intention of plundering her house.

She had, however, planted a seed. *By God, she's hiding something!* he would say to himself. Maybe she did have a cache of gold or jewels. The more he pondered it, the more he convinced himself it must be so.

He came reluctantly to the conclusion that he would not stay much longer. Now he understood why the other hired men had moved on. Nor did he doubt any more that Rose had poisoned her father. The woman was demented, and her long years of labor on the farm had made her strong enough to be dangerous to any man.

But he stayed because he wondered what she was hiding. Each day he postponed his departure once again. *I'm a damned fool,* he would scold himself; but he stayed nonetheless.

Meanwhile, he tiptoed through the days like a soldier approaching a picket line in the dead of night, not knowing when a single misplaced footstep might draw the sentry's fire.

Inevitably the day came when Rose had to make a rare journey into town to buy supplies. McGrath declined the invitation to mount the buckboard with her, pleading a headache. (And not altogether falsely: he'd been feeling downright poorly for the past few days, always tuckered out and unable to relax.) She accepted his excuse and drove off, leaving him alone in the house.

He gave her half an hour's start before he assayed the cellar door. Had it been locked, there would have been an end to it, he would have let it be. But to his mild astonishment, it wasn't. He lit a lamp and descended the stone stairs, wading slowly into the dank air. It closed over his head like water.

"My God, it stinks down here!" he said out loud.

He had half a mind to turn around, pack his few belongings, and be gone before Rose came back from town. There was nothing down here worth stealing; and even if there were, he was not a thief. He wasn't even a busybody, and he never would have been tempted to snoop if Rose hadn't accused him of it.

Why forbid him the cellar? Surely no one would want to come down here except to fetch things out of storage. By the light of the lamp he could see that Rose kept her whiskey here, and roots and herbs, sealed casks, preserved fruit in glass jars, and other household items.

He advanced a few steps into the murk. Lamplight trickled over a heap of rags piled against the fieldstone wall.

Now that's strange. What's she want with a bunch of tattered old clothes? And men's clothes, to boot.

Rose worked in men's clothes, to be sure; but these she washed thoroughly when they were soiled, and mended carefully when they were torn. Moreover, she was a frugal person, and it wasn't like her to throw old clothes into a pile in the cellar—not when any farmer could find a hundred uses for the rags.

And these were filthy. Dappled with dark stains, and smelling of . . .

Blood. And sweat, and piss, and even shit. All mixed together with mildew in a uniquely sickening fetor. Now that he realized what it was, McGrath felt his stomach roll like a beaten dog playing dead. But still he advanced for a closer look.

These were not Rose's clothes. Her personal tidiness was remarkable, she would never let any garments she owned get into such a state as these. Shirts, trousers, woolen underwear, stockings, bandanas: all were stiff with dried and drying blood. It was as if she had stripped the dead on a great battlefield and brought their clothes back here. A jumble of skulls and bones could not have offered a more charnel sight.

"Take a good look, McGrath."

He nearly dropped the lamp when he spun around and saw her. So intent had he been on his discovery that he hadn't heard her come down the stairs. Now she stood there like a dragon guarding its hoard, a terrible grin on her face. She held an ax in her hands.

"Thought I'd gone to town, didn't you?" she said. "Did you really think I'd be so stupid? *You* were the stupid one, Mc-Grath. I set my trap and you fell into it."

He understood it all now. Soon his own bloodstained clothes would join this moldering collection, unless he somehow found the means to preserve himself.

"Where are the men, Rose? Where did you bury them?"

"You're standing on them."

He shuffled his feet uncomfortably and she laughed—the indescribable laugh of a woman who murdered men and buried them in her cellar floor. His eyes darted about, desperately seeking something he could use as a weapon.

He thought he saw movement in the shadows behind her, thought he heard faint scrapings and rustlings as of a crowd quietly jockeying for the best view. But it was nothing.

"*Why*, Rose? Why did you kill them?"

She laughed again. "Idiot! They were all thieves—all of them! They'd steal the teeth out of my mouth, only they wanted more than that. And I gave it to them!"

McGrath shook his head. He was standing next to some rickety shelves that held a number of broken and discarded items. He clutched at the shelves for support. His fingers touched rusty metal—an old iron sash weight. By small, subtle movements he gained a grip on it.

Rose grimaced at him. He'd never dreamed a woman's face could be so monstrous. Madness—or was it something else?— coarsened her features. Her nose had started bleeding again, and the blood was running freely down her lips and chin. She ignored it.

To McGrath it seemed that the air crackled all around them. His short hairs rose, his skin prickled.

God help me, am I going mad, too?

Saint Elmo's fire, pale and fairylike, danced around the

head of Rose's ax. Rose herself wore a halo of it. Her eyes shone red.

He screamed, and the scream released him from the spell. He leaped at her, getting so close that she couldn't strike him with the ax, and brought the sash weight down on the center of her forehead, driving it with all his strength, feeling her skull crumple. The shock of the blow rippled through his arm; but only death could have jarred the bludgeon from his hand.

Rose dropped the ax. She froze in her tracks, a red crater crushed into her brow, her eyes pressed nearly out of their sockets. She grinned at him.

He hit her again and she fell.

Still screaming, he sank to his knees and hammered at her skull, breaking it, splintering it, showering himself with blood and brain. His hand went numb.

Somehow his lamp broke. Fire bloomed. The clothes began to burn. He felt their heat on his back, and it finally prodded him to his feet.

He was out of his mind, and he knew it. As flames sprang up from the dead men's clothes, he thought he heard a crowd of phantoms jostling around him, gabbling in unknown tongues. He thought he felt their lurid eyes on him, leering at the blood that soaked his hands.

He screamed again and fled from the house, leaving it to burn.

He wandered dazedly until a constable saw him and arrested him. The blood on his hands, face, and clothes was more than enough to convict him. In Rose's cellar, the rags had burned to ashes, the fire going out when it encountered the clammy walls and the damp, earthen floor.

McGrath never took the stand, never told his tale, not even to the priest who tried to save his soul before he met his executioner. He didn't want to tell it and end his days in a lunatic asylum. He could have asked the police to dig in the floor for the hired men's bodies, but a numbness of spirit had fallen over him, and if they were determined to hang him, he had no desire to oppose it. He had no will to live. Telling his mad tale would not save him. Better it should die with him.

As indeed it did.

4

For the first time since the conclusion of his hypnosis sessions, Virgil had a nightmare. It wrenched him from his sleep and then fled before he could remember what it was.

He lay next to his sleeping wife in the friendly darkness of his bedroom and wondered if he was, after all, as sane as Dr. Lauther had assured him he was.

He got to thinking about the story Carrie had told him earlier. Whatever the ambiguities, it was a recorded fact that murder had been done at the Smollet house, and the county had hanged the man who'd done it.

But why did it trouble him? It had happened over a hundred years ago.

And my school stands on the site of that house.

Virgil was willing, just barely, to keep an open mind on haunted houses; but could a patch of *ground* be haunted? Could land itself take on a supernatural taint? There was a time when he would have laughed off the whole idea, but that time had passed. There was nothing to laugh at anymore.

He thought he had purged himself of that old horror in the janitor's closet, rid his mind of it. Why hadn't it stayed purged?

He lay awake for hours, wondering if his own experience was somehow born of the other horrors that unhappy place had known.

Chapter Sixteen

1

"What's that?"

Cosmo Iacavella pointed to the dime-store crucifix that hung around Rudi Fitch's neck on a length of blue yarn. Rudi didn't understand what he was talking about at first, and he turned around to see if it was something behind him.

"No, no, you dummy! I mean the plastic Jesus around your neck. You ain't Catholic."

Rudi wished Mr. Iacavella wouldn't confuse him. The crucifix had nothing to do with being Catholic. Rudi didn't go to the Catholic church, St. Jerome's, so how could he be one?

"Mrs. Giddens bought it for me," Rudi said. Mrs. Giddens owned the house where Rudi lived. She was the landlady; he was her boarder. She helped him take care of his money and cooked his suppers for him.

"Why'd she do that? She ain't Catholic, either."

"I asked her to. I asked her to buy me one."

At seven-thirty this Monday morning, Cosmo already had the feeling it was going to be a long, long week. All he needed right now was Rudi showing up for work with a crucifix around his neck. Cosmo shook his head and turned on the coffee machine, needing something to take off the dampness of the boiler room.

"I ain't tryin' to step on your freedom of religion, Rudi," he said. "Hell, no. You wanna to be a Catholic or a Jew or a Buddist, more power to you, you got a right. I'm only askin' because I'm curious, that's all. *And* I wanna make sure nobody's been talkin' you into somethin' you don't understand. You don't wanna tell me, fine. I ain't gonna ask you again. But for the love of Pete, kid, how come you're all of a sudden wearin' a crucifix?"

He could have asked that without so many words, Rudi thought.

"Mr. Iacavella, you'd get mad at me if I told you. You'd think I was making something up."

"Son, I know you *never* make things up. You ain't got the brains for it."

He didn't mean it in a nasty way. What he meant was that he knew that Rudi always told the truth—or at least as much of the truth as he could hope to know. Encouraged, Rudi tried to explain why he needed a crucifix.

"Mr. Iacavella, this school is getting really *bad* lately. Don't you know there's ghosts in it?"

"No, Rudi, I didn't know that."

"Well, there is. And I seen one, plain as day." He told the older man about the boy with no clothes on who'd walked into the music room and wasn't there when Rudi looked inside, and how he had to unlock the door before he could take a look. Mr. Iacavella let him go on without interrupting, but he had a look on his face like the story hurt his feelings, somehow. Rudi was sorry for that, but he had to tell the truth.

"Ain't you ever *noticed*, Mr. Iacavella? There's whispers in the halls when nobody's there, and footsteps going up and down the stairs; and sometimes when I open up a classroom in the morning, I find chairs moved around from where I left 'em when I locked the room up the day before. You gotta have noticed some of that! *I* sure have. And the way I figure, it's gotta be ghosts. Just like on TV."

"So naturally," Mr. Iacavella said, "you told Mrs. Giddens all about it, and she said you ought to wear a crucifix to keep the ghosts away."

Rudi beamed. "That's right, Mr. Iacavella! That's exactly what she said! How did you know?"

Cosmo sat down behind his desk, put a hand over his face, and shook his head.

"You told Mrs. Giddens?"

"Sure."

"You didn't happen to tell anybody else, did you? Like Mr. Bradley, or the police, or the Board of Education?"

"No, sir! They'd think I was crazy," Rudi said. "You and Mrs. Giddens know me better, though."

Mr. Iacavella ran his fingers through his sparse hair and sighed. For a long time he didn't say anything. Rudi waited. He knew Mr. Iacavella didn't believe in ghosts, and knew it'd be hard for him to believe the story.

Finally Cosmo spoke. "Will you do me a favor, Rudi?"

"Sure, Mr. Iacavella. Anything you say."

"Don't tell nobody else about this, willya? You gotta promise me you won't say another word to anybody."

"I promise. But—"

"Good boy," Mr. Iacavella rubbed his face some more, like he was still trying to wake up and get out of bed. "Like you said, they'll think you got a screw loose. You might get fired."

"I won't tell."

"Good ... good." Cosmo paused to contemplate the interlocked rings of coffee stains that decorated the top of his desk. "Now go and open up the building, okay? Let's just go to work. I gotta think about this."

Rudi took the keys and left Mr. Iacavella pondering in the boiler room.

* * *

He walked down to the far end of the hall. It was still rather dark outside, and the light bulbs in the hall were dirty, so the corridor was kind of dim. It was supposed to rain again today, after all the rain they'd had Friday and Saturday. Wasn't it ever going to stop?

He was about to turn and go up the stairs by the library when he saw a man coming down.

He was too startled to yell. He froze, open-mouthed.

It was an old man, lean and pale, wearing rimless glasses and a musty-looking pale suit with baggy pants and wide lapels. His jacket was unbuttoned, revealing a stiff white shirt and a black bow tie. He stopped halfway down the stairs and looked at Rudi.

And his feet shot out from under him, and he fell, tumbling head over kiester down the hard stone stairs—*bump-bump-bump-bump-crack!* He hit the bottom step with his head and skidded almost to Rudi's feet and lay there staring up at him. Thick ropes of dark blood, almost black, began to uncoil from his nostrils.

Rudi screamed and bolted back toward the boiler room.

"Mr. Iacavella! Mr. Iacavella!"

He ran into Cosmo as the older man was coming out the door and almost bowled him over. Mr. Iacavella grabbed him by the arms and shook him.

"Rudi, what the fuck is this, what's the matter? Get ahold of yourself, boy!"

Rudi tore loose and pointed frantically back down the hall.

"An old man! He fell down the stairs!"

"What old man! What're you talkin' about?"

"Come on!" Rudi dragged him down the hall. He was too strong to resist, and Cosmo had to go with him.

But there was no old man, and not even a spot of blood on the yellowed linoleum floor.

Rudi couldn't believe it. For some moments he was speechless. Mr. Iacavella fired questions at him, but Rudi couldn't hear them. It took another vigorous shake to snap him out of it.

"Now what *is* all this shit, damn it!"

"There was this *old man!* He was walking down the stairs and he fell, right here! And he was hurt, he banged his head *real* bad, there was blood—"

"All right, all right! Calm down, fer chrissake! He ain't here now, is he?"

Rudi stared at the blank floor. He couldn't believe that that was all he could see. He shook his head and muttered, "No, sir. He ain't."

"Come with me, Rudi."

Mr. Iacavella led him back to the boiler room, sat him down, and made him sip a bit of vodka from the bottle he kept in his top drawer. The vodka burned its way down Rudi's throat and sat on his stomach like a coal, but it did shake him up a little, and in doing so, calmed him.

"I'm sorry, Mr. Iacavella." He croaked a little when he said this. How could Mr. Iacavella drink this stuff? "Jesus, I guess I must have seen another ghost."

Mr. Iacavella held him by the shoulders.

"Listen to me, Rudi. Are you listening?"

Rudi nodded.

"There ain't no ghosts. Whatever you saw or thought you saw, there ain't no ghosts. There's *no such thing.*

"Now, sometimes a fella can honestly *think* he sees somethin'—only it ain't there. It's only in his imagination. It don't necessarily mean he's crazy, but it sure as shit is gonna sound crazy when he tries to tell somebody else about it. So you ain't gonna say a word about this to anybody. Not a fuckin' soul. You gotta promise me you won't."

"I won't. But—"

"But *nothin'!* Shit, Rudi, I know what your problem is. You been watchin' too many screwy things on TV. They fuck you up. Make your imagination run away with you. You gotta stop watchin' those scary TV shows. Will you do that for me?"

"If you want. But Mr. Iacavella, I saw—"

"No, Rudi. You *thought* you saw. And that's all there is to

141

it. Look, you sit here for a little while, okay? I'll open up the building. I want you to take it easy today. You got scared, and you'll get scared again if you don't relax."

After silencing whatever protests the boy wanted to make, Cosmo went alone to unlock the doors and turn on the lights in the halls.

He didn't like it, not one bit. If he didn't know the kid so well, he'd swear Rudi was losing his marbles. But that couldn't be. The kid was dumb, not crazy. He was saner than nine out of ten people you'd meet on the street, you could bet your ass on it. But if he was sitting up in his room all night watching horror movies and spook shows, no wonder he was seeing things. Probably the poor dumb cluck just wasn't smart enough to understand—*really* understand—that all that shit was make-believe. Special effects and trick photography. Like those Vietnamese hillbillies they brought over after the war. Never saw TV in their lives, never even *heard* of it. They came over here and watched TV, and everything they saw, they thought was real. Some of 'em *died* after watching monster movies: they got nightmares so bad, it gave 'em heart attacks. Those poor bastards didn't know any better than Rudi.

Anyway, being alone in this fuckin' place was enough to give anyone the heebie-jeebies. It was too dark, the lighting sucked; too many shadows. Lousy construction, too. The place wasn't solid, so things *moved*. Expanded and contracted with changes of temperature or humidity, shifted ever so slightly under the sheer, poorly distributed weight of the building. It was old and it hadn't been maintained properly. And it smelled.

Cosmo made his rounds, unlocking doors, switching on the lights.

He'd have to protect Rudi, keep him quiet, until the kid got over this. No way did he want to lose him. Rudi was the best damn help he'd ever had, and being a little feeble-minded probably made him better than he'd be if he were normal. But if

142

he went around babbling about ghosts, they'd drop him like a hot potato.

He'd get over it. It was the TV shows, nothing more.

But Cosmo knew that the school's first principal died in a fall down the stairs, just the way Rudi saw it. *Explain that.*

Fuck it. Everybody here knew that story. Rudi'd have to be stone-deaf not to have heard it. And they had the old fart's picture hanging in Mr. Bradley's office. Rudi had seen it there hundreds of times.

"Fuckin' television," Cosmo grumbled to himself, as he made his way back to the boiler room. "Shit, if I lose that kid, I'll *sue* the motherfuckers!"

2

"Sorry, Virg, but I am *not* going to recommend that we expel them. Albany wouldn't like it, and I don't want *those* monkeys on my back. Tough it out. You'll be rid of them at the end of the school year, anyway."

That was Dr. Noonan's answer, as Virgil had expected it would be. You could always trust the superintendent of schools not to stick his neck out. Still, Virgil gave it one last try.

"Bob, if you look at their records, you know those boys are out-and-out sociopaths. At least Rizzo and Dudak are; maybe the Diehl kid just plays follow-the-leader. They're not going to grow out of it. The district's going to have problems with them right on down the line. They simply don't belong in a public school environment. If the state wants 'em educated, let 'em get their education at a state school."

Noonan said, "Forget it, Virgil. I'm not going to have a hundred Department of Education bureaucrats crawling up my shirt. Grin and bear it."

Virgil gave up. With the school winding down its last year of existence, nobody wanted to do anything that would make it any better. Just let it die, the general feeling seemed to be. The board hardly allotted enough money for super-basic maintenance. They weren't about to risk being taken to court by Mr. and Mrs. Diehl, or Officer Rizzo. It cost money to go to court.

Thus the three little creeps were back in school this morning, and Virgil could only hope the janitors wouldn't notice for a while. *(Of course they'll notice: those boys will brag all day about how they pissed on Rudi's sandwich. Every kid in the school probably heard about it before the bell rang this morning. How long before Rudi catches a couple of them laughing at him? Nice school you're running here, Mr. Bradley.)*

Well, Bob Noonan didn't care whose feelings got hurt, as long as he didn't have to *do* anything but pontificate at school board meetings. Ed-u-ca-tors, thought Virgil, are the bane of education.

He peeked at the clock on his desk. *Almost time for lunch. Gee, time sure flies when you're talking to people who make more money than you in education without ever having to set foot inside a school.*

The hell with it.

Virgil took sincere pride in his handling of teachers; and the proof of it, he thought, lay in the fact that he could sit down to lunch in the faculty room without inhibiting his staff one iota. Some principals walked into their faculty lounges like Jack Palance in a gunfighter suit stepping into a saloon and shutting up even the player piano just by looking at it; but that was ego-tripping, Virgil thought. When he came in to lunch, he left his principal's hat outside. "I ate my lunches here for eleven years before I became principal," he'd explain. "You can't expect me to hole up in my office all day." He never criticized a teacher for anything that was said or done in the lounge; he never even mentioned anything he saw or heard there. This was the teachers' turf, and he was there only to eat his lunch and socialize with his fellow human beings.

The teachers hardly noticed him when he dropped in for lunch, and that was just the way he wanted it.

3

No one was noticing Diane Phelps, either, as she pretended to read a Robert Ludlum book and waited for Joanne Wilmot to bite into her daily apple.

The apple had a razor blade in it.

Diane knew, because she was the one who'd put it there.

She had expected it to be some days before she got an opportunity, and here it came up the first day she brought the razor with her. Wilmot, after setting up her lunch, went out to take a leak or something. The other teachers were still in the cafeteria, buying lunch. All Diane had had to do was get up and wedge the double-edged blade into the apple. The way she positioned it, Wilmot would get a real mouthful.

She wasn't worried about getting caught. Halloween would be there in a couple days, and they'd think some kid did it. She wouldn't even be suspected.

In a few minutes the room was full of teachers, all wrapped up in lunch and small talk, and Diane became invisible. Mr. Bradley was there, too, but that didn't matter.

Now they'd see who had a strong stomach, Diane thought.

Charlie wasn't in today, though, damn it. He must've gone out for a drive or something, even though the weather wasn't what you'd call inviting. Diane wanted him to be here, but she wouldn't hold up the show for him. Whether he saw it with his own eyes or not, she had a feeling he'd get the message.

4

If Diane could've seen Charlie at that moment, she'd have been flabbergasted.

Under the leaden sky, with rain threatening, a lone figure huffed and puffed around the quarter-mile cinder track at the county park beside the riverbank. It was Charlie, who during the past dozen years had maybe *once* sprinted ten feet to catch an elevator. Clad in a sky-blue warmup suit that he'd bought over the weekend, he was taking his first steps toward rejuvenation.

And they were painful steps. He wasn't halfway around his first lap and already he had a stitch in his side and funny-colored dots were swimming before his eyes. But he persevered.

Gotta do it! No pain, no gain. Every day I don't have lunchroom or playground duty, I gotta do it. Rain or shine, never mind, gotta do it all the time. And again when I get home. I'll get in shape if it kills me.

It might just do that; but he knew it'd kill him faster if he didn't.

5

Wilmot had playground duty today, it turned out, so she'd be in the teachers' room for only half an hour. Diane watched the clock fretfully as twelve-thirty drew near. Only a few minutes now, and the silly little bitch still hadn't touched her apple.

Wilmot was sitting next to Richard Bennett, who was regaling her with a recipe for some kind of carrot jelly. She beamed at him and waved her pretty hands around, and he couldn't take his eyes off her. Silently, Diane ground her teeth. What did men *see* in Wilmot? Across the room, Peter Ludovics was getting an eyeful, too. Nobody was looking at Diane.

She had never really noticed it before, but the whole damned school was half in love with Wilmot. Even Otto Reimann opened doors for her. Next thing you knew, Cosmo Iacavella would be writing sonnets to her.

She looked up at the clock. Twelve-twenty-eight.

"Do you think it'll rain?" Wilmot asked the group. The other teachers who had playground duty today had already gotten up to put on their coats.

"You can stand under my umbrella if it does," said Ludovics, getting a laugh from the teachers and a comely blush from Wilmot. Even Mr. Bradley was smiling placidly.

Wilmot got up, leaving the apple on the table. "Just as long as it doesn't rain on the Halloween parade," she said, crossing to the rack where the coats were hung.

Damn it to hell, was this going to be the one day all year when she *doesn't* eat her shitting apple? *I don't believe it. I fucking can't believe it.* She put on her coat.

Somebody said, "Hey, Joanne! You forgot your apple."

"Now, what makes you think I'd do a thing like that?" She went back to the table, picked the apple up, and put it in her purse.

Diane died a little death.

"When are you gonna break down and have a doughnut for dessert like the rest of us mortals?" one of the teachers asked.

"All that processed sugar!" said Wilmot. "I wouldn't touch it with a ten-foot pole."

"The kiddies are waiting, Jo," a teacher said.

Wilmot took a step toward the door, then turned and reached into her purse. She took out a folding rain cap, shook it loose, and put it on her blond head.

"You know what I always say . . ."

"Spare us, just this once!"

With a puckish expression on her face that plainly said *So there!,* she plucked the apple from her purse and chomped down hard on it.

147

6

The blade got stuck deep between her two front teeth.

Diane's heart stopped when she bit into the apple; and for a moment that couldn't have lasted longer than the time it took for the signal to flash from Wilmot's mouth to her brain, but seemed to last forever, Diane felt like she was going to pass out before she could see whether her trick had worked or not.

Then Wilmot spat out a strangled scream, and with it a gout of bright red blood, and went into a dance of pain and shock and horror, and the faculty lounge went mad with her.

She was spraying blood everywhere; every time she tried to scream, she slashed her lips. Everybody was jumping up at once. Everyone was yelling. Diane got up and started yelling, too: protective coloration.

Wilmot was trying to tell them what had happened, but she wouldn't win any enunciation prizes with a razor-blade stuck in her mouth. All she could do was flail her arms, roll her eyes, gabble like a chicken, and bleed.

And then Mr. Bradley had her, and held her, and had somehow managed to maneuver her into a chair, where her heels, in her panic, drummed a tattoo on the floor. He had her mouth open and you could see the blade protruding from her teeth. Below her nose, her face was a mask of blood.

"Back up, people—out of the way!" he cried. "Give us some room! For God's sake, somebody get Doreen! We need a nurse!"

Richard Bennett, his face the color of spoiled milk, bolted out of the room. Diane wondered if he'd be able to find Doreen; sometimes she went out for lunch.

Wilmot kept groaning the same three syllables, over and over again: *Unh-unh-unh, unh-unh-unh!* Mr. Bradley put her in some kind of gentle headlock between his left arm and shoulder, bent over her like a dentist, and deftly pulled the razor out from between her teeth. It made her squeal; her feet shot up from

148

the floor on spasmodically stiffened legs. Mr. Bradley had her blood all over his hands and shirt now, and some was spattered on his face, but he didn't back away from her.

"Should I call an ambulance?" Ludovics wanted to know. The room had suddenly gone quiet, except for Wilmot's frantic panting and burbly whimpering.

"You'd better!" Mr. Bradley said. He held Wilmot close to him and rocked her a little. "It's all right, Joanne, we got it out, we'll take care of you."

"My God!" somebody said, in tones of awe.

"Stitches. She's gonna need stitches."

"Who could've done this? Who could *do* a thing like that?"

"Kids. Some dirty rotten stinking kid ..."

"Come on! She teaches *kindergarten*. Those kids are too young even to think of pulling—"

"Doesn't matter. Some older kid could've gone into her room when she had her class out for recess ...."

"Would you all please be quite!" Mr. Bradley snapped.

Glaring at them with that mess of blood plastered across the front of his shirt, he got his way.

149

Chapter Seventeen

1

Doreen rose to the occasion.

Once she got Mrs. Wilmot's face cleaned up—a losing proposition, because she continued to bleed—she realized that the damage was essentially superficial. As unlucky as Mrs. Wilmot had been to bite down onto the razor on her very first bite of the apple, she'd made up for it by setting the blade firmly between her teeth. That had stopped it from cutting very far into the gum or the lips. True, her upper and lower lips were badly lacerated; but it could have been worse. The doctors at the emergency room wouldn't have any trouble stitching these cuts.

The scars would be kind of ugly, though. Maybe a little plastic surgery could take care of that.

As for the psychological trauma—well, that wasn't Doreen's department, thank God. *I know I'd be a basket case if it happened to me . . . but it didn't.*

Anyhow, she'd performed calmly and efficiently, and that was something. Mr. Bradley had complimented her in front of everybody. "You really handled that well, Doreen. I don't know what we'd have done without you." That was something, too.

But now that the crisis was past and she was alone in her clinic once again, Doreen was coming down with a bad case of the shakes.

She couldn't stop trembling. Oh, Christ, how she needed a belt of wine right now! She had some children's cough medicine in the cabinet and she tried a swig of that, but it was too weak to do her any good unless she drank the whole bottle, and she wasn't about to do that. No: her drink would have to wait until she got home—if she could hold out that long.

Oh, Lord, somebody did *that to her! Actually put a razor blade in her apple. Holy Jesus Christ!*

Would it be Doreen's apple next? She had an apple for lunch, once in a while. Or maybe it'd be something different, more creative. A copperhead in her desk drawer, perhaps, or ground glass in a slice of cherry pie.

Everybody liked Joanne. Even Doreen liked her.

It just went to show that anybody could be a target, at any time.

Doreen's nerves were shot. Once she had to turn around in her chair because she thought she heard the cot creak, as if someone had just sat down on it ... or gotten up. But there was nothing, of course. Nothing but her nerves.

She fancied she heard whispers in the air around her. *Stop it! Cut it out! It's only the pipes in the walls. It's only the heat coming on, stupid.*

She was a nurse, she knew what was happening to her. When Mr. Bennett came bursting through her door and she followed him to the teachers' room, her system began to pump her so full of adrenalin that she felt as if she could have run up the side of the World Trade Towers. Now the need was past, but she was still awash with adrenalin, still pumped up like a sky-diver making his first jump. Everything she was experiencing was just a reaction to it, a common post-stress reaction. She'd have to wait for all the glandular white lightning to be absorbed by her system. Then she'd be herself again and she'd stop hearing things.

Or so she hoped.

2

Virgil had to go home to change his shirt. Carrie nearly fainted when he came through the door.

"Take it easy, I'm all right—it's not *my* blood," he said. As briefly as he could, and while he stripped off his shirt and undershirt and took the stained clothes out to the kitchen sink to be hand-washed, he told her what had happened. It drained the color from her face.

"But Virgil—that's horrible! God, will she be all right?"

"Doreen and the paramedics seemed to think so," he said. "Physically, at least. I'm more worried about the effect on her mind. It was a pretty traumatic experience, to put it mildly."

He cleaned blood from his chest with a wet paper towel. When he was finished, Carrie held him.

"Poor Joanne!" she said. "What kind of monster would do a thing like that to her? To anybody?"

"Oh, hell, Carrie, it beats the shit out of me. Some perverted kid, I guess. We've got our share of 'em." He shook his head so that her hair caressed his cheek. "Sometimes I feel like I just don't know the score anymore. Sometimes I wonder whether I'm in charge of a grammar school or a zoo. I just don't know what to expect from people anymore. For two cents, I'd just stay home."

She made him sit on the couch with a glass of milk while she brought him clean clothes. After he put them on, he was still depressed.

"I'm not kidding," he said. "I've just about had it. I'm this close to picking up that phone and calling in my resignation."

"Honey, it was an isolated incident—"

"Was it? Honest to God, Carrie, I don't know. Somebody did this. Somebody in *my* school. And unless that somebody shoots off his mouth and brags about it and some other kid actually has the decency to turn him in, we'll never know who did it. We'll just have to wait for the next time."

Carrie tried to be reasonable. "Virgil, you don't *know* it was somebody in the school. Somebody could have tampered with that apple in the store where Joanne bought it. That's horrible, too, but it happens. There are a lot of sickos roaming around out there."

"And I've got some sickos in my school, too, but Noonan won't let me get rid of 'em." He told her about his unfruitful phone call to the superintendent. "To tell you the truth, this razor blade incident has all the earmarks of a Johnny Rizzo prank; and I wouldn't put it past that Dudak kid, either. They're both sick."

3

But Mike Dudak only *wished* he'd put the razor into Mrs. Wilmot's apple.

By the time the dismissal bell rang, the story had spread all over school; everybody knew about it. And on the way home, Rizzo swore he hadn't done it. Mike had kind of thought he had.

"Are you nuts, Dude? What would I want to mess up Mrs. Wilmot's face for? She's the only pretty teacher in this dump. Anyway, a razor in an apple, that's too much. They put you *away* for somethin' like that, man!"

Mike still wished he'd done it. Shit, he wished he'd at least *seen* it. Damn, she must've bled like a stuck pig.

He couldn't stop thinking about it, trying to imagine it. Ma heated him up a turkey pot pie for supper and he could hardly taste it, he was thinking so much about Mrs. Wilmot and the razor. There must've been blood all over the teachers' room. Shit, what was it *like* to bite into a nice, sharp razor? And what had it done to her face?

After super he went up to the bathroom and took Daddy's razor out of the cabinet, opened it, and took out the blade. The fucker sure was sharp. It cut soap like it was air. Just the slightest little touch of it cut the ball of his thumb—painlessly, effortlessly parting the skin before he even felt it. He put the razor back in the cabinet and sucked the blood from his thumb. He wondered if the blade in the apple had sliced Mrs. Wilmot's tongue off, or split it in half like a snake's.

With Daddy on the road, Ma was fixing to tie one on tonight. He'd told her not to drink anymore, but he wasn't here right now, so screw him. She didn't even notice when Mike put on his jacket and went out the back door.

At first he planned to see if Rizzo could come out and mess around a little, but once he found himself alone on the sidewalk, he lost the desire for company.

It was a misty night, with unshed rain coming down as fog. It was kind of clammy out there, but Mike didn't mind. He was all alone, and it made him feel free, like he had the streets and sidewalks all to himself.

He wandered, still thinking about Mrs. Wilmot and the razor blade, still excited by it. He felt strong. He felt like beating someone up just for the hell of it. But he wasn't likely to run into any other kids tonight. Not unless he went downtown—he could do that. But tonight the bright lights held no attraction for him.

After a time, he found himself heading toward the school-yard.

Well, shit, why not? That was where it happened. He could stand by one of the doors and imagine them taking Mrs. Wilmot out to the ambulance, her face a shredded, bloody mess. Maybe he could find some of the drops she must have left behind. He didn't know why, but he thought he'd really like to do that.

As he approached the playground, a low-voltage current of fear ran through him. He'd conked out the last time he was here. He felt fine tonight, he didn't think it would happen again—but it could, couldn't it?

But he could have no more turned away from the school, this close to it, than a compass needle could turn from the north.

The fog was really getting thick, now. He could see the spotlights along the rim of the roof. In the dense fog, they looked like the eyes of dinosaurs. And blind eyes at that. You couldn't see shit out here tonight.

He walked onto the playground. When his feet touched the mushy ground, his heart began to race. He felt like he was about to get into a fight: muscles tensing, stomach rolling into a clenched ball, all keyed up and ready to go. He wished he could run into Ned Bradley right about now. When he got done with him, Mr. Bradley'd really have something to squawk about.

Somebody was in the building.

Mike stopped and stared. He was looking at the back of the school, the big white wall with the new wing and the gym stretching out on the left side.

There were lights in the kindergarten windows, and upstairs on the second floor of the main building.

But they weren't the school's regular lights, no way: those burned brightly, and showed you the insides of the rooms. These lights showed you nothing.

They flickered from window to window, pale and cold, with the fog swirling all around like smoke. The lights moved, like lanterns being carried around inside the building. They seemed very far away, and they had a quality that made Mike think of lights shining up from the bottom of a muddy lake at night, if such a thing were possible.

He heard voices, too. A lot of them, all talking at once so he couldn't make out the words, all coming as from far away. It was like when you were coming up to the playground and were still a block or two away, and you could hear all the kids carrying on long before you saw them.

It was too dark, the fog was too thick. Mike didn't see anybody.

He began to walk up to the school.

He heard running footsteps. Laughs. Yelps of pain. A grown man cursing. No words, just sounds. If he closed his eyes he would swear he was moving through a crowd, he could swear there was a mob of kids playing on the blacktop. He could almost—but not quite—feel them running past him.

He wasn't afraid.

Up on the blacktop there was a little porch where the kindergarten kids went in. On the steps stood a man. Mike thought the man was waiting for him, and had been waiting for him for a long time. He walked faster, wanting to keep his appointment.

"Hello, Michael." He seemed to hear the man's voice inside his head, as if he were dreaming it. But he knew he was awake.

It was the same old man whose picture hung in Mr. Bradley's office, the picture that had fascinated him while Mr. Bradley was trying to chew him out for peeing on Rudi's sandwich. Who was he? He had to be somebody important for his picture to be hanging in the principal's office. Meeting him made Mike feel important, too.

He felt something else: a low thrumming that went right through him, the kind of thing you felt sometimes when you stood by the power station beside the NYP freight line and could hear the electricity in the wires. The school seemed to be generating electricity tonight; right now Mike wouldn't have touched one of the metal doorknobs on a dare. Even the blacktop felt like it was vibrating. He could feel it through the rubber soles of his sneakers.

The old man smiled at him. In person, he was just as faded and colorless as the picture.

"You can feel it, can't you, Michael?"

Mike nodded. "Yeah."

"It's because of what happened here today. You can see me and talk to me right now because of all the energy that was released by that incident in the faculty lounge. You feel it yourself, don't you?"

Mike couldn't have explained, in words, what the old man meant; but at a deeper level of his being, where words were not used, he understood. Somehow, because of what had happened to Mrs. Wilmot today, the school had come alive.

Mike heard the babble of many voices and the tread of many feet within the building, up and down the empty corridors. Now he thought he could see shadows milling around in the darkness on the other side of the windows. He thought he could see pale faces peering through the windows in the kindergarten door, just behind the old man on the steps.

The old man held out a white hand. A vague patch of light rippled in the fog. It floated up from the steps, or poured out through the door, or seeped in from all directions—Mike couldn't say which. He only knew he was watching a person ooze out of the fog from somewhere: maybe someone who'd been in the fog all along and had only been waiting for the old man to call him out.

A boy.

He was a big, husky kid, like Johnny Rizzo, only his eyes glowed flatly, like a cat's: a pair of greenish-yellow discs shining in the dark. The rest of him Mike couldn't see that well, just enough to know that his long hair was slicked straight back from his forehead, and he wore some kind of black leather jacket. His face was as white as bleached bone, with dark lips that were almost black. The old man laid his hand on the boy's leather-clad shoulder.

"There are many of us, Michael. More than you would ever dare to think, and all one big, happy family. We all live together in our happy little house."

Mike wanted to cry then, because he knew exactly what the old man was talking about *(You just go on and on, forever, forever and ever, and no one can tell you what to do, and no*

157

one can stop you from doing what you want to do, forever), and he wanted it so badly, he could taste it—and there was no way he could have it, no way that he knew. But the old man seemed to understand and smiled comfortingly at him.

The kid reached into a pocket, and suddenly he had a knife in his hand. It took Mike a moment to realize it was a switchblade. The blade shot out when you pressed a button. Mike had always wanted a knife like that, but Daddy said they were against the law.

Pale light danced along the blade. It was beautiful.

"Pay attention now, Michael," the old man said.

The kid held the knife in his left hand and brought up his right so that his palm was touching the tip. Without flinching, he shoved his hand down. The steel tip popped up through the back of his hand. You could barely hear it going through. Louder was the patter of blood dripping onto the concrete steps. Mike felt a little sick to his stomach, but he didn't turn away.

The boy slid the knife out of the wound. The dripping blood made a sound like the beginning of a heavy rain. He held up his palm and wriggled bloody fingers. Mike smelled the blood. The boy jiggled his left thumb and the blade withdrew into the handle.

Then the boy began to fade, like an elaborate fireworks display blowing away in the breeze. But before he went, he flipped the knife to Mike. It bounced off his chest and fell before he could catch it. He heard it clatter on the asphalt at his feet.

"Take it," said the man. "Use it as you like. It's yours."

His head pounding, Mike bent to pick it up. The handle was warm and slick with blood. He had no doubt it was real.

When he straightened up again, the man was gone.

4

In his bedroom, seated on the edge of his bed, Mike played with the knife, shooting the blade out over and over again. Ma was too far gone to notice if he started setting off M-80's in the toilet bowl, but he was quiet nevertheless.

He washed the blood off it, dried it carefully, and put it under his pillow.

What dreams he had!

They came one after another, an avalanche of dreams, each one better than the last. The knife figured in all of them.

In one he straddled a screaming Ned Bradley and scalped him like an Indian. In another he cut his father into little bloody pieces. He roared up and down the halls of the school and everybody in it fled before him.

He woke with the front of his pajama shirt stiff with blood, and his lips and chin caked with it. He'd had another nosebleed in his sleep, and a big one, from the looks of it. But it didn't scare him anymore.

He dressed in a hurry, eager to get to school. This time he'd be showing up on the playground with a switchblade in his pocket, and anyone who messed with him was going to die. Maybe he hadn't put a razor blade in Mrs. Wilmot's apple— but they'd forget all about that when he was through. He reached under his pillow for the knife.

"What the *fuck?*" he cried out loud.

It was a useless chunk of rust. It was caked with dirt. Rusted solid. He couldn't even *find* the release button, much less spring the blade free. God damn it, it didn't even look like a knife anymore! Nothing but a piece of junk. Shapeless. Worthless.

Flecks of rust and dirt came off in his hand.

Chapter Eighteen

1

Virgil was a little late getting started Tuesday morning.

He hadn't slept at all well. He hadn't awakened screaming, but he'd tossed and turned all night. He kept dreaming, over and over again, that he was compelled to go to the janitor's closet; and every time he opened the door, he came face-to-face with a shrunken, distorted caricature of his nine-year-old self, squatting like a monkey on the rim of the sink. Or else he dreamed of being held by ropes of flesh, held in the dark, waiting for ... he never found out what.

But at least he woke to a sunny morning, for a change, and that raised his spirits. If he had to go back to Dr. Lauther for another session or two, he'd go, that's all. No big deal. He didn't think he'd have to. After what had happened yesterday, he should have expected bad dreams.

Carrie insisted on making him pancakes for breakfast, which raised his spirits even more.

"I'm gonna be late," he said. "Have you sent Ned off already?"

"I didn't want him plaguing you with questions while you ate. An extra twenty minutes in the fresh air won't hurt him. Anyway," Carrie said, "who's going to yell at you if you're a couple minutes late? You're the principal."

"Damn right. The hell with 'em," Virgil said, and pitched into the pancakes. By the time he arrived on school grounds, the children were lining up at the doors to be let in. The bell would ring in just a few minutes.

He headed for the girls' entrance. They didn't line the kids up by gender anymore, but the two front entrances still bore the legends "Boys" and "Girls," carved into their white granite lintels. A few of the kids piped up, "Hi, Mr. Bradley!" He ruffled a few heads of hair. Children played, darting in front of him like minnows. He wanted to snatch them up and hug them. They tugged at his heart.

He had many moments like that. It was why he'd gone into teaching, it was why he was a school principal. He couldn't imagine himself pursuing any other line of work. What could be as important as the nurture and education of these little ones? And what could be a fraction as rewarding? It was all he could do to continue on up the steps and through the doors, bound for his office, where he would flounder in paperwork and worry. The real work was out here with the children. With a pang, he went inside.

As he mounted the stairs, his eyes chanced to stray to the gray wall of the stairwell. There was a message scrawled there in black crayon.

SUCK RAW DICK

Virgil shook his head and sighed.

161

2

In the hangover she brought with her to work that morning, Doreen found her expectations for the day less than high.

She had drunk too much last night, and now she was paying the price. But it was worth what she was getting from the wine. When Doreen went to bed last night, she wasn't fretting about a thing.

No one bothered her all morning, and in three hours she was feeling almost human again. Her head only ached a little, and her stomach had settled down nicely.

She even felt up to visiting the teachers' room at lunchtime. Why not? She'd done a good job there yesterday, and everybody knew it.

"It was amazing, Doreen: everybody calmed right down the moment you walked in. I know I was never so glad to see anybody!"

"Do you think she'll be all right, Doreen? What do *you* think?"

"I just wish you'd brought some smelling salts for *me!*"

"You really took charge, kid."

Doreen could listen to this stuff all day. Usually she didn't enjoy being the center of attention, but she was enjoying it now. One thing she could always do was handle the sight of blood. For a while, at least. Long enough to do her job. And it was nice, for a change, to be appreciated for it.

Most of these teachers were still shaken up from yesterday, some more than others. Christ, Mr. Hall looked terrible, and he hadn't even been there!

Well, Doreen thought, everybody knew Mr. Hall had a thing for Joanne, and maybe that was why it had hit him so hard. He looked like death warmed over, sitting alone over there by the coffee machine. Face doughy under its artificial tan, gray circles under his eyes, deep lines at the corners of his mouth. And he hadn't helped himself by dying his hair a deeper shade of black; it made him look like he'd dipped his head in shoe polish. And was that actually *makeup* on his cheeks? He must really be losin' it, she thought.

Almost reluctantly, Doreen got up to go back to her clinic as the end of the lunch hour drew near.

Along the halls, Halloween decorations had sprouted everywhere. At Victory School it was a tradition, on Halloween Day, to allow the children to wear their costumes during afternoon classes and conclude the day with a parade around the building. Doreen looked forward to that: it was colorful, and it reminded her of her own childhood, which had been a lot happier than her adulthood had turned out, so far. But she was almost happy today. She smiled at the orange pumpkin faces that festooned the walls outside the classrooms.

What the hell, maybe she'd get invited to a Halloween party this year. And this time she'd go. Have some fun, for once.

She unlocked the clinic, stepped inside, and stopped short, all thoughts of Halloween parties driven instantly from her mind.

The room reeked like an opened grave. Doreen had never stood beside an opened grave, but it couldn't be any worse than this. Her guts began to squirm.

There was a little vestibule between the door and the clinic itself; standing in it, Doreen could see only her desk and the window. The window was closed, the desk was just as she'd left it. But the stench was overpowering. She clapped a hand over her nose and held her breath.

Her first thought was that the toilet in the washroom had backed up, spewing raw sewage onto the floor. If it had, she'd be out of business for the day while they had the plumber in to deal with it. Still fighting an intense nausea, she forced herself to go ahead to see what was causing the odor.

She saw.

Two children sat side-by-side on the cot, waiting for her. They looked up at her when she entered the room. One was a little boy, the other a little girl. Both had long black hair and dark skins. Both were naked.

But they were clothed with filth. Patches of fuzzy mold mottled their skin. Their limbs were streaked with black mud. Clumps of dirt and humus clung to them. Earth matted their hair.

The boy's throat was gashed, revealing the pale tube of his windpipe. One arm was dislocated at the shoulder. A flap of skin hung raggedly from his narrow chest, showing brown ribs.

The girl had one of her cheeks torn away; Doreen could see her molars. An incision, red and raw, ran from her collarbone to her crotch.

They were dead, long dead, beyond question or dispute. And their eyes rolled up to meet her. Pieces of leaf-mold dripped from their jaws.

Doreen screamed and screamed again, but they didn't go away.

3

A few doors down the hall, Rudi, under Cosmo's expert supervision, was wiping a stubborn stain from the floor. When they heard the screams, they dropped their work and came running.

Cosmo couldn't outrun a hippopotamus in a wheelchair, and Rudi got there well ahead of him. The woman's screams rebounded down the hall. Cosmo was convinced someone was being murdered; he'd better call the cops. Jesus H. Christ, he thought, after that mess in the teachers' room yesterday, what was it this time? The screams were coming from the clinic. He hustled down the hall, keys clanking from his belt.

He charged into the clinic and almost ran down Rudi, who was standing there like a moonstruck moron while the school nurse screamed and screamed. Cosmo had no idea what she was screaming about. He grabbed Rudi and shoved him back out into the hall.

"Go get Mr. Bradley! Go on, Rudi, move it!"

Rudi's face was as white as milk, and he seemed to have gone deaf all of a sudden. Cosmo shook him out of it. "Damn it to hell, Rudi, go get Mr. Bradley!" Rudi turned and fled.

Miss Davis screamed. Cosmo ran back into the clinic and grabbed her. She twisted in his grasp like a fish, and he had to hold on for all he was worth. She was almost too strong for him.

"It's all right, it's all right!" he shouted into her ear, and wondered if she could hear him. She didn't seem to notice he was there at all, not even when he shook her. *Aw, shit!* He had a fuckin' hysterical broad on his hands. Was he going to have to pop her one, like they always did in the movies? But he couldn't figure out a way to do it; he couldn't let go of her long enough to hit her. The screaming was driving him up the wall, meanwhile. "Cut it out, damn it!" he growled, shaking her harder. "Will you cut it out, lady? It's all right!"

Maybe if he got her onto the cot ... but when he tried to steer her toward it, she fought twice as hard and screamed twice as loud. He couldn't force her any further without hurting her, or maybe getting hurt himself. He couldn't do a blessed thing except hold her in a bear hug and pray for help to get there before she got loose and tore him apart. He felt like he was wrestling a mountain lion.

She was still in hysterics when Mr. Bradley arrived on the double, followed by Rudi and a couple of the teachers. "What happened, what happened?" the principal cried.

"I don't fuckin' *know* what happened, damn it! Gimme a hand!"

"Lay her down on the cot," Mr. Bradley said.

"Whattya think I been tryin' to do, fer chrissake? I can't!"

Mr. Bradley lent a hand. The two of them together could hardly budge the nurse. She screamed and flung her head around, just missing Cosmo's nose. Furious, he strained his head back toward the doorway.

"Damn you to hell, Rudi! Give us a hand here!"

Rudi came forward with a confused look on his face, gawking at the little white cot like it was King Tut's solid gold bed. But Rudi was strong, and with his help they were finally able to drag and push the struggling woman across the floor inch by inch. They almost had her to the cot when she suddenly went limp on them.

They laid her on the cot and stepped back, Cosmo sweating and panting like a piano mover. His ears rang with the screaming, and the sudden silence seemed unreal. For a moment he was sure the nurse had dropped dead on them, but a closer look showed she was still breathing. Her face looked like it was made of wax.

Mr. Bradley called the police and asked for an ambulance, using the phone on the nurse's desk. By now there was a small crowd of teachers and children buzzing around by the doorway.

"It's all over, folks!" the principal said. "Please, go to your classrooms."

"Is she dead?" one of the kids asked.

"No—of course not. She's fainted, that's all. Everything's under control. Teachers, please—get the children out of here. You're all just getting in the way."

The crowd dispersed. Cosmo ached to sit down, but he was afraid to, in case Miss Davis woke up and went batshit again.

"You don't know what this was all about?" Mr. Bradley said.

"Aw, hell, no!" Cosmo groaned. "Look, me and Rudi were out in the hall when she started screamin'. She never said *why*. She just kept carryin' on until she fainted. Fuck if *I* know what set her off."

The principal had to settle for that. He knelt beside the cot and looked closely at the nurse, but didn't touch her. If he was afraid to, Cosmo didn't blame him.

4

Diane Phelps walked slowly back to her classroom, ignoring the questions a couple of her kids were slinging at her.

She'd had a bad night, too, but it hadn't been because of drink. After being as high as a kite all yesterday afternoon, she came crashing down around suppertime.

She didn't know why. It certainly wasn't her conscience come gunning for her. Wilmot was out of the way; she'd be jumping Charlie's bones again any day now. Wilmot had pit her youth and self-assurance against Diane, trying to steal her lover, and fully deserved what she got. Diane would do it again in a minute.

But her depression remained a fact, and it was still with her when she woke in the morning.

And now this, Doreen Davis flying off the handle, right out of left field. *Am I next?* Diane wondered.

After all she'd done to get Charlie back, that'd be a laugh, wouldn't it?

Chapter Nineteen

1

Cosmo had to sit down for a while. He was getting too old to be wrestling berserk women.

Safe in the boiler room, with the door closed against the rest of this fucked-up school, he sipped vodka and wondered what the place was coming to. The people seemed to be falling apart with the building.

"Who'd of thought she'd go bananas?" he said, more to himself than to Rudi, who was sitting on his stool, watching Cosmo drink. Cosmo was only marginally aware of his presence. "I mean, I always thought she was kind of flighty, but this ... Jesus. What got into her?"

Rudi knew the answer to that. *Mr. Iacavella, you'd scream, too, if you saw what she saw.*

Rudi had seen them, the two little kids sitting on the cot, looking like something you'd find under the porch when the smell got bad enough to make you crawl under for a look. And they were gone when he came back with Mr. Bradley—vanished like that kid he'd followed into the music room not too long ago, and the old man who fell down the stairs the other day.

But they sure as shoot had been there, and that was why Miss Davis screamed.

He didn't know how to volunteer that answer, though, without making Mr. Iacavella mad at him. He'd stopped watching horror movies on TV, just as he'd been told, and he hadn't seen any ghosts since then ... until today.

But Mr. Iacavella *hadn't* seen them. Rudi didn't get it, because Mr. Iacavella had been right there, he could've reached out and touched them. All the same, it was as plain as the nose on your face that *he* hadn't seen them. And Miss Davis *had.* How could that be?

Maybe there were people who just couldn't see things like that, same as there were people who couldn't see colors, like Mrs. Giddens. She always dressed kind of funny because she really couldn't see what colors her clothes were.

"Mr. Iacavella?"

"Huh?" Cosmo put his bottle down. "What, Rudi?"

"Mr. Iacavella ... when a person is seein' things ... can somebody else see 'em, too?"

"Now what kind of tomfool question is that?"

Rudi felt embarrassed. He knew he wasn't putting this the right way. He wished he were smarter. He wished he knew how to ask Mr. Iacavella about this without letting on that he'd seen the ghosts, too. A smart man could do it. Rudi could only try.

"I mean, if somebody was *imagining* something, could another person imagine the same thing, at the same time?"

"Shit, no, of course not! What're you gettin' at, Rudi? You ain't makin' sense."

So if two people saw the same thing at the same time, then it was really there, wasn't it? Had to be. That was what Rudi wanted to say; but you didn't have to be a genius to see that Mr. Iacavella wasn't in the mood for it right now.

"You didn't see nothin', Mr. Iacavella? Up there in the clinic?"

"Rudi, weren't you listenin' when Mr. Bradley asked me that? All I saw was a crazy broad screamin' her cotton-pickin' head off, same as you and everybody else. Why don't you go out and sweep the hall for a while? I need some peace and quiet."

So Rudi swept the hall, and wondered unceasingly why Mr. Iacavella hadn't seen those poor kids, too.

2

In the hall outside the emergency room at County General, Virgil cooled his heels until an intern told him he could see Doreen. A Tianoga policeman waited with him, in case anything came up that the police should know.

"Is she all right, doctor?" Virgil asked.

The young man smiled; he still got a charge out of being called "doctor." "She's suffering from shock, but she'll come out of it. She ought to stay here overnight, though—maybe a couple nights. We'll want to run a couple of tests, and observe her."

Virgil followed the patrolman into the emergency room. It didn't look too busy at the moment. They found Doreen resting on a cot, with movable cloth screens around her on three sides. She was still clothed in her school nurse's whites and a gray cardigan. She was pale, her eyes hooded. She looked half-stunned.

"How do you feel, Doreen?"

She twitched her shoulders listlessly, evidently not caring much how she felt.

"Doreen, please . . . I know you'd rather be left alone, and I promise you we won't stay long. But we do have to know what happened up there in the clinic. The school's security might be at stake. Just tell us what frightened you, and we'll go."

"You're safe here, ma'am," the cop added. "And the doctor says you're gonna be all right."

"What happened, Doreen?"

She looked at them bleakly. When she spoke, her voice was painfully hoarse, almost a croak, from all that screaming.

"I don't understand it." She spoke slowly, and Virgil had to strain his ears to catch the words. "I locked the clinic when I went to lunch. It was still locked when I came back. And they were *in* there, on the cot. *Waiting* for me."

"*Who* was there, Doreen?"

She shook her head feebly. "Two kids. A boy and a girl. They were . . . all messed up. Dirty. Filthy. Bloody all over."

This wasn't making any sense at all, but Virgil knew he had to keep the questions simple. Cosmo hadn't said anything about anybody else, any children, being in the clinic when he came in. They must have run out when Doreen started screaming, gone before Cosmo and Rudi could arrive.

"Which two kids, Doreen? Did you recognize them?"

A hint of weeping crept into her voice. "You don't understand! They were naked. They were dead!"

The policeman said, not unkindly, "How did you know they were dead? What makes you say that?"

Her eyes were wide open now. She stared at the officer.

"They were *moldy!* Mold grows on dead bodies. They were cut open. They . . . they *smelled!* They were covered with dirt and they *smelled* like dead bodies. Of *course* they were dead. I'm a nurse, I ought to know. . . ."

"Did you recognize them?" pressed the cop.

She shook her head. "No. I didn't know them, they weren't any kids I know. They were naked. They were all cut up."

"What did they *look* like, ma'am? Under all that dirt, I mean."

Doreen couldn't take her eyes from the policeman's badge. She seemed to be psychologically clinging to it, Virgil thought.

"I don't know," she muttered, still shaking her head. "Like little *Indians*, I guess. Little dead Indians. They had dark skin. They had long black hair. They were dead."

"Ma'am, the janitors didn't see any children when they came

171

running to help you. Nobody saw any. What happened to them?"

"I don't know ... I don't know. ..."

This couldn't go on, Virgil decided. Another few seconds of this and she'd be screaming again, sedative or no sedative. He cast an admonitory look at the policeman, then patted Doreen's hand and caressed her brow. Her skin was cold and damp.

"You rest now," he told her. "Everything's going to be all right. We have to go now, but you're going to be fine. Just rest."

Obediently, she closed her eyes; and he was glad not to be looking into them anymore.

"She was hallucinating," the cop said as he drove Virgil back to school. "I'm sorry for her, but there's nothing more I can do. She's had a nervous breakdown, and that's no job for the police."

I'm going to need another nurse, Virgil was thinking. He couldn't imagine any way Doreen could resume her duties. They'd have to put her on indefinite sick leave.

He sighed. The board would want to know all the whys and wherefores. Were there any drugs in the clinic that shouldn't have been there? Did anything funny turn up in Doreen's urine? Why hadn't anybody seen this coming?

It must have been that thing with Joanne yesterday. It must have shaken up Doreen worse than anybody thought. And the police were investigating that ... not that Virgil expected ever to know who'd put the razor blade in Joanne's apple. Carrie was right: it could've been done anywhere, by anyone, one of those acts of random violence that were so common these days.

But why *Indians?* What kind of hallucination was that? One little, two little, dead little Indians ... and judging by the way Doreen had reacted, they must have been horribly real to her. Sitting on the cot in her clinic. No wonder she'd resisted so hard when they'd tried to put her on the cot.

172

And that made two of them, he thought, remembering his own vivid little encounter in the janitor's closet. *Two of us in the same school.* Was there ergot in the bread they were selling in the cafeteria, or what?

There was something wrong, very wrong, with this school of his, he told himself.

3

Virgil knew what small ordeal would be waiting for him when he came home, but he couldn't think of any way of avoiding it.

Ned had already told Carrie some wild story, he was sure. Enough of the children had witnessed the bedlam in the clinic for the rumors to multiply like cancer cells before the dismissal bell rang. Virgil heard snatches of conversation in the halls when he got back from the hospital, ranging from the bizarre *Didja hear? Mr. Iacavella strangled Miss Davis!* to the merely preposterous *Guess what, Miss Davis found a giant rat in the clinic.* And the rumors current among the teachers weren't much closer to the truth.

His wife and son started questioning him as soon as he came through the door.

"Dad, is it true Miss Davis went crazy?"

"What happened, Virgil? Ned says the nurse had to be taken away in an ambulance." Carrie tossed the boy a stern look. "That's the only part I've been able to believe."

Virgil went to the kitchen for a beer, and they followed him. He would have paid good money to shelter his son from a thing like this, but it was too late even to try.

"Miss Davis had a nervous breakdown, son. She had to go to the hospital."

"Virgil!"

"I've been to see her, hon," he said. "I spoke to a doctor, and he said she's going to be all right."

173

Ned's eyes shone with excitement. "What's a nervous breakdown? *I* heard that Mr. Iacavella tried to kiss her!"

"Oh, for God's sake, Ned!" It was almost laughable, but not quite. "No, Mr. Iacavella tried to help her, that's all. He couldn't handle her by himself, though, so Mr. Fitch and I had to help, too. Then she fainted, and the police and the rescue squad came."

"Phil said it was the guys in the white coats from the insane asylum."

"Sorry to disappoint you. It was just the Tianoga Valley First Aid Squad. They sent their new ambulance, the one we saw in the Fourth of July parade."

Virgil took a sip of beer and continued. "A person has a nervous breakdown when he has problems that he just can't solve and it gets to be too much for him. I don't know what Miss Davis's problems are, but I know she had a big one yesterday, taking care of Mrs. Wilmot when she was hurt. I don't know if that really has anything to do with it—she *is* a nurse, it's her job. But I'd been thinking she looked kind of unhappy lately. Maybe a little jumpy, too."

"Why?" Ned asked.

"I don't know, son. I never asked. Now I wish I had."

"Don't blame yourself, Virgil," Carrie said. "You can't possibly be expected to intervene in your staff's private lives."

"So what was she screaming about, Dad?"

"I'm afraid she was having a hallucination," Virgil said. "That's when you think you see something that isn't really there."

"So she *did* go crazy!"

Carrie cuffed the boy's shoulder just hard enough to let him know how she felt about his choice of words. "Theodore Bradley! If you're not grown-up enough to show some compassion, you can go to your room. That poor woman had a frightening and painful experience, and God knows what she suffered before she finally broke down. You ought to be ashamed of yourself!"

"Aw, Mom, I didn't mean to make fun of her!"

"We know you didn't, Ned," Virgil said. But children *were* inclined to be callous, he thought, even the best of them. And only the best of them, he was afraid, really ever grew out of it.

"What did she see, Dad? I mean, what did she *think* she saw that scared her so bad?"

It was natural that the boy would want to know. And he had asked with such intensity. But Virgil didn't think it proper to tell him, no matter how badly he wanted to know.

"Son, Miss Davis's feelings would be very badly hurt if she thought any of the kids in the school knew that. She'd be embarrassed. Believe me, she has enough on her plate right now without that."

"You wouldn't like it," Carrie pointed out, "if something like this happened to you and everybody in school knew all the details. This is Miss Davis's private business, Ned."

"But Dad knows!"

"I'm the principal; I had to know," Virgil said. "I had to be sure there was no danger to the school. What if she'd seen a prowler who'd gotten into the building somehow, or a poisonous snake or something? That was why I had to ask her about it. But if I weren't the principal, I'd have no right to know, either."

"I wouldn't tell the other kids."

"That's not the point. The point is that you have to respect a person's privacy—just as you'd want other people to respect yours. You understand that, don't you?"

"Yeah, but—"

It wasn't like Ned to wheedle, not like him at all, but he kept it up until Carrie told him he could go to his room and start his homework, or go to the living room and watch *The People's Court,* but one way or another, he was going to shut up about it. He submitted grudgingly and had to be scolded again at the supper table. When he gave it one more try after supper, Carrie sent him downstairs to the rec room.

"I don't know what's gotten into him," she said as she rejoined Virgil in the living room.

"He does seem to have a bee in his bonnet, doesn't he?" Virgil said. "Well, it's understandable. These last two days at school have been very unsettling for all of us."

"Was it really bad, honey?"

He sighed and pulled her close to him. They were sitting on the couch, waiting for the eight o'clock movie on TV.

"It was absolutely the pits," he said. "Honest to God, I've never seen anyone throw a fit like that. Cosmo, Rudi, and I all had hold of her, and the three of us could barely control her. I was afraid she was going to have a stroke."

And not to gossip, but because it was a heavy burden and he needed his wife to help him bear it, he trusted her not to repeat it to a soul and told her all the rest.

4

Ned listened at the cellar door until his parents turned on the TV, then tiptoed back down to the rec room. They'd have skinned him if they'd known he was eavesdropping, but he had no choice: he had to get the rest of the story.

He spread his schoolbooks around the floor to make it look like he'd been studying, in case they checked, and stretched himself on his belly, his chin propped in his cupped hands, to think.

He knew from horror movies that monsters waxed powerful because nobody would believe in them until it was too late. All right, he was too old to believe everything he saw in the movies. But on the other hand, he didn't truly know why there *couldn't* be vampires and other monsters. It was just something that adults *said.* No such thing as this, no such thing as that. Ned didn't distrust adults, but he knew they could be wrong.

He'd learned that in school. Once upon a time, they were

wrong about the world being flat. They were wrong about the sun revolving around the earth. They dug up dinosaur bones and said they belonged to sinners who drowned in Noah's Flood, and they said no one would ever be able to build a machine that would fly. They said the space shuttle was perfectly safe, and then it blew up and fell into the sea with that nice lady teacher and all those astronauts aboard.

So they *could* be wrong when they said there was no such thing as this or that; and you had to figure that *maybe* there was just an itsy-bitsy chance, say one in a jillion but still a *chance*, that Dad and the doctors were wrong about Miss Davis, too. They said she'd *had a hallucination*. And probably they were right. But what if they weren't? What if she really *had* seen two dead little Indians sitting on the cot in her clinic?

Ned's problem was that he'd seen something impossible, too. A man in Revolutionary War clothes going into the boys' room and disappearing there. *Sorry, Ned, we know you* think *you saw him, but you were HAVING A HALLUCINATION, get it, you were SEEING THINGS . . .*

No, sir. He'd followed that man right into the bathroom, and he was *gone*, ladies and gentlemen! Presto! Now you see him, now you don't.

I saw a ghost.

And if *he* had, Miss Davis could have, too—couldn't she?

But how could he tell anybody without winding up in the hospital right next door to poor Miss Davis?

Chapter Twenty

1

The president of the neighborhood PTA hoped recent events wouldn't be allowed to interfere with Victory School's annual Halloween party. "I mean, the kids shouldn't be punished because the poor nurse flips out—right?"

So the story was loosed on the town already. Poor Doreen. By the time she was ready to come back to work, they'd have her climbing the school flagpole naked, screeching that the British were coming—again.

"We don't want to break tradition, do we, Mr. Bradley?"

This would be the second year of the tradition's existence. Virgil refrained from mentioning it.

The school was to be open Friday night. Chaperoned by PTA members and teachers who had volunteered, the children would assemble in the gym/cafeteria for a monster movie—*Godzilla 1985* had been rented for the occasion—and Halloween snacks (just in case they hadn't had enough by then, even after trick-or-treat the night before). Virgil had gracefully resisted a suggestion by the PTA president's husband that he don ghoul makeup and introduce the movie "like one of those guys on

TV, the kids'll love it." The PTA president's husband didn't want to do it himself: as a Little League coach, he had to maintain his dignity.

"There's been no change in plans, and there won't be," Virgil promised; and with that he was able to get off the phone.

The school board had already persuaded Arlene Penkul to come out of retirement for a little while, so Victory School had a nurse today. Arlene was willing to stay the remainder of the year if Doreen couldn't make it back, so the administrative end of it was settled. Virgil just wondered whether Doreen *could* make it back, ever. He'd have to call the hospital later to see how she was doing—although what could be expected in twenty-four hours, he didn't know.

Oh, God, it's only Wednesday morning!

He'd have to ask how Joanne was getting on, too: in all the furor with Doreen yesterday, he'd never gotten around to it.

His mind drifted back to those two weeks he'd spent this summer at Poway Lake, in a rented cabin with a dock. He replayed his favorite scenes: teaching Ned to row a boat, kissing Carrie under a stand of pine trees, building a campfire by the lake shore and toasting marshmallows under the stars. Two solid weeks of it. Man, he was beginning to miss the point of the other fifty. Why was he *here,* when he wanted to be *there?* He wanted to grab his wife and son and flee back to the lake, and never again have to see a teacher go to pieces.

But at Victory School, that kind of thing had been going on forever, as he learned later in the afternoon when Millie Stanhouse brought him the staff lists.

"It's amazing how many people you actually forget, even after you worked with them for a couple years," Millie said.

Small wonder, Virgil thought. It was a huge list, and out of all proportion to the size or age of the school. Victory used up teachers the way World War I used up armies. Central School's staff list for the same period probably had only about a third as many names.

Millie went over the names with him, rattling them off like a desk sergeant recalling the year's police work in the naked city. This one had gambled, that one was a drunk. Speed freak, tranquilizer junkie, shoplifter. Mrs. Pawl, anorexia. Mr. Birnbaum, hauled away for sexually abusing an eight-year-old niece. Divorce with all the trimmings: child custody wars, cross-complaints, courtroom mélées, other teachers on the witness stand, tongues wagging all over town. Domestic violence.

"Right from the word go, we had trouble," Millie said. "Look under 1946, these two names, Annette Couch—*she died!* Illegal abortion: it was a dangerous operation in those days. And Mrs. Suratte—they fired her. She beat the living daylights out of one of the little boys in her second grade. So that's two in the first year we were open."

Two in the first year. It reminded Virgil of an ancient Roman custom: when the Romans first fortified their city, they immured two slaves, a Gaul and a Greek, alive in the foundations. And we lost two teachers in our first year, almost as if they were a sacrifice. But that sounded fanciful, and he kept the thought to himself.

"What's wrong with this place?" he wondered out loud.

"It's not the place," said Millie. "It's the people."

"The people, then—what's wrong with them?"

"Damned if I know, Mr. Bradley. We live in troubled times. Lots of troubled souls."

"We've had more than our share, wouldn't you say?"

Millie only shrugged.

After school, Virgil took Ned to the drugstore to buy a Halloween mask.

Ned still didn't have a costume for tomorrow, but that was
okay. They had some neat rubber masks at the pharmacy, and
once you had yourself a good mask, the rest of the costume was
easy.

The masks in the store hung from a wire over the center
aisle, flaccid and grotesque, looking like the war trophies of
some nameless tribe of savages. It was a weird mix of monsters
and celebrities: the President of the United States rubbing latex
cheeks with Frankenstein; a saggy, weepy-looking Joan Rivers
trapped between Dracula and the Fly.

Ned stood under the display, looking up, trying to choose. It
didn't take him long to make up his mind.

"That one, Dad!"

He'd opted for Blob Man—a shapeless gray thing, a mass of
oozing lobes and nodules that covered the whole head. The
rubber had been treated to make it slimy to the touch. It reminded Ned of *The Incredible Melting Man,* who, at the end
of the movie of the same name, melted down into a shapeless
pile of gunk and was swept into the garbage by a janitor. It
wasn't much of a horror movie, but that ending stayed with you
long after you'd forgotten the rest.

Dad plucked the mask down from the wire for him, and he
tried it on.

"That's beautiful, Ned. I'm glad I raised a son who has such
impeccable taste."

Poor Dad. He was trying to get into the spirit of Halloween
and not quite making it. He was still upset about Miss Davis
popping her cork yesterday, and that thing with Mrs. Wilmot
the day before. He'd rather not be here. For the first time in
his life, it struck Ned that the old man was a pretty good sport,
and that sometimes Dad acted happy when he wasn't, so he

wouldn't spoil something for somebody else. And in that lay Ned's first real intimation that his father was a living, feeling person in his own right, and not just a part of his son's world.

They paid for the mask and went back outside.

As they walked home, Ned took his father's hand. Normally he wouldn't have, it'd make him look like a baby. But he did it now because he knew it'd make the old man happy.

At home, Mom helped Ned with his costume while Dad sipped a beer and watched.

"You want to go for high fashion, kid, or are you just lookin' to freak people out?" she asked.

"Could we melt a shower curtain onto some old clothes?" was Ned's idea.

"Sure—if we don't mind dropping dead from breathing the toxic fumes. Wait, I have a better idea."

She had him put on his Sunday School suit, then the mask. She took him upstairs so he could see himself in the full-length mirror on his parents' bedroom closet.

"Well?"

"All right!" Ned said. The combination of the neat suit and the hideous mask really blew him away. "Just don't spill anything on that suit tomorrow," she warned him. "I'll take it out of your hide if you do."

3

Mike Dudak's mother was in no shape to help him with a costume, but Mike wasn't concerned about that.

He was at the schoolyard again tonight, still hoping the old man or the kid in the black leather jacket would give him a new knife, one that wouldn't turn into solid rust when he put it under his pillow.

Anyone seeing Mike just now would have thought him dangerously ill. He reeled around the blacktop with blood dribbling from his nose, moving like a boxer who'd taken one too many to the head, muttering incessantly to himself, batting feebly at the empty air. But it was dark, and there was no one there to see him.

And he wasn't talking to himself.

"... *Come on, damn it, come out, let me see you ... I won't tell, cross my heart and hope to die ... damn it ...*"

He heard them, hundreds of them, inside the school, partying away. Kids and grownups, yelling and laughing and mumbling and cursing. Some of them were crying and some were screaming, all jumbled together inside his head. They were all inside, and he was outside, locked out, alone. He couldn't get in and they wouldn't come out.

When he touched the brick wall, he felt a kind of humming, a low vibration that coursed through his hands and right down into the blacktop through the soles of his sneakers. It was like touching a refrigerator, only a thousand times bigger and more powerful. He felt the power and wanted to be part of it; but when he took his hands from the wall, there was only a brief tingling in his palms, then nothing.

It made his nose bleed, but he didn't care about that.

It never occurred to him to bring Johnny and Bob out here and see what they thought of it all. No way he was gonna let them horn in on this. *It's mine! I'm the one, I'm the only one, I'm the one they want. . . .*

And by now he knew about the old man. That man used to be the principal here, a long, long time ago, back when the school was first started. Mike's teacher, Mrs. Praize, told him that yesterday.

"What happened to him?" Mike asked.

"Oh, I don't know, I'm afraid it was before my time. Long before my time! Anyway, he's been dead for years," Mrs. Praize said.

They were all dead. Mike didn't need any crummy teacher

183

to tell him that. But it was a different kind of dead ... not like a squirrel run over by a car, not like a dead bird you found in someone's yard.

This kind of death set you free.

And Mike wanted it. He kicked and pounded on the kindergarten door, begging to be let in, hearing them whooping it up inside, beyond the door ... but they only hid themselves in the dark; they wouldn't let him in.

If he could only get *in* one of these nights, they'd have to take him then. He'd stay until he was one of them.

"You promised!" he reminded them.

But there came no answer.

Chapter Twenty-One

1

The sun came out for Halloween and the afternoon's parade.

During the lunch break the children donned their costumes, as did many of the teachers. Peter Ludovics became Indiana Jones, complete with hat and bullwhip, and Miss Vollmer amused her kindergarteners by turning herself into a big, soft, orange pumpkin with her arms and legs in bright green tights. Those were the two teachers Ned thought had the best costumes.

As for Mr. Hall, he came to his desk wearing a brown paper bag over his head with slanting eyeholes in it.

"What're you supposed to be, Mr. Hall?" asked a girl in a cheerleader's outfit.

"A pornographic mailing," said Mr. Hall—whatever that was supposed to be. "Now let's get to work, or this class won't make the parade this afternoon."

The paper bag was an improvement, Ned thought. Lately Mr. Hall was looking like something the cat dragged in, and in the afternoon he had B.O. He was doing something at lunchtime that made him sweat, but nobody knew what it was and nobody dared to ask. Whatever it was, it wasn't doing him much good. He had bloodshot eyes all the time now, and deep lines on his face. And he'd bite your head off for the least little thing.

Somehow, he put a damper on what was supposed to be a fun afternoon. Ned wouldn't have been surprised if he gave them homework, even though he knew the kids would want to trick-or-treat tonight. But when two o'clock rolled around and he still hadn't done it, Ned began to breathe easier.

Virgil stood with his arms folded, watching the parade, trying to enjoy it, a dutiful smile plastered to his face.

The word on Doreen Davis wasn't good: they still had her at the hospital, still on sedatives. Meanwhile, Joanne Wilmot stayed at home, hiding her lacerated lips. How badly her psyche had been wounded, Virgil didn't want to guess.

The kids were enjoying the parade, though, and the teachers seemed to be getting into it. A host of parents had turned out, too, to take pictures and drive their kids home when the parade was over. Carrie was floating around somewhere with her Polaroid.

The little costumed figures paraded past, as precious as gems. There was a tiny kindergarten boy whose mother had turned him into a flannel mouse with big floppy ears; a girl ballerina; an oversized milk carton with a child's face peering out of a round hole in it; a little sheik in flowing white robes; and the usual assortment of ghosts, witches, vampires, Indians, and soldiers. Watching them, Virgil felt a pang, wishing he could throw down his burdens and join them.

Ned marched past in his Blob Man suit, and Virgil couldn't help grinning at him. Ned waved and went on.

Millie Stanhouse was standing next to Virgil. "That son of yours—he's something else," she said. "Where does he get his ideas?"

"Horror movies," Virgil said. "He's addicted to them."

"Could be worse," Millie said. "Maybe he'll grow up to be the new Stephen King."

"I think he wants to be an archeologist."

"Smile, Virgil!"

Carrie had sneaked up on him with her camera, and Virgil had to strike a happy pose.

Diane Phelps marched past with her kids, and a face that would curdle milk. What was *her* problem, Virgil wondered.

2

Ned went out trick-or-treating as soon as he got home from school. This was the only time of the year he could get as much free candy as he could carry. If he did a good job of collecting, his loot would last him till Thanksgiving.

He went out with Phil and the McManuses, Marty grumbling at having to take his kid sister trick-or-treating when he could be sinking foul shots down at the CYO gym. Mrs. McManus had bought Halloween makeup kits at the A&P and done a great job of turning Patty into a green-faced little witch and Marty into a grimacing skull. Phil had on his Little League uniform and a rubber pig's-head mask from the drugstore.

"What're you supposed to be?" Patty said.

"A designated pig," he said. Nobody got it.

For two hours they filled their bags in Rivertown, then split up and went home for supper. Pickings were good this year. Ned deposited his take in one of his mother's half-gallon mixing bowls, almost filling it.

"I don't know if it's a good idea to let you eat all that candy," Mom said. "It'll wreck your teeth."

"Not if I brush 'em."

"Heck, I feel guilty about giving out these Tootsie Roll Pops," she said. A bowl of them stood ready in the living room.

"I should've bought something nutritious, like apples. Or those little seaweed cakes they have in the health food store."

Ned goggled at her and was about to yelp out a strenuous objection, when he realized she'd pulled his leg. She laughed at him.

3

Johnny Rizzo and his friends waited until after dark to go out.

Johnny was dressed up as G.I. Joe and Bob Diehl as a hard-hat construction worker. Mike Dudak had one of his old lady's stockings over his face.

As soon as they got together, Johnny took off his costume and stashed it in a neighbor's empty garbage can.

"This way," he explained, "if anybody squeals on us, they won't be able to say it was a kid in a G.I. Joe costume, and Pop won't believe 'em. You too, fatso. Take that hard hat off."

"How we gonna trick-or-treat without costumes?" Diehl said.

"Just do it, asshole."

The fat kid got all whiny. "But I wanna trick-or-treat!" he complained. "I want candy!"

"Tell you what, then, jerkoff. You go trick-or-treating by yourself. You'll only slow us down, anyway."

Diehl beat it, then—a little too quickly, Johnny thought. That left him with Dudak, and he wasn't altogether happy about that. He hadn't seen Mike these last couple nights, he didn't like the way Mike dodged around telling what he'd been up to, and the Dude had been acting kind of crazy these last few days at school.

Johnny had his own way of trick-or-treating. Let the little suckers go from door to door in costume: Johnny would hide behind parked cars or bushes and snatch their candy from them when they went by. You had to be careful, since there were plenty of parents walking around with their kids, but this way you could get a lot of candy fast—as long as Dudak didn't mess it up.

He couldn't see Mike's face with that stocking over it. He wasn't sure he wanted to. Something about the fucker was giving him the creeps tonight.

"We grab the candy and run," Johnny said, "and that's all. No stopping to fuck around. You got that, Dude?"

"No problem, man. Let's get started."

They hid behind a mailbox about a block from Johnny's house. Johnny's old man was on patrol tonight, but that was at the other end of town. They waited until they heard a couple of little kids coming down the sidewalk, then jumped them.

"Trick or treat, suckers!" Johnny yelled.

The two kids squealed. Johnny snatched a paper bag full of candy before the little girl who held it knew what was what. But the boy, dressed like a soldier with a plastic helmet, tried to hold onto his bag when Mike grabbed for it. Mike rapped him in the nose and knocked him down, and the kid yowled like a fire siren. Johnny and Mike ran until they were out of earshot, stopping around the corner.

"What'd you do that for?" Johnny snapped.

"The little fuck wouldn't give me his candy," Mike said. He was still holding the stolen bag, but it was empty now; it had been ripped in the tug-of-war, and all the candy was lost. Mike crumpled it disgustedly and threw it aside. "Shit! I should've kicked the little snot's head in!"

"I'll kick *your* head in if you don't get ahold of yourself," Johnny said. "We won't get nothin', if you got the whole damn neighborhood watchin' out for us."

Mike mumbled something which Johnny chose to interpret as agreement. But the next time they struck, it was worse.

Mike hit a little kid from behind and knocked him face-first to the sidewalk, and dropped onto him knees-first, like a wrestler. The kid screamed. Mike laughed. Johnny had to pull him off. The victim cried.

Johnny didn't dig this at all. Mike struggled, twisting all

around and cursing like a maniac, but Johnny had him from behind and he couldn't get loose. The little kid got to his knees and fled, weeping.

Normally Johnny would've just let Mike have it, pounded him into submission as he'd done fifty times before. But that was when Mike was normal, and he wasn't normal now. Johnny couldn't think of a time when Mike had flat-out defied him before. He had a feeling that once he started on the Dude tonight, he wouldn't be allowed to stop until he'd *really* flattened him. So he only held him until he calmed down.

"You shit! You let me go!"

Johnny shook him. "Not until you fuckin' take it easy! What's the matter with you, man?"

Mike wouldn't say. Johnny searched his mind for an idea.

"Shit, Dude, ease up! Look—whattaya say we go down by the Cliburn School and play a few tricks on the rich folks, huh? Give 'em a little taste of what Halloween's all about. Can you go for that?"

Mike sighed and said, "All right, damn it. Let's go."

Around the Cliburn School, in the southern part of town, the houses and the cars were new, the lawns were wide and expensively landscaped. There was nothing like it in Rivertown. Johnny and Mike walked there without incident, then paused to get their bearings. Down here it was hard to believe you were still in Tianoga.

"Lookit these rich stiffs!" Johnny said, waving an arm to take in an entire block. "They must be loaded."

"You bet," Mike said. During the walk, his surly mood had evaporated, and he seemed just about back to normal now.

"I mean, my old man busts his ass, right? Same with you. Your dad drives his fuckin' truck all around the country. Can we afford anything like this? *Lookit* these fuckin' houses, man!"

Johnny shook his head as he ran out of words. He wished he had a nickel for every time his old man bitched about the people down here: how they expected the cops to come running every time some rich fucker lost a dime—yet at the same time, the cops couldn't get a decent raise if their fuckin' lives depended on it. According to Officer Rizzo, that was the fault of these rich sons-of-bitches. Something to do with taxes and the police budget. Johnny didn't understand all of it, and he wasn't exactly in love with his old man, but he knew what was right. And these fat fucks having all that money, that wasn't right.

"Let's boogie," he said.

They sneaked into back yards and tore up chunks of costly sod. They cut up lawn furniture with Johnny's penknife. They spilled garbage cans, slashing plastic trash bags and stuffing them into bushes. Most of the houses had garages, and most of the cars were safely locked away, so that part of their repertoire had to be left out of the program. But they smeared gook from the garbage cans onto aluminum siding and unlit windows, and really went to town when they discovered a dirty gas grill and were able to get a couple rags loaded with greasy soot. *That* would be a bitch to clean up. They wiped it on people's windows.

They didn't bushwhack any more trick-or-treaters; after an hour or two of creative vandalism, Mike was all calmed down. Johnny put his G.I. Joe costume back on and went home.

Mike stripped the stocking off his face and threw it away.

It was sodden with blood.

Chapter Twenty-Two

1

Charlie dropped his class off with the art teacher and wondered if he ought to use the free period for an extra jog around the track.

Jesus, Mary, and Joseph, he was beat. He hoped like hell it meant he was getting fitter.

The scale this morning said he weighed two-forty. The ideal weight for a man six feet tall (well, five-eleven), according to the chart he'd clipped out of last Sunday's paper, was one hundred and eighty pounds, which meant that after a week of getting physical, Charlie was still sixty pounds over the mark. He shuddered to think what he must've weighed *two* weeks ago, before he'd started doing anything about it.

Oh, what a week! Now it was Friday morning, and looking back, Charlie was kind of surprised he'd made it this far. He'd cut out *all* alcoholic beverages, quit smoking flat, given up red meat and sugar, and cut his food intake down to about a thousand calories a day. At the same time, he was getting up at six in the morning and jogging around the block, again when he had a free lunch period, and once again before he went to bed.

Charlie felt like hell.

Lesson plans, he ought to work on next month's lesson plans. There was just no time for an extra quarter-mile today. Reprieved, but too groggy to feel it, he headed back to his classroom.

There he found Diane Phelps waiting for him, seated on the corner of his desk and smirking at him like she was the Queen of the Nile.

And she looked it, for all Charlie cared right now. Cleopatra herself could be sitting up there bare-ass naked, and it'd do about as much for him as an old tintype of Queen Victoria. He'd have traded all the dancing girls in Moslem heaven for a single cigarette, anyway—and he wasn't even allowing himself to smoke.

"Hello, Charlie."

"Hi, Diane. Whattaya want? I gotta do lesson plans."

Had Charlie been less wrung out, he would have seen something flash through her eyes that would have scared him.

"It's too bad about Joanne," she said.

Joanne? It took him a second to remember who Joanne was and what had happened to her. "Oh, that. Yeah, that's terrible."

"Charlie, are you sick?"

"No. I'm fine."

"You don't look fine. You look like you've just been initiated into the Living Dead fraternity."

"Just tired, that's all." Christ, he couldn't *stand* here ... he walked around her and sat down.

"I saw your name on the chaperones' list for tonight," she said, "so I volunteered, too. I thought we could have a drink or two afterward. Get back together again."

Charlie didn't even remember signing up for the fucking kids' party. What the hell, if his name was on the list in the office, he must have. He didn't want to debate it. All he wanted was to rest. So he just said, "Sure."

"I still don't see how you could have dropped me for that silly little slut, Charlie. She wasn't worth it."

The words bounced off Charlie's brain. He didn't know what she was talking about and he didn't care. He felt a headache coming on. He had a pain way up inside his nose, a dull ache that never let up.

"Whatever you say, Diane."

She got up. "That's settled, then. Good. I knew you'd come to your senses. I never doubted it."

The only thing she did doubt was whether she'd done a good enough job on Wilmot to warn her off Charlie permanently. But that would have to wait until the bitch came back.

As she walked back to the teachers' room, Diane tried to concentrate on her reunion with Charlie after the kids' party tonight. This was difficult to do. She seemed to have a kind of buzzing or humming in her head; and she knew by now that when it went away, it would leave her with a whopper of a headache. These last few days at school, she'd been absolutely plagued with it. But never at home, thank God for small mercies.

The stroll from Charlie's room to the faculty lounge should only take a minute or two, three at the most. Diane hadn't been giving it any conscious thought—until suddenly she was surprised to find herself still only halfway there, still walking down the long, deserted corridor. She felt like she'd left Charlie's room half an hour ago.

And there, up ahead of her, right in the middle of the hall, stood Charlie. Diane stopped. He couldn't be there, he couldn't possibly have passed her, not unless he ran right by her in the hall. . . .

Without a word, without a sound, he turned and went through the fire doors to the stairs leading down to the girls' entrance and the basement. His name was on Diane's lips, but he was gone before she could speak it.

She hurried after him. She pushed the doors aside and looked down from the landing, but he was already out of sight. She couldn't hear him on the stairs.

"Charlie?"

No answer but an echo.

That, and the humming in her head.

2

Before he went home, Virgil stopped to see how the PTA volunteers were progressing with their work in the cafeteria, preparing it for the evening's festivities.

Cosmo Iacavella stood beside the entrance, watching with the air of a janitor who refused to believe the PTA's assurances that the party wouldn't mean a minute of extra work for him, they'd leave the gymnasium spick and span. Rudi Fitch, though, had thrown himself enthusiastically into the work and was presently setting up a ladder so a volunteer could climb up and hang black and orange streamers.

"How's it going?" Virgil asked his head janitor.

"Why can't they have parties at home?" Cosmo grumbled.

"Because the PTA thinks it's better to have the kids all here, where someone can keep an eye on them. And it helps build school spirit."

"*That's* a waste of time!"

He was cranky, Virgil knew, because he was sure he would have to come in Saturday morning and wash and wax the big floor. Virgil could have pointed out that at least he wouldn't have to come in tonight and open and close the building, because Virgil would do that himself; but there was no point in trying to cheer up Cosmo when he was in one of his moods. Virgil wasn't feeling all that cheerful himself, anyway.

"Watch that ladder, Rudi!" Cosmo bellowed. "You put a scratch in that floor and I'll brain you!"

Rudi grinned sheepishly and tightened his grip on the ladder.

3

Marty McManus absolutely refused to go to the party: there was a St. John's game on the tube tonight, and he'd had enough of Halloween for one year. But a family fracas had been averted by Ned and Phil, who had agreed to take Patty.

"And we're not goin' home without my water pistol!" Phil said.

"If the door's unlocked, we'll get it," Ned promised. "Unless he locked his desk."

"Fuckin' thief—I wouldn't put it past him!"

The fuckin' thief was Mr. Hall, who'd confiscated Phil's new Mini-Uzi water gun when the kids came back in from lunch break and he caught Phil showing it around the classroom. He hadn't been squirting anybody with it, but Mr. Hall was in a pissy mood and took it anyhow, shoving it into the top drawer of his desk.

"And let that be a lesson to you, Mr. Berg—gun control is an idea whose time has come, and what better place to begin than in the grammar school classrooms of this great and noble land?"

"Can I have it back after school, Mr. Hall?"

"*May* I have it back, Mr. Berg. *May* I. Speak English, for God's sake."

"*May* I have it back?"

"Of course not."

The other kids had laughed, Phil having been made to look

like an idiot. But he planned to have the last laugh. Tonight he'd sneak out of the gym during the movie and steal the gun back—provided the classroom door and Mr. Hall's desk were both unlocked.

Chapter Twenty-Three

1

There was a simple stage at the far end of the gymnasium built for just such occasions as this. Above it hung a movie screen, waiting to accommodate Godzilla.

A couple of tables had been pulled out from the wall to hold refreshments—Halloween cupcakes, home-made brownies, liter bottles of orange soda, coffee for the adults. Tonight the refreshments were free.

The rest of the floor was bare, providing ample room for over a hundred kids to sit down and watch the movie. At the moment, most of them were on their feet, waiting to see who'd be best at bobbing for apples or pinning the hat on the witch. Crepe-paper streamers fluttered from the ceiling, and the foot of the stage was lined with a display of carved and painted jack-o'-lanterns. Jointed cardboard skeletons hung from the walls.

Halloween now technically over, the children hadn't bothered to put their costumes on again. But the spirit of the holiday was still very much in the air.

"I need these calories like I need a hole in the head," Carrie said to Virgil, flourishing an orange-iced cupcake.

Virgil laughed at her. After the horrors of Monday and Tuesday, he was finally feeling like a human being again. He put his arm around her and gave her shoulder a squeeze. "I don't see anybody making you eat that cupcake, lady."

She was overjoyed to see him snapping out of it at last, but for fear of making him self-conscious about it, she didn't say anything.

This was Victory School at its best, she thought, and solid evidence of how good a principal her husband really was. Before he took over here, nothing like this party would have even been contemplated. She wondered if he knew how much he meant to the community; she wondered if anybody knew. He made his contribution in a quiet way, and she suspected people were inclined to take it for granted.

"Guess I've just got the Halloween spirit," she said. "This is such a *nice* party, Virgil! Everybody's having such a good time."

2

Diane Phelps, however, was most emphatically *not* having a good time.

Never in a thousand years would she have volunteered for such a wasted evening as this; she was here only because she'd expected to go out with Charlie afterward and get *laid,* damn it.

And the stupid son-of-a-bitch never showed up.

She didn't delude herself: if he wasn't here by now, he wasn't coming, period. And now, while she was stranded with a grinding headache amid a goddamned babel of squealing brats, *he* was probably out hitting on a barmaid or a waitress somewhere. Count on it.

She was this close to telling Mr. Bradley she had a headache and going home. The only reason she didn't was because she couldn't bear the thought of going back to stare at the four walls of her living room before she went to bed. Her husband was out bowling tonight, but with her luck he'd come back early, and he was worse than no company at all. If Ed's mother had ever known what a miserable, boring fool she was about to loose upon the world, she'd have sealed her womb.

One of the wretched children shrieked right in Diane's ear; it went through her skull like a nail. If she hadn't been holding onto the edge of one of the tables, she'd have swatted the little snot.

Well, Charlie, you can run, but you can't hide. Not forever. You're going to have to pay for this little trick. You're going to have to learn your lesson. This is *me* you're dealing with, not some insipid little wimp like Joanne Wilmot. And we all know what happened to her, don't we?

3

Godzilla came on, roaring mad and ready to kick Tokyo into the sea.

The children squirmed and fidgeted on the floor, loving the way the roars reverberated in the big gym, loving the way the bright screen stood out in the dark. A lot of them had already seen this film on television, but that didn't lessen their enjoyment. Godzilla was a lot more of an eyeful on the big screen.

Ned would have liked to see the whole thing, but a promise was a promise, as Phil reminded him the moment the lights went out.

"Will you quit elbowing me, damn it?"

"Let's go, then!" Phil whispered.

Aided by the darkness and the spell cast by the movie, they crept through the crowd of kids, drawing a few curses as they passed. After a few seconds of not looking at the screen, their eyes adjusted to the darkness and they stopped bumping into people. Soon they were at the back of the gym.

Grownups were supposed to be flanking the entranceway, guarding against unauthorized excursions, but at the moment the coast was clear. Ned and Phil crawled into the hallway and made their way quietly through the doors into the new wing.

"Where are we going?"

"Oh, no!" Phil groaned under his breath when they discovered that Patty had tagged along. "Get outta here, willya?"

"No way—I'm goin' with you."

"If we stand here arguing about it, we'll all get caught," Ned said. "Come on, let's get this over with."

He led them silently down the hall. The lights were on, but the lighting in Victory School was lousy in the middle of the day, and at night they were worth hardly anything at all.

Ned couldn't help thinking that any minute, that guy in the Revolutionary War suit was going to come floating right through one of the freakin' doors. Swear to God, this place gave him the creeps sometimes. But you never see ghosts, he reminded himself, when there's anybody around to see them with you.

They rounded the corner by the boys' room and ran right into Johnny Rizzo and his friends.

4

"Well, if it ain't the little Jewboy!" said Bob Diehl.

The three of them were standing by the water fountain next to the boys' room door—Rizzo, Diehl, and Mike Dudak. Ned hadn't seen them at the party earlier; they'd probably sneaked in.

Ned wanted to retreat back to the gym, but Dudak had already circled around them, cutting them off. He figured he and Phil could get past Dudak, but not Patty. And damn it, with the freakin' movie going full blast, no one in the gym would hear them if they yelled. Not this far away.

Diehl sauntered up to Phil and backed him toward the fountain.

"So whattaya say, Berg, how about forkin' over a few quarters? I need money for snacks tomorrow."

"Sorry, I don't have any extra," Phil said. Ned thought, *C'mon, man, what's the matter with you? Give him the money and let's get out of this.*

"Whattaya mean, you don't got any extra? I thought you kikes were *loaded.*"

And of course Phil, God damn him, had to say, "You don't need any snacks, asshole. You're already a big fat slob."

Diehl, who could have lifted Phil's father on a seesaw, slammed Phil hard against the wall. Phil's glasses almost flew off. Ned balled his fists and got ready to go down swinging.

"Don't smart-mouth me, you little hebe. You wanna get turned into a lampshade?"

At this point, Ned thought, Phil could still hand over some money and get out of there. But Diehl had been picking on him forever. Phil had taken all he was going to take, and he wasn't thinking straight.

"Your mother should've got an abortion," he told Diehl, "but she was already so goddamn fat, the doctor at the whorehouse couldn't tell she was pregnant."

Diehl gaped like George Steinbrenner would if some third-string rookie walked up and slapped him in the face. Phil's insult had been so unexpected, so all-embracing in its offensiveness, that it was taking a moment to register. Ned glanced around wildly for an opportunity to escape.

And he saw Mike Dudak standing behind Patty, his eyes as glazed as any werewolf's, holding a butane lighter to her hair and getting ready to set her on fire.

Ned didn't even think about what he did next. All he knew was that his fist shot out and nailed Dudak right in the ear, knocking him back a step and making him drop the lighter.

Ned grabbed Patty's arm and shouted *"Run!"*, darting between Diehl and Rizzo and pulling Patty with him. Phil ducked under Diehl's attempt to grab him and followed Ned and Patty up the main stairs.

5

Dudak would've caught Patty if they'd tried to run back to the gym, so the stairs and the second floor were the only way to go. Ned practically dragged Patty up the stairs, expecting at any moment to be collared from behind and dragged back down. But the only thing that was catching up to him, for the moment, was a chorus of threats and curses from the bullies.

They fled up the hall, hearing Rizzo and his friends pounding up the stairs after them. Ned ran all the way to the end of the hall, then dodged left and bolted through the pair of fire doors next to the office.

Phil was nearly hysterical, giggling uncontrollably as they barged down the stairs. They hit the first landing and saw the chains on the doors of the boys' entrance: no getting out that way. Above them, the fire doors crashed open.

"Here we come, you shits!" Rizzo's voice boomed in the stairwell. Ned and his friends rushed down the stairs to the basement. Before they reached the floor, they heard a yell, a series of muffled thumps, and an explosion of cursing from Dudak.

One of the bullies had fallen down the stairs. That was good, that would slow them up for a few seconds ... and Ned could only hope that would be enough.

He broke into the corridor that led from the boiler room to the library, intending to escape up the flight of steps that led up past the girls' entrance. That ought to do it—from there they could get back to the gym.

But as he reached for the door at the landing, he looked

through the windows on it and saw somebody coming *down* the stairs.

Great! They figured it out, they cut us off!

There were only two choices left: to hope somebody had left the library unlocked, and try to hide in there; or to duck into one of the little stairwells from the basement to the blacktop and just hope to hell that Rizzo didn't come in after them.

Without pausing to dope it out, Ned darted away from the door and ran straight to the library. He seized the doorknob and almost fainted with relief when the door swung open.

There was no need to give instructions: they all knew they were going to try to hide in the library. Phil had stopped his cackling and had the presence of mind to pull the door shut after him.

In the school library, unlike the public library, all the books were on the walls. There were no stacks on the floor. That left only two real hiding places: behind the counter that enclosed the librarians' work area, or the little storeroom—the "annex," they called it—at the other end of the library.

Ned sped to the storeroom, found the door unlocked, and pushed Patty inside. Phil brought up the rear and closed the door. Within seconds the three of them were crouching on the floor, waiting for Rizzo's gang to barge into the library.

The little room smelled of books and papers slowly succumbing to decay.

Cartons of unused books, taken out of circulation because of broken spines or outdated information, lined the walls. It was dark in there, but not completely. The library had a couple of windows that faced River Street, the annex door had a window in it, and a little bit of light seeped into the room from the streetlights outside. There was just enough to see by, if your eyes were adjusted to the dark.

Ned crouched and hardly dared to breath, listening for noises out in the hall. All he heard was his own heartbeat, which sure as shit seemed loud enough. If there was any way Rizzo could fail to look for them in the library, Ned couldn't think of one.

It was a mistake coming here, it was running into a trap....
When they find us, we'll have nowhere left to run.

Too late for that now, though. Now they could only wait.

Ned had been in here only once or twice before, and he hadn't even noticed how really cruddy it smelled. It wasn't just mildewed paper and dissolving ink and paste, either. There was a spoiled-meat smell, too, that made him want to puke. He wondered if Phil and Patty noticed it. Under the circumstances, though, he didn't dare ask.

As his pupils dilated further, he was able to make out a little more of his surroundings. *Holy cow, there must be a million books in here!* The cartons were piled all the way to the ceiling, and there were more boxes on the floor. There was barely enough room in here for three kids to hide.

Something moved.

He saw it in the corner of his eye. For a better look, he didn't even have to turn his head. Only his eyes had to move.

Some kind of *flower* was growing out from between two stacks of boxes.

No, not a flower ... it was more like one of those whatchamacallits you see on *Nature,* those animals that kind of looked like flowers, which lived in the ocean, anchored to rocks.

And it was balanced on a stalk—a thick, pink stalk that reminded Ned more of a gigantic earthworm than anything else.

Even as he looked at it, it drew back like it was hiding from him, withdrawing and vanishing between the two stacks of cartons. Ned jumped.

"What's the matter?" Phil whispered in his ear.

"Nothin'! Shut up!"

"I think they're gone, man. They missed us."

Ned could have socked Phil. But now that he thought of it, they *had* been in the annex for a couple of minutes at least, and they hadn't heard the door of the library open, hadn't heard anybody moving around.

Cautiously, Ned inched up to peek out the window in the door. All he saw was the empty library, with the door still closed.

Patty got up, but Ned grabbed her.

"Hold it! They might be hiding on us. You wait here."

Slowly, like a man defusing a bomb, Ned opened the annex door. He tiptoed across the library and crouched to listen by the door. If there was anybody outside in the hall, they were keeping awfully quiet.

They couldn't stay there all night, he reminded himself. Still not hearing anything, he teased open the library door just a crack. Rizzo and the boys might be just out of his line of sight, waiting to pounce.

Incredibly, the basement corridor was empty. Ned stepped outside and took a good, long look. By then Phil had come up behind him, Patty close on his heels.

"They're gone," Phil said, wonderingly. "They must've thought we went up the other stairs."

"But they—" Ned started to say, then cut himself off. Obviously he'd only thought he'd seen somebody on the other stairs. *That's what happens when you panic.*

"Can we get back to the movie now?" Patty said.

It hit Ned then, like a slushball in the face, that neither Patty nor Phil had seen what Dudak had been about to do with that cigarette-lighter. Well, he'd be damned if he was gonna be the one to tell 'em. Jesus, Dudak was going to set her *hair* on fire! He wouldn't like to be around if Mr. and Mrs. McManus ever found out about *that.*

Phil started to giggle again. "Hey, did you see the look on that fat fuck's *face* when I made that crack about his mother? I thought he was gonna have a fuckin' heart attack!"

Patty giggled, too, and for a second Ned was almost the one to have the heart attack. The sound of their giggling bounced all the way down the hall, and probably up the stairwell.

But Rizzo and his asshole buddies failed to materialize, and Ned began to breathe normally again.

Chapter Twenty-Four

1

Johnny didn't know who he was madder at, Bob or Mike. Bob had started it, trying to shake the Jewish kid down for money; but fuckin' Dude was gonna set the little girl's hair on fire. Johnny felt almost grateful toward Ned Bradley for stopping Mike with that Sunday punch.

Bradley, the little girl, and the Jew had gotten away. Johnny thought he was going to catch them when he slipped and fell on the stairs. Damn near cracked his skull, and the Dude practically broke his neck trying not to trip over him. That gave the three wimps the time they needed to escape up the other flight of steps, and hide in the cafeteria, where their mommies and daddies and teachers would protect them. Johnny hadn't even bothered to continue the chase, giving it up when he reached the basement hall and realized they'd just gone up the other steps. Slowly boiling over, he led his friends back outside.

Dudak was still hopping mad about that punch to the ear.

"Let's get 'em on their way home! We know which way they go, we can ambush 'em...."

"Mr. Bradley's at the party," Bob said. "He'll be with 'em. Anyway, I bet they got a ride home."

"You fat booger! If it wasn't for you bein' so fat and slow, we'd'a caught 'em. If it wasn't for Johnny fallin' down the stairs—"

But Johnny wasn't going to listen to that. Before Mike could say another word, Johnny spun around and creamed him with a forearm to the jaw, knocking him right down.

"You funkin' crazy jerkoff! You and your fucking fire! You know what happens if you do that? You dumb shit! We *all* get sent to the juvenile home, all three of us, and all because of *you!*"

Johnny was on the point of going berserk. He was a bully, but he wasn't crazy. He liked to scare kids, even liked to punch kids out, but he wasn't out to send anybody to the hospital. Shitfire, Dudak could've *killed* that girl if he'd actually set her hair on fire. Johnny was sure you could kill someone that way. And he had no doubt what would've happened if they had. Officer Rizzo had told his delinquent son all about the electric chair, in the vain hope of scaring him into acceptable behavior. They weren't electrocuting anybody right now, Officer Rizzo said; but they sure as hell hadn't thrown the chair away, either, hadn't even let it get dusty. It'd be ready to go again in a minute.

"It fries you like a hamburger, Johnny. Next time we go to MacDonald's, listen to the burgers sizzle when they throw 'em on the grill. That's what a person sounds like when he's in the electric chair."

Well, Johnny was damned if he was going to go to the electric chair because of some bright idea of Dudak's. Okay, no one had really been hurt—this time. But just having been subjected to the risk infuriated him.

So Johnny hit him hard, and Mike went down. Johnny yelled at him and Mike got up for more.

Johnny was so surprised, he actually retreated half a step. Dude had never *attacked* him before. Now here he was, coming right at him, screeching like a cat with its tail caught in a door. He was absolutely the craziest son-of-a-bitch Johnny had ever seen, and the fact that he was short and scrawny as a chicken didn't mean jack shit right now. Mike would kill him if he could, and Johnny knew it.

Johnny had beaten the crap out of any number of boys whose daddies had told them that a bully always chickens out if you stand your ground against him. He wasn't about to run from a little shrimp like Mike, no matter how crazy he was.

Mike tried to get him in the eyes. Johnny grabbed him, shook him, and threw him back down. Mike tried to bite him in the ankle and got kicked in the face for it. Mike tried to push his legs out from under him, but Johnny caught his head in a scissor-lock and pounded the living daylights out of his unprotected back—and enjoyed doing it.

But even that didn't finish the Dude. He managed to slip his head out from between Johnny's legs and roll away, still making that awful noise that was half-scream, half-growl. Johnny was really mad now, too, and all set to teach Mike a lesson he'd never forget. He wasn't going to wrestle with this little fucker anymore.

"C'mon, you little turd, I got some more for ya, I'm gonna mess your fuckin' face—"

Mike charged again, head down. Johnny caught him in a front headlock, shifted it to a side headlock in his left arm, and began to batter his face with his strong right hand.

Bob had seen Johnny and Mike fight before, but nothing like this. Not ever.

He was good and scared. Shit, all he'd wanted to do was shake a kid down for a little money. Johnny did it all the time. And then Mike had to go and take out his lighter. . . .

As clearly as if it were on display in flashing neon lights, Bob suddenly realized that his friends were heading straight for trouble. Not just *trouble*. Police, judge-and-jury, jailhouse trouble. The kind of trouble that sucked you down like quicksand. And if he stuck by them, it was going to suck him down with them.

No one would believe, or even care, that *he* hadn't wanted to set anybody's hair on fire. He'd just be one of the gang that did it. And if it wasn't that, it'd be something else equally bad. Mike and Johnny were not just bad; they were flat-out crazy.

No doubt about it, they were gonna kill somebody someday—if Johnny didn't kill Mike right here and now. He kept hitting him and hitting him, and there was blood flying all over, and Bob wanted to scream. But he didn't dare, because he was afraid Johnny would come after *him* if he did.

So Bob did the next best thing. He ran away.

Johnny worked off his anger on Mike's face. When he'd cooled off enough to notice that his hand was hurting and the Dude wasn't fighting anymore, he released the headlock.

Mike lay bleeding in the schoolyard dirt. Johnny's hand was killing him. He was gasping for breath. And Bob Diehl, that fat fairy, was nowhere to be seen.

For a moment he was afraid he'd gone too far: killed Mike, or turned him into a vegetable. Johnny was as strong as a lot of eighth-graders, and he'd hit Mike with all he had.

Fighting a strong impulse to turn and run, he dropped to one knee and turned Mike over.

Mike's face looked like wild horses had run over it. You couldn't recognize him: it might be anybody under all that blood and dirt. Johnny couldn't see his eyes.

Unnerved by what he'd done, Johnny left him lying in the dirt and hurried home.

Should he tell, or shouldn't he?

They'd gotten back to the cafeteria in time for the climax of *Godzilla,* and as far as Ned could see, they hadn't been missed. At the end of the movie, the lights came on and there they were, right where they were supposed to be.

The end of the movie was the end of the party. Parents and kids put on their coats and went home. Volunteers stayed to clean up as much of the mess as they could for the janitors, and Dad stayed to close the building after them. Ned went home in the car with Mom, with Phil and Patty in the back seat, pushing each other around and rehashing their favorite parts of the movie.

They thought he'd punched Dudak to create a diversion so they could get away. Phil couldn't have seen around Bob Diehl, Patty didn't have eyes in the back of her head, so they had no idea what the fourth-grade weirdo had been about to do when Ned popped him.

Ned imagined himself appearing on *The People's Court,* trying to sell his story to Judge Wapner.

"But Your Honor—"

"Son, didn't you hear what your witnesses just said? They didn't see it. They can't help you. It's your word against these three other guys'."

"But Judge, they're creeps! Ask anybody! They're liars, you can't believe anything they say—"

"It doesn't matter what I believe, son. You've made a charge. You have to prove it. Where's your proof? Would you want a judge to rule against you just because of something one person said?"

Ned knew the judge's speech by heart. People were *always* going up there, trying to win their cases without proof, no matter how many times Wapner explained you had to have it, and they always lost. So Ned knew that even if Dad, say, believed him, he wouldn't be able to do much about it. You couldn't kick kids out of school without proof, and Ned had no proof.

No more than he had proof of the ghost in the boys' room, or the weird flower-animal in the library annex. *(Jesus, what was that?)* He knew the building had termites, carpenter ants, cockroaches, mice, and maybe even a rat now and then—but something that looked like it belonged on the bottom of the ocean? Something on a stalk that dodged out of sight when you looked at it, like a night-crawler ducking down its hole?

What're you trying to tell me, Ned? That's what Dad would say. *Ghosts? Coral-reef animals in the library annex? Come on, what's the punch line?*

Mom dropped Phil off, then Patty, then took Ned home. Before they got out of the car, she asked, "Do you feel all right, kiddo? You're awfully quiet."

Even if she believed the part about Dudak, she'd never believe the rest. She'd think he was making it up, she'd say he was watching too many horror movies. . . .

"I ate too many cupcakes," was all he could tell her for the time being.

Maybe tomorrow he would try the truth. See how he felt after he'd slept on it.

3

Mike didn't remember sneaking back into the school, but there he was: scrunched under a desk in the dark, hearing voices in his head.

Hello, Mike old buddy, glad you finally made it!

You're safe now, Michael, we're going to take good care of you.

He was surprised to be alive. The last he remembered, Rizzo had him in a headlock and was bashing his brains out. He felt like he'd fallen off a cliff, landing on his face. How he'd gotten into the building and found this hiding place was a complete mystery to him.

He didn't know where in the building he was. Even if it hadn't been pitch-dark, his eyes were swollen shut. Pain made him give up trying to open them.

Rest, Michael, rest! Soon you'll be seeing things you never dreamed of. It won't hurt anymore.

He'd never been beaten up like this before, not even by his old man. Shit, Rizzo must've thought he'd fuckin' killed him. He didn't believe Rizzo could have hit him any harder. Goddamn. He'd taken Rizzo's best shot—maybe a hundred of his best shots, for all he knew—and he was still here. Kind of banged up, but still hanging in there. That was the kind of thing Daddy would be proud of. Not that it mattered anymore what the old man thought.

Mike tried to figure out how badly he'd been hurt. His nose was clogged with drying blood. It hurt when he touched it, and its shape was wrong. It was broken, for sure. His tongue found a few holes where teeth used to be. The tongue was sore and ragged, all torn up from being mashed against his teeth. His lips were swollen, split in several places. His fingers found bumps all over his face, blood in sticky patches, most of them gritty with dirt.

The rest of him wasn't much better off. It hurt to take a deep breath. His neck screeched with pain when he moved his head, even slightly.

It's all right, Mike, it won't hurt much longer, soon you'll feel just fine. . . .

Funny—he wasn't all that mad at Rizzo. Johnny'd whupped him plenty of times, this was just the worst. *And the last, man.* It was never going to happen again. Mike knew that.

What *really* pissed him off, what made him grind what was left of his teeth, what nearly gave him the strength to get up again, was that goody-two-shoes principal's shit-hole kid. Ned Bradley—who had sucker-punched him, who had fucked up the absolute neatest trick he'd ever thought of—was the one who really got him going. Ned Fucking Bradley.

Oh, he was going to kill Bradley, no doubt about it. He was going to find a knife and cut that fucker's guts out. He was going to stomp on his face. The thought of Bradley made his guts slither with rage.

The voices roared approval.

Right on, Mike! You're gonna do it, baby, you're gonna get that motherfucker!

I have faith in you, Michael. I know you'll make us all proud of you.

That's the spirit, boy! "Don't Tread on Me," that's our motto! Be bold!

He's all yours, Mike. . . .

And there were voices that spoke a language Mike didn't understand, but their meaning came across loud and clear. They were all pulling for him. He had his own cheering section here. He had a crowd around him like a hero.

He had to get out of here, though. He couldn't just sit around under a desk until they found him and sent him home. Now that he was here, where he wanted to be, he never wanted to leave again.

Shit, that hurt! Every movement stuck a knife into him. For a moment he didn't think he was going to make it . . . and then he was out on the floor, on his hands and knees, gasping as explosions of pain went off inside his skull.

He tried to see where he was, but his eyes would only open to slits. He couldn't see worth a damn, anyway: too many blobs of dull purple swimming in front of him.

Don't be afraid, Michael. We'll take care of you. We know all the hiding-places, we'll find one for you.

He felt around for the desk, found the top of it, clutched it, and hauled himself to his feet. A rush of nausea nearly knocked him back down, but he clung to the desk until he fought it off. He was dizzy, too, and there was a tinny ringing in his ears.

But in a way that wasn't quite *seeing*, but somehow just as good, he was aware of people all around him, pressing in close on him, wanting him to make it. They wouldn't let him pass out again. They wouldn't let him fall. He couldn't touch them, but his skin tingled all over because they were so near, like they were electricity in the air.

He still couldn't see, but he could walk. He let them lead him out of whatever room he'd been in, out into one of the corridors. They were so close.

Somehow he knew that the Halloween party was over, that all the people had gone home, that the building was locked up tight with all the lights turned off. But it was far from empty. The hall was full of voices.

That's it, Michael. This way. Easy does it.

It's all right, man, trust us, we got just the place for you to hide. They'll never find you.

Good lad! Be steady, we don't want to lose you. You're almost one of us now.

One of us . . .

One of us . . .

Chapter Twenty-Five

1

Ned was at the McManus's front door, holding Patty by the hand. Her head was a round black ball of charred skin and flesh, with a cooked tongue sticking out of her mouth and cooked eyes bulging from their sockets. All her hair was burned away. She was dead, and Ned wished he could die, too. That'd be better than having to face Patty's mother.

Sick to his soul, he rang the doorbell. After a moment or two, the door swung open.

But it wasn't Mrs. McManus who had answered him. It was that old guy whose picture Dad had in his office, the old principal, Dr. Hargrove, the one who'd died so long ago. He stood in the doorway looking down at Ned, impossibly tall, dry and pale as an old bone; and he grinned suddenly, showing a hundred sharp and dripping fangs.

2

"We're all done here," Cosmo said.

Virgil stood beside him at the entrance to the gymnasium, watching Rudi push the waxer across the big floor, now as clean and shiny as the floor in Carrie's kitchen. Rudi was smiling, proud of the job he'd done.

"This is the last time I'm comin' in here on a Saturday morning," Cosmo said, as he always said on such occasions. "You tell the Board of Ed they can keep their overtime, I gotta get my rest after bustin' my ass all week. For two cents, I'd retire."

"Don't it look nice, Mr. Bradley?" Rudi said. "You'd never think there was a party here."

"Neat as a pin, Rudi," Virgil said. "I really appreciate you and Mr. Iacavella coming in today and doing this for me."

"Let's get this equipment put away and get outta here," Cosmo said. "You want us to lock up, Mr. Bradley, or are you gonna stay awhile?"

"I'll lock up. What with the parade and the party and all, I've really fallen behind on my paperwork. I'll have to stay for a few hours to catch up."

"Doesn't hardly seem worthwhile, what with the place gonna be closed for good come June."

"That's the problem," Virgil said. "That's why I've got twice as many forms to fill out as I ever had before."

"Better you than me. Come on, Rudi. See you Monday, Mr. Bradley."

Virgil stood for a moment in the gym while the janitors wheeled their machines back down to the boiler room. The builders of the school, he reflected, had never spared a thought for the janitors who'd have to lug their equipment up and down all the stairs in here. The new school, Cliburn, had only one floor.

Well, at least the party had been a success. The second and last annual Halloween party.

What a waste. But the school board had the numbers. He only hoped the demographics were right, and the board wouldn't have to come begging to the taxpayers for a new school a few years down the road.

Meanwhile, he had to keep up with the paperwork. He felt like a man planning his own funeral. Quietly, he closed the gym and headed down the new wing toward his office.

3

"I'm going over Mr. Fulham's for a while, Ned. Want to come?"

"No thanks, Mom, not today."

"No mischief while I'm gone."

"You want it to wait till you get back?"

Mom laughed, ruffled his hair, and left him to finish his breakfast alone.

He still hadn't told her about Dudak and the lighter. Hadn't told Dad, either. And now they were both out, so he couldn't tell them if he wanted to.

As far as the Dudak thing went, Ned decided his parents would believe him. They could usually tell when he was fibbing, anyway. They knew he wouldn't make up a thing like that about another kid—especially Dudak. Why bother to make things up about *him?* That'd be like saying Darth Vader had B.O. Dad already wished he had some way he could kick Dudak, Rizzo, and Diehl out of school for good.

But this wouldn't help him do that. All it'd do would be to make trouble. *Trouble for me, mostly,* Ned figured.

Yeah—but Dad was the principal, he was always saying how he needed to know everything that went on in the school. Then again, he hadn't brought Ned up to be a tattletale. He made a

218

point of never asking Ned about stuff that happened on the playground and wound up having to be settled in the office. "I don't want people taking advantage of you," he would explain. "They can't help assuming you have a special access to the principal. But if they think you come running to me every time you see the least little thing wrong, you're not going to have a very happy grammar school career."

But this wasn't the least little thing, was it? Hey, he *could* have set her hair on fire! He was trying to. And he would've, if Ned hadn't hit him.

In the end, it was the nightmare that made up his mind for him. *"Well, gee, Mrs. McManus, I guess I did know what Mike was up to, but I didn't want to start a bunch of trouble over it. . . ."* Ned didn't *ever* want to have to say anything like that.

4

Virgil wondered what they would do with all these forms and reports he was toiling over today, once they closed the school. Probably stick them in a file somewhere and never look at them again in a hundred years. He was only here because the Tianoga school board, like all bureaucracies great and small, had a mindless compulsion to hoard paper.

When his back started griping him, he went out to the front office for a cup of coffee. He drank it standing up, resting his eyes on the *Smithsonian* poster on the wall over the coffee machine—the famous one showing the three-toed sloths lounging on deck chairs. Millie Stanhouse was an animal nut, and the decor of the front office proved it: china figurines of cats and frogs, another poster of meerkats standing erect beside the entrance to their burrow, a North Shore Animal League calendar.

He finished the coffee and decided to go for a stroll down the hall to stretch his legs.

He hadn't turned the hall lights on, and the light coming in through the windows was gray and watery. The weatherman was predicting rain again, lots of it.

Virgil walked slowly, postponing the inevitable return to his desk. He noted that most of the Halloween decorations were down already, making the walls outside the classrooms look bleak and forlorn. Well, in a couple of weeks, they'd be putting up Thanksgiving turkeys and cardboard Pilgrims; and after that came Christmas. He didn't want to look much beyond that. *Othello's occupation's gone,* he thought glumly.

A door slammed shut.

"Who's that?"

Jesus, he was glad Millie Stanhouse wasn't there to hear *that. That* being the sound of his voice. Screaming and holding back at the same time, he'd squeaked. Squeaked like a gerbil, in a way that was more startling than the sudden slamming of a door *(What door?)* somewhere inside the empty school.

He had almost reached the end of the hall and the main staircase. Now he stood stiffly, listening.

Could it really have been a door? If someone had slammed a door in here, there ought to be echoes of it running up and down the halls, like ripples on the surface of a quiet pond.

There weren't any.

He didn't feel too good about this, not at all. Had someone sneaked into the building while he was absorbed in his paperwork? It could be; he might not have noticed. Maybe somebody looking for something to steal. It happened. Only two years ago, thieves broke into the high school and carried off a dozen electric typewriters. You could find a lot of fenceable material in a schoolhouse these days. Personal computers, TV sets. Not that Victory School had any—but a passing thief from outside the community wouldn't know that.

The hairs on the nape of his neck began to twitch. He looked at his arms and saw gooseflesh. He felt like he'd just scuffed his way across a carpet on a rainy day, and knew he'd get a shock if he touched a metal doorknob.

He heard footsteps. They seemed to be coming from no direction in particular, neither approaching the stairs at his feet nor moving away from them. Just a couple of shoes clumping down the hall somewhere, just out of sight. A sound you heard a thousand times a day during the week, when the building was full of children and staff. Clop, clop.

Oh, shit, oh, shit ... it's starting again. Frozen where he stood, he recalled the last time he'd thought he'd heard something, the time he'd poked his nose into the janitor's closet and seen a shrunken phantom of himself. He thought of the first time, too: that incident—real or imagined—Dr. Lauther had dredged from the deepest part of his mind with hypnosis. *Oh, shit ...* Where was Dr. Lauther *now?*

Abruptly the clatter of footsteps ceased, as though someone walking down the hall had stopped in his tracks and decided to stand still. The sound was simply cut off. It did not resonate.

It was some punk looking to vandalize the school, some thief looking to make an easy score.

His heart raced like a poorly tuned engine.

The janitor's closet. All he had to do was go down the stairs and hang a left at the boys' room, and he'd be right there. Open the door and step inside....

Virgil cleared his throat, assured himself that he would sound like an adult male human being this time, and called out his challenge.

"Whoever you are—I've heard you, I know you're there! Come up to the office and identify yourself now! I'll call the police if you don't."

His voice boomed in the hollow corridors. Jesus, it made him sound like Pavarotti. The echoes filled the building, then gradually died away. He stood and waited for an answer.

Behind him, a shrill cry rang out. He wheeled around and saw nothing.

Behind him again, from down at the foot of the stairs, came a voice: "Mr. Bradley, I presume?"

5

Dad would have to promise to keep it to himself. If he did, Ned would tell him. If he didn't, no deal, Ned reasoned as he walked to school after his late breakfast. Dad had to know about something as serious as this: he had to be made to understand just how far off the deep end Dudak had gone. But he had to make sure it would never get out that Ned told him. Shit, maybe he could call Bob Diehl into his office Monday morning and scare *him* into telling. Then Ned would be in the clear. Diehl was chicken-shit, he'd probably fink on Dudak if Dad got him alone.

Ned approached the school by way of River Street, which ran past the front of the building. There was a green lawn with hedges out in front of the school, with the flagpole in the middle of it and a couple of tall old spruce trees. Off to one side of the building was the teachers' parking lot; to the other side, the new wing.

From a distance the lawn and the spruce trees made the place look kind of nice, but they lost their power to do that when you got up close. Once you were on school grounds, you could see that the white trim around the windows was dirty, the paint was peeling, the brick facade was darkly stained and weathered, cuss-words had been carved into the front doors, and there were cracks in the concrete steps. It really was a raunchy old building, Ned thought. Under the heavy gray clouds that were beginning to choke the sky, it almost looked like the setting for a horror movie. Something about a haunted schoolhouse.

That made him think of the ghost in the boys' room, and he shivered under his jacket. *The sooner they close this stinkin'*

222

place, the better, he thought. He hoped they tore the sucker down.

With Dad working in there alone, only one door would be open. It was sure to be the boys' door, since that was closest to the office. Ned tried it and found it unlocked.

Sure is dark in there. Dad was saving on electricity again. Only his office was lit, probably. Ned went inside and up the stairs down which he'd fled from Rizzo and his friends just hours ago.

"How's it goin', fuckstick?"

Ned was halfway up the stairs. He hadn't seen anybody come out onto the landing above him; but when he saw who was there now, he stopped like he'd run into a wall.

For half a second he didn't know who the hell it was. All he saw was a pair of fell eyes gleaming through two slits in a crusted monster-mask of dirt and dried blood, and a filthy red grin with a few white teeth in it. Blood had dried in the speaker's hair, leaving it standing up in spikes like a punk haircut. The nose was smashed nearly flat.

Even the outline of the face was distorted, as if it were part of a badly focused frame in a movie, or as if the head were made of clay, and its maker had squeezed it out of shape. Around the eyes and lips, it was swollen out of recognition.

But he recognized Dudak by his clothes.

The fourth-grader had a knife. He held it out in front and beckoned to Ned with both hands.

"Come on up, shit-hole! Come on up and see what I got for ya!"

Ned forgot all about his dad, who should have been sitting in his office just beyond the fire doors above. He didn't know what had happened to Mike, but whatever it was, it had pushed him clean over the edge. He had no doubt whatsoever that the crazy little shit would try to kill him if he got close enough.

"Or come on down here, if that's what you want!"

Ned turned and yelped. Only his panicked grip on the bannister kept him from falling.

Mike was down *there*, too, at the bottom of the stairs, beckoning for him to come down. Ned shot a glance over his shoulder.

There were two Mike Dudaks, identical in every way. They both had knives, and he was trapped between them on the stairs.

6

Virgil's skin tried to creep away without him.

He stood at the head of the stairs, rooted there because his thoughts had fallen into bedlam.

Up the stairs, one step at a time, straight at him, came Eric Hargrove.

There was no mistaking him. He was exactly as he looked in his portrait, down to the gold stud on his brown tie and right-to-left parting of his thinning pale hair. Perhaps the portrait, despite its age and less than optimal condition, was a tad more colorful. This Dr. Hargrove, the one who loomed in front of Virgil as solid and three-dimensional as his mother's old Frigidaire, seemed faded, like old drapery that had hung in the sun too long. He was like an image on a color TV set that needed its tint dial readjusted. But he was *there*, right there on the main staircase, which had been as deserted as Troy a second ago.

"After all this time, Mr. Bradley, I'm so happy we can have this chance to meet. I've been looking forward to it. I feel as though we're already close friends."

Virgil moved his jaws and something that sounded like *ubba-dubba* came out. His brain was screaming. *No! No! This isn't real! You're dead! I can't be seeing this!* He tried to remember his psychiatrist's advice, but all he had was a chaos of meaningless noise.

"Mr. Bradley—may I call you Virgil?"

Hargrove's voice was as dry and lifeless as a snake's shed skin, and it seemed to be coming from speakers planted randomly around the hall. Maybe Virgil was hearing it inside his head. He didn't know. Suddenly he wasn't tracking well at all.

Behind him, someone screamed. He didn't dare turn to see who it might be.

I've got to get out. I've got to get away.

He backed up. Now he was only a step away from the fire doors that separated the second floor hallway from the stairs that led down to the girls' entrance. But that was locked, the chain was on, it'd take him too long to find the key and stick it into the padlock. . . .

He would have to retreat all the way back down the hall and take the stairs down to the boys' door.

"That's right, Virgil—the stairs. Let's have a little run down the stairs together, shall we? Race each other to the bottom, like children. You've got a little head start on me, but that's all right . . . run. I'll be right behind you."

It came to Virgil that Hargrove had died in a fall down the stairs. With whom had *he* been racing? All the stairs inside Victory School were worn down in the middle, by generations of children marching up and down. *Easy to fall and break your neck on stairs like that.*

He continued to back away. Hargrove had come all the way up the main stairs now and was following him down the hall, a sere grin on his pallid face.

Virgil retreated down the hall. He reached out and felt the fire doors at the boys' stairs. He pushed through them and was on the landing. *Walk, don't run, down the nearest stairs! Walk right out of the building.* All he had to do was cling to the rail, just take it slow: refuse to be stampeded. He took the first steps downward.

Hargrove pushed the doors in. They came to a complete stop just before they touched the walls and didn't swing back, in

225

defiance of all the rules of gravity and momentum—like a chair swing, after a hearty push, freezing to a dead stop at the highest limit of its arc. Not possible.

Hargrove paused at the top of the stairs, smiling down at Virgil. Blood began to seep from his ears. It was almost black— by far the most vivid thing about him. It dripped in dark, dime-sized blotches onto the shoulders of his nearly colorless tan suit.

Virgil groaned, turned, and fled down the stairs without even running his hand along the rail.

At the first landing, he threw himself forward through the fire doors, into the vestibule at the boys' entrance. He hit the bar full-speed and burst into the safety of the open air.

And tripped headlong over the body of his son.

Chapter Twenty-Six

1

Mike ran up the basement corridor, screaming in wordless frustration because Bradley had escaped him.

He hardly hurt anymore. Just a little. Twelve hours ago, he never would have thought it possible he could ever run again—and now he ran full tilt, with just the merest twinges of pain to remind him that he still had a body.

Two bodies now! He didn't even know which was the right one: you couldn't tell them apart. All he knew was that one of them was going to go on and on forever.

Meanwhile, he ran, and a crowd ran with him. He ran effortlessly; he felt like a leaf swept up by the wind. His double ran beside him and did everything he did. A mob of still barely seen phantoms hustled him up the hall, carrying him along. He couldn't have stopped if he'd wanted to.

He'd tried to chase Bradley when the no-balls coward ran out the door, but he couldn't force himself to venture out of the safety of the school. He was part of *this* now, he couldn't go out there.

He felt like he was *plugged in* to the school, like an electrical appliance plugged into the wall. All the power was here. He was conscious of a source—an energy that existed apart from himself and all these others, yet fed them, powered them, and without which neither he nor they could long endure. It wasn't part of them, but they were part of *it*. And it permeated the schoolhouse. He could almost taste it in the air as he ran up and down the halls, up and down the stairs.

The old principal ran beside him, touched his shoulder. Now he could almost feel it. Soon he would.

"Feel it, Michael! This is your new life, the life you'll share with all of us. The life that lasts forever!"

Mike laughed, exulting in his new freedom from pain and weariness, hunger and thirst. He felt it, all right.

The hall was thronged, and he laughed again because finally he could see the phantoms clearly. Men, women, children. They wore strange clothes, historical stuff; it was like being at a neverending Halloween party.

"I feel it!" he screamed. *"I feel it!"*

2

"Aw, shit, Dad!"

It dawned on Virgil that his son wasn't dead. He'd fallen over him, probably knocked the wind out of him, but he wasn't dead.

But I damn near bought it there. In charging out through the boys' doors, Virgil had lost his balance and pitched forward. If he hadn't fallen over Ned, he'd have surely fallen on the porch steps and cracked his head open on the concrete sidewalk. It would have been a much worse fall than the one the boy had given him.

They were both exclaiming at once.

"Ned, what are you—"

"Let me up, Dad, damn it—"

"Are you all right—"

"We gotta get outta here!"

Ned thrashed. Virgil forgot his own panic as he tackled his son, restraining him. Ned fought him.

"Lemme go, lemme go, shiiit—!"

Ned got loose. Virgil was too shaken up from his fall to hold him. Ned actually ran a step or two before he stopped abruptly and turned around, staring at the doors.

"Ned, hold on a minute—"

"Damn it, Dudak's in there!" Ned pointed at the entrance. "He's got a knife, he was gonna kill me—Jesus Christ, Dad, *there was two of him!"*

Virgil got up gingerly, amazed his legs still held him. The fall had knocked the panic out of his system, leaving sheer confusion in its place. The confrontation with Dr. Hargrove was already like a fading dream. Simply too bizarre to be real. *But I was awake, wasn't I? I didn't dream it. I couldn't have dreamed it.*

And what was the matter with Ned?

"You say Mike Dudak is inside the school? With a knife?"

"Yes!"

Virgil squatted down in front of Ned and took him by the arms above the elbows. Ned didn't even look at him; he remained staring at the doors.

"Son, calm down. Get ahold of yourself. Tell me what happened."

For another second or two, Ned behaved as if Virgil weren't there; then, suddenly, he grabbed his father by the lapels of his shirt.

"Dad! You came out that door like a bat out of hell! Did you see him? *Did you see him?"* Ned shook him. He didn't stop until Virgil hugged him and patted his back.

So tell him! Tell your son you saw a ghost, buckaroo. Dr. Hargrove, as I live and breathe. Tell him you were chased out of the building by a man who died over thirty years ago. See how that goes down, eh? Virgil let Ned go and stood up, pain shooting

229

through his right knee as he straightened the leg. He didn't know what to say.

Ned started to cry.

"Shit, Dad, the school is haunted, there's a ghost in it. I saw it, and I saw some other thing, some ugly, wormy pink thing . . ." He broke down, unable to continue.

Virgil picked him up, still crying, and carried him around the corner of the building to the teachers' parking lot, where the school no longer blocked what little sunlight remained in the sky. He wished there were a place to sit; but there was no way he was going to go back inside the building just to sit down. Not even on the steps.

He held Ned until the boy stopped crying, then put him down. Ned dried his eyes with the sleeve of his jacket.

"It's all right, kiddo."

"It's not all right. I was gonna tell you, Dad. Honest, I was comin' here to tell you. . . ."

"You can tell me now. What is it?"

"Oh, man . . . cryin' like a baby. That's gross."

"There was nobody here but me," Virgil reassured him. "Nobody saw you."

Ned stopped sniffling. Although not ashamed of him for crying, Virgil was proud of the way he tried to reassert his dignity. *He's going to grow up to be either a good man or a successful politician.*

"Dad . . . did you see Dudak?"

The question struck Virgil as possessing the quality of an induction, like a riddle posed to an Arthurian knight at the beginning of a story. If he answered it, it was going to take him someplace where he was pretty sure he didn't want to go.

But he also had a feeling that he was going to go there anyway, whether he wanted to or not.

Virgil hadn't thought about the temperature when he ran out of the school without his jacket. Now that he'd heard Ned's story, however, he felt deeply and thoroughly chilled.

"Well? You don't believe me, do ya?"

But he did. He didn't need to dope it out logically, argue it pro and con. He believed because the truth of it hit him like a draught of cold air. He didn't understand half of what Ned told him, but he believed it all.

"Son, I believe every word of it. I don't get it, but I believe it." He had to. He saw a ghost. He saw two of the same person at the same time—and it was him. And he saw a long pink tentacle. Saw a hell of a lot more of it than Ned did.

What had Dr. Lauther said? Something awful happened to him when he was nine years old, and he unconsciously recast it as a fantastic nightmare? Is that what he did? Great. Fine.

Only tell me this, Doc.

What in the holy hell is my son doing in the same nightmare?

"We have to call the police," Virgil said. "They'll have to get Dudak out of there. Can't leave him hiding in the building."

"Are you all right, Dad? You look like you're gonna be sick."

"I'm fine, Ned. Look, I'm going to go across the street, right there, to Mr. Thompson's house and call the cops. You keep an eye out, okay? From a safe distance. I'm just going to use the phone, then I'll come right back out. You watch the boys' doors. If Mike tries to sneak out, that's the only way out."

Ned agreed to watch the entrance—from the other side of River Street. Bill Thompson, who lived just across the street from the school, belonged to the PTA and had a daughter in Ned's class, was surprised to see Virgil, but didn't put up a fight about letting him use the phone. "There's a problem in the building," Virgil explained.

When he got through to police headquarters, he kept it short and simple. All they needed to know was that there was a boy with a knife hiding in the building.

The dispatcher put him right through to a detective who was glad to get the news.

231

"We've been looking for that kid, Mr. Bradley. Seems he went out last night and didn't come home. Sit tight, we'll be over in a jiffy."

3

Two patrol cars showed up, followed by the detective in an unmarked car. Four patrolmen went into the building while the detective stood outside with Ned and Virgil, asking questions. Virgil told him about the party last night, but didn't volunteer anything more.

"Well, there were some lively goings-on here," said the detective. "Officer Rizzo's kid was involved. Him, this Dudak kid, and another boy went outside before the movie was over, and Rizzo and Dudak got into a fight. Johnny beat the hell out of Dudak, beat him up so bad that the third kid got scared and ran home. When Dudak didn't come home and his mother called the third boy's house to see if he was there, the kid broke down and told his folks what happened. But by the time we were called, the Dudak boy was nowhere to be found. We've been looking all over town for him since last night."

4

Mike still couldn't follow the others into any of the locked rooms. His new body could, but he had to remain outside in the hall.

Watching himself pass through a solid wooden door like it wasn't even there made Mike feel there were great things in store for him. Soon he'd have only one body again, and it'd be that one—the magical body that couldn't be stopped by doors and locks. In mad ecstasy he howled and pounded on the door.

He stopped when he suddenly noticed he was alone. Even his new self was gone.

"There he is. Hey, over here!"

A cop?

Mike's perspective had been altered. He stared at the approaching policeman without comprehension, as if the man were a dragon creeping up on him. He didn't know what to do.

"Take it easy, kid, everything's gonna be all right. We gotta get you to a doctor."

A second cop appeared behind the first. They were coming on slowly, like they thought Mike might be dangerous. He still didn't know what to do, though.

The old principal told him. He heard the voice inside his head, clear as a bell. As he listened and began to understand the meaning of his instructions, he began to smile.

(You're one of us now, Michael. They can't do anything to you. Don't be afraid. But you can hurt them. . . .)

So it was all coming true. His new self was just about ready. What happened to his old self didn't hardly matter anymore.

Raising the knife, screaming and laughing at the same time, and spraying blood from his nose, Mike attacked the cops.

Officer Boggs, unable to believe what he was seeing, waited a bit too long to get out of the way.

Jesus, the kid was so little . . . and his face! Holy God, another kid did that to him? Rizzo's kid did that?

Boggs had never seen a child's face so badly battered, not even in pictures. The kid's whole chest was a bib of blood, some of it shiny and fresh. He had trouble believing the boy was actually alive.

Then the kid's berserk shriek and sudden burst of movement froze Boggs in his tracks; and before he knew it, there was a fucking knife slicing into his left thigh. He didn't even feel it, just yet, but he sure as hell saw it. It was like he was seeing it on a movie screen: the knife-blade coming down, the momentary glimpse of white skin as his uniform pants tore, and then the incredible gushing-forth of bright red blood.

That was when he almost fainted just from the sight of it; but some self-preserving reflex enabled him to grab the boy's skinny wrist before the knife came down again. And that was when the pain hit and Boggs screamed.

He was still screaming when Officer McGovern grabbed the kid from behind and pulled him off him. The kid was screaming, too, and McGovern was yelling, and somewhere not far away, the other two policemen in the building, Barnes and Shamsky, were yelling, too. Somehow Boggs heard the knife clatter when it fell to the linoleum floor. Boggs was falling, too, but he was out before he hit the floor.

5

"Officer down!"

A patrolman burst through the door.

"It's Harry!" he cried. "The kid cut him real bad. Got him in the leg. Sarge, he's bleedin' like a stuck pig!"

"Get an ambulance," the detective said. The officer threw himself into one of the patrol cars and seized the radio.

A second cop came out, dragging, by the wrists, a wildly struggling creature that Virgil at first had trouble recognizing as a boy. Ned jumped and clung to his father's arm.

Sweet Christ! Virgil wondered. *What is this?*

The boy screamed and thrashed as though he were willing to lose his hands at the wrists if that would get him out of the policeman's grasp. Virgil wouldn't have known him in a hundred years. The boy was the right size for Mike Dudak, but there the similarity ended.

"I got him! I got him!" the policeman cried.

He dragged Mike through the doorway and down the steps. The detective moved to lend a hand; but the moment Mike's feet touched the sidewalk, his struggles ceased instantly, and he went totally limp. Virgil was sure he'd died.

234

"Shit!" the detective said.

The patrolman laid Mike on the grass and knelt over him. "He's alive, Sarge, but I think he's in shock."

"What about Boggs?"

"Fainted. Matt's trying to put a tourniquet on, but we sure as hell are gonna need an ambulance."

"We got one on the way," said the detective, having gotten the thumbs-up from the cop in the patrol car. He knelt down for a closer look at Mike, and shook his head. "Jesus!" he said. "What a fucking mess. Rizzo's kid's in real trouble this time!"

6

Virgil and Ned gave the detective terse statements while the Rescue Squad did its thing. When the ambulance had departed with Mike and the wounded policeman strapped to stretchers inside, the detective concluded his questioning for the time being, sent his two squad cars back to headquarters, and followed them in the unmarked car, leaving Virgil to secure the building. This he did as quickly as possible while Ned waited for him outside.

"Let's go home, Ned."

"Dad, you never told me. What made you come running out of the school like that? If you didn't see Dudak, why were you so scared?"

Even now, Virgil wanted to shelter his son. But how could he? What could he say that would be any more traumatic than what Ned had just seen?

"Let's walk, Ned. I'm too cold to be standing around here any longer." He offered his hand and Ned took it.

Not lingering on details, but not skipping them, either, he told his son the whole thing as they walked home. He didn't want to, but he had to. He started with his recent hallucination (if it *was* a hallucination; he couldn't be sure of that anymore)

235

in the janitor's closet and finished with his meeting with Dr. Hargrove at the main stairs.

It sounded like a bad LSD trip, but Ned believed him.

"Jesus, Dad ..."

Virgil drummed up a watery, defeated smile. "Pretty crazy, ain't it, kid?"

Ned stopped. "Dad, Miss Davis ... it happened to *her,* too—didn't it? Just like us."

"You know about Miss Davis?"

"I heard you tell Mom. I wasn't eavesdropping, I just—"

"It's all right, Ned. Yes, Miss Davis, too."

"The school is *haunted,* Dad! Oh, man, we got a *haunted school!*"

Virgil hated the sound of that. But he was right. What else could you possibly call it? And by God, it had been haunted from Day One! That's why all those teachers went to pot. The place was haunted—corrupted, polluted, tainted, *whatever*—when he was nine years old, and it was haunted before that, too: in the days of Dr. Hargrove, who was *still here.* Still pounding his beat in the halls. *For God's sake, I'm haunting it. . . !*

How a ghost of himself at nine years old—shrunken, distorted, but nevertheless a recognizable facsimile—could be haunting the school, while he occupied the office of principal at forty, Virgil was hardly willing to conjecture. But it was true.

Ned tugged on his hand.

"Dad, you gotta have it exorcised!"

"Thus speaks the true horror-movie buff. Come on, Ned—what do you think Mr. Frye would say if I went up to him after services tomorrow and asked him to stop over and exorcise my school?"

Mr. Frye was the pastor at Our Redeemer, the Lutheran church attended by the Bradleys. Virgil would no more think of asking him to perform an exorcism than he would think of asking him to referee a ladies' mud-wrestling match.

"Ask the priest, then!" Ned said. "The priest at the Catholic church. They must have one."

"Father Stokowski would think I was crazy, son."

"We gotta do *something!*"

Virgil felt helpless. "I can't think of what. Give me a break, Ned. Until today, I thought it was all in my head. That's why I went to see a psychiatrist. Now I've got to rethink everything."

Well, at least Dad believed him. That was better than nothing, Ned guessed.

He didn't see how Dad could take any time to *rethink* everything, though—not when *he'd* seen a ghost, too.

And it was more than just ghosts. What about that other thing, the thing that looked like a gigantic worm? The thing Ned saw in the library annex; the thing that grabbed Dad when he was a little kid and stuck its stinger up his nose. That was no ghost. And it lived in the school.

But Dad didn't even want to *talk* about that. Not now, he said. He'd had enough for one day.

What did he want to do, though? Sit around *thinking* about it until it grabbed someone else? Wait for someone else to see the ghosts and go crackers, like Miss Davis?

They were almost home. Home was just around the corner. Overhead, the sky was blackening. In another minute or two, it'd be raining cats and dogs. You could feel it.

"I want you to do something for me, Ned," Dad said.

"What?"

"Don't say anything about this to your mother, will you? Give me some time to think it over. Then *I'll* tell her. Okay?"

"Dad, Dudak—"

"Mike's being taken care of, Ned. He won't be going after anybody else. And he was dangerous, a lot more dangerous than any ghosts. Let's be thankful we've got that problem out of the way."

Ned could have kicked his father in the shins, but he held back. The old man just wasn't taking it very well. Being chased by a ghost ... well, it just seemed to have taken an awful lot out of him. You couldn't blame him for that.

"All right," Ned said. "I won't tell Mom what happened to us today. What we saw. But Jesus, Dad, you can't just do *nothin'!* God, there's some kind of *monster* in that school! We both *saw* it! And the ghosts, too. We gotta think of somethin'."

Dad sighed. "I'm *thinking,* Ned. I'm thinking!"

"Just don't think too long, man. That's how the monsters get you."

Dad groaned and said, "Yeah, yeah, I know—that's the way it happens in the movies all the time!"

The rain came, then, and they had to run the rest of the way home.

Chapter Twenty-Seven

1

"There were hardly any Indians here when the first settlers came," Carrie said, over the supper table. "If it rained like this back then, it's no wonder."

It was like living in a house built under a waterfall, she thought. This was supposed to go on all weekend.

"I'm sorry, hon—what'd you say?" Virgil made an apologetic gesture with his fork. "The rain kind of sent me off woolgathering."

"I was just telling you what John told me today," Carrie said. "He wanted to take the history of the school property all the way back to the Indians, only there were no Indians. There was hardly a soul in the valley when the white man found it."

Normally Virgil was interested in something like that. He didn't seem himself this evening, Carrie thought. *Working too hard lately.* And this hadn't been exactly a red-letter week for him.

But it could be just the weather. Even Ned was down: they'd heard hardly a peep out of him since they sat down to eat.

"John says it's funny about the Indians," she kept trying.

Virgil *might* talk, and Ned ought to find this interesting. "The Tianoga valley was settled pretty fast. The land was great for farming, the water was sweet, and the hunting and fishing was excellent. All the oldest reports say so, according to John—and he met with the county historian the other day. It really struck the settlers as strange that there were no Indians living here. There were Indians all *around* the valley."

She was gratified when Virgil responded: "But not *in* the valley?"

"Nope. And there seems to have been a reason for it."

"Are you going to tell me, or make me guess?"

"You don't want to try?"

"I'm too worn-out to guess. Just tell me. I want to know."

Carrie felt like a singer who'd lost her audience before she'd finished her song.

"Well ... the county historian thinks a meteor fell here. There was some kind of Indian legend about a false sun that fell out of the sky and landed in the valley, and that's why the Indians were afraid to live there. At least that's what they told the settlers."

2

They played a little poker after supper, family poker that used just chips instead of money. "You might as well learn poker early in life," Dad always used to say, although he didn't bother saying it tonight. "You'll need these skills when you're at college and you run out of spending money." To which Mom would always reply, "If you don't gamble, you won't run out of money."

They played for a while; then Mom and Dad decided to watch a movie on TV about two jerks falling in love, and Ned drifted off to his room.

He closed the door on the movie dialogue and listened to the rain.

How could his father sit there and watch a freakin' movie?

Dad thought their worries about Dudak were over when they took him away in the ambulance. *Doesn't he listen?* There were two identical Mike Dudaks in the school; Ned had seen them both at the same time; and when he tried to get away, the one at the bottom of the stairs hadn't been able to stop him. Hadn't even slowed him down. You didn't have to be Sherlock Holmes to figure out that *that* Dudak was a ghost. Ned had never heard of a ghost of someone who was still alive, but now he'd seen it, so he wasn't going to argue about it. And it was still in the school. *Waiting for me to come back on Monday.*

Ned wasn't particularly worried about sitting in a classroom with twenty-five other kids and a teacher. It was the thought of being *alone*—anywhere in the building, for any amount of time—that gave him the willies. And Dad thought he was going to go back and sit alone in that office of his, with Whatsisname's picture on the wall? Was he nuts?

Dad had made it perfectly clear to Ned that there was a curse on that spot of ground where Victory School stood—even though, apparently, he hadn't made it clear to himself at all. But what else would you call it? All those bad things happening to kids and teachers, from way back when the school started; and even worse before that, before there was a school—if that wasn't proof of a curse, what was? Shit, even the Indians stayed away from here. They must've figured it out.

Ned went to bed, and dreamed of being chased by doubles and triples of Mike Dudak, all with knives, down empty corridors that never ended.

The sentience took notice of the rain.

It was seeping into the ground in unprecedented quantity, where it was absorbed by a network of fine, fibrous rootlets that carrried it, molecule by molecule, to the body from whose existence the sentience was virtually independent. But at times like this, the sentience was forced to respond to gross physical stimuli.

It willed the rootlets shut. Too much water would unbalance its metabolism.

There was another problem posed by the water, but the sentience was not equipped to deal with it. It was aware of it, but that was all.

Over the years, the sentience had grown into the artificial structure raised by the prey organisms and thronged by them at predictable intervals. In a way it had become the building. Its sensory tissues permeated the structure top to bottom: not a step was taken, not a word spoken, but the sentience was aware of it. And larger organs, of use in physically subduing the prey, and evaluating the energy patterns of individual prey organisms, threaded their way through a maze of plumbing and heating pipes, electrical wiring systems, and small vacancies created by neglect or decay.

And so the sentience knew that the structure was losing stability. Was that why the prey was preparing to abandon it? But the sentience could not evaluate the more abstract patterns of the prey's brain activity. It could only note that this latest accumulation of water under the foundations was weakening the structure at key points.

It took no notice of the phantoms that pranced and gibbered in the deserted halls. These had no mass, so their prancing failed to register with its pressure sensors. Their cries and babblings did not produce any physical vibrations in the air, so these failed to register on its sound sensors. They were only *waste energy generated by the sentience's consumption of the prey, and its energy sensors had long since learned to screen them out.*

But it kept its sensors trained nevertheless. It had recently captured one organism outside the building's regular hours of occupation, and it was hungry enough to lie in wait for more.

Chapter Twenty-Eight

1

In spite of the rain, which as yet showed no sign of letting up, the Bradleys went to church on Sunday morning, Ned going to Sunday school while his parents attended services.

The pews were half-empty. The incessant drumming of the rain seemed to cut the church off from the rest of the world, making some of the worshippers feel like the last men and women on earth. There were few enough of them to make the opening hymns sound thin and watery; the choir, too, had its share of absences this morning. When he stood behind the pulpit and looked over his sparse congregation, Mr. Frye looked like he had half a mind to send everybody home. But he refrained from making any remarks about fair-weather Christians, and the services proceeded as usual.

Virgil prayed for guidance, hardly hearing the pastoral prayer that rumbled from the pulpit. *What am I going to do? Please, Lord, tell me!*

He received no inspiration. Here, in the familiar church he'd attended since his childhood, the bizarre experiences of yesterday were neutered by a sense of utter unreality, rendered dreamlike. But he knew they would be real again the moment he walked out the church door, like bailiffs waiting to seize a fugitive who'd claimed sanctuary.

Maybe, for the time being, it was enough to feel there was a sanctuary.

2

Charlie tried to run, but he only made it once around the block before he gave it up. Getting fit didn't include drowning.

But he couldn't just sit around his apartment all day long. *Gotta burn off calories.* What he wanted to do was to dry off and go back to bed; he felt like he could sleep all day, right around the clock to Monday morning.

Instead, he went out and shopped for an exercise bike. *That* he could do if it rained till Christmas.

3

It seemed inevitable that Carrie would get wise and demand to know why he and Ned were moping around; but as Sunday wore on and she didn't, Virgil stopped worrying around it. Probably she put it down to the rain. The family watched the Jets game on the tube and didn't say much.

Meanwhile, all Virgil could think of doing about his problem was to advise the Board of Education that in his opinion Victory School was no longer structurally sound, and to recommend an early closing—at least a temporary one, while the borough's building inspectors made a thorough investigation.

He thought they might buy it. Everyone complained about the funny smells, and with all this rain, the place ought to smell funnier than ever. That ought to get the Board of Health interested.

It was awfully thin, however. The board already knew the building was in a state of less-than-optimal repair. He'd already reported the leaks, the drafts, the patches of rotting wood, the lights that sometimes didn't come on even after the janitors changed the bulbs. They weren't about to renovate a facility that was to be abandoned in a few months. As long as there was no danger of the school falling down over its occupants' heads or suddenly bursting into flame, the board probably wouldn't want to hear about it.

Still, this rain just might do it. Maybe, when he came in the next morning, he'd find Cosmo Iacavella complaining about big chunks of plaster falling from the classroom ceilings. That might justify a temporary closing.

Carrie got up and looked out the window.

"You'd think it was never going to stop," she said. "Did you hear what Marge Hollis told me after church this morning? The river's rising. She says half the county park is flooded. I just hope our cellar doesn't spring a leak."

They'd had it sealed before adding wood paneling and a linoleum floor in the rec room half, but that had been a couple years ago and this was an unusually heavy rain.

"I'd better go have a look," said Virgil.

"You do that. And I might as well start supper."

Ned followed him down to the work shop, where Virgil poked around for any sign of water coming through the concrete walls, the cement floor. The room smelled damp, but it still looked pretty dry.

"Well?" Ned said. "You figured out what to do yet?"

"Yeah: pray the rain washes away the building."

"*Dad!*"

Virgil shushed him. Overhead, he could hear his wife rattling around in the kitchen.

"I'm afraid to go back there, that's all," Ned said.

Virgil sighed and squeezed the boy's shoulder. "I know, son. And I don't blame you. So am I."

4

Diane couldn't wait any longer for the rain to stop.

It was boiling her brain, this constant drumming on the roof. Snapping at her husband wasn't helping any, either. She had to get out of the house, rain or no rain. After supper, with it still coming down in sheets, she went to the kitchen and sharpened a six-inch utility knife. She put it in her purse, put on her coat, and went outside.

Just climbing into the car, she was soaked through her coat and clothes. "Shit fuck!" she growled as she grappled with the door. It finally came open and she sloshed inside, feeling mad enough to bite the steering wheel.

The engine sputtered when she turned the key. "Cocksucker, motherfucker . . . !" It was going to fucking *die* on her, it was going to give up and die. Her knuckles turned white as she pinched the key and stamped furiously on the gas pedal. Then, with the perversity of machines, the engine turned over and the car was ready to roll.

She was going to Charlie's, that much she knew. Beyond that, she wasn't altogether clear. She'd temporarily forgotten having packed a knife in her purse.

Charlie lived in one of the new apartments way out on Harrison Street, out past the high school, on the edge of town. Diane had only been there once or twice, but she could have found it blindfolded.

He'd stood her up Friday night, the shit: gone out bar-hopping while those miserable little bastards at the school jumped up and down on her headache. He said he'd be there, but he wasn't.

She ground her teeth and pushed the car through the rain.

Even with the wipers on high speed, she could barely see past the hood. She could feel the wheels hydroplaning on the slick film of water between the tires and the road, but she didn't slow down. Her mind was shut to the risk of accident.

The thought of him coming into school the next morning, and hanging his coat in the faculty lounge like nothing had happened, while she could only watch and burn inside . . .

She cackled shrilly. "It's not going to be that way, Charlie!" she cried out loud. "It won't be the way you want it this time!"

Charlie pumped the pedals of the bike, oblivious to the way his efforts made things jump on the shelves around his living room, hearing nothing but the hammering of blood through the veins inside his head.

He'd set the bike to maximum resistance—in effect, he was toiling up a never-ending grade. The timer rang a minute ago, but he hadn't heard it.

Gotta hit the wall, gotta hit the wall and bust on through, gotta go, gotta go . . . His lungs felt like they were being dipped in acid, his legs were *this* close to falling off, and he was as drenched with sweat as if he'd been riding in the pouring rain— but he continued.

His headband, saturated with perspiration, had slipped down over one eye. He couldn't shake it clear, but he refused to stop to adjust it. Once he stopped, he knew he'd never be able to start again. His warmup suit clung wetly to his body.

All he could see in his mind's eye was the haggard, raddled, *aging* face he'd seen in the boys' room mirror a hundred years ago.

Or so it felt.

Diane stopped somewhere in the parking lot of the apartment building—she couldn't see whether she'd found a parking space or not, and didn't care—and got out of the car. The rain washed her hair into her eyes.

The parking lot was a shallow pond, ankle-deep. She waded through it, stepping onto the sidewalk with feet that were already going numb. She clutched her purse to her body with both hands, like a football, and nearly shrieked with the torment of the frigid raindrops machine-gunning her scalp.

It was a two-story, L-shaped building with a pale brick facing. Diane charged around the shorter leg to get at Charlie's back door. Her sodden pants wanted to fall down, but she willed them not to.

His drapes were drawn, but light showed through them: he was home, no doubt about it. Home and ready to die, whether he knew it or not.

She tried to turn the doorknob, but the door was locked. She made a fist and pounded on the door, not bothering with the bell. She hit it hard, feeling the shock all the way down to her toes, but no pain.

"Open up, you bastard! I know you're in there!"

Charlie didn't hear her. He wouldn't have heard a gun go off six inches from his ear. He wouldn't have seen the muzzle-flash, either. It would've been just another one of the many bright streaks of color that were shooting past his eyes.

He was dead from the waist down, but somehow his legs still moved, somehow he continued to pump the pedals. If he could have stepped aside and watched, he would have seen the bike's back wheel revolving with the slowness of a cement mixer winding down.

He'd busted through the wall, although he was no longer thinking about that. He wouldn't have felt a cat-o'-nine-tails laid across his back. His mind seemed to be drifting away from his body, drifting into a blank nirvana beyond weariness or pain. It was almost pleasant; but he was beyond pleasure, too.

Do you hear me? Let me in!

Diane's voice cracked. Her throat was on fire. In spite of the cold rain, she was burning, her blood was molten. She would have gladly torn her clothes off and thrown them aside, if she'd thought of it.

But she did think of the knife in her purse. She fumbled with the zipper, unable to feel it with her numb fingers, unable to see it for the rain in her eyes. She bit her tongue and drew blood.

The zipper suddenly tore open. She dropped the purse, spilling its contents on the sidewalk. Cursing, she went down to her hands and knees and felt around for the knife.

She had it. She lurched back to her feet and began to hack at the door. Splinters flew. She had to grip the slippery handle with both hands.

She gouged away at the door until the knife fell from her hands and was lost; she didn't have the strength to get back down and look for it. Sobbing and cursing, she fell against the door and beat on it with her palms, painlessly shredding them of the splinters.

"You fucking bastard, Charlie . . . you fucking bastard . . ."

Charlie didn't know when he'd stopped peddling, nor for how long he'd been sitting up there, slumped over the handlebars, without moving.

He wanted to get off, but his legs wouldn't budge. There was a pain in his lower back that was the equivalent of being struck there, over and over again, with a mallet. His head spun.

He didn't feel it when he hit the floor.

Her wallet, with a week's pay in it, lay on the sidewalk by Charlie's back door, where it had fallen from her purse; but Diane had forgotten it, and now, as she trudged numbly back to her car, it lay there still, along with the purse, the knife, and everything else.

Vaguely she realized she had a fever. All she wanted was to go home and collapse into bed. The thought of it kept her on her feet.

She found the car, somehow. She'd left the door ajar, and the seatcovers were drenched. It didn't register. She fell into the driver's seat and found the key still in the ignition. She was too crushed to appreciate the miracle of the engine starting the first time she turned the key.

She drove home, weaving from lane to lane. Since she had the road to herself in the storm, the quality of her driving hardly mattered.

Unceasingly, as if it were a mantra, she muttered repeatedly, *"Fucking bastard . . . fucking bastard . . ."*

Chapter Twenty-Nine

1

He knew this day was going to be a bitch, so Cosmo Iacavella was in no hurry to get it started. He added a wee drop of vodka to his first cup of coffee and wished he had a cigar.

No shit, he and Rudi would be tramping back and forth among the classrooms all day, mopping up leaks and spraying Pine-Sol to cover up unappetizing smells. You'd think a teacher could grab a couple of paper towels and wipe up a little puddle of rainwater from the floor; but they always sent for the janitors, no matter how trivial the cleaning job.

He wondered if he ought to add a drop of coffee to his vodka.

The boiler room door swung open, ending his privacy. Without looking up from the cup in his hand, he said, "You're late."

"Sorry, Mr. Iacavella. But I couldn't ride my bike across the playground! Have you seen it this morning?"

"No, Rudi. I gotta work, I ain't got time to stand around gawkin' at playgrounds."

Rudi began to unfasten the yellow slicker he wore on rainy days. It had finally stopped raining, but Mrs. Giddens had probably persuaded him to wear it just in case.

"I wasn't gawking, Mr. Iacavella. I was tryin' to get across. You should see it. Water all over! It's like the whole playground's one big gigantic puddle. And the school looks like an *island* in the middle of it! A magic island."

"Like Alcatraz."

"Well, I had to go back and go all the way 'round the block," Rudi said. "It ain't so wet on the front side of the building."

"I'm glad you had so much fun gettin' here, Rudi, 'cause we gotta get right to work. We gotta go up to the new wing and clean up a big mess somebody made for us on Saturday afternoon, right after we cleaned up the big mess they left for us in the gym. Get a bucket ready."

"Man, this is gross!" Rudi said as he plied the mop under Cosmo's expert supervision. "The guy bled all over the hall!"

"He sure did." Cosmo spotted another bloodstain on the wall and wiped it off.

"I could have told you, though—that Mike was a bad kid," Rudi said. "I knew he'd hurt somebody. I'm sure glad they caught him while he's small, before he grows up. I sure hope that poor policeman's gonna be all right."

"Mr. Bradley saw 'em take the cop away in the ambulance. Damn it, I wish he'd have called me when it happened, instead of waitin' till Sunday night." Cosmo sneezed, a real boomer, then shook his head. "Hurry it up, Rudi. I'll go ahead and unlock the classrooms."

Rudi had finished by the time Cosmo had made his round of the doors. Cosmo inspected the hall and couldn't find any bloodstains. Not surprising, he thought. *The lights in these hallways suck. You could go blind workin' here.*

He headed back to the boiler room, wondering what kind of cop lets himself get cut to the bone by a scrawny little fourth-grade kid. Maybe Tianoga needed tougher policemen. *Jesus, a teenager would'a killed the guy.*

He found Rudi staring down at the floor.

"Mr. Iacavella—did you see this?

"All these cracks." Rudi pointed. "Look!"

The surface of the boiler room floor was a webwork of cracks: most of them hairline-fine, but a few of them considerably wider. They showed up as pale lines on the dirty concrete surface.

"What about 'em?" Cosmo said. Actually, he hadn't noticed them. Then again, he wasn't in the habit of admiring the view of the boiler room floor.

"What about 'em?" Rudi cried. "The floor's fallin' apart!"

"It's just some little cracks in the concrete. All that rain we got this weekend, there must be a lot of water under the foundations. That'd make the building settle unevenly, Rudi. It never did settle right, anyway."

"If this is from water, how come there ain't no water on the floor?"

"Leaked out through the cracks, I guess."

"What're we gonna do, Mr. Iacavella? I'm worried—"

"Don't bother," Cosmo said. "The place ain't gonna fall apart on us just yet. If the cracks get worse, we'll just buy some fresh cement and fill 'em up."

But Rudi *did* worry. He didn't like the looks of this, not one little bit. If the building's foundation was moving around, wouldn't it eventually pull everything apart? Sure it would: like when you have a stack of boxes and you pulled out one of the boxes on the bottom. The whole darned thing fell down.

He knelt for a closer look.

"Poo! That smells bad! Can't you smell it, Mr. Iacavella?"

"With this cold? I couldn't smell an outhouse on a summer day if I was standin' in it."

Well, Mr. Iacavella was lucky he couldn't smell this, Rudi thought. *Wish I couldn't.* It reminded him of that aquarium full of tadpoles Mr. Ludovics had in his class a while ago: all the tadpoles died one weekend, because Mr. Ludovics had left

254

the tank on the windowsill and the sun killed 'em; and when Rudi opened the classroom the following Monday morning, all the pollywogs were floating on their backs, puffed up like marshmallows, making an unforgettable stink. That's what *this* smelled like.

He wondered how deep the cracks went, but he sure as heck wasn't going to stick his fingers in to find out. Not for a million bucks. The ones that were wide enough to admit his fingers looked like they'd snap shut as soon as he reached inside. Anyhow, he didn't really *want* to know how deep they were.

There were a lot of things about this school that you didn't really want to know, he thought.

2

Virgil sat at his desk, not knowing what to do, wishing he could get rid of Dr. Hargrove's portrait without anybody asking why. But he didn't even dare to turn its face to the wall.

Millie Stanhouse came in to give him the daily disabled list report. The term failed to amuse him this morning.

"Are you all right, Mr. Bradley? You mustn't let things get to you." She already knew about Mike Dudak and the wounded cop. How, he had no idea. He hadn't told her.

"It made for a hard weekend, Miss Stanhouse."

"Of course it did. And all that rain didn't help, either. Mrs. Phelps is in the hospital with pneumonia."

Virgil felt like saying *Aw, shit*, but contented himself with, "What?"

"Her husband called. He had to rush her over last night with a hundred-and-three-degree fever. Apparently she went out for some reason and got a real soaking, plus a bad chill. Mrs. Rasky will be in to sub for her."

Phelps was his senior teacher—it didn't seem fair. "I hope she pulls out of it soon," he said.

"I'm sure they'll fix her up just fine."

Virgil sighed. Millie continued.

"Joey Wilmot's home taking it easy. She won't come back until they take the stitches out of her mouth. I thought she sounded pretty good over the phone, all things considered. She said she's sure somebody booby-trapped her apple while it was still in the store, she doesn't think it was any of the kids in her class—or in this school, for that matter."

"When are the stitches supposed to come out?"

"The end of the week, she said."

At least she seemed to be healing quickly. Virgil nodded. Joanne was an upbeat little woman, and the school needed her.

"Brace yourself for this, though," Millie said. "Doreen Davis called. They let her out of the hospital yesterday, but she's still on a sedative. I tried to get her to talk to you, but she refused. She says she's going to resign, you'll be getting her letter soon. I think she means it. She still sounded pretty rattled to me."

"I'm not surprised," Virgil said. "And I can't say that I blame her. Thank you, Miss Stanhouse."

"You try to take it easy today, Mr. Bradley."

Maybe he ought to phone Doreen, he thought.

Hi, Doreen! Hey, you know those ghosts you thought you saw? Well, cheer up, they were real. You weren't having a hallucination. How do I know? Well, just the other day, I saw one, too! And my kid saw another one. Turns out the place is lousy with 'em.

Oh, yeah—that ought to bring her back to work on the double.

Maybe it'd be kinder to let her think she'd had a hallucination. It might be easier to get over that.

What in God's name am I supposed to do?

Mr. Hall looked like he was going to drop dead any minute, Ned thought.

All the kids noticed, but none of them dared to ask their teacher how he was feeling. He also looked like he'd knock the head off the first kid who opened his mouth. It made for a very quiet classroom that morning.

Maybe he had dropped dead, Ned thought. With the kind of stuff that was going on inside this school these days, Ned kind of scared himself with that one. Maybe he'd open his mouth and *worms* would fall out. He'd try to write something on the blackboard and his hand would fall off at the wrist.

Stop it! Cut it out! No wonder Mom and Dad say you watch too many horror movies.

From the next desk, Phil flipped him a crumpled wad of paper. Ned opened it up and read the note.

Now he knows how we feel when we have to listen to those stupid jokes of his.

Ned made a face and stuck the note in his desk. If he knew Phil, the little jerk was probably hoping Hall would keel over right now so he could get his Uzi water gun back. He wondered if Phil had heard about Dudak yet. They'd had rides to school this morning, he hadn't had a chance to tell him about it.

Wanna try to tell him you saw two *Dudaks?*

Not much, Ned thought.

"There's some exercises I want you to do in your English books before boys' gym this morning," Mr. Hall said—or croaked. His voice was wheezy, and Ned didn't know how they could hear him at the back of the room.

Boy oh boy, he looked like dog meat today. The tan seemed to be washing off his face; but worse than that, the whole face seemed to be sliding off the bones, like it was melting. Ned had never seen such saggy cheeks, except on a few of the really old people who went to Our Redeemer. And you'd swear Mr. Hall was using makeup now, like a lady. Miss Poretti's face some-times looked *sort of* like that, and Ned had heard his dad gripe about her using too much makeup. What would he think when he saw Mr. Hall today?

4

He kept them busy doing textbook work, then took the boys to the gym, the girls to art.

"Man, is he a mess!" Phil said when Mr. Hall left them at the gym. But before Ned could answer, Mr. Reimann started yelling at them to hurry up and get in line, he didn't have all day.

"Ground's too wet to run laps around the playground," Mr. Reimann said, "so it'll be calisthenics indoors today."

"Can we play kickball, Mr. Reimann?" somebody asked.

"'Can we play kickball, Mr. Reimann?'" The phys ed teacher strained his voice into a high-pitched, mousy squeak, making fun of the kid. "This is physical education, not kindy-garten playtime! Stand at attention, you punks! Count off by fours!"

He was in one of his military moods. They made four lines on the gym floor and started doing calisthenics. *Bor-ing!* Ned thought. Push-ups, sit-ups, jumping jacks. Deep-knee bends. Running in place. Touch your toes, touch your hips, reach for the sky. He hoped they wouldn't have to do this crap when they went to middle school.

"You call that a push-up, Myerson?" Mr. Reimann yelled, picking on one of the fatter kids. "Get that gut up off the floor, fer chrissake!"

"My arms are gettin' tired, Mr. Reimann!"

For some reason, that really ticked him off—at everybody.

"You think you're tired *now!* Make that *forty* push-ups, sis-sies! Look at you, you make me sick! Sittin' home, watchin' dirty movies on your daddies' VCRs, eatin' doughnuts all night long—no wonder you're tired! I never saw such a bunch of flabby little kids in all my life. But I promise you this, *girls*, and I don't care if it kills you—you're going to be physically fit when you get out of here in June! You think I want Bob Thomas up at the middle school getting on my case because I sent him a bunch of misbegotten *weaklings?*"

Ned looked up from the floor. Mr. Reimann had gotten up a full head of steam, they must be able to hear him in the boiler room. His face was like a setting sun.

He reached out with his foot and pushed a kid flat to the floor.

"*All* the way down, Feldman! Don't you wimps know how to do a goddamn push-up yet? All the way down and all the way up!"

Ned didn't know about push-ups, but he knew teachers weren't supposed to yell "*goddamn*" at the kids. He was pretty sure they weren't supposed to step on kids' backs, either. Reimann was really nutso today.

"You make me wanna puke, you kids! Do you hear me? You make me wanna fuckin' puke!"

That was when Mr. Reimann's nose started bleeding.

He didn't notice it at first, he was so worked up. The blood crept out of his nostrils and down his face in two shiny streams like red satin ribbons. All the kids who saw it stopped and stared. That got him even more worked up: he wasn't just yelling at them anymore, he was screaming, hopping up and down. He started to spray blood around. One of the kids sat up and pointed at him, trying to tell him he was bleeding, but Reimann couldn't hear him.

The blood began to *pour*. It poured into his mouth.

He must've gotten a taste of it, then, because he suddenly stopped screaming and clapped a hand to his face. He felt the blood and stared at his fingers. Ned heard him mutter, "Oh, shit . . ."

For a moment silence reigned. Now all the kids were staring.

Mr. Reimann groped his pocket for a handkerchief, whipped it out, and held it to his nose. His brick-red face was rapidly going pale.

"What're you staring at!" he yelled. "It's just a little nosebleed. You never saw a nosebleed before?"

But he was scared, no doubt about that. He looked like he was going to throw up. Ned felt kind of queasy, too.

"Bradley!" Ned shot to his feet. "Go tell Mr. Ludovics I can't take his class next period. Gotta get this taken care of. The rest of you line up by the door—and no talking! Mr. Hall'll be coming to get you in a couple of minutes."

5

"Got a nosebleed, did he?" Mr. Ludovics turned to his class. "Not to worry, boys—I'll run your gym class today." And back to Ned. "Tell the man he owes me a free period."

So Mr. Ludovics didn't think it was any big deal. It made Ned feel better. He thanked Mr. Ludovics and headed back to the gym.

Coming down the main stairs he saw Mrs. Phelps crossing the hall from the front door to the new wing, as if she'd been out on the steps having a smoke. He didn't think anything of it until she stopped and gave him a look that kept him from coming the rest of the way down the stairs.

Ned didn't have the words to describe that look. It was like she had half a mind to eat him. It was some kind of evil smile like he'd never seen before, not even in a movie, and it gave him the galloping creeps. He felt the hairs jump up along the back of his neck, and his skin broke out in gooseflesh.

She only stared at him like that for a second or two, then moved on. Ned remained on the stairs, feeling like it was more than his life was worth to go on down.

But he had to. He didn't want to get Reimann going again.

Shit, he didn't want a crazy man with a nosebleed yelling in his face. Ned descended the stairs as quietly as he could. When he turned into the new wing at the boys' room, Mrs. Phelps wasn't in the hallway anymore.

He felt inordinately grateful for that, and hurried down to the gym.

6

Mrs. Penkul was one of those old-fashioned school nurses who didn't take any shit, not from anyone. She made Otto lie down on the cot and wouldn't let him up.

"I know all about it, Mr. Reimann. Carrying on like a lunatic! Bursting a blood vessel in your nose. Well, you're not leaving this room until your blood pressure gets back down to normal, so just try to calm yourself."

Otto tried to relax. She took his blood pressure when he first came in, and it was up there, all right. One ninety-five over ninety-five. A bit too high for comfort, Otto admitted to himself. All right, a *hell* of a lot too high for comfort. Shouldn't have let those kids get to him like that.

He'd been having a lot of nosebleeds lately. Headaches, too: real thunderers, like a couple of bighorn sheep staging their rutting battles inside his head. But he didn't tell Mrs. Penkul any of this—she'd ship him off to the hospital as soon as look at him.

The nose wasn't bleeding anymore. It hurt, though. Christ, it hurt! And way up there, too. No shitting around anymore, he'd have to learn to take it easy. Couldn't keep getting riled up like this. You could get killed that way.

She took his pressure again after he'd rested for twenty minutes or so.

"Well, that's better," she said, and in a way that implied she wasn't convinced of her patient's good health. "One forty-five over eighty-five. That's still a little high, Mr. Reimann. Not a good sign. I'm going to make an appointment for you to see Dr. Keene after school today. I think he'll want to put you on medication, and maybe on a diet, too. And if you want to keep working, you'd better keep the appointment."

"I'll be there," Otto said.

"Another thing, I want you to keep your cool this afternoon. I don't care what the kids do—if I hear you've raised your voice even once today, you're out of here. I'd send you home right now, only we're already so short-handed today, I don't want Mr. Bradley winding up here, too. You behave yourself, young man—hear?"

"Yeah, yeah."

Otto sat up and rolled his sleeve back down. No question about it, he'd have to play it cool for a while. He nodded to the nurse and walked slowly out of the clinic.

"And lose some weight!" she called after him.

Chapter Thirty

1

As the day progressed, Cosmo found his cold growing worse. Every two minutes he had to blow his nose; by noontime it was raw and red. His head felt like it was stuffed with soggy cotton.

Having to clean up Mr. Reimann's blood from the gym floor before lunchtime didn't do any wonders for his morale, either.

"What is it with all this blood, all of a sudden?" he whined as Rudi wiped the spots from the linoleum.

"Mr. Reimann had a bloody nose," Rudi said.

"If it ain't too much trouble for you, Rudi, could you just once tell me somethin' I don't already know?"

"I'm sorry, Mr. Iacavella. But Mr. Ludovics said—"

"Skip it. I don't want to hear it."

Having finished that chore, they had to pull the tables out of the wall and unfold the chairs for lunch period. Cosmo let Rudi do most of it.

Back in the boiler room, he couldn't taste his coffee or his sandwich. He gave up on both of them.

"Rudi, I'm gonna have to go home. I just can't hack it today,

I gotta go to bed. I'll help you clear up after lunch, but then I gotta take off. You'll be able to hold the fort for one afternoon. I'll be back tomorrow morning."

"How did you get such a bad cold?"

"Aw, who the fuck knows? Must be the weather, I guess. And it's damp enough down here today to grow moss on the walls. That ain't helpin' any."

Rudi ought to be able to handle the job by himself for a few hours, Cosmo thought. If he couldn't now, he'd never be able to. Cosmo was going to retire soon, anyway; he couldn't nursemaid the kid for the rest of his life. Besides, they'd finished all the big jobs for the day. The afternoon ought to be a piece of cake, even for Rudi.

"I'll take care of everything, Mr. Iacavella. You'll see. You go home and get better. I can see you're really sick."

"A nice, dry bed'll put me right."

"You bet."

Cosmo poured a little vodka into his coffee and finished it. The alcohol went down smooth. He'd have a proper drink or two when he got home, then hit the hay. It was the only thing you could do for a cold like this.

He had Rudi pass the word to Miss Stanhouse. They cleaned the cafeteria and put the tables and chairs away. Cosmo was about ready to curl up and sleep on the floor. But he stayed awake and returned to the boiler room for his coat and hat.

"Mr. Iacavella?"

"What now, Rudi?"

"These-here cracks. What am I gonna do about 'em?"

Cosmo groaned. "Aw, Rudi, *forget* the goddamn cracks for now! If you're so worried about 'em, *watch* 'em. Just watch 'em. And if they look like they're gonna gulp down the building, tell Mr. Bradley and let *him* worry about it. Just don't tell *me*. *I'm* goin' home to bed, and I don't want to hear from nobody until tomorrow morning."

Rudi did watch the cracks, and he didn't like what he saw.

He didn't like what he smelled or heard, either.

It still smelled like dead pollywogs down there, only stronger now ... worse. Like a whole swampful of 'em. If Mr. Iacavella hadn't had such a rotten cold, he'd have smelled it, too. A little more, and you'd be able to smell it out in the hall.

If he got on his hands and knees, and lowered his ear so it was almost touching the floor, he could hear water trickling around down there—and something else. Something that was swishing around, rustling ... crawling. It made Rudi think of snakes, and he shuddered. Could there really be snakes down there? He hoped to God not. That was one thing he couldn't handle.

A little while after Mr. Iacavella left, Rudi had to go up to Mrs. Pfeiffer's room and clean up after a kid who'd gotten sick. On the way back, Mr. Bennett caught him in the hall and asked him to wipe some cuss-words off the wall outside his classroom door; someone had written them there during lunch. So he wasn't able to watch the cracks all afternoon.

They were wider by the time he got back to them.

It was the water, Rudi thought, it was the water that was doing this, Mr. Iacavella said so. It was only water.

He paced around the boiler room. The cracks weren't actually growing wider as he watched them, they weren't moving—but they sure *looked* wider. Rudi climbed up on his stool and watched them from what felt like a safer vantage point. A few of the cracks really were quite big. *You could probably stick a finger in there....*

He wondered if the floor was cracking all over the building. He'd have to tell Mr. Bradley, if it was true. He wasn't supposed to bother Mr. Bradley unless it was for something really important, and he wasn't supposed to phone Mr. Iacavella for any reason—but if there were cracks all over the building, he had to tell someone!

It was hard to see any evidence of that in the basement hallway, unless the linoleum squares on the floor were a little out of line. Rudi couldn't say for sure whether they were or not. And the crummy lighting made it awfully hard to tell.

At least the walls weren't cracked; they still looked solid enough.

More worm-holes, though ...

Son-of-a-gun, why hadn't he noticed that before? How could he have missed it? Patches of the brick wall down here were riddled with the little holes, some of them no bigger than the tiny airholes you saw on the sand when a wave receded back into the ocean. Sometimes when you dug where the little holes were, you found those weird critters, those sand fleas: shells with a bunch of crazily kicking legs. Rudi wondered what he'd find if he dug out *these* holes. He'd have to show them to Mr. Iacavella tomorrow.

He drifted into the library, where the third-graders were picking out books. Boy, you could really smell the mildew in there today! But the kids didn't mind, and the librarians were used to it.

"Hi, Rudi! Do you want something?" Mrs. White, the librarian who was there now, smiled at him.

"Lookin' for cracks in the floor," he said. "Have you seen any, ma'am? Mr. Iacavella says it's because of the water."

"I haven't noticed any," Mrs. White said. "But get a whiff of this place! Whoever thought of putting the library in the basement was no genius, I can tell you that."

Rudi spent more time than he meant to in the library. A few of the kids wanted to show him their library books, and more than a few asked him to get books down from high shelves that they couldn't reach. He didn't get back to the boiler room until it was almost time for the bell to ring.

When it did ring, he hardly heard it. He was sure now that the cracks were getting wider. There were cracks running under the boiler.

Maybe he ought to get hold of Mr. Bradley, the principal, before he went home for the day. Get him to come down here and see this for himself.

But Mr. Iacavella would be ashamed of him if he went off halfcocked like that. He didn't want that to happen the one day Mr. Iacavella trusted him to do the job alone. He at least had to make sure how bad the damage really was before he went bugging anybody about it.

From the tool table he selected a yardstick and a putty knife. Rudi didn't know how thick the floor was, but he figured if he could stick the yardstick all the way down one of the cracks, that'd be worth telling Mr. Bradley. The putty knife was for those hairline cracks, to see if they were just skin-deep or went down a ways.

He got down on his hands and knees. The dead-tadpole smell was really getting hard to take. Something was rotten down there, you bet.

He was still wearing his little plastic crucifix around his neck, and glad of it. He'd been wearing it under his T-shirt, where Mr. Iacavella couldn't see it, so he wouldn't start ragging him about it. Mr. Iacavella knew a lot, but he didn't know everything. And he couldn't see ghosts: hadn't seen them up there in the clinic, where they were sitting on the cot as plain as a pair of frogs on a lily pad. If *he'd* been able to see them, Rudi thought, he'd be wearing a bigger crucifix than Rudi had.

He probed a wide crack with the yardstick. It wouldn't go in very far, but he could tell it was because the cracks must be as crooked going down as they were running across the floor. What he really needed was a steel tape measure that would follow the cracks down; but that was clipped to Mr. Iacavella's belt. A straightened coat hanger might be useful, too.

But for the time being he kept poking around with the yardstick. And suddenly he thrust it down so deep he almost lost it.

267

Ooh ... He was able to wiggle the stick a little, enough to show that he'd poked it into some big empty space under the floor. If he let go of it, it'd fall out of sight.

He felt like he'd walked out to the middle of a frozen lake and found a "Danger! Thin Ice" sign that had fallen down.

He pulled the yardstick out of the crack. It didn't come out quite as easily as it had gone in.

The last eighteen inches came up dripping slime.

Rudi trembled. *Holy cow, what's down there?* The stick looked like he'd dragged it through snot—and smelled worse.

Something like a slimy, gigantic pink worm darted up from one of the cracks and threw itself around his wrist.

Chapter Thirty-One

1

Although it wasn't raining anymore, the sky was still oppressively dark. At three o'clock it looked like five, and nobody wanted to stay much later. Victory School was virtually deserted within fifteen minutes of the dismissal bell.

Millie Stanhouse made Virgil leave early.

"The last thing you need is to hang around here any longer," she said. "And if you do, Rudi'll think it's because you don't think he can close the building by himself. You've got to show some confidence in him, Mr. Bradley."

Thus admonished, Virgil dropped his plan to stop by the boiler room to see how Rudi was getting on. He declined Millie's offer of a ride, saying the short walk home would clear his head.

And it needed clearing. All day long he'd sat at his desk, muddling through his paperwork, completely unable to come to grips with what he'd experienced here on Saturday. The school had such a host of mundane problems that it was almost possible to forget that it had ghosts, too.

He'd called the police that afternoon to check on the Dudak boy and received a mildly chilling report.

"They got him up at the hospital, Mr. Bradley," Chief Lockwood told him. "He's in some kind of coma, and they can't seem to snap him out of it. They think he might have brain damage from what Neil Rizzo's kid did to him. County's holding *him*."

"I'm sorry for Officer Rizzo," Virgil said.

"You and me both. It ain't his fault. The kid takes after his old lady, and believe me, Ellie Rizzo was a tramp. Well, the poor bastard did the best he could, after she run out on him. He brought the kid up himself. He's a good man, Rizzo—but he couldn't work miracles."

"How about the policeman who was hurt? Is he all right?"

"Boggsy? Yeah, he's just fine, they patched up his leg okay."

Virgil supposed he ought to be relieved, at least, to be rid of two of the school's worst problem kids; but it just left him numb. Well, maybe without the other two, Bob Diehl would straighten out. That'd be something.

"How did it go, honey?"

Carrie kissed him when he came in the back door. In spite of having put in a relatively short day, he was dog-tired. He hung his coat over the back of a chair and told her about the two boys.

"You knew they were headed for trouble, Virgil," Carrie said. "It's too bad they finally got there; but there was no way you could've stopped them. I do feel sorry for the parents, though."

"It just was another helluva day, Car. We're so short on staff, it's a wonder we can continue to function. Cosmo Iacavella had to go home early today, with a cold. Diane Phelps came down with pneumonia this weekend and is in the hospital. And Otto Reimann has high blood pressure. He was yelling at some kids today and he broke down with a nosebleed."

"I know. Ned told me."

"That was Ned's class?" Virgil hadn't realized that. "Where is Ned?"

"Down in the rec room. He told me about it just a few minutes ago. Mr. Reimann used some very improper language, I'm afraid. Ned says he's been terribly hot-tempered lately: the least little thing wrong, and he blows up. And according to Ned, Mr. Hall wasn't in very good shape today, either."

"You could say that." Virgil decided to have a beer. "Charlie did look pretty sick. I'm glad he came in, though."

The phone rang. Carrie picked up the receiver while Virgil popped open his can of beer.

"It's for you, hon . . . Rudi Fitch."

And Virgil knew it couldn't be anything but some new debacle. He knew it as surely as a teenager's father knows the first time the kid takes the car without permission that the phone wouldn't be ringing now except to try his soul.

Rudi babbled. It took a minute or two to get him to make sense. He wanted to go into some kind of spinout, but Virgil cut him off. "I'll be right there, Rudi. Just stay calm and try to get Mr. Iacavella again. I'll be with you in just a few minutes. Everything'll be all right." He hung up before Rudi could get in another word.

"What's wrong now?" Carrie said.

"Oh, I don't know!" Virgil snatched his coat from the chair. "Something about the floor cracking up, and Mr. Iacavella not answering his phone, and Christ knows what else. I won't know until I see it for myself."

He wanted to get out of there fast, before she saw how much it really bothered him, before she started asking questions. "I won't be long," he said, and barged out the door while he was still buttoning his coat.

271

Ned had been about to open the cellar door and come out when he heard his father say that Mrs. Phelps hadn't been at school today. She had pneumonia; she was in the hospital. That stopped him cold.

But he had seen her!

Seen her ghost, you mean.

But she wasn't dead!

And neither was Dudak.

Then the phone rang, and Ned was still standing at the top of the cellar stairs, trying to get his brain in gear, when Dad went out. He pushed the door open and ran into the kitchen.

"Dad! Is he—"

"Take it easy, Ned," Mom said. "Your father had to go back to the school for a little while, Mr. Fitch is having some kind of problem with the floor."

"Did he say the floor was *cracking?*"

"Something like that. Mr. Fitch wasn't too clear about what was wrong."

Ned ran back to the living room closet for his jacket.

"Hold your horses, kid! Where do you think you're going?"

"I gotta talk to Dad!"

"You can talk to him when he gets back. It's too cold and wet outside for you to be—"

But Ned was already out the front door and sprinting down the sidewalk.

Virgil walked briskly, eating up the ground with long strides, afraid of what he'd find when he reached the school, but unable to dawdle.

He understood one thing clearly: Rudi was as scared as he would ever be if he lived to be ninety. Cracks in the boiler room floor, no matter how wide, wouldn't have scared him like that.

But if there was structural damage, that was all he needed to get the board to close the school. That was how he'd get a thorough investigation of the building.

Ned ran. He jumped some puddles and splashed through others, hardly noticing he was now soaked from the waist down.

He had to catch his father before he got there and tell him about Mrs. Phelps's ghost. Nobody should be in that building anymore. It was too dangerous. They had to get Mr. Fitch out of there and close the place down, before somebody really got hurt.

If Dad didn't want to tell the board the place was haunted, all right—Ned could understand that. People didn't believe a thing like that unless they saw it for themselves. Let Dad tell the school board whatever he liked, as long as he got the place shut down.

He wasn't going back there, no matter what they did! He'd seen enough. He didn't want to see any more.

He caught up to his father on River Street, right out in front of the school. Virgil heard him coming and turned around.

"What's the matter, Ned?"

Ned gulped to catch his breath. "You can't go in there!" he managed to get out. "You gotta get Mr. Fitch out of there!"

Ned told him why. Virgil listened without giving him an argument. He knew he was telling the truth.

"I still have to go in there. I have to find out what's wrong."

"Jesus, Dad, you already know what's wrong! The place is haunted!"

"Ned, Mr. Fitch wants me to see the floor. He thinks it's breaking apart. It's very important for me to see it for myself, ghosts or no ghosts. But if it's true, I can get them to close the building. Now go home before you catch a cold. I'll be back soon."

Go home and *wait?* Ned shook his way violently. "No, sir! I'm stickin' with you."

273

"There's really no need for you to come in with me, Ned—especially not when you're already this scared."

"Don't make me go, Dad. Let me stay with you."

"Ned ..." Dad stuck his hands in his pockets and sighed. "All right, come on. Mr. Fitch is waiting. Let's just get this over with."

3

Rudi heard them coming and walked out of the boiler room to meet them.

His face was nearly gray with fear and there was a thick streak of grime across his forehead. Virgil was as tempted as a man could be to turn around and walk back out; but he was principal here, and that option wasn't his.

"Hello, Rudi," he said.

"Hi, Mr. Bradley! Boy, I'm glad you're here! I don't know what to do, and Mr. Iacavella still doesn't answer his phone. He must've took his medicine and gone to bed."

"It's all right. Let's see what the problem is," said Virgil.

Rudi conducted them into the boiler room and pointed to the floor.

Virgil gulped. Some of the cracks were an inch or two wide. The sight made him think of earthquake damage.

"They were only *little* cracks this morning!" Rudi was saying breathlessly. "And Mr. Iacavella, he said it was the water, the water from the rain was doing it, and all we hadda do was pour some cement in 'em ... but I been watchin' 'em all day, Mr. Bradley, all day long, and they keep on gettin' wider, and I'm afraid the building's gonna fall down!"

"We'll have to let the building inspector have a look at it, Rudi."

"You don't understand, Mr. Bradley!"

"Rudi, it *looks* like water damage—"

"It ain't!" It was so unlike Rudi to interrupt him that Virgil fell silent with astonishment.

"Mr. Bradley, there's somethin' down there! And there's *ghosts* up here! I seen 'em, I seen the ones Miss Davis saw, I seen more than that.... You're gonna think I'm crazy, but I *seen* 'em, honest to God!"

Virgil put an arm around Rudi's shoulders. He was trembling like a spooked horse.

"It's all right, Rudi. It's all right. I don't think you're crazy. I believe you."

But Rudi jumped away. *"But it ain't just ghosts!* I'm tellin' you, there's somethin' down there, under the floor. Look!"

He turned and snatched something off the top of Cosmo Iacavella's desk, and thrust it at Virgil.

For a moment Virgil could make no sense of what he was seeing. It was a flabby, rubbery *length* of something, ribbed like a worm, pink shading to gray....

"It grabbed me when I was tryin' to measure the cracks, Mr. Bradley. I cut it off with a putty knife. But there's more of 'em down there. If you bend over the cracks and listen, you can hear 'em movin' around. Can't you *smell* 'em?"

Virgil did smell something, a cloying, rotten meat-like odor. And it brought him back ... all the way back to that nightmare in the janitor's closet when he was nine years old.

"That's like the thing I saw, Dad," Ned said. "Only that one had like a flower on the end of it. This is the same thing, though. It's like the one—"

"I know, Ned." God, how he knew. And he wished he didn't.

He thought he could hear the floor slithering under his feet, a furtive rustling that filled the room, just above the threshold of audibility.

"Put that in a safe place, Rudi. I'll want to show it to the building inspector when he comes."

The thing gleamed with slime. Rudi dropped it into a plastic bucket. It plashed when it fell.

"Have you got a sledge hammer down here? A pick?"

"Well, sure ... I think. Wait a minute." Rudi rummaged around in a corner and came up with a grimy old pick. "What do you want it for?"

"I want to knock a hole in the floor, over the cracks where that ... that thing came out," Virgil said. "I want to see what else is down there."

"I don't know, Mr. Bradley. Maybe we shouldn't't."

"Please, Rudi. Just do it."

Destroying public property? But the objection was almost laughable. Even if it weren't, Virgil wouldn't have heeded it. Under the floor was something that had tainted his life. He wanted to expose it and destroy it.

Rudi was strong. He swung the pick with a force that was almost frightening, making the heavy head whoosh through the air. Ned jumped back when the point slammed into the cement floor, along the cracks.

Rudi chopped at the floor, sending fragments flying. Virgil didn't move when some of them bounced off his shins. He had himself on a very short rein. He would see this or be damned. He would learn the nature of this thing if he had to have Rudi tear the school down brick by brick.

Something snapped loose. Rudi yelped and almost dropped the pick. With a low rumble, a section of the floor fell in, creating a round hole as wide as a man could jump. Cement dust billowed over it.

"Jesus, Dad!"

Virgil took his son's hand. The rumbling continued: it sounded like a minor rock-slide.

"Oh, boy, we done it now!" Rudi cried. "What's Mr. Iacavella gonna say when he comes in tomorrow and sees *this?*"

"Be quiet, Rudi. *Listen.*"

The rumbling subsided. The dust settled. Up from the crater in the floor rose a stench that was like an invisible fog. Ned and Rudi coughed, but Virgil disregarded it. He stepped up to the brink of the pit and looked down.

A rough circular shaft stretched down immeasurably into

darkness. There was no way to judge its depth, because it was full.

It was like peering into a cauldron full of eels. A seething, slimy mass of them, impossible to number, boiled and writhed within two yards of Virgil's feet. It seemed to be sinking slowly downward, as though withdrawing from the open air.

More dropped from countless holes around the shaft, adding imperceptibly to the filthy pink mass, a medusa-head of vileness.

"My God!" Virgil muttered. "Who'd have thought there'd be so many of them?"

Chapter Thirty-Two

1

Carrie felt abandoned.

It was after four now, and still no word from Virgil. Should she start supper? How long was he going to be? Whatever the problem at the school, it must have turned out to be something pretty major. He must be up in his office now, making phone calls. She saw a vivid mental picture of him at his desk, harried and tiring, frenetically dialing his phone as he tried to track down various school district officials who'd already left their offices for the day.

All to save a school that they'd take away from him in a few months, anyway.

For the first time, she began to think that maybe her husband would be better off without Victory School. The things that had been going on there lately were enough to give anyone gray hair. And it was getting to Virgil: she could see it in his face. That episode over the weekend, the one involving the Dudak boy, had really knocked him for a loop. He couldn't take much more.

It was time she got back to work, anyway, she told herself.

Ned was old enough to look after himself for most of the day. She could find a nice teaching job and still be home when she was needed. She'd take summer refresher courses, she'd read the NEA literature, she'd substitute-teach a couple of times a month. She'd have no trouble getting back into the swing of things.

But for the time being, her husband was stuck at that damned school, their son with him; and it looked like it could start raining again, too.

Well, she'd be damned if she'd let Virgil walk home in the rain after all this. Supper could be a little late tonight. Maybe they'd just pick up a pizza on the way home, and the hell with cooking.

She put on her raincoat, checked her purse to make sure she had her car keys, and went out.

<h1 style="text-align:center">2</h1>

As the mass of tentacles continued to withdraw, the beam of Rudi's flashlight described a deep, wide chimney in the earth.

The smell issuing up from it was inutterably foul, and mixed with it was a hint of ozone, a whiff of air molecules shattered by electricity. There was unseen lightning in the air, and it prickled Virgil's skin.

"Jesus, Mr. Bradley! *What is it?*"

Virgil shook his head, unable to respond. Whatever it was, it was alive; and it had assaulted him once, leaving a reservoir of horror that had lasted more than thirty years. But whether it was one great, massive thing or an incalculable swarm of evil little things he couldn't tell.

"It's alien," Ned said softly. "It's not from here. It must've come down with the meteor Mom told us about."

Virgil didn't know about that, either. All he knew was that it was alive and that it had to be destroyed.

God, how long had it been here, he wondered. Since creation? And had it poisoned this place for all that time? Was this the reason for all the tragedies that happened here?

He couldn't believe he'd been the only victim. There must have been many. Hundreds, maybe thousands ... who could say? Who would ever know? How many had ventured into some dark corner of the school—or some preceding structure—to be seized by one or more of these fleshy tentacles, held fast, and violated in some profound and loathsome way? It was too unspeakable to be remembered consciously.

What if he hadn't been taken once, but several times? *Many* times? What kind of chemical had this thing shot into his brain?

He remembered, now—Christ, it came rushing back at him!— a visit to the doctor shortly after the ambush in the janitor's closet, to see about his nosebleeds. *("The boy must've stuck something up his nose, Mrs. Bradley. A pencil, maybe—kids'll do that sometimes. But it'll heal.")* He'd had a *hole* up there, a wound. He'd been injected with something, or something had been siphoned out of his head. Or both.

God, how many? How many had been subjected to that?

But he was still here. He could do something about it now.

"You got a rope, Rudi?"

"What for, Mr. Bradley?"

"I'm going down there," Virgil said.

"Really, Mr. Bradley, I don't think that's such a hot idea."

Virgil looked down into the pit. The writhing mass had sunk below the reach of the flashlight, but he could still hear it moving. He could still smell it.

"We're going to kill it, Rudi," Virgil said. "It has to be destroyed. But first I have to get a better look at it. We have to know what's down there." He had to know, at least. He couldn't stand not knowing.

"I want you to lower me down on a rope so I can get a good look. Don't worry—you'll pull me up if it looks dangerous. I don't plan on taking any crazy chances."

Ned couldn't believe what he was hearing. Sure, Dad did a

280

lot of rock-climbing in the summer, he could punt a football pretty far—but who did he think he was? Han Solo? And Mr. Fitch was strong; but could he really pull Dad up fast enough if things got hairy down there?

He caught himself saying, "Dad, let me go down there. I'm little, you and Mr. Fitch can pull me up real quick."

The two men just stared at him.

But he wanted to go. He had to see, too. He couldn't imagine getting out of there without having seen what was at the bottom of the pit. If he didn't, it would haunt him for as long as he lived. It'd be worse than the ghosts, which he *had* seen, like it or not. Seeing it'd be bad, but *not* seeing it would somehow be worse. He knew that without being able to explain it to himself.

"It'll be safer for me than for you," he told his father. "I don't weigh as much."

"Ned, if you think I'm going to let you do this, you need your head examined."

"I don't think anybody should do it!" Rudi said. Dread made him speak up where normally he would maintain a deferential silence. "Let's just get out of here."

"Rudi, I'm the principal. This thing is under my school. I *have* to see it!"

"Dad, you're too *big!* We won't be able to pull you out of there fast enough."

"No, Ned. Rudi, let's find that rope."

3

Carrie pulled into the teachers' lot and parked. She was surprised not to find any other cars there. What was Virgil doing?

She climbed out of her car and looked at the sky. It was getting dark fast. How much rain could they get around here, anyway?

She saw a light in Virgil's office.

4

I must be crazy, Virgil thought.

The thick hemp rope, left behind by painters several years ago, was firmly knotted under Ned's arms and anchored to a support beam in the ceiling. Ned had been rock-climbing with his parents several times, he knew how to make the descent safely. And he only weighed seventy pounds.

Is this what I really want to do—put my son at risk? Lower him down there like bait on a hook?

Still, he and Rudi could haul Ned out of the hole in a matter of seconds. And if something tried to hold the climber back, he and Rudi would be a lot more likely to be able to rescue Ned than Rudi alone—Ned's help hardly counted. Sending Ned was the logical thing to do. And it was only a reconnaissance: they weren't sending him down there to fight.

"I'm ready, Dad."

Virgil bent down and kissed him.

"You're to yell if there's any threat to you at all, no matter how small—understand? You're coming out of there if you even *think* it's about to get dangerous."

"I will, Dad."

He was sending part of himself down there, Virgil thought. In a way, the biggest part. But it had to be done.

It grabbed me once, but it never took him. It saw him once and didn't try to take him. That must mean something. God knows how many chances it had to take him since he first came to this school....

"Be careful, Ned."

Ned took the flashlight and went over the edge of the pit, slowly, Rudi and Virgil playing the rope out inches at a time.

* * *

Going down the hole was no big deal; he'd done harder things on Dad's rock-climbing trips. All he had to do was keep his feet in contact with the chimney, so he wouldn't spin around. Hold onto the rope with one hand, aim the flashlight with the other. Anybody could do it.

He shone the flashlight beam straight down, but he couldn't see anything. He raised it and played it around the chimney.

The earth was packed hard here, and the chimney seemed almost as smooth as if it had been dug by a machine. That made him think of UFOs and alien robots, and it wasn't a lot of fun to think about when you were hanging from a rope with only a flashlight for a weapon. But animals, he remembered, dug pretty smooth burrows, too. Like the ants in the ant farm Mom had got him last Christmas.

"Ned! Are you all right?"

"I'm fine!"

"What do you see?"

Ned made another sweep with the flashlight.

"There's about a jillion holes in the wall down here. Like giant worm-holes. They must've come out of these holes and crawled down this tunnel. I don't see 'em yet; they're down too deep. The flashight doesn't reach."

Shit, there were round holes *everywhere!* If there was one of those wormy things for every hole, they'd need an atom bomb to get rid of 'em all.

Ned's excitement ate up most of his fear. He was being a hero, an honest-to-God hero, just like in a movie. Sigourney Weaver would be proud of him.

He wished Dad and Mr. Fitch would let him down a little faster. How far would he have to go before he saw the worms' nest or whatever was at the bottom?

He could hear them. This flashlight wasn't very strong; they sounded close enough that he ought to be able to see them.

Now the chimney was a round black hole a little below his feet: the end of the tunnel already. Looking up briefly, he could still see the boiler room's ceiling overhead. He wasn't that far down.

Suddenly his feet danced on air. He bumped into the wall of the chimney and almost dropped the flashlight.

"Ned!"

"I'm okay! I just got to the end of the tunnel, that's all."

"You touched bottom?"

"No! It's like I came to a big hole, that's all. Like an empty space. Let me down a little lower."

He aimed the flashlight. They let him down like they were trying to lower a piano onto a bed of eggs. In another minute or two he was dangling freely in the air, with the thick rope biting at his armpits. He started to spin, but slowly.

He had entered some kind of vast underground cave. The flashlight beam showed him an earthen ceiling, with dead tree roots sticking out of it like whiskers.

He lowered the beam.

Holy shit, what am I looking at?

It was like looking straight down into one of those sea anemones they showed on *Nature*. Those slimy things weren't worms. They were arms ... tentacles. A huge teeming crown of them, like a sea anemone's crown. And he was the little fish who'd get stung and eaten if he got too close.

But that was only part of it.

"You gotta see this, Dad! Oh, man, I don't believe it!"

He spun around a little faster. He felt dizzy, and for a moment he suffered a strange longing to be let down among the tentacles, right into the restless, seething mass of them, and let them have him. He fought it off.

"I need more light!" he cried.

He heard his father ask Mr. Fitch if they had any highway flares, but couldn't hear the janitor's reply. He spun around and around, playing his flashlight back and forth, seeing only little bits and pieces of the one impossible hole.

"We're pulling you up, Ned!"

And up he went, a little faster than he'd come down. Up into the chimney. He propped his right foot against the earth and stopped spinning.

A tentacle threw itself around his left ankle.

Chapter Thirty-Three

1

Carrie was pretty sure the boys' entrance would be open; that was the door Virgil customarily used. She pranced up the steps, found the door unlocked, and entered the building.

She could have taken the flight of stairs that would put her down in the basement, right next to the boiler room; but she took the flight up instead, thinking to find Virgil in his office on the phone. She made the choice with no hesitation at all, never thinking he might still be downstairs in the boiler room. Not after all this time. He was an administrator, not a custodian.

Up the stairs and through the fire doors: she'd come this way before, many times. It was going on five now, she thought. He was coming home with her if she had to drag him by the hair. Home to beer and pizza!

She paused when she entered the second-floor hallway. For some reason it smelled rainier inside the school than outside. She actually thought she could hear water in the ceiling. What a ruin this building was! Why hadn't they maintained it better?

To her left the office door was closed. But light shone through the translucent window in the door, and she took a step toward it.

2

Virgil was already getting ready to climb down the rope with a flare when Ned's scream came loud and terrifying from the pit.

He looked over the edge and saw the flashlight's beam waving around wildly in the darkness, but he couldn't see his son.

"Ned!"

"Dad! It's got hold of me! Pull me up!"

Showing his teeth, Rudi heaved on the rope, gaining a yard or two before it fought him to a stop. Ned cried out in pain.

"Stop pulling—you'll hurt him!"

Rudi's eyes rolled. When he gave up a little bit of slack, that much of the rope snaked over the lip of the crater in the floor.

"C'mon, Dad, get me outta here!"

"Can you hold the two of us?" Virgil snapped. "Just hold the rope, so we can climb up?"

"I think so, Mr. Bradley! Yeah, I can hold."

Virgil leaped to Cosmo's desk and stuck the putty knife in his belt. He broke the flare apart and lit it. The bigger half spat fire.

"I'm going down to get him, Rudi. Whatever you do, don't let go!"

Rudi gritted his jaws and nodded. Virgil grabbed the rope, looped some of it around his left leg, and began his descent.

It would be a dangerous climb, but he didn't stop to think about that. He'd made dozens of trickier climbs, up and down the sheer rock faces in the Shawangunks, in the Adirondacks, in the Catskills. Fueled by an adrenalin surge, he went straight down, rapelling on his right foot, holding the flare clear of the rope.

"I'm coming down, Ned! Hang on!"

"I can see you! Hurry up, Dad!"

He had to make an effort not to go too fast. Around him, the flare lit up the earthen shaft brilliantly. The rope never slipped an inch.

He neared the end of the rope. When he looked down he saw Ned's face. Most of the fear had gone out of it with his approach, but it still seemed pale and drawn.

"Are you all right?"

"It's got me around the foot!" Ned said. He didn't seem to be in any pain. "Look." He dipped the flashlight.

Stretched almost unbelievably thin and taut, a band of shiny pink flesh tied Ned's ankle to a squirming bed of tentacles some yards below. For the moment Virgil couldn't take the time to look beyond that.

"Can you bring your leg up any? Try, son!"

Ned grimaced and pulled against the tentacle. He was able to gain a few inches.

Slowly, carefully, Virgil extricated his left leg from the rope and inched down closer to the boy. There was no way he could get access to the putty knife in his belt without letting go of the flare, and he didn't want to do that. He reached down and touched the chemically-fed fire to the pink flesh.

The tentacle held for a moment longer, then parted suddenly, burned through. It snapped down like a broken strip of stretched rubber. The remainder clung lifelessly to Ned's sneaker.

"Are you hurt?"

"I'm okay now. God—can you *see* that thing?"

Virgil looked down. The flare gave much more light than the flashlight, revealing an immense round cavern in the earth. Virgil couldn't even guess at its dimensions.

And it was full. It was more of a cocoon than a nest. Virgil cried out at what he saw below, under the ruddy light cast by the flare.

The myriad tentacles were withdrawing, slowly, into a bulbous fixture that reminded Virgil of a tapeworm's head, blown up to the size of his upstairs bathroom. As he watched, a circular, leathery orifice was imperceptibly closing on the tentacles as they retracted into it. And the head itself was withdrawing, sinking down into a yawning cleft.

It was closing up. The whole damned thing was closing up, like a snail pulling into its shell.

Below the head, around the open cleft, he could just make out a dark, round mass that nearly filled the great cavity in the earth. He discerned dull flashes where the light bounced off a rounded surface of smooth, hard chitin, like an insect's armor; and pale, fleshy-looking rings where the immense chitinous sheets were joined together.

The armored bulk was propped against the earth by jointed, sharply bent appendages, gray lobster legs, each joint as thick as a construction girder. *Jesus God, they'd be twenty or thirty feet long if you could straighten them out. . . .*

And how much weight were they supporting? How many *tons?*

"Mr. Bradley! Are you still there? Are you all right?"

Rudi's yell cut through a fog of astonishment. Virgil yelled back, "Hang on! We're coming back up!"

"Want me to pull you?"

"If you can!"

To his wonder, both he and Ned began to ascend: slowly, to be sure; but Rudi was hauling them up. Virgil was just barely able to maneuver a safety loop around his left leg.

He looked back down, past Ned, to the alien thing below—hating it, disgusted indescribably by it, yet marveling at it all the same.

They were directly over the head, with its gorgon's crown of tentacles. Virgil wanted to hurt it, kill it, pay it back for centuries of pain and madness.

He held the flare out at arm's length, took a moment to aim, and let it fall.

Carrie heard footsteps on the stairs behind her. She turned from the office door.

"Virgil? Is that you? Ned?"

Tramp, tramp ... but no answer. She went back to the fire doors and looked through the windows.

Up the stairs came a woman in a man's clothes, carrying an ax.

It didn't register right away. She thought it was a teacher, although she hadn't thought there were any still in the building. She almost spoke to it.

But what teacher would come clad in filth, her hair a spongy mat of blood? There was blood all the way down the front of her shirt, dark and almost dry, with bits of dirt stuck to it. Blood that left a trail on the steps behind her. That squelched in her shoes as she came.

Up she came, one step at a time, cradling the ax. Carrie, her thoughts lagging behind the insane message transmitted by her eyes, was actually on the point of speaking to her—babbling out some inanity, like, "Ma'am, are you all right?"—when she reached the top of the steps and looked up.

Her face was a pure shambles. Over her right eye, her skull was crushed in like a crumpled hat, the pressure of the blow springing the eye from the socket so that it dangled whitely on the bloody cheek, hanging by the optic nerve like a Christmas tree ornament. The rest of her features seemed crowded onto the other side of her face.

But the other eye was where it ought to be, and its stare went through Carrie like an arrow.

The woman's mouth split in a leering grin. She changed her grip on the ax and began to raise it over her ruined head.

Carrie screamed and fled into the office.

4

There was a sound like the hissing of fat burning off a hot skillet, louder than the combustion of a forest of pitch-laden pines.

Virgil saw nothing. The flare dropped into the midst of the tentacles and sank at once into darkness. But he heard desperate movement, like the stirrings of a giant tortured in his sleep.

His head swam with exultation.

He knew, now, what to do next. He couldn't wait for Rudi to pull him out of the shaft. Hand over hand, feet braced against the earth, he climbed the rope. Ned called out to him, but he couldn't hear it. Rudi froze in surprise when he saw his head rise out of the pit, but didn't let the rope slip back. Virgil climbed out of the hole and helped Rudi pull Ned up. They had him out in a few seconds.

"You got floor wax? Drums of floor wax?" Virgil snapped.

"Sure, Mr. Bradley, we got lots of it, we—"

"Cleaning fluid? Solvent?"

"Yeah . . ."

"Bring it over here. A couple of drums of each!"

Rudi obeyed instinctively. Ned let himself out of the rope.

"What're you gonna do, Dad?"

"We're gonna *burn* this baby, Ned! We're gonna burn it right to hell! Rudi, where do you keep those flares?"

Rudi came up lugging two brightly labeled buckets.

"I put 'em on the desk, that cardboard box right there."

"Open the drums!"

Virgil went to the desk and began to stuff flares into his belt, as many as would fit. He stuck a few in his pockets, too.

"Dad—"

"Not now, Ned! We don't have much time. It's closing itself up, trying to hide in its armor. We got him now!"

"I got 'em open, Mr. Bradley," Rudi said.

"Good! Now get us a lighter rope so we can lower 'em down."

Virgil knew exactly what he wanted to do: easiest thing in the world, if only he had time. He widened the noose of the thick hemp rope and fixed it around his chest, under his arms. Rudi came out of a corner with a new clothesline.

"Lower me back down there, Rudi, and hold me there when I yell for you to stop. Ned, you lower these drums down to me. Be careful not to spill 'em."

Rudi and Ned both had questions, but Virgil was on a roll; he couldn't stop to listen to them. Rudi took up the hemp rope again, while Ned broke out the clothesline and started tying it to the handles of the drums.

Virgil took a firm grip on the rope with both hands and began to climb back down the shaft, rejoicing when he heard the tentacles writhing wetly in the dark. He still had time. It hadn't closed up yet.

The smell was worse now. His flare had burned some of the thing's flesh, and the reek of it was slowly rising up the shaft. Well, let it—he'd burn it all before he was through.

Chapter Thirty-Four

1

The office door was unlocked. Carrie tore it open and threw herself into the room, and yanked the door shut after her with a crash.

"Virgil!"

She fumbled clumsily with the knob, trying to lock the door; but that could be done only with a key. She stared through the frosted-glass window and saw a dark shape looming up outside. She dropped the knob and made a run for the principal's private office.

The door was ajar. She heard the front office door crash open behind her. She slammed the principal's door shut and pressed herself against it, sobbing as the frantic exertion pushed the air from her lungs.

The principal's door was solid oak, without any window, and fit snugly in its frame. Now that she had it closed, she couldn't hear anything outside.

She groped the doorknob, found a manual lock, and turned it so that it clicked shut.

But she has an ax—sweet Jesus, she has an ax! She'll get through, she'll chop her way in. . . .

Holding her breath, as if there were any hope of not being found, once the woman with the ax saw that she hadn't tarried in the outer office, Carrie stepped back from the door. She couldn't take her eyes off its wooden blankness. In her imagination she already heard the booming of the ax, almost saw the blade gouging its way through the wood. But it was a solid, heavy door. A full-grown, healthy man would take a while to hew his way through that. . . .

She's dead. She can't be alive, not with her skull crushed in and her eye popped out. Dead! Oh, Christ, all that blood . . .

Carrie put her hands over her face. The name of Rose Smollet jumped into her mind.

Rose Smollet: murdered by her hired man, right in the cellar of her own house. Right here, where the school stood now. Bludgeoned to death. Right here!

"No!" said Carrie under her breath, shaking her head. No! That was a hundred years ago, she was killed a hundred years ago . . . the dead didn't walk. They didn't come after you with axes.

No sound passed through the heavy door. Except for the beating of her own heart, and the faint whoosh of air in and out of her mouth, all was silent.

Where's Virgil?

Where's Ned?

Carrie trembled. She couldn't go back out, even if the woman with the ax showed no sign of coming in.

An inspiration came to her. The telephone! Virgil had a telephone. She could phone the police for help. She turned reluctantly from the door, afraid to stop watching it; but the only hope she had was Virgil's phone.

Virgil's chair was turned to the wall, and a man was sitting in it, not moving. She hadn't had an inkling he was in the room. She saw only the back of a head, and an elbow on the arm rest, but that was enough to tell her that he wasn't Virgil; and he sure as God wasn't Rudi Fitch.

Slowly, noiselessly, the man swung the chair around to face her.

"Well—Mrs. Bradley! Isn't this a nice surprise!"

Her eyes darted from the man in the chair to the man in the picture over Virgil's desk, and saw no difference.

2

Virgil hung over the well of darkness, listening to the alien rustlings below. He plucked a flare from his belt, broke it open, and struck the flame.

The thing was no less awesome than it had been at first sight; and he saw it better now, unencumbered by Ned and dangling below the earthen chimney.

"Hurry up with that first drum!" he called back up the shaft.

The tentacles squirmed below his feet, as though agitated by the flare's light. The thing moved slowly: it still hadn't retracted all its tentacles, the head was still being pulled down into the cleft of the gigantic body.

Ned was right, he thought. This was literally not of this earth. It couldn't be.

The drum came down on the clothesline. Virgil guided it with his free hand and called up to Ned to hold it when he had it where he wanted it. By flare-light he read the label.

FLOOR WAX
CAUTION: HIGHLY FLAMMABLE

All to the good, he thought. He held the flare out of the way and tipped the bucket, pouring a stream of liquid wax onto the nightmare below.

"Another one!" he cried. "More wax! Hurry!"

The thing stirred below him, ponderously, as though its movements were geared to a different scale of time. Another bucket of wax came down, and another. He emptied three drums of highly toxic cleaning solvent, too, holding his breath as he poured it. The fumes made his eyes water.

He would have liked to pour more, pour an ocean of poisons over this poison thing below. He kept remembering his terror when it seized him and immobilized him with a sharp probe up his nose. All the poison in the world wouldn't be enough.

But he was running out of time.

He dropped his flare; and before it fell, he was reaching into his belt for another.

The wax ignited, burning brightly. He smelled the solvent. He lit the second flare and threw it down, and the third.

Where the flames danced on the creature's armor, they soon went out. But Virgil had been careful to pour most of the wax onto the tentacles, and into the open cleft that was waiting to close over the head. There the flames found good hunting.

A fourth flare. A fifth.

He felt like jumping down there and going at it with a hatchet, a crowbar, his bare hands. He lusted to tear the thing to pieces. But all he could do was throw flares, and he threw them with a vengeance, pegging them one after another into the growing thicket of fire. He felt the heat of the blaze reach up and gnaw at his feet, but he hadn't had enough, not yet. He roared curses, threw flares.

There was no noise but the gluttonous crackling of the fire, and the whoosh made by the flames as the updraft of air began to suck them toward the chimney. The alien entity made no sound at all. No screams of rage or pain; no bellows of threat or fury. No shrieking, no whining, no unbearable high-pitched squeals. Even with a fire burning in its belly, it was silent.

But it began to move.

The timber-like legs flexed slightly, shifting the armored mass on its bed of earth. Joints creaked with the sound of steel boxcars being bent in half.

Bombs of dirt, some of them bigger than Virgil's head, began to rain down from the ceiling of the cave.

He felt himself being drawn upward.

Still cursing, he lit the last flare and threw it down.

3

Carrie had been in Virgil's office before. She knew who Dr. Eric Hargrove was. He had died thirty years ago.

But he lounged in Virgil's chair as if he owned it, smiling inscrutably at her, holding a pencil in his fingers like a cigarette.

"I'm so glad you could come." She heard his voice inside her head, she heard it all around the room. "I'm afraid Mr. Bradley has been detained, but I don't think you'll miss him."

Blood was trickling from his ears, from his nostrils, down across his smile. His picture frowned at her.

He put his pallid hands on the desk and slowly stood up.

A tremor rumbled through the floor.

Caught off-balance, Carrie fell.

Chapter Thirty-Five

1

The flames chased him up the shaft.

Ned looked over the edge and saw his father silhouetted against a round pool of fire, like a fallen angel climbing out of hell. Mr. Fitch was pulling him up, but he was helping a lot by rappelling off the chimney.

A fist-sized piece of cement broke off the lip of the hole and fell down.

"Dad! Did you get him?"

But his father couldn't hear him; the fire was too loud. Ned never would've thought you could get so much fire out of three drums of wax, three drums of solvent, and a bunch of highway flares. He really and truly hadn't thought that thing would burn. He'd tried to say so; but now it looked like a good thing his father hadn't listened to him.

"Hurry up!" Ned yelled at Mr. Fitch. "It's gettin' *hot* down down there!"

Virgil heard that. His mind had only just started to clear, he was only just becoming aware of how sore and muscle-weary he was. The air he breathed was starting to burn his lungs. His face ran with sweat. He thanked God for the rough hemp rope that his sweaty hands could still get a grip on.

The fire poured its light up the shaft. Virgil could see rocks and pebbles in the earth, and the profusion of small round holes like a swallows' nesting colony in a clay cliff.

A few tentacles, broken off by what must have been an uncharacteristically swift retraction of the creature's head, were oozing sluggishly from their holes and dropping down into the blaze. They seemed to retain some purposeless vestige of life and blindly crawled until they fell. One landed on his shoulder, twitched there for a hateful moment, bringing him close to panic, and then dropped off.

Then he was out of the shaft, expending the last of his strength to scramble over the rim and crawl onto the floor. Ned tried to help him up. Rudi dropped the rope and almost collapsed.

"You did it, Dad! You did it!"

The floor stirred under him. Overhead, something cracked like a rifle shot. A few more chunks of cement broke off and fell down the shaft. Rudi yelped.

"That was a support beam, Mr. Bradley! Oh, we done it now! We gotta get out of here!"

Virgil tried to stand. Rudi had to help him.

The cracks in the floor were widening, and some of them were running up the walls. Black smoke was beginning to rise from the pit. It smelled like a fire at a toxic dump. Virgil clung to Rudi with one hand and reached for Ned with the other.

"All right," he said, "we've done all we can do. Let's go."

2

Plaster rained down from the ceiling. A few periodicals toppled from Virgil's bookshelf.

Carrie pushed herself up to a half-kneeling position and

glanced back over her shoulder. Hargrove still stood behind the desk, smirking at her. Behind him, his picture had been canted.

"Surely you don't mean to leave me so soon, Mrs. Bradley. I'm not sure I would want to leave this room if I were you. Here, let me help you up."

He moved toward her and Carrie was at the door before she knew it, screaming for help, for Virgil, pounding on the door with one hand and groping for the lock with the other. She found it, released it, yanked the door open with both hands, and burst into the front office.

The woman with the ax was standing by the window. The floor shook harder this time, overturning the coffee machine and throwing Carrie against the wall. That kept her from falling; and as the woman with the crushed skull raised her ax, Carrie darted past her and out into the hall.

The linoleum floor was powdered with plaster dust from the elaborately cracking ceiling. Something ran madly back and forth, howling and screaming, but the hall was so dark and full of dust that she couldn't see anything in detail. Most of what moved seemed to be children.

A myriad of fleshy ropes swung from holes in the ceiling. Some fell down and writhed spasmodically on the floor. They lay everywhere, like an infestation of snakes, spreading trails of slime in the dust, coiling around air. Some sprouted delicate, fanlike flowers; others brandished slender, wicked-looking rods that spattered drops of fluid from their tips. The hall smelled like a charnel house.

Carrie lunged for the fire doors. Below her the stairs were thronged with struggling shadows and the stairwell reverberated with unintelligible cries. But it was the only way out of the building.

She charged. She felt buffetings against her like quick gusts of wind and saw gleaming eyes and rotting faces. She was screaming but she didn't know it. Her only conscious thought was to fight her way down the stairs and out the door.

Down in the flames under the school, a giant was dying, and dying violently. Even as they reached the door out of the boiler room, a huge piece of the floor broke up and avalanched down the pit.

What have I done? thought Virgil.

Rudi pushed him out the door. The hallway was full of smoke. Ned coughed uncontrollably while clinging to his father's hand. Plaster bombs rained from the ceiling. A pipe ruptured overhead, spewing foul-smelling water and a severed tentacle.

Virgil tried to find the stairway, but Rudi manhandled him in the opposite direction. Disoriented by noise, smoke, and fatigue, he let Rudi push him into a small dark space; then heard a crash and felt a sheet of cold air wrap itself around his face.

"Go on, Mr. Bradley! Straight up that way!"

We're going out the back way, out to the blacktop. All right, Rudi—I hadn't thought of that. He stumbled up the short stairs, tripped on the threshold, and felt asphalt under his palms.

They were out. They'd gotten out alive. The thought revived him. He got up without any help and as his vision cleared, made for the end of the blacktop. Ned hung onto him, still coughing. There was a cold drizzle in the air that blended with his sweat and cooled him. It felt good until it got under his clothes.

"Are you all right, Mr. Bradley?"

Virgil nodded. "Yeah, I think so. I think I breathed too much of that smoke when I was down in the hole, but I'm okay."

At the end of the blacktop, they turned.

Ned thought he was going to faint. He'd gotten a big whiff of smoke, he was dizzy, he was sick to his stomach—but the fresh air was going to save him, he knew that now. Jesus! If

Mr. Fitch hadn't let them out the back way, they might not have made it.

He stared in disbelief at the school.

Lights were going on and off in all the windows, like there was a silent thunder storm inside. Smoke boiled out through the door of the little white shed that protected the back stairs.

He thought he saw faces in the windows.

Holy shit! How many of 'em are there?

There was a crowd inside the building. There must have been a thousand ghosts in there. Pale faces pressed against the windows, leering and grimacing. White hands beckoned.

They want us to come back.

Above the windows, along the edge of the roof, the gutters glowed—softly, like weak fluorescent tubes. The air hissed and crackled. The wire mesh in the window of the kindergarten door burned bright red, melted the glass, then went out, leaving the door smoking. A weird bluish light emanated from the brass doorknob and danced along the metal rail of the kindergarten porch.

"Jesus God, what's happening?" Mr. Fitch muttered. Ned looked up and saw him fingering a plastic crucifix that hung around his neck.

"It's okay, Mr. Fitch! It's dying, we killed it! It's burning up!"

Then Dad screamed:

"Carrie! No!"

Virgil, too, had been spellbound by the gallery of phantoms at the windows, and the unaccountable electrical display along the gutters and the metal fixtures of the doors. Instinctively he recognized it all as the death throes of the thing beneath the school.

Somewhere in that hell was the ghost of him. Him as he was at nine years old, when he first peeked into the janitor's closet. But it wasn't a real ghost, was it? It was only part of what that monster did to me. It was a part of him: left over from something that was taken from him thirty-one years ago. Something that bound him to the place for all this time. He wondered if

302

it was dying with the monster. He wondered if its death would set him free.

Somehow his eye strayed from the building to the teachers' parking lot and found Carrie's car there.

His wife was in the building. It took a moment to sink in; when it did, he screamed.

Rudi caught him, held him back.

"No, Mr. Bradley! You can't go in there!"

"Let me go!" he cried. "My wife's in there!"

He fought, but his strength was at an end, and Rudi held him as if he were a child.

"Damn it, that's her car! Don't you see it? I have to get her out of there!"

"You can't make it, Mr. Bradley! You won't make it!" Rudi shook him until he stopped struggling. "The whole darned place is catching fire, Mr. Bradley. You wait here. I'll go."

Virgil stared stupidly. Gently, Rudi forced him down until he was kneeling on the blacktop; then released him and turned to go.

Smoke was billowing out the back door, a black ocean of it. The tarpaper roof of the little shed was smouldering. Seeing a hint of flame in the stairwell, Virgil suddenly understood what Rudi was about to do.

"*No!* Rudi—wait—"

There was a blinding flash and a wave of shock that knocked him flat against the asphalt, then a blast that swallowed all.

4

The sentience was dying.

Which was to say that its physical structure was sustaining irremediable damage. The sentience had no conception of death. It was incapable of such cogitation.

It was aware of the fiery assault on its body. The mode of life evolved for its kind—armored underground giantism—made the likelihood of serious physical damage virtually nonexistent. Which, over thousands of millenia, had contributed to a functional separation between sentience and body.

It could not conceive of its own nonexistence; nor did it concern itself with the independent existences of other entities.

It had monitored the brain activity of these individual prey organisms. For the first time the sentience encountered vigorously hostile others. For the first time it was actively under attack.

It was encountering the impossible, the inconceivable, the inexpressible. Its conceptual framework could not accommodate the circumstances. It was incapable of logical response because it could not adequately perceive the threat.

All it could do was continue to withdraw into its armored shell, continue its attempt to achieve dormancy.

Under the armor, its flesh was soft and biochemically receptive to the flames. Key neural pathways had already sustained damage, slowing its withdrawal into its vast shell, rendering certain movements unproductive. Where the fire burned, flesh bubbled like frying fat.

The sentience made a decision to thrust unfertilized spore packets deep into the earth.

That was the closest it could come to desperation.

Unable to conceptualize its own death, it had no fear. Nor did it experience pain as earthly organisms knew it.

But it burned.

Chapter Thirty-Six

He couldn't hear anything, but when he was finally able to sit up, he could see.

Boiler must've blown, Virgil thought.

The boiler room had been tacked onto the side of the school, almost as an afterthought, and there was no second story over it. Now there was no roof, either . . . just a jungle of flame.

The shed over the back stairs was burning. All the windows, even on the second floor, had been blown out. Over the boiler room, the school's west wall was falling down. Cracks appeared in the whitewashed wall over the blacktop.

Flames marauded through the interior. One after another, the first-floor windows were lit by fire as if demons were turning on red lamps.

Virgil heard a ringing in his ears, but still no sound.

A few feet in front of him, Rudi was groveling on his hands and knees, trying to get up. Virgil wanted to speak to him, but his brain couldn't seem to generate any words.

Ned was beside him, clutching at what little shelter was offered by the blacktop. He trembled all over.

Virgil watched his school die.

The whole west wall fell in, from the roof on down, opening up that side of the building and sucking up fire from the basement. Soundlessly, glass exploded from the second story windows. The blacktop shivered. The main chimney disintegrated and rained a hail of bricks into the chaos of smoke and flame below.

Fire spewed from the windows. Virgil felt the heat of it on his face. Flames crowned the roof. The gutters fell, arrested somewhat by what bolts and brackets remained in place, so that their collapse resembled a slow-motion replay and was not complete. They hung from the roof like broken wings.

The ringing in Virgil's ears intensified, then began to fade, giving way to the roaring of the blaze, the rumble of falling bricks, the cracking of wooden beams. Far away a fire siren keened.

All around, people were coming out of their houses, staring, pointing, calling inaudibly to one another. A thick pall of smoke began to spread across the sky.

Rudi got up first, but only to stand transfixed by the destruction.

Virgil reached for Ned, who was still pressed to the asphalt like a soldier demoralized by an artillery barrage. He squeezed the boy's shoulder, kneading it gently until he got him to roll over and sit up. His face was blank with shock.

There was a great crash as a central portion of the roof fell in. It seemed to startle Ned out of a trance.

"The school . . ." he muttered.

"The school's finished," Virgil said. "Look at it. No way anyone can save it."

"The alien . . . we killed it. We *did* kill it, didn't we?"

"Son, if this doesn't kill it, nothing will."

"Mom. You said Mom . . . she . . ."

Virgil got up. He felt empty inside, devoid of life, all feeling stripped away, leaving a man-shaped husk that would walk and talk and work, but never live again.

* * *

Ned shivered. He opened his mouth to say something to his father, but then decided not to let it out. Dad's face looked a hundred years old.

Ned saw Mom's car in the parking lot, too, and even from this far away, he could see she wasn't in it. She had to have gone inside the building.

But stayed inside? She couldn't have. She wouldn't. And anyway, the new wing wasn't on fire yet, the new wing was fine. . . .

Seizing the idea that came to him, Ned broke loose and ran for his mother's car.

"Ned! Damn it, come back here!"

Virgil wanted to chase him but could muster up only a feeble trot. Rudi, roused out of his stupor, ran on ahead. Virgil saw them both make a wide turn around the broken, burning corner of the building and disappear behind a wind-blown veil of smoke.

His body was depleted; he couldn't run a step. It had begun to rain. He walked. This close to the fire, the heat dried his skin as soon as the drizzle landed. He paused beside his wife's car and touched the fender. It was hot.

"Mr. Bradley!"

Ned came running. Behind him toiled Rudi, carrying Virgil's wife in his arms. Virgil woke back to life.

"The grass, Rudi! Put her down on the grass!"

"She's all right, Dad! Mom's all right! She was outside!"

Carrie winced when Rudi set her down. Virgil held her. Ned held them both.

"Virgil . . . ?"

"It's all right, hon. You're safe now. I've got you."

She opened stunned eyes. "What happened?"

"I think the boiler blew up. Jesus, Carrie, how did you get out? I thought . . ."

307

"I *ran* out! Where were you?"

Fire sirens howled, closer now. Virgil's mind raced.

"Listen, everybody," he said. "They're going to want to know what happened here—right? Rudi?"

"What do you mean?" Rudi said. " *'Course* they're gonna want to know what happened!"

"And when they ask," said Virgil, "tell them this. The foundation was cracking, and the boiler went. And that's *all.* That's all I want you to say." He sighed and shook his head. "No one'll believe the rest."

"But Dad! They'll *find* it!" Ned cried.

"If they do, they'll believe us. Then we can tell the rest. But for the time being—the boiler. Everybody got that?"

"Virgil! *I* saw—"

"I know. We all saw. Rudi and Ned, too."

"You don't understand! That man ... that man in the picture, in your office ... I saw him! *He was there!*"

The first fire engine was pulling up to the curb on River Street. Virgil squeezed his wife.

"I saw him, too," he said. "And more. We can talk about it when we get home. We have to. But for now, it was the boiler. Rudi, have you got that?"

"Mr. Bradley, wouldn't it be lying—"

"For God's sake, Rudi!"

Rudi flinched. He shook his head sadly. "All right, you're the boss. The boiler."

"Jumpin' Jesus!" the fireman cried. "Are you folks hurt?"

Epilogue

1

Cosmo woke with the alarm the next morning and decided he felt well enough to go to work. For a couple of hours, anyway. He could play it by ear from there.

He'd been a good boy yesterday: two big belts of vodka, a Nyquil chaser, and off to bed. He'd slept like the dead. And even after all those hours of sleep, the alarm clock had to jangle in his ear for a full minute before it woke him. *I must'a been sicker'n I thought.*

It was a dark morning; he could still feel rain hanging in the air. Much more of this, and the town fathers'd have to start building an ark. He made himself oatmeal for breakfast, and added a pop of brandy to his coffee to take the chill off.

When he stepped outside, he smelled smoke in the air mingled with mist. *Smog? We got smog now? That's progress.* The sky was like a gray horse blanket. Cosmo put his hat on—an L. L. Bean roll-up that looked like it had been used to wipe down radiators—and buttoned his coat to his neck. Tucking his umbrella under his arm, with the morning paper tucked inside that, he trudged off to school.

It was only three blocks away, but he was already tired half-way there. He walked with his head down, avoiding the wet spots on the sidewalk. *Gonna get triple pneumonia, comin' to work on a day like this.*

You think you got troubles now? Wait'll it starts snowin'.

He looked up, finally, when he realized there were already cars in the teachers' parking lot.

Police cars.

Cosmo's gaze traveled further.

The school was gone . . . except for heaps of charred timbers and tumbled bricks. Pieces of blank wall were left standing like stage flats. A smell of charcoal that'd make you gag hung in the air. Cops and fire marshals poked around the ruins.

He felt his guts turn into water.

"Oh, my God, Rudi," he said out loud, but didn't hear himself. "Oh, my God. I leave him alone for one lousy afternoon, and *this* is what he does!"

2

Charlie Hall woke in a hospital bed and tried to figure out what day it was . . . or what night, rather. His room was already dark.

He remembered a doctor telling him he'd had a wee bit of a heart attack Monday afternoon, trying to squeeze in a few laps around the track before it started raining again. Of the heart attack itself he now remembered nothing.

Well, that's what came of being out of shape. *Hey, a few weeks ago, I could've had it walking up the stairs—right?* If they thought he was going to let this stop him, they were out of their minds. *I wouldn't've survived it if I hadn't already made a good start on getting myself back into shape. If it hadn't been for that, I'd be pushin' up daisies right now. Bet your ass.* As soon as they let him out of here, he'd pick up right where he'd left off.

A rectangle of white light appeared in the darkness as some-one opened the door to his room. Charlie smelled a woman and woke up a little more. Did they have any really hot nurses in this place? He hadn't seen any so far, but there was always hope.

The woman surprised him by closing the door after her and not turning on the light. *Now that's a hot nurse!* Hey, right about now, he could use some of what she had to offer—never mind the heart attack.

"Charlie? Are you awake?"

That whisper sounded familiar. Couldn't be, though. But Charlie didn't care. This was shaping up to be his lucky night.

"Over here, doll."

Clothing rustled. A soft but considerable weight settled onto the side of his bed.

"It's me, Charlie."

"Diane? What—"

"Shh!"

He shut up. He knew he wasn't supposed to have visitors at this hour; but if Diane Phelps missed him so badly that she had to sneak up here in the middle of the night, he wasn't going to complain. The world of women wasn't exactly beating a path to his door just now. He hadn't been with old Di in quite a while; it'd be nice to make up for lost time.

"Lie still, Charlie."

He obliged her. They'd have to be quiet so as not to wake the old geek in the next bed.

Making no more sound than the flutter of a moth's wing, she found the top of his sheet and slowly pulled it down past his knees. For some reason, the passive role suited him tonight. It was giving him a helluva kick. He was already getting a hard-on when he felt her pull up the hem of his johnny-coat, right up to his chin. His heart began to race. His cock felt like a telephone pole. Her fingers made a light tracery over his bare chest.

When he felt the steak knife plunge into his stomach and rip

311

him all the way down to the crotch, his heart blew out on him before he'd finished screaming.

3

"Actually," Fielding Jones was saying, "the site'll probably fetch a higher price with the school already demolished than it would if the buyer had to do the job himself."

Virgil and Carrie nodded. Fielding had dropped in for a cup of tea to bring them up to date on the findings of the fire marshal and the building inspector.

By the time the fire was put out, Victory School was a total loss. Most of the new wing still stood, and the gymnasium; but even there the interior was gutted. There was a chance the gym could be restored, but there was no point in spending the money.

"The boiler blew, all right," Fielding said. "Basically, Virgil, you were right. Parts of the foundation were pretty badly undermined by water damage over the years, and these last heavy rains were the straw that broke the camel's back. Seems when they poured the concrete in 1944, they used the cheapest stuff they could get. Didn't hold up well—especially right under the boiler. So the floor buckled, the stress was too much for the boiler, and *kaboom.*" He shook his white head. "Thank God it didn't happen a few hours earlier."

Virgil threw a look at Carrie, but she didn't need it. *"I'm* not going to tell Fielding Jones I saw a ghost!" she'd said half a dozen times since the explosion. "This little girl didn't see nothin'."

"How extensive was the damage to the foundations?" Virgil asked.

"Extensive enough. We're not gonna do any architectural autopsies, though. The building's gone, and everyone who had anything to do with putting it up is long gone, too. Nobody was hurt, nobody else's property was damaged, so why bother? Let's just forget about it and get our kids reassigned to the other schools before they miss too much."

4

Diane Phelps was charged and indicted for the murder of Charles Arthur Hall, then remanded to a state institution for the criminally insane until such time as she might be found competent to stand trial.

Michael Dudak, comatose, almost certainly brain-dead, remained hooked up to life support systems at the taxpayers' expense.

Johnny Rizzo—whose degree of responsibility for his friend's condition could not be determined until Mike died and pathologists looked inside his skull—was assigned to a county juvenile facility. His father, Officer Neil Rizzo, made no objection.

5

The ruins of Victory School acquired an unsalubrious reputation among the policemen who guarded it by night.

Officers Shamsky and McMullen chased three silent vandals—two juveniles and a tall, thin adult male—into the empty shell of the new wing one night and lost them there. That part of the building had been secured, and there was no way the intruders could have eluded the patrolmen. Shamsky and McMullen filed a brief report of the incident and refused to discuss it with their friends or families.

Officer Weinstein saw a woman prowling amid the rubble on his night and did not report it. He didn't even mention it to his wife. The woman had been walking noiselessly, easily, in areas where a bird couldn't find firm footing. She went behind the remains of a partition and could not be seen again. The officer wanted only to forget her.

Others heard faint whispers, faraway laughs and cries, unintelligible mutterings.

But after a time, no one saw or heard anything at all.

6

Within a week, the Board of Education put its emergency reassignment scheme into operation.

Ned Bradley and his friends were sent to Central School, where classroom space had been reshuffled, extra desks squeezed in, and extra supplies purchased. They had Mrs. Praize now, Mr. Hall having been murdered in the hospital by Mrs. Phelps—a topic whose fascination eclipsed even that of Victory School's sudden end. "She hadda be crazy all along!" Phil Berg said. But Ned never liked to talk about it much.

As the reorganization was implemented, Mrs. Fulham, the principal at Central School, surprised the board by filing for retirement, effective at the end of the current school year. The reason she gave was uncomplicated: her husband, John, had been retired for two years now, and she wanted to join him and have some fun. She was eligible for her full pension by now, and had given the district good service for twenty-six years. Her request was approved.

The board slated Virgil Bradley to replace her.

Joanne Wilmot returned to work just before Thanksgiving, joining the jury-rigged staff at Central School. Her mouth was healed, and she wore lipstick to cover the scars on her lips.

Her husband had retained a private investigator in an effort to find out whether the razor had been pushed into Joanne's apple at the school, or at the supermarket where she'd bought

314

it. "If it turns out to be either of 'em," he told her, "it's lawsuit city. We'll sue their fuckin' pants off." As time went on, nearly every teacher who had worked at Victory School with Joanne found himself answering the investigator's questions. No one was able to tell the man anything enlightening.

"I just want to forget it," Joanne told her friends, "but Goeff is still too mad to let it go."

Otto Reimann, meanwhile, was on indefinite sick leave, by recommendation of the district's physician. "He could have a stroke right in front of the kids," Dr. Keene said. "His blood pressure is too damned high, and he can't control his temper. See if a new diet and medication can straighten him out. If it doesn't, can him." But the language of Dr. Keene's formal recommendation was a lot more elegant.

Before the board could fully consider the case of Doreen Davis, she left Tianoga and was never seen or heard from again.

7

Ned looked forward to Christmas, Little League, and—far down the road, it seemed to him—going on to middle school.

Things were a little unsettled at home, and he didn't like that. Mom was looking for a teaching job for next year. Dad was working at the school board office as a consultant, whatever that was, waiting for reassignment to half a year of teaching before he became a principal again. They were keeping themselves busier than he'd ever seen them—like they knew he wanted to talk about what had happened at Victory School, and this was their way of ducking him.

He kept waiting for workers to dig into the ruins and find whatever was left of that thing down there, and for questions to be asked; and for the Bradley family to provide what answers they could; and for some scientists to come out and *explain* the whole freakin' thing. *Tell us what it was, where it*

315

came from, how long it was under the school. And what it really did to people.

Tell us it's really dead. Tell us it's never coming back.

But the workers only came and carted the bricks and beams away in dump trucks. They knocked down what was left on the walls before they could fall and hurt somebody, brought in several truckloads of fill, and bulldozed the spot flat. Later the town put a storm fence around the site and boarded up the new wing and the gym to make sure nobody would break in. These would be torn down in the spring, the newspaper said.

Ned didn't dream about it. He wasn't afraid to walk alone down the halls in Central School. But he thought about it quite a lot.

"How can we be heroes if nobody knows what we did?" he asked his father when he got the chance. "*We* don't even know what we did! Did we kill it? How do we know unless they dig it up?"

"See what happens when somebody develops the property and puts a new foundation in," Dad said. "See if they find anything. But nobody's going to spend taxpayers' money to see if we really killed a monster, son. They'll think we're crazy. We *did* kill it, and that's the only thing that matters. We burned it. It's dead."

Ned wasn't satisfied with that, but what could he do?

All he wanted was to tell what happened, hear what other people thought: make some sense out of it. He couldn't tell anybody now, but he'd grow up someday, he wouldn't be a kid forever. Maybe then. Once he was grown up, nobody could stop him from telling.

"Hey, didja read that book by that guy Bradley?"

"Yeah, man! He sure knows how to write a horror story."

"Can't wait till they make a movie out of it."

Just like in the UFO movies, Ned thought. They never believe you.

316

Virgil didn't want to tell the tale, and he wouldn't, unless future developments forced it out of him.

He walked past the site one Saturday morning and stopped to watch a light snowfall powder what was left on the blacktop.

He was able to view the site with more equanimity than he'd ever thought possible. It didn't make him heartsick to look at it.

I was never happy there. How could I have ever thought I was? What did I ever do there but try to plow furrows in the sea? His former attachment to the place seemed unreal, like a bizarre action taken in a dream.

The nightmares were over. He hadn't had one since the explosion.

I'm free of it now. For the first time since I was nine years old, I'm free of it. He didn't pine for it, he didn't miss it, he didn't brood about it. He could hardly wait to take over for Harriet at Central. *Think of that—a school where kids and teachers don't go mad. Think of it!* He could leave Victory School behind as easily as a long illness.

This, more than anything else, proclaimed to him that the horror under the school was truly dead. It had had a hold on him, and the hold was broken.

Dead, he thought. *And I'm alive, and all my family with me. Alive and free.*

Thanking God, he turned and walked home through the snow.

TERROR LIVES!

THE SHADOW MAN (1946, $3.95)
by Stephen Gresham
The Shadow Man could hide anywhere—under the bed, in the closet, behind the mirror . . . even in the sophisticated circuitry of little Joey's computer. And the Shadow Man could make Joey do things that no little boy should ever do!

SIGHT UNSEEN (2038, $3.95)
by Andrew Neiderman
David was always right. Always. But now that he was growing up, his gift was turning into a power. The power to know things—terrible things—that he didn't want to know. Like who would live . . . and who would die!

MIDNIGHT BOY (2065, $3.95)
by Stephen Gresham
Something horrible is stalking the town's children. For one of its most trusted citizens possesses the twisted need and cunning of a psychopathic killer. Now Town Creek's only hope lies in the horrific, blood-soaked visions of the MIDNIGHT BOY!

TEACHER'S PET (1927, $3.95)
by Andrew Neiderman
All the children loved their teacher Mr. Lucy. It was astonishing to see how they all seemed to begin to resemble Mr. Lucy. And act like Mr. Lucy. And kill like Mr. Lucy!

Available wherever paperbacks are sold, or order direct from the Publisher. Send cover price plus 50¢ per copy for mailing and handling to Zebra Books, Dept. 137 , 475 Park Avenue South, New York, N.Y. 10016. Residents of New York, New Jersey and Pennsylvania must include sales tax. DO NOT SEND CASH.

THE FINEST IN SUSPENSE!

THE URSA ULTIMATUM   (2130, $3.95)
by Terry Baxter

In the dead of night, twelve nuclear warheads are smuggled north across the Mexican border to be detonated simultaneously in major cities throughout the U.S. And only a small-town desert lawman stands between a face-less Russian superspy and World War Three!

THE LAST ASSASSIN   (1989, $3.95)
by Daniel Easterman

From New York City to the Middle East, the devastating flames of revolution and terrorism sweep across a world gone mad . . . as the most terrifying conspiracy in the history of mankind is born!

FLOWERS FROM BERLIN   (2060, $4.50)
by Noel Hynd

With the Earth on the brink of World War Two, the Third Reich's deadliest professional killer is dispatched on the most heinous assignment of his murderous career: the assassination of Franklin Delano Roosevelt!

THE BIG NEEDLE   (1921, $2.95)
by Ken Follett

All across Europe, innocent people are being terrorized, homes are destroyed, and dead bodies have become an unnervingly common sight. And the horrors will continue until the most powerful organization on Earth finds Chadwell Carstairs—and kills him!

DOMINATOR   (2118, $3.95)
by James Follett

Two extraordinary men, each driven by dangerously ambiguous loyalties, play out the ultimate nuclear endgame miles above the helpless planet—aboard a hijacked space shuttle called DOMINATOR!

Available wherever paperbacks are sold, or order direct from the Publisher. Send cover price plus 50¢ per copy for mailing and handling to Zebra Books, Dept. 137, 475 Park Avenue South, New York, N.Y. 10016. Residents of New York, New Jersey and Pennsylvania must include sales tax. DO NOT SEND CASH.